Finding something you need

is never an accident . . .

THE
HOPE
MERCHANT

Free Wish with Every Purchase

Adam Berkowitz

Published by Leviathan Press 2013

Published by
Leviathan Press
leviathanpress@gmail.com
PO Box 5888
Pikesville, MD 21282

Layout & Design	Block Design/blockdesign@gmail.com
Cover Art	Luana Kauffman
Editorial	Leah Kampf, AJ Samuels, Roberta Chester, Marcy Willow

ISBN: 978-1-881927-12-9

Distributed to the trade by Ingram Book Group

Printed in the United States of America and Israel

ACKNOWLEDGMENTS

My publisher suggested I write acknowledgements. My initial reaction was passive resistance. It's not that I don't have anyone to thank, it's that I have so many people to thank so deeply that a printed page seems trite and inadequate. The opportunity to thank my wife, however, is one I embrace.

A woman is *malkhut*, the kabbalistic aspect of majesty that allows the sun to continue to shine beyond its physical limits and to bring its deeper light to the darkest corners where it is needed most. This is my wife in every way. I have learned that *malkhut* brings my dreams down into this world, closing off so many 'might-be's, focusing them all into one grand 'will-be' that gives my dreams a reality that transcends me. A life, a home, a family—and even this book—are dreams come true. That is my wife's ongoing gift to me.

I would like to acknowledge my gratitude to my publisher, Shimon Apisdorf. He took a seed and saw a forest sleeping inside. He had more faith in my visions than I did, ignoring my murmurings of impatience, nurturing it until it grew to its full glory. How strange to find a friend wandering through my dream, and how deeply appropriate.

I would like to thank my mother for teaching me to believe in your children's dreams, in the simplest and most practical manner. It is a lesson I yearn to pass on.

I would like to thank my abba for helping me from heaven. Though you didn't live to see it, I never could have done this without you.

CONTENTS

The Book of Life

And above all, watch with glittering eyes the
whole world around you because the greatest
secrets are always hidden in the most unlikely places.
Those who don't believe in magic will never find it.

—ROALD DAHL,
Charlie and the Chocolate Factory

We shall grow old together, discovering new dreams
hidden along the way. My dreams are seeds, brought
by angels, sent by God, seeds that will grow into
trees, bearing sweet fruit to heal a hungry world.

—BENJAMIN JACKSON,
Free Wish With Every Purchase

BOVINE OVERTURE

BIG BRAD

single bird call roused Hanna from her bed to greet the dawn with hope reborn, determined to leave her fears and nightmares behind in the rumpled bed sheets. She left her cabin, dressing lightly and in haste, shivering in the pre-dawn chill but welcoming the cold into her body as it drove away the dregs of sleep. She climbed the hill, a cloud of breath leading the way. The ragged edges of her dress were soaked with dew when she reached the top but she had arrived in time to greet the sun. She stood for several long moments before the words finally came. Hesitant at first, they increased in speed and volume with each breath, like the first light rain of spring, building into a downpour that revives the parched fields.

"Though my body is still weak, my spirit remains firm and strong. I greet this new day as a gift, and I accept it with thanks for the blessing of this place where I am restored. I hope for all my heart can hold: a man to share love and children to prove that love. I will make this day a tribute to the One who gave it to me. And if

I am blessed to see this sun set, I will dream again, dreams that are strong enough to last a lifetime and more. And if you will it, I will come to this hilltop tomorrow to tell you of those dreams, too."

The cold air filled her chest like water from a spring. As she finished, her eyes closed and her chin lifted for a few moments, allowing her pale face to glow like the fading moon. A lone cow called plaintively. Hanna shook herself as if waking a second time. She descended into the valley, smiling, as more cows joined in.

She didn't notice the large man standing a few yards behind her, drinking in her words with an expression of awe on his face. He watched her until she arrived at the herd, singing and clapping to gather the animals. His lips moved in silent prayer, his eyes closed. He stood, motionless like a gnarled tree, waiting until she disappeared into the milking parlor, and then followed her down.

THE
BOOK
OF
PRAYER

JACK

"**D**amn it!"

Jack slammed his fist on the steering wheel. He was pushing his beautiful Mercedes hard, while the radar detector beeped angrily in the background like a soundtrack echoing his mood perfectly. He was driving back to the firm's headquarters to meet with his boss, the senior partner. For the last two years under the tutelage of Mr. Jonas, he'd tried hard to transform himself into a serious corporate lawyer who thrived on pressure. Last year, a junior partner, slightly older than Jack, had keeled over from a heart attack in the middle of a marathon six-digit contract negotiation, after which he was relegated to milder cases that generated meager billings. Corporate litigation meant high stakes and big money. And killer stress was nature's way of weeding out the weak. With his new client, Jack was getting a real taste of what that pressure was like.

His C-180 was capable of doing zero to sixty in under five-and-a-half seconds; but that became instantly irrelevant when two tractor-trailers appeared jackknifed across the highway. Jack chewed his lip, thankful for his daily workout at the pricey health club without which he might have a heart attack at moments like this. He cursed as the state troopers set out reflective triangles, warning motorists to stop. Any idiot with enough brains to operate a motor vehicle should be able to understand that two massive trucks parked across the road meant 'Go No Further'. Jack disdained the police and their slavish devotion to often irrational and inconvenient traffic laws. After he passed the bar, he had taken an oath to uphold the law; but in his post law school life Jack learned that in the real world, the law could be used and even abused, becoming a burden rather than an aid to society.

These were the tricks of the trade he had learned from Mr. Jonas, and he used this approach to earn kudos and big bucks, advancing the interests of his client along the way. Once in a while, when he thought of his father's career in law, his old idealism would surface. His father's alma mater was his as well; like his father he had the distinction of being editor of the law review. At his commencement, the Dean of the Law School spoke of father and son in glowing terms. Jack was deeply moved by his words. His father died young while in the course of defending a pro bono client falsely accused by a corrupt cop. The client, a young man with no money, was later exonerated due to Jack's father's tireless efforts.

But for Jack and his mother there was no court of appeals. She sat in the front row at the graduation, beaming up at him through her tears. It was a moment he would always cherish.

Jack became adept at squelching any moralistic misgivings he might have had before joining the firm. The time he spent with his father taught him to respect honesty and integrity; he was certainly not oblivious to the contrast between his dad and Mr. Jonas. But the incredibly plush office, the roster of wealthy clients, and the fact that Mr. Jonas singled him out from the other recently hired young lawyers, settled the argument. He was proud that Mr. Jonas had given him so much responsibility with this distinguished client, and he was determined to prove that he could more than meet the challenge.

The biotech company's directors were a bit concerned that Jack was playing a dangerous legal game, but he _was_ keeping them ahead of their competition. Jack was becoming a hard driver, on the road and in life, and so far, it paid off. Until now, tweaking the law codes had worked for him and his client. Deftly, he created a legal tangle, a master performance of intellectual Aikido that used a federal regulation to prevent the competition from catching up. This was exactly what his client wanted. They were a veteran company whose name had become synonymous with toxic waste. The mother company hid behind a maze of mergers and spin-offs, but the stubborn smell of past transgressions lingered. Jack helped the company avoid trouble with the feds, assisted by a handful of savvy lawmakers whose election campaigns had been generously supported by several board members. Jack learned these skills under the tutelage of Mr. Jonas.

But lately his master plan threatened to unravel. A District Attorney had made a few inquiries that seemed merely procedural, but the situation was becoming delicate. Jack hit the books, studying harder than he had for the bar exam, pulling all-nighters and writing briefs to counter any action the DA might bring against them. He thought his position was shaky but manageable until Mr. Jonas called him back for a serious sit-down. He was worried, in spite of Mr. Jonas' jovial tone. Mr. Jonas had many guises: patrician, elder statesman, and gentle mentor of a new generation of brilliant young attorneys. He had guided and coached Jack every step of the way. It seemed like an amazing opportunity for such a new arrival. When Jack was assigned this multi-million dollar client, he felt sure that he was being fast-tracked for junior partner. He immediately leased the luxury car that he couldn't afford, justifying the expense as necessary for the commute from the city to the biotech firm's headquarters hidden away in the country.

He worked hard and everything seemed to be on track. Until two days ago. Mr. Jonas had called, sounding friendly and upbeat on the phone. Once, Jack witnessed Mr. Jonas flash a big smile just before ripping into a green attorney who had messed up. He was an acquaintance, a former schoolmate two years ahead of Jack. That sacrificial lamb was at the beginning of his career, just starting to pay off his heavy student loans, but by the time Mr. Jonas finished chewing him out, it was clear that he had no future with the firm. There were even rumors that he left law, using his legal degree as a decorative wall hanging and a calling card for a meager management position. Jack, like all the newcomers, had received a personal invite to the meeting to watch Mr. Jonas make mincemeat of the poor young lawyer. The show was clearly intended as an example of what could happen to each of them. It was nothing less than diabolical the way Mr. Jonas smiled the entire time, like a great white shark in a business suit showing its healthy teeth to a plump seal that crossed its path. Jack kept that image in his mind while revving himself up to give a power presentation to Mr. Jonas about the great job he was doing for their client. If it weren't for that damn accident, I'd be doing that already, he thought.

He was sitting in traffic grinding his teeth, a habit from childhood, when his phone rang. Caller ID flashed the number of the assistant to the CEO of the company he was representing: June, the ice princess, was slim, long-legged and distractingly attractive in Furstenberg business suits. She undoubtedly had a pocket in her Chemise for her cell phone. She was a top business school grad, but many of her equally bright classmates were languishing in entry-level positions. Her fashion model looks and man-eating attitude opened doors closed to others. Since she and Jack were always the youngest in the boardroom, they pretended to flirt, putting on a show for the old men; but Jack had a feeling that June was the source of many of his problems, whispering nasty rumors in her boss's ear.

He flashed a toothy smile before answering. "Hey, June bug. Did you call to flirt, or is there something serious on your mind?"

Her voice was a thin sugar coating of icy permafrost. "Hey, lover boy. Where did you run off to? I thought I'd be seeing your gorgeous face today."

Jack wondered if he was on speakerphone, with June performing for all the old execs who couldn't tell the difference between a young woman's passion and barefaced greed. "You've got me blushing. I've just got to run back to the office to tie up a few loose ends."

June's voice turned colder while Jack's grip on the steering wheel turned his knuckles white. "We got a letter from the DA's office this morning. It was a bit of a surprise. Bo Plus is ready to go and a delay at this point could be very costly. You know that." Her voice was unmistakably patronizing.

Jack gritted his teeth, but his voice was deliberately nonchalant, a technique he learned directly from Mr. Jonas. "I got the same letter, darlin'. It doesn't mean a thing. We tested Bo Plus and the FDA loved the results. If the tree huggers want to talk, they're gonna have to put their money where their mouth is and finance their own independent tests. A couple of hysterical parents and an angry lunch room lady just don't have that kind of juice."

"The DA decided to file an injunction because Green Global filed a petition. Those angry parents and the lunchroom lady just called in their big brother. And the green in Green Global isn't just from hugging trees. They're multinational tree huggers and have enough lawyers and money to make it sting. They could delay Bo Plus and maybe even convince some idiot judge to take it off the shelves. And it hurts me to say this, lover boy, but some of those lawyers might be cuter and smarter than you."

Jack took a deep breath, while his fingers numbed from his death-grip on the wheel. He needed a quick response. The words he found would have made Mr. Jonas proud. "That's the best thing I've heard all week. I was worried because there's no money in suing tree hugging mommies and daddies. I spoke to Jonas last week and suggested slapping them with a lawsuit just to get them off our backs. He said it was a waste suing a PTA for peanuts. If Green Global wants to play rough, let them try. I'll sue them for more money than Bo Plus would have made. That's why Green Global didn't get involved until now. They were afraid of getting sued by us. Now, that nasty letter from the DA just gave me the green light to sue Green Global for all they are worth. A lot of dolphins are going to miss their free fish this winter." There was a pause on the phone as his words sunk in. He grinned, almost for real this time. "And if I catch you looking at their paralegals, I'll just have to make them uglier by smacking them in the face."

He could hear the murmurs around the conference table before she spoke. "We're glad to hear that, Jacky. When am I going to see you again so we can discuss strategy and other important things?"

"Don't worry, June bug. I can't stay away from you for too long. I just need to hold Mr. Jonas' hand for a few days and then I'll come running back to you. If you have any other good news for me, don't hesitate to call."

Jack dialed the next number from memory, too impatient to use speed dial. Canned music played while he watched the dumbstruck highway patrolmen wander around the trucks as if they were beached whales that had mysteriously appeared in the middle of the interstate. A voice came on just as Jack was about to fling his phone at the dashboard. Jack began to speak, barely containing his anger.

"Hey, Jeff. It's Jack Nathan. How are you buddy?"

The voice on the other phone sounded apologetic, making Jack even angrier. "Hi, Jack. I don't think I want to speak to you anymore. We've handed it over to Green Global. They've decided that, in light of recent developments, they will pursue the matter with their resources."

Jack was incredulous. "I'm shocked. I thought we had a good working relationship. We were totally transparent with the testing. You got the results when we did and they looked fine. Bo Plus is a great development in dairy farming and is going to make milk a lot cheaper for all calcium-deprived school kids."

"Well, actually, that's what I wanted to talk to you about. We contacted the DA and he asked the lab for their results. He had to threaten them with an indictment. The results they gave him didn't match what you showed me. The results indicated . . ."

"I don't know what you are talking about. I have a double latte every day before I start work so I drink the stuff. There is no way I would want bad milk to hit the shelves."

By the pause before Jeff spoke Jack could tell he had pushed the other man too far. "Jack, I am sorry but that's not what the results showed. Also, the name of the company the lab was working for was Creves Corporation. You told me you represented Herdsman."

Jack shuddered. "Herdsman might be a subsidiary of Creves but the accountant at Herdsman is the one who signs my paycheck."

"I'm willing to give you the benefit of the doubt and assume you didn't know. Herdsman is a front that Creves created to sell Bo Plus

13

to dairy farmers. Normally, Green Global wouldn't get involved in this. Their area of concern is global ecology. When it looked like Herdsman was a small, local, company with a new product that might be contaminating milk, they referred us to other non-profits that deal with the FDA. As soon as they heard Creves was involved, they jumped in to give us their full support. Jack, these people invented chemical warfare and now they are making additives for milk. Doesn't that bother you?"

"Listen, Jeff, it's not an additive. It's a supplement that enhances . . ."

"No, Jack, I won't listen. You've lied to me twice. Maybe more. You knew the lab results were tampered with and you knew who you were working for. When I first approached you with my concerns, you seemed like an honest man I could work with. Frankly I don't know who you are anymore." Jeff took a deep breath. Jack realized that his mouth was hanging open. "I'm sorry, Jack, but I don't want to talk to you again. You can address your concerns to Green Global's legal department. There are plenty of people there who would love to talk to you." Jack began to reply, but the wimpy little pushover had already hung up on him.

Swearing loudly, he swung the car's tail around. Braced for impact he pumped the gas, pushing the car in the opposite direction with no thought of the flagrant violation of several traffic laws. A collision would destroy his expensive car and open him up to a massive lawsuit, but he'd risk it. He was on a mission, a hard-driving attorney with no time to waste. Violating traffic laws in a dangerous and public manner didn't worry him. A couple of hours in traffic court might even be an interesting diversion, a chance for him to embarrass the idiot cop stupid enough to pull him over. He needed to get back to the city right away. Events were coming together that would determine the future of his career. Developments over the next couple of weeks would decide whether he would trade in the two-seater for an expensive sedan or have it repossessed.

He turned down the exit ramp onto a country road, one he'd seen as a blur from the highway on the drives to his weekly war sessions at the biotech headquarters hidden away in a sleepy corner of the state. Cutting-edge technology was revealed at the last meeting that was ahead of what the law was ready to permit. Any delays between research and production would give the competition a chance to catch up. Corporate theft was common in the multi-billion dollar jungle of biotech R&D. Being first on the market meant exponential returns on a preliminary investment of millions.

The law was being written in the courts at the same time as the technology was being grown in the laboratory. No one knew what the scientists would dream up tomorrow or whether the courts would permit it. Jack worked hard and got results. If he continued to be successful he would be the hottest lawyer in a rich new field of practice that few lawyers understood. The industry was riding high because of the legal lag; but if any legislation stalled them, Jack would be known as the counsel that dropped the golden egg laid by a cloned goose.

He considered running the next red light, but a glance in his rear view mirror stopped his foot just as it touched the gas pedal. A state trooper was parked behind him, talking on the radio. Jack's phone began to beep, confusing him for a second. It seemed as if the trooper was calling his phone from the police radio. Jack realized he was jumpy and needed to relax. When the light turned green, Jack pulled over and let the police car slide past. Flipping open the phone, he saw a number that made him feel weaker than the phone's dim signal. He cut the engine and got out of the car so he could pace while he talked. As always, the low raspy voice coming out of the phone made him feel like a scared kid.

"Hello, Jack. How is everything? I expected to see you in the office this morning."

"Everything's fine, Mr. Jonas. I had to meet with the CEO and his assistant late last night to discuss recent developments." He listened to himself. He was so nervous he wondered if Mr. Jonas could hear him sweat. "There is an unexpected complication in the strategy you suggested. Everything was fine, moving along just like you said it would. The ad hoc citizens' group seemed satisfied with the doctored lab results we gave them. But one of them called the DA; he got curious and subpoenaed the lab. Now Green Global is getting involved and their legal department is a real concern. The people at Herdsman were a bit worried but I assured them it was all perfectly legal and under control. I feel the situation is not under control and faking those lab results could blow up in our faces."

"Jack, you are starting to sound like a little boy who got caught with his hand in the cookie jar. Scared little boys don't earn the kind of money we are paying you. I know all about the DA and Green Global."

"Changing the lab report was illegal. If the DA investigates . . ."

"It wasn't illegal. Would I suggest it if it weren't proper? Every law firm does it. It's the kind of real-world legal practice they don't teach you in law school. Listen, Jacky my boy, just come in and we'll talk about it."

Jack tried to calm himself. "Okay. I should be back in the office in a couple of hours. There was a major accident on the highway and I had to take a detour."

Mr. Jonas paused before he spoke, his voice slightly less upbeat. "No problem. I'm sure that gorgeous car of yours will get you here fast enough. Come straight to the office. I'll order lunch from Giorgio's; I'm sure the good news I'm expecting will justify the expense. I'll wait for your report before I order the wine."

Mr. Jonas had bullied most of the top restaurants into delivering haute cuisine as if it were cheap pizza. Jack knew his boss always worked until midnight. As senior partner, he could afford to do whatever he wanted, including retire; but two divorces and an unending battle with alcohol proved that, like many successful attorneys, he was better at litigation than real life. His idea of a serious relationship was comparing prenuptial agreements over cocktails and candlelight.

"That's too tempting to pass up. I'll be there. You can count on me."

Back in the car, Jack turned the key, but the starter didn't catch. He forced the key as the engine wheezed and coughed. The computerized diagnostics were supposed to tell him all the inner secrets of the finely tuned engine in an alluring female voice, but they were strangely mute. Jack could only stare in disbelief at the only gauge that was still illuminated. He was out of gas.

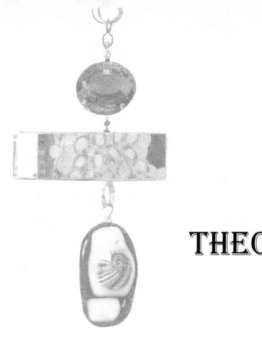

THEO

Theo looked up from his small stack of corn cakes. "Tell Big Brad to take his boots off," he warned Mother. Heavy footsteps thudded outside and the door opened. A large man filled the doorway. Mrs. Meyer turned from the stove and sighed. "Take off those boots, Brad," she sighed. "Theo mopped the floor before breakfast."

Big Brad stopped in mid-stride and looked down at the muddy boots that were just about to leave their mark. He shook his head and stepped back out, returning in heavy wool socks. Theo's mother put a steaming plate of corn cakes on the table in front of him. Brad dropped his chin and closed his eyes. Theo stopped chewing long enough to watch the large man's moment of prayer. No one noticed as Theo tilted his head slightly to one side as though struggling to hear a distant sound. "Mother, you might want to get Hanna's medicine from the fridge. She forgot to take her pills again."

Mrs. Meyer pursed her lips in annoyance. "I swear she does that on purpose. How does she expect to get healthy if she doesn't take her medicine?" The question hung in the air as the door opened again. Her husband entered, followed by a young woman in a calico dress and floppy cotton socks. At twenty, she was gaunt and pale but pretty with long dark hair and large hazel eyes, and the grace and energy of a dancer. They took their places silently at the table. Mother put another heaping plate of cakes in front of her husband and the young girl was given a dish with several colorful capsules. Hanna looked over at Theo. "You snitch."

Father smiled. "You should thank him for keeping an eye on you. We all want you to get well. When you showed up on our doorstep last year, you were looking like something the cat dragged in, too ragged and bony to eat, too tired and sad to throw back."

"Something Theo dragged in is more like it." Brad's voice was a gravelly rumble rising up from the depths of his barrel chest. Hanna stared at the pills, color rising to her cheeks as her anger grew. "I want to get well and am grateful to you. I just don't want to take pills. They're made by strangers who know all about how to kill disease but nothing about what I need to keep on living. For them it's about war; for me . . ." The room was suddenly quiet except for Hanna's panting.

Mother looked up from the pan. "Hmm? We're listenin'."

Hanna sighed. "For me, it's about faith, love and acceptance. I'm rediscovering my healthy self."

"That's a lot of self-improvement to digest on an empty stomach," said Father. "Swallow those pills and then you can tell us more about that while you have some breakfast."

Mother put a glass of fresh squeezed orange juice next to Hanna's plate. "You're right about the pills," she said, "but you have been getting better. You're looking like a pretty little flower sprouting out of a cow patty. Last time you tried breakfast without your pills, you had to scoot out pretty fast. So unless you think my cooking tastes better coming up than going down, you'd better quiet down and take those pills."

Hanna glanced at her then at Theo, who said softly, "You promised."

Her defiance wilted. She scooped up the pills and took a swallow of juice, pushing them painfully down her throat. As soon as the first bite of corn cakes hit her stomach her scowl vanished. Theo watched her display of anger but his eyes saw only the woman whose prayers accompanied the dawn. With the light banter of breakfast conversation, her smile grew and her glowing spirit began to shine.

Theo took his empty plate to the sink. "I'm going into town this morning."

His parents exchanged a look of mutual concern. Father spoke to the back of his son's head while Theo washed his dish. "Do you need me to pick you up later?"

Theo pulled his baseball cap off a coat rack and set it firmly on his head. "No thanks, Dad. I won't be long."

His mother's eyes pleaded silently while her husband nodded. He knew what his wife wanted him to say. "I've got some errands to run. Maybe I'll meet you later and drive you home?"

Theo paused for a moment, his hand on the doorknob. Finally he turned and smiled at his father. "Thanks, Dad. That would be swell." He turned and ran out before he could hear a combined sigh of relief.

Theo parked his bike behind the garage and rummaged through the collection of cast-off car parts until he found a large crate with small wheels. He rolled it out to the sidewalk. Still too early to open for business, the stores were closed and the streets were empty. Small towns wake up quietly. People in towns closer to the city were already coping with traffic jams and reading the financial pages. Here, the day had not yet begun. This was not the route of choice for city-bound travelers. If a person in a rush passed through, it was usually by mistake.

Theo opened the front of the crate to shelves of odds-and-ends that looked like leftovers from a garage sale. As he began rearranging the items, the garage mechanic showed up. The mechanic began his day as he always did, greasy and smelly, anger burning yellow in his eyes. A patch on his coveralls spelled "Lance" and under it, in smaller letters, "Manager/Owner." It was true that Lance owned the garage, but "Manager" was a joke. The coveralls were bought and embroidered many years ago when, in an uncharacteristic burst of enthusiasm, he decided to expand his business. He had, in fact, hired a few employees and supervised them, but none stayed and his enthusiasm quickly soured. He was a difficult boss and there wasn't enough business for a full staff. These days, it was all he could do to manage himself, and some days the garage was full to overflowing with just him and his fury.

"Why don't you jus' git ohn home? Your junk is an ah-sore. It's jes' chasin' ma customers away."

Theo didn't look up. He pulled a folded piece of notebook paper out of his back pocket. "A deal's a deal." He unfolded it and laid it on top of the crate. "I have your signature right here on this contract." He cleared his throat, "I, Lance Higginbottom, will permit Theo Meyer to run his roadside business in front of my gas station for a period of not less than but not exceeding one month. I willingly do this in exchange for a Ford Mustang water pump, used, but in fine working condition, that Theo is providing me this day." Theo stopped reading and looked up. "Dated and signed by" he pointed to Lance's embroidered pocket. "Lance. Manager. Do you want to read it for yourself?"

Lance ignored Theo, leaving the ragged contract on top of the crate as the boy continued putting his merchandise in order. Lance glared at the piece of paper, his fingers itching to snatch it up and rip it to shreds. He was used to people giving him a wide berth. This boy's calm was different and unsettling. Theo ignored him, intent on the small objects that filled the rough wooden shelves.

"I don't know where you picked up dat water pump and I don't rightly care. You probl'y stoled it off ma shelf when I waren't lookin'. It don't matter none. It waren't worth dat much anyways."

The boy stopped and looked up at the face blackened with several days of grease. "You charged two hundred dollars for putting in that pump. And because of the deal you made with me, the pump didn't cost you a dime."

"Maybe, but it didn't cost you nuttin', neither. You probl'y foun' it by the side of the road." The man put his hand on the crate, ready to topple it over. Theo put his hand, clean and small, on the man's grimy paw. The man felt his strength drain away.

"Maybe I did, but a deal's a deal. You made two hundred dollars and it didn't cost you anything. Except for letting me stand out here a couple days a week."

"You waren't doin' me no favors. I coulda ordered it. It'a gotten here soon anuf. It'a bin wort' da money. Dat shore woulda bin bedduh den listenin' to yore lip an' watchin' you standin' here tryin' to sell garbage. It done cost me plenny in nerves an' aggervation."

Theo lifted the dirty hand off the crate and rubbed at the spot where it touched. "That's right. I didn't do you any favors. But you aren't doing me any favors. We aren't really doing business; this is a public sidewalk. I could stand here all day for free. I asked your permission as a courtesy. My business was with the owner of the car. I needed to make that deal with you so that lady would get home on time. Her father was dying, and she didn't have time to wait for a new water pump."

"How you knowin' dat?"

The boy looked into the man's face; fear had replaced the anger and Theo could have enjoyed that power. He chose instead to focus on the reason he'd come into town. He could have lingered and seen more but it made him ill to look into the angry man's soul. A white lie would suffice for an explanation and sometimes the truth was a powerful weapon best kept in reserve. "I heard her say it on the phone in your office. The favor was for her. She was headed in the wrong direction when her car broke down. She never would have found out until it was too late. Now if you don't mind, I have some business to attend to."

"I do be mindin', so you bes' be mindin' yo own manners, boy." Lance pulled a crumpled pack from his shirt pocket and stuck a half-burnt cigarette into the corner of his mouth. The boy reached down without looking and handed him a box of safety matches. Lance glared at him before taking them, lit up, and pocketed the matches with a look that dared the boy to reclaim them. He blew a stream of smoke towards Theo. "It waren't much of a favor for her neither. Her pa died anyways."

"Yes, but she was there when he died."

"What good's that doin' eeder of 'em? He's still dead and she's still gonna be without a pa. An' better off if ya askin' me. In de end, we all jus' worm food. Dead is dead. Whatit matter who watches it happen?"

The boy stared into the man's rheumy eyes. "I didn't ask you."

Lance plucked the cigarette from his mouth and ground the stubby remainder onto the piece of paper, burning a black hole in the center. "Well, ya gots two mo' weeks. An' you bestest not be thinkin' ya can find anudder water pump. Dat wus a one-time deal. If I sees ya around here in two mo' weeks and one day, I'll be settin' my dawg on ya."

"You don't have a dog."

"I'll git me one. Da meanest, ugliest critter I kin find jus' so he kin bite you. Den I be takin' him out back and shootin' im dead."

Theo stared into his face until the man turned away nervously to unlock the gas station. Theo gazed up the street towards town, where the asphalt swayed under heat waves. A delivery van swerved around a tractor and pulled into the gas station. Lance pumped gas as a passenger stepped down from the van.

Theo smiled. "Hey mister! Wanna buy something?"

Jack's expensive suit was dusty and wrinkled. His tailored shirt was grimy, soaked with sweat, and his silk tie was loose at the collar. He watched the gas pump for a few moments, then turned towards the boy.

"Hey, kid. Are you from around here?"

Theo smiled. "Sure. Do you want to buy something?"

Jack glanced at the crate and shook his head. "No. I really need to get out of here. My car ran out of gas a couple of miles back. I've got to fill up and get home." He nodded towards Lance. "As soon as he finishes with the van, I'll need to talk to the gas station owner."

Theo shook his head. "He won't help you. In the meantime, you want to see what I'm selling?"

Jack looked up and saw the van drive away. He left the boy's question hanging in the air and walked over to speak to the greasy mechanic. Theo watched the two men haggle. Out of the corner of his eye, he saw his father's tractor drive towards him. The conversation beside the gas pump grew louder as the big machine got closer. It pulled up in front of the boy's roadside stand, the heavy diesel engine drowning out the sounds of the argument. Mr. Meyer switched off the motor just as the argument ended. He looked down at his son for a moment, thankful to see him.

"Let's go, Theo."

The boy smiled. "My name isn't Theo."

"Well, that's what your mother calls you and she's the one who sent me out to drag you back home. If it bugs you so much, I'll call you Thelonius."

"I hate that name."

The father smiled. "So give it back."

"I've tried. The warranty expired before I was old enough to talk." They both smiled, the mirrored grins making them look even more like father and son. "I can't go yet. I have a customer."

"I don't see anyone here except us."

Jack suddenly appeared, walking up to Theo, still annoyed, ignoring the boy's father. "Is there another gas station in town? That man is the biggest thief I ever came across."

Mr. Meyer got down off the tractor. "Lance isn't a thief. He just takes what he can grab, whether it's his or not. He isn't half-smart enough to steal, just mean and angry. Some say he's got good reason to be, from his past. He gets away with it because he's got the only gas station in town, which is why most of us have learned to fix our own engines. I'd rather get my hands greasy than do business with him. Engine grease washes off. Anger tends to stick around."

Jack looked at Mr. Meyer, not sure if he were being contradicted or agreed with. Mr. Meyer stuck out his hand. "I'm Fred Meyer. Around here we generally introduce ourselves first. After that it's okay to interrupt."

Jack looked down at the rough and calloused hand, before shaking. He ground his teeth, impatient with these local yokels. He put on a discounted version of his game face. Realizing he was at their mercy, he feigned politeness. "Sorry if I was rude. I'm

Jack Nathan. I've got to get back to New York City by tomorrow morning. My car ran out of gas a few miles from here. I don't know how it happened and I feel stupid that it did. I thought I had plenty and then all of a sudden the gas dropped a half a tank. I'm an attorney and I guess I was distracted thinking about some high-level negotiations. I need to get some gas and get back to my car. That man wants to charge me twenty-five dollars for a gallon of gas in a gas can and another hundred and fifty dollars to drive me out to my car! It's robbery but I'd pay it if I could. He said he only takes cash and I don't have that much cash on me. I have plenty of plastic, but he says there are no ATM's in this forsaken place."

Mr. Meyer shook his head. "I've heard of Lance doing that kind of thing and I don't like it. The bank over in Lawrence might be able to help you out, but they don't open for another hour and you have no way to get there, anyway." He paused for a moment, looking at his son as if he were asking permission. "I've got a few things to pick up in the store, but after that I can take you out to your car."

Jack shook his head, his annoyance obvious. "And how much do you charge? Half price? I just need to know where I can hire a tow truck. The normal kind with normal rates."

Mr. Meyer glanced at his son again before answering. "You know, if someone holds out his hand to help you, it would be better not to spit in it. I don't charge for helping out when it comes my way. It won't cost you a thing, except maybe a 'thank you'. And I won't even hold you to that if you feel the price is too steep."

Jack hesitated. "Sorry. I'm under a lot of pressure and I'm running late."

Mr. Meyer nodded and pointed across the street. "There's a hardware store right across the street. They'll sell you a two-gallon jerry can for five dollars. Or you can borrow mine for free.

Jim over in the hardware store takes credit cards. If you don't want to buy gasoline from Lance, I could sell you two gallons of gas from my car. We could just siphon it out when we get to my house. You could pay me for it or not. I won't mind either way. Two gallons should get you to the next town and they have three gas stations there. Competition keeps them honest." Jack's mouth fell open. He stuttered twice, and then simply nodded his head. "In the meantime, I've got some errands to run. Why don't you take a look at what the boy has to sell before stepping over to buy that gas can?"

Mr. Meyer pulled a crumpled list from his back pocket and walked towards the general store on the corner. Jack looked down at the assorted items on display. He picked up a hood ornament, the unmistakable flying 'B', recognized by well-heeled status seekers as "Bentley". An ungainly chunk of shiny steel, ugly to look at, easy to ignore if you didn't understand the power and wealth it signified. Holding it in his hand sent a chill up Jack's spine. Bentleys were handmade, big and luxurious, with an overpowered motor that sounded like a contented tiger while running at twice the speed limit. The car was so expensive ordinary mortals were excluded from even entering a Bentley dealership. Jack reluctantly put the hood ornament down and laughed nervously. "I always wanted one of these. Actually, I want the car you took it from. The senior partner in my law firm has a nice one. I was going to go to the dealer next month and see if maybe I could extend my credit until it squeaked, trade in my merely luxurious ride for one of these truly decadent babies." He picked it up again, turning it over to watch it sparkle in the sun. "How much?"

Theo shook his head.

Jack polished the chrome on his shirtsleeve.

"C'mon. It will look good on my desk, inspire me to work over-time. How much?" He pulled out his wallet. "I'll give you twenty."

The boy shook his head. Jack dug into his wallet again. "Considering what your father is doing for me, I'll sweeten the deal. I'll give you fifty. That's way more than a kid like you has ever seen. Fifty dollars will buy a lot of comic books." He held out the bill but the boy ignored it, shaking his head and looking into Jack's eyes.

"It's not for you."

Jack laughed. "I get it. You'll never see another one of these babies drive through here again. I guess I'll just have to steal the one from my boss's car." He put the hood ornament back and turned to get the gas can. Something caught his eye and he turned back. On the top shelf was a baseball card, crumpled and worn. He picked it up and studied the faded image on the forty year old rookie card. "Wow! I had this same card when I was your age. Do you know who this is? He's long retired now, but in his day he was the best. He used to smoke 'em in. I saw him pitch in the first game my dad took me to. It was his last full season and by then he was working out of the bullpen. He was my dad's favorite." He looked at the card, flipping it over to read the stats. "How much?"

Theo smiled. "Do you really want it? I might just sell you that hood ornament if you want that more."

Jack stood looking at the card, deep in thought. "No. I don't want that. I can always pick up another one in the city. Maybe even rip it off of my boss's car when the parking lot's security camera isn't looking." He flipped the card back over to look at the player's picture. "But I haven't seen one of these cards in twenty years. How much?"

"Your cell phone."

Jack laughed. "Get real. This card is old but it isn't a collector's item. I'll give you twenty dollars."

The boy shook his head.

"Fifty? Okay. It's not worth it, but it is to me. I'll give you one hundred dollars."

Theo shook his head. "I want your cell phone."

Jack put the card down on the wooden crate. "My cell phone is brand new. I paid three hundred for it just a couple of months ago. It's worth way more than this baseball card."

Theo smiled. "I don't want to keep the phone. I just want to hold it for a minute."

"You can't use it to make a call. The battery ran out just about when my car ran out of gas. Otherwise I would have called a tow truck."

"I don't want to call. I just want to hold it."

"That's it? And I get to keep the card?"

The boy nodded.

"How do you stay in business, kid?" He handed him the cell phone and put the card in his shirt pocket.

Theo looked at the cell phone for a few moments before quickly pressing it against his forehead, his knuckles turning white with the effort. He groaned. The cell phone started ringing wildly, playing tones the manufacturer never intended. Theo shuddered and groaned, "It's broken. What good is a phone that lies to you?" He mumbled, "Phones are important. They should tell you what you need to hear. I gotta fix it. There are so many important things for you to say but this phone can't do it yet. There are so many lies, so many words, and wrong words for bad reasons. It's time to fix all that."

Theo went on mumbling, his words drowned out by the chirping cell phone. Jack was frozen in place, both confused and fascinated. The phone continued to blare out a painfully loud and distorted electronic cacophony. Wild scales, short song clips played at twice the normal speed, and what sounded like animal sounds recorded in reverse, drowning out Theo's groans.

The sounds got louder and faster; Theo, swaying, almost falling, then catching himself on the wooden crate and nearly toppling it over. Then, silence.

He held the phone against his forehead for a few moments, panting and sweating. His hand shook as he held it out to Jack. The phone hung in the air between them before Jack finally took it, staring at it in his hand, not knowing what to expect. The phone remained strangely silent.

Theo started packing up the crate. "You better go get your gas can. I've got to close up and put my stuff away before my dad gets back. Mom will be worried if he takes too long." He closed up the crate, pushing it forward slowly, and disappeared behind the garage. Jack waited for a few minutes before crossing the street to the hardware store.

⁂

Mr. Meyer drove the tractor, Theo perched high on the left wheel cover enjoying the breeze, while Jack, perched on the right, held on to the roll bar. Ten minutes later, the tractor arrived at the house where a small crowd of mildly curious cud-chewing cows witnessed the unlikely sight of Jack climbing down from the tractor. Mr. Meyer carried the groceries into the kitchen. He put them away while Jack watched impatiently from the open doorway.

"Can we go? I'm in a rush. I've got a meeting in the city and my boss wants me there before noon."

Mr. Meyer closed the refrigerator. "Do you want a cup of coffee before you go? You look all done in."

Jack gritted his teeth. "No, thank you. It's a very important meeting. If I'd known it was going to be like this, I would have called the firm and had them take care of everything from their end. They would have sent a limo and a tow truck. They need me at that meeting."

Mr. Meyer put the pot on the burner. "Well, I'm sorry to be such a bother. If you don't mind, I'll start some coffee brewing. Siphoning gasoline always leaves a bad taste in my mouth. A good cup of coffee will take care of that. I'll just start it now so that when we're done I can slurp it down." Jack opened his mouth to object but thought better of it. "Why didn't you call your boss before?"

"My cell phone died right after I finished speaking to my boss. Can I use your phone? I need to tell the firm that I'll be a little late." A loud buzzing came from Jack's pocket. Puzzled, he reached in. He flipped open the cell phone, glancing at the number on the display before putting it to his ear. Jack was surprised to hear Mr. Jonas already speaking, but not to him. Mr. Jonas was in mid-tirade, talking about Jack but seemingly unaware that Jack was listening. Jack tried to interject but the phone seemed to be stuck on mute. He was forced to listen to Mr. Jonas without being able to defend himself.

"I don't know where the little weasel is. He doesn't have the brains or the guts to run. He should have been here by now."

A voice that Jack didn't recognize answered. "An investigation like this takes time."

Mr. Jonas laughed bitterly. "Just keep those marshals where they are. Once he sees their guns and badges he'll confess to the whole thing. He's a lousy lawyer and this whole project was just another example of his disrespect for the law. As senior partner, I was always reining him in. He was greedy and put money before ethics, thinking this is how you play it in the big leagues. I tried to set him straight, but I guess it wasn't enough. That stupid switch he pulled with the lab reports was the last straw."

There was a pause on the line. "The District Attorney certainly appreciates your cooperation, Mr. Jonas. It saves us a lot of digging."

"Not a problem. I wouldn't want you to waste your time and get your hands dirty from sifting through all our dusty files. I've been in this profession for a long time and I plan on being around a lot longer. Mistakes do happen, and in my experience it is always better to cooperate. We were happy to turn over the relevant files. It's a pity about Jack but he brought it on himself. He didn't understand that if you don't play by the rules you get burned. He went off on his own and doctored those lab reports and now he's going to have to pay the price. He may be like a son to me but this time he's gone too far. More than once I needed to give him a slap on the wrist to keep him on the right course. Maybe this will finally set him straight."

The other voice hesitated. "The marshals will stay in his office for a little while longer, if you don't mind. An assistant DA will come over to tie up a few technical loose ends. The state police spotted Mr. Nathan on the road a couple of hours ago, so this should be wrapped up fairly quickly, especially since he doesn't know we are looking for him."

The line cut out and the phone turned dark. Jack pushed the "on" button but the battery was dead. His hand shook as he tried to put the phone in his pocket. It slipped from his fingers and he had to wipe his sweaty palms on his pants before picking it up.

Mr. Meyer poured two cups of coffee, putting them on the table between them. "Theo messed with your phone, didn't he?"

Jack stared at his phone in a daze, holding it away from him like the incomprehensible object it had become. He nodded slowly.

"You gotta watch that. Theo has a way of making things go weird. He means well and everything works out in the end, but he makes getting there feel like an unexpected trip to the county fair with a couple extra loop-the-loops thrown in. My guess is that you have time for that cup of coffee now, isn't that right?"

Jack nodded again, putting the phone into his pocket. He sat in the chair across from Mr. Meyer. A frown creased his brow. He stood up.

"I need to use your phone."

Mr. Meyer sipped his coffee. "Why don't you have a cup of coffee first while you figure out if that's really a good idea? It looks to me like you're in a big hurry to go somewhere you don't want to be and talk to some people you don't want to talk to. That doesn't make much sense, does it?"

Jack was about to contradict him, object strongly like in court, but thought better of it. His objection would have been overruled, all the evidence supporting Mr. Meyer. He sat back down and lifted the cup of coffee. "You wouldn't happen to have any soy milk? I'm lactose intolerant."

Mr. Meyer shook his head. "That stuff comes from tofu cows. All we got are the old-fashioned kind made out of leather and beef." Mr. Meyer glanced over his shoulder. "Theo, stay away from that coffee pot. You know your mother doesn't like you to drink coffee. And if you're going to mess with people, you should at least have the decency to sit down and hear about the can of worms you helped stir up."

Theo stepped away from the coffee pot and poured a glass of milk, joining the two men at the kitchen table.

His father turned to Jack. "Maybe you want to tell us about it."

"You wouldn't understand."

"Probably not. But sometimes telling someone else helps a person sort out things in his own head. See, it comes from having your ears so close to your mouth. There's no time to think things through if you're all alone. So telling it to someone helps straighten things out. By the time it crosses the table and gets to the other person, it makes more sense to both of you than when it just churned around in your own head."

Jack's hands shook as he lifted the cup to his lips. "There are marshals at my office waiting to arrest me, for god's sake! They must have issued a subpoena and would have slapped it on me if my car hadn't broken down. And if my phone didn't go bonkers, I would have walked right into it. My office is probably under lock and key. I can't even go home. I knew I was testing the limits of the law, but I didn't think they would arrest me. Mr. Jonas should have said something. I was just following his instructions."

"I thought you said you were an attorney. You folks are supposed to uphold the law, not break it."

"The problem is that the legislation isn't keeping up with the technology. If you follow the rules, you end up being too late and the competition grabs all the profits. The first one to market is the only one that counts."

"That's how Bonnie and Clyde got famous, staying one step ahead of the law. Until they didn't. It's a hell of a business."

Jack grimaced. "We weren't robbing banks. This was an important client for my law firm. They deal in biotech research, the stuff that helps farmers. You can appreciate that. For me, it would have meant being on top of a whole new branch of practice. I fought tooth and nail to get assigned, got results, and there was talk of me being made a junior partner, but I was riding the edge. Oh, they were worth a fortune, on paper. The top employees were mega-rich in stock options that were one step away from becoming a stack of worthless papers. So we had to stay ahead or everything would fall apart. And I was the key player, holding it all together by working double overtime and bending the rules big time." He sighed and took another sip. Then he continued. "Mr. Jonas made a few suggestions that went out of bounds but he said, 'that's how we play it in the major leagues.' I didn't want to, but he threatened to fire me. He could easily replace me with someone hungrier, who played to win. I did what I was told and now everything's blown up in my face."

"He really set you up, didn't he," Mr. Meyer said, his matter-of-fact tone lacking the compassion his words might have implied.

"Well, I assumed that if there was a problem, the firm would stand behind me and Mr. Jonas would back me up. Instead, they're hanging me out to dry, blaming me for going rogue. Now I'm looking at probable disbarment and possible criminal charges. Hell, I could even go to jail. The cops are looking for me. Mr. Jonas is cooperating to limit damage to their assets. He's selling me to the cops in order to save the firm. I can't go to work, I can't go home, and I can't even use my credit cards if I want to stay out of jail. It's a good thing I paid for that gas can with cash."

"Is Mr. Jonas big?"

Jack stared at the farmer, trying to understand the incongruous question. "Of course. He's a senior partner, one of the founders of the firm."

Mr. Meyer shook his head. "That's not what I meant. If Mr. Jonas smacked you in the face, would you be eating lunch through a straw?"

Jack was confused. "No. He's old and has a nasty temper but I wouldn't be afraid of him if he came at me. What's it matter?"

"Does he have a gun?"

"No."

"Does he hire big goons to rough people up?"

"Of course not."

"Maybe he's got a big dog trained to kill on command?"

Now Jack was getting annoyed. "What's your point?"

"When he told you to do something stupid, you should have smacked him hard as you could and told him you weren't nobody's fool. You don't seem much more than half stupid. You knew that what he was telling you to do would end up coming back and biting you in the rear."

"He's my boss."

"And not a very good one. You know that it's not a crime to tell someone else to break the law. The guy who ends up with the handcuffs on is the one fool enough to listen to stupid advice. You're running from the police while he's sipping a martini."

Jack felt his anger rise but it cooled as he let the words sink in. The hick was right. He knew that Mr. Jonas gave him bad advice but he followed it anyway. He thought that his new position and the money that came with it would lift him into the stratosphere of the untouchably rich and important. He was sure that Mr. Jonas was opening up the door to the executive suite and inviting him in. And all he needed to do was get those reports altered enough to calm down the critics of Bo Plus. He thought that Mr. Jonas would stand by him like a father if anything went wrong. Jonas had said so himself, or something to that effect. Now he felt used and foolish.

Mr. Meyer sipped his coffee, watching Jack consider his words. "Do you feel like turning yourself in?"

Jack sighed heavily. "No, but I don't see any alternative. Maybe they'll take it easy on me if I do."

"It seems to me that there is a lot riding on your tail getting cooked all the way through, so that no one else even gets a little bit burned." Mr. Meyer and Theo's eyes met in silent agreement. "We'd better hurry up and get your car before a trooper finds it. A flashy car like that attracts attention, especially parked by the side of the road."

Jack looked at him in a daze. "What are you talking about?"

"The city is a long way from here. We could park your car in the barn and no one would ever know."

"I can't just hide in your barn until the police forget about this."

"You've got that right. You're going to have to learn to milk a cow if you're going to stay around."

HANNA

Jack's Mercedes started right up even without the siphoned gasoline, its German engineering humming away with eerily quiet precision. The gas gauge decided to change its mind and was now claiming a half tank of hi-test fuel in the tank. The idling car purred away as if nothing had ever gone wrong. Big Brad clucked his tongue. "It was probably an electrical short circuit. That would explain your cell phone. I can fix that." When he went to pop open the hood, Jack slammed his hand on the hood and tried pushing the big man away. "Don't touch it. This is a Mercedes, not your piece of junk tractor. If anyone works on it other than a company-certified mechanic, it cancels out the warranty. You got that, Tonto?"

Brad looked down at Jack and calmly placed a hand calloused like tree bark over the smaller pale one, hiding it almost entirely. "I got that. I was just trying to help." He squeezed slightly, making Jack wince. "Don't call me Tonto." He climbed onto the tractor as Theo scrambled onto his perch. Brad popped the clutch, the big wheels spinning before catching. He ran through the tall gears with the hand throttle jammed down, the throaty growl and half-burned diesel lingering in the air after they disappeared around a bend. Mr. Meyer got into the passenger side of the two-seater, listening to the engine hum, not saying a word until the turn-in at the farm's front gate.

The car was small enough to slip into a tool shed behind the barn. It was a tight fit. Jack put down the convertible top to climb out over the trunk. He watched his gleaming new car disappear behind the unpainted wood door and realized, with a sense of desperation, that a chapter of his own life might be closing. For the first time in a long while, he felt his own vulnerability. All the material expressions of the façade he had so carefully constructed as a successful, brilliant, and enviable young attorney had abruptly vanished. He tried to start up a discussion about escape routes, alibis, and false identities to present to the police when they arrived. The others listened politely but did not join in. Big Brad walked away first, forgetting his anger at the previous slur. The broad, dark expanse of his forehead furrowed, first in annoyance and then in confusion, as Jack babbled away as if he were still billing two hundred dollars an hour for talking fast. Hanna mumbled something about having a chore she forgot to attend to and hurried off, the frayed hem of her calico skirt swishing against her black gum boots. Mr. Meyer politely interrupted and told Theo to attend to their guest and set him up in a room. Jack carried on but felt foolish plotting to evade police arrest with a twelve-year-old boy. Theo listened intently, fascinated. Jack finally realized that he might as well be talking to a blank wall and fell silent, suddenly aware that his heart was pounding.

Theo looked him over. "You're about my dad's size. We could lend you some of his clothes to get you by. I figure you'll need two sets of work clothes. You'll still have to do a wash every day. I'll help you with that. Do you have any regular clothes packed in your car?"

Jack felt helpless, a disturbing condition to be in when standing in front of a boy. "How long do you think I'll be staying here?" The question was out before Jack realized it was a question the host should be asking the guest and not the other way around.

Theo answered as if it were a natural question to ask. "Not too long. A week or two at the most. Maybe three."

Jack was about to ask how he knew that, but Theo had already walked away, calling back over his shoulder. "My dad wants me to get you set up. We'd better get to it if you want to be in time for the night milking." They went back to the house and came out loaded down with bed linens and some casual clothes. Perched on top was a pair of old work boots, soft and comfortable from years of use. The boots were a little big but thick socks would help them fit. Jack walked blindly behind the pile of clothes, following Theo's voice out to the barn. They put down their load on bales of hay by the ladder that led up to the loft.

"I'm sleeping here?"

Theo nodded. "The loft is nice this time of year. It's high up and right off the south field so you get a breeze night and day. It keeps the skeeters away. You have plenty of room and if you keep the loft doors open, you'll get a nice view. It's a good clean smell and it's private. That makes for good alone-time thoughts. You can even have visitors if you want. You can keep a jar of iced tea but I wouldn't keep cake or biscuits around. It'll attract ants."

"What are you talking about, kid? What visitors?"

Theo smiled. "Me, and maybe some others. I usually sleep out here this time of year. You'll find a nice mattress up there and a couple of decent books. The batteries in the lantern are new, but the moon is coming on full so you won't need the lantern except for reading."

Jack smirked. "I figured the batteries work. I've seen how you recharge them. Do you think you can charge my phone again? I need to make a few calls."

"Who did you want to call? Your friends at work are pouring coffee for those marshals, admiring their guns, and slipping them clues on how to find you. How many of your old friends do you think are siding with you and how many do you think are trying to save their own careers?" Jack was dumbfounded. Theo's wry grin seemed out of place on the face of a young boy. Mildly toxic sarcasm is a vice reserved for grown-ups, like nicotine and caffeine. For the most part, Theo looked and acted like a boy. But when Jack looked closer, there were tiny lines around his eyes that made them look inexplicably old.

Theo's words echoed in the empty barn as images of faces drifted through Jack's mind. He felt lost, strangely dizzy, and light-headed, almost losing his balance as he realized those faces were all part of his identity as a high power attorney. It was a highly developed network of mutually parasitic relationships. Calling one would mean dealing with the whole lot and thinking of that made him nauseous. The colleagues who were high enough on the ladder to be able to help were the ones with the biggest interest in selling him out to the authorities, dead or alive. The ones who couldn't help would sell him out to the bigger fish for the price of Jack's place on the ladder. He had done the same, avoiding other attorneys who were in Mr. Jonas' bad graces. Friendship perished quickly in the furnace of a high-pressure law firm.

Jack realized he was alone in a barn, all but stripped naked. He had little cash, couldn't use his credit cards, and if he took his fancy overpowered car on the road it would draw police like flies to cow patties. His tailored suits, worn to intimidate adversaries and subdue clients, were at the dry cleaners one hundred miles away, perhaps already confiscated by the District Attorney as evidence. He would be wearing borrowed clodhopper clothing until this mess got sorted out. His real talisman, the one he wielded with the most devastating effect, was his cell phone, but that was literally out of power. Or at least not under his power but under the spell of a child who could make his cell phone live or die without a power cord.

Theo interrupted his thoughts. "Milking is in an hour. That will give you just enough time to settle in and grab a sandwich."

Jack sat down, feeling tired and helpless. "I don't know how to milk a cow. I barely know how to open a carton of milk."

Theo smiled even wider, with the same crooked grin. "That's okay. Big Brad will teach you."

Jack slumped down, straw poking him through his silk pants. It had been a long time since he actually cried. Theo came in with a big pile of peanut butter sandwiches for Jack to take to work. In his borrowed work clothes and tall black gum boots, Jack followed Theo out to the cowshed. Big Brad was walking slowly through the field, clapping his hands and singing a low tune. The cows that were lying down got up slowly and ambled into the pen adjacent to the milking parlor, jostling each other gently, their large jaws incessantly chewing. Jack kept hoping he would wake from this nightmare but it just wasn't happening.

Big Brad closed a gate and punched a button, starting up the sprinklers that washed the bottoms of the cows. Theo and Jack sat silently in the office, avoiding conversation, waiting for the shower to finish. When the water turned off, Brad turned on a large portable stereo. Jack was surprised to hear a chamber quartet playing Pachelbel's Canon in D. Brad flipped a switch, starting up the air pumps that ran the milking system. A gate opened and a string of cows strolled in, taking their places at the milking stations. Each cow had a small bowl full of oats to munch while the machine sucked away at her udders. Theo led Jack into the sunken trench where the milkmen worked. Jack caught on quickly to the repetitive work but he had to hurry to keep up with Big Brad, who moved with a dreamlike calm.

Jack found some relief from his problems in the mindless, rhythmic movement of his hands. The cows gave him slow stares as they walked past as if they were checking him out. When he wasn't looking, an enormous tongue, rough as sandpaper, ran down his forearm, coating it with a layer of goo. Jack felt like he had been thoroughly tasted. As the milking wore on, Jack imagined the cows were ignoring him and their looks turned disdainful. He needed to keep reminding himself that they were dumb animals too stupid to have an opinion. One cow decided to let loose a surprisingly long stream of pee as it passed him, splattering gallons in total disregard of Jack's dignity. Jack was unavoidably and fragrantly soaked, angry with Brad for laughing. Jack glared at the huge Indian, then decided to shrug it off.

"I've been pissed on much worse than that in courtrooms from lawyers a lot more stupid than that cow."

Brad stopped in mid-chuckle, a surprised look on his face. Jack jumped as the big man broke out laughing twice as hard, the booming noise welling up from deep in his chest like a geyser of mirth. Brad's outburst of laughter was the first sound the big Native made all night. The last cow to enter the parlor, an old dowager, refused to be coaxed or crowded. She stood off to the side, waiting until all the other cows finished. Her stride was slow, her big bony hips swayed gracefully. It occurred to Jack to pat her udder gently before attaching the machine. The cow twisted her head around, strands of hay hanging from her mouth, to stare at the new milkman. She tossed her head and a slightly chewed clump of straw landed on Jack's arm. He looked up at the cow as she watched him. He dipped his head in a nod of respect, saying "Thank you, m'lady" before placing one of the less damp stalks in his mouth and beginning to chew. When the old dame finished, Jack turned to see Brad staring at him. Brad nodded before commenting.

"Maybe the boy is right. You might be good for something besides baiting bear traps."

Jack grinned. "I'm glad you think so."

"Don't get your hopes up," Brad said as he headed out the door. "I'm not convinced yet and I was looking forward to some fresh bear steak."

Jack wondered if he was serious, disturbed that it wasn't so clearly a joke. He smelled like the inside of a cow, but the milking parlor had a shower room and washing machine. Jack showered and put his filthy work clothes into the washer. He headed back to the barn. He was sore from the unaccustomed physical work, but thankful that he was too tired to think about the difficult choice facing him, whether a catastrophic career change to avoid imprisonment was worth the risk of having his scalp hung over the cow shed's front door.

He considered closing the large open window as he fell onto the thin mattress. The night was warm and there was a pleasant breeze, but city living had made him a bit agoraphobic. He was accustomed to living behind walls of glass and concrete eternally lit by humming electric lights. Here, the open windows and flat fields scared him, making him too nervous to fall asleep. Being surrounded by nature made him feel as though he was living an Animal Planet safari. He was half expecting a whispered voice with a British accent to begin describing the ravenous nocturnal predator stalking its unwary prey, a fat and succulent attorney, unarmed and helpless.

Something else bothered him. After several minutes of intense concentration he figured it out: It was too quiet. He missed the deep rumble of the subway and the constant traffic noise of "the city that never sleeps." The night sky wasn't tinted by pollutants and he could actually see the stars and the moon. City sounds had been his lullaby; the absolute quiet of the country night made him jumpy. He closed his eyes and tried counting. When he got to one hundred and convinced himself that he was beginning to feel drowsy, the barn door squeaked. He sat up. A soft tread crossed the barn floor, softly brushing over the loose straw. He stared through the dark to where the ladder should be. The shape of a head, darker than its surroundings, appeared at the top of the ladder. A girl's voice whispered. "Theo? Is that you?"

Jack reached over and turned on the electric lantern. The soft light filled the loft. Hanna looked at him in surprise, but her expression quickly changed to anger.

"What are you doing here?"

Jack fumbled for an excuse. "Theo told me to sleep here. He said I might have visitors but I thought he meant himself."

"That's typical of Theo. That boy is full of surprises." She hesitated before climbing up the rest of the ladder and sitting on a hay bale. "I am the mystery visitor he had in mind. I come here every night when he sleeps out here. But being Theo, he didn't tell you the details."

"He's a strange kid."

Hanna shrugged. "You don't know the half of it." She hesitated as if she wanted to say more. Jack waited but she decided not to continue.

"That roadside stand of his is a joke. He'd make more money selling ice cream in Alaska."

Hanna plucked a straw from the bale and began to chew it. "Theo's business is a lot of things but it isn't a joke. Far from it! That's actually why I'm here on the farm. He gave me a journal. I write in it every night before I go to sleep. Part of the deal was that I would come here to work for six months."

"That's a steep price for an empty journal. I guess I got off cheap. I just lent him my phone for a couple of minutes."

"No, I got a good deal. I'd left home and had no place to stay, and nothing to lose. I was in a rough space. I thought his parents would have a fit but they genuinely seemed relieved when I told them about the deal. They told me I could stay as long as I wanted and it seemed like they really meant it."

"You're old to be running away from home."

She threw a handful of straw at him. "Yeah. I moved back in with my folks for a little bit. I thought it would help get me through a rough period. It didn't. So I moved back out."

"Trying to save on rent?"

"Something like that. I had a problem to work out and I thought my parents could help. They couldn't deal with my issue, or me, so I left. I wasn't very good at dealing with my problem on my own but at least the only one suffering was me." She turned quiet. Jack's instincts told him not to push. "The six months are almost up and the journal is almost full. I write in it every night."

"And you keep it up here?"

She shook her head, a worried look on her face. "No. I have the journal." She took a small book out of the baggy pocket sewn onto her skirt. "I found out later that he sold me the journal but not the key that opens it. He kept that and refused to sell it to me. I stole it once but it disappeared from where I hid it. I had to apologize to Theo and admit that I stole it. He thought it was hilarious and couldn't stop laughing. I didn't understand why he was so amused. I got angry, telling him the key was lost and now we would have to ruin the journal to get it open. He laughed and showed me that it was back where it always was, right under his pillow. I tried breaking the lock with a screwdriver. It looks like it's made of fake metal but I sweated for an hour and a half for nothing. I even tried ripping off the cover but the book must be made of iron. After a month I got used to asking him for the key. I started reading him all the stuff I wrote. I even got to liking it. It's like reading him a bedtime story except I need it for me to fall asleep."

Jack nodded. "That sounds like the deal I made. I lent him my cell phone and now I can't use it without him. I thought I was getting a baseball card and the next thing I know, I'm sleeping in a barn." They both laughed, ending in a shy silence. "What deal did he make with Brad?"

"I don't know. Brad was here before me. He doesn't talk much. I get the feeling that Brad doesn't have the same relationship with Theo. Brad doesn't need anything. I think Brad is teaching Theo."

"Teaching him what? How to shoot a bow and arrow?"

Hanna gazed at him, a confused look on her face. "No. I think he is teaching him how to pray. If you spend any time with Brad, you'll see a lot of that. I tried asking him about it once. I asked him to teach me but he just shook his head. I kept pushing, asking him every day but he refused to talk about it. One day Theo told me that Brad didn't like my asking so I stopped."

Jack thought about it for a few moments but it didn't make any sense. Hanna stood up. She put her journal back into her pocket. "I guess I'll have to go find Theo if I want to keep on writing."

Jack nodded apologetically. "I wish I could help you but I don't have the key. I just made up my bed and there weren't any keys around." He reached under the pillow and was shocked when his fingers felt a ribbon that hadn't been there five minutes before. He pulled it out and dangling from the end was a small key. Confused, he looked over to see her smiling, almost laughing at him.

She took the key and opened the small book, pulling the electric lantern closer. Jack watched as she began to write in the journal. She ignored him, intent on her writing. Jack turned to the books Theo had left for him. He expected a selection of comic books or science fiction. He was surprised to find a copy of Thoreau, a book on American history, one about quantum physics without the math, Rumi, Kerouac, and a volume from the Tolkien trilogies. He glanced at Hanna. She had finished writing and was watching him.

"Is this what he usually reads, or did he bring these books up especially for me?"

"My guess is both. He wants you to feel at home."

"That's sweet but he should have brought me a recent law journal."

"Is that all you read?"

"It's what I do. It's what I am."

She laughed bitterly. "Not anymore. Now you milk cows for a living. And unless some kind of miracle happens, the only bar you'll care about are the ones keeping you in a jail cell. You'd be smart to face up to facts. It's your own damn fault so stop complaining."

Jack bristled. Hanna looked angry, but soft in the moonlight. Her barbed comment stung, because he knew she was right. He hadn't thought constructively of his predicament and hadn't even begun making plans. He spent all his time angry with Mr. Jonas for turning him in. Now that he was too tired and sore to be angry, he realized that it wasn't Mr. Jonas' fault. He went along despite his own better judgment. The money was simply too tempting.

Like the cutthroats say, you can't rape the willing. Mr. Meyer had said it and now Hanna confirmed it. He had been greedy, took a gamble and lost, and now he was going to have to pay the price. He hadn't thought about solutions because there were no solutions and no excuses. Eventually the police would catch him and no evidence existed that could help him. He had been trussed up like a turkey ready for the oven. What particularly bothered him was how he allowed himself to become so blinded by greed and ambition, and that Mr. Jonas, the real culprit, would walk away looking like the wise mentor disappointed by an unworthy apprentice. Begrudgingly he realized that the time on the farm was a gift, a vacation before an ugly losing battle he would be forced to fight alone. He might as well enjoy it while it lasted.

Hanna saw that her comment hit home and that the atmosphere had changed. She stood up, ready to leave. "Give me the key. I need it to lock the journal. I never leave it open."

He held out the key but snatched it away as she was about to take it. Her irritated look made him smile. He shook his head. "I want the same deal as Theo. I'm bored. Tell me a bedtime story." He realized he was flirting with her.

Sparks flashed in her eyes. "You aren't Theo. And I am not here for your entertainment!"

Her anger made the teasing more appealing. He shook his head and held the key out of her reach. She glared at him for a moment before slumping her shoulders in defeat. Jack laughed in triumph. But quicker then he could react, she swung her fist into his stomach, driving the air out of his lungs as he doubled over. The key dropped onto the straw-covered floor. She fell to her knees and began desperately sifting through the straw.

He sat down heavily on his bed, gasping for breath.

She muttered as she continued searching for the key.

He coughed a few times before speaking in a raspy voice. "I may not be Theo. But my guess is that you'd be better off making the same deal with me, anyway." He held up the ribbon, the key spinning at the end, sparkling in the moonlight. She snatched the key out of his hand and tried to lock the journal. The key refused to fit into the lock. She tried to force it but the key slipped from her fingers, bouncing once before falling over the edge of the loft into the darkness below. She almost fell over the edge trying to catch it and then started to scramble down the ladder but was stopped by Jack's sharp laugh. She turned to see him still sitting down, out of breath, holding the key by two fingers. He put the string around his neck and leaned back against a hay bale, waiting to be read to.

She glared at him and opened the book. "I'll read to you from the beginning." She moved closer to the open windows, holding the book at an angle to catch more of the moonlight. She began to read.

"Writing is thoughts given shape, the process by which our thoughts become real. The words flow slowly, letting you see yourself more clearly, but you risk setting the memory in stone, taking away the gentle winds of time that allow the past to live after it has drifted away. Thoughts are the butterflies of time, going back and forth without reason, carrying tiny droplets of nectar, precious dreams, those that were and those that have yet to be. They bring flashes of beauty to the moment, coming from we don't know where, and leading us away from the trails we were following. We can sometimes catch them with our nets and remember a part of their beauty by writing them down. It's important after you catch them to set them free again or their beauty will fade. Beauty held too tightly becomes dogma, a faded moth in a museum, studied until it is no longer appreciated, only understood. The butterfly of your dreams and inner thoughts may not be real, but its splendor and truth are more real than anything you have built or bought. Your hopes and dreams, what you lack, say who you are more than anything you have done. People may know you for your past, for what you have been, what you are. But only love can open the cocoon where your dreams lay sleeping and only a lover can see you for what you are going to be. A journal is a forest where your hopes may live in dim shadows. And dreams are the seeds from which prayer can grow. With my face towards . . ."

She stopped reading, hesitated, and then closed the book. Jack reached across and held her wrist. "A deal is a deal." She shook her head and Jack realized that she was about to cry. He was baffled. He had just met this girl and already they had gotten into a fist-fight and now she looked like she was about to start crying on his shoulder. She was a strange mixture of country calico and work boots. He took the book from her hands and laid it gently on her lap. "Please, when you are ready." She looked down, her dark hair covering her face. After a minute, she looked up and read.

"With my face towards death, red and real as the setting sun, I have no choice but to use the time I have to live my dream and to finally feel good about just being me, the best possible me I can be. I have been given a great gift. Even though I may not have much time, I will spend it in the best possible way here on this farm where I have discovered what it means to truly be alive. Though I spend most of my day with cows, I have learned how to communicate with them and they with me on the level of the purest and simplest of feelings, that of tenderness."

In spite of himself, what Hanna wrote struck a chord, and Jack, the Ivy League graduate and sophisticated lawyer, was moved by her heartfelt words. They were about her but they could also apply to him as well. He hadn't been the best possible person he could be, and, in fact, he wasn't even sure who he actually was.

He understood something, but it was an uncomfortable understanding that he quickly pushed away.

She closed the book and stood. She was halfway down the ladder when Jack called out, "Same time tomorrow night?"

"Bastard!" She glared at him for a moment, breathing hard. She took two steps down and stopped. She hesitated, her head just visible. "It seems I have no choice if I want to keep writing." She hurried down the ladder. Jack heard the barn door open and close. He was about to follow her when his phone rang. Digging through the pile of clothes he finally found it.

He heard a young woman's voice with a chirpy southern twang. "Hello, Mr. Nathan. My name is Candace and I'm calling from The Baby Shop. We've been trying to reach you for three days but couldn't get through. Your order is ready to ship but there was a problem with your address. Probably a pesky computer glitch wiped it. I just need to confirm your address and we can ship it out right away."

"Is this some kind of scam? I didn't order anything from a baby store."

The woman hesitated but continued in a professional tone. "I assure you this isn't a scam. The order has been paid for and is ready to ship. We just need to confirm your address."

"What did I order?"

"There's a lot. It looks like you chose The Baby Shop to provide all of your newborn's needs. Let's see . . . You ordered a full bedroom set with sheets. I also see a stroller-car seat combo. There is a long list of toys and accessories; diaper bag, bottles, breast pump. Gosh that's nice. Breast feeding is becoming popular again."

Jack stood at the open window, looking in the direction of New York, imagining he could see the city lights. Even hiding out from the police, tele-scammers could still find him. This promised to be a pleasant distraction. People went into tele-scamming because they were incompetent and ignorant but too lazy to flip hamburgers. He ate these guys for breakfast. This could be a light snack, a pleasant diversion to take his mind off his own problems. "Nice try. I imagine the next step is that I'm supposed to give you my credit card number. This is the stupidest scam anyone has ever tried on me. I don't have a baby, am not expecting a baby, and have no intention of having a baby now or ever. The only thing I hate more than half-baked telephone credit card scams is crying babies and their lactating mothers. Leave me alone and get a job!" He pushed the button to disconnect the call but the phone was already off. He tried turning it on but the battery was dead. He chuckled as he lay down. That outburst released just enough tension to let him fall asleep. He was gently snoring a minute after his head hit the lumpy pillow, a small grin on his face. If he had continued standing in the open window for a few more minutes and listened to the quiet country night, he would have heard Hanna, fifteen feet below, gently hitting her head against the tree, sobbing softly.

Jack's intense fear of Brad was becoming a strong curiosity. He didn't know how long he would be hiding from the police or how long he would be on this farm. He imagined himself suffocating from boredom. There weren't many options for entertainment. He could spend the time thinking about how messed up his life was or he could spar with the yokels. He chose the latter option, which would pass the time until the inevitable caught up with him. The Indian had pissed him off and even physically threatened him. He wanted to know more about how an Indian came to be milking cows instead of sitting around the reservation complaining about the lack of buffalo to hunt. After they finished milking, he followed

Brad and Theo outside. They walked until they were well into the field separating the dairy from the road. He watched in fascination as Brad kneeled down on the ground. Theo kept walking towards the road. Jack assumed he was heading into town to set up his roadside stand. Brad was singing, his voice carried across the field on the wind. Jack stepped closer to hear better, but the song had no words.

Big Brad took a deep, shuddering breath. "Good morning, Jack."

"Morning, Brad," he croaked. "How did you know I was here?"

His shoulders shook with silent laughter. "It was either you or a lame cow wearing cheap after-shave." Big Brad stood and turned to face Jack, the smile half-gone from his face. "Now it's your turn."

"My turn to sing?"

Big Brad shook his head, his long, shiny black hair swinging in the bright sun. "Nope. It's your turn to pray. We should thank God for the milk He just gave us. I also pray before milking, asking for milk."

Jack shook his head. "That's ridiculous. Cows give milk. It isn't a case of divine intervention. It's biology. It's what they do and they're too stupid to do anything else except maybe sit on a plate waiting for steak sauce and a glass of red wine."

"Just because science can explain it, doesn't mean God isn't there."

"That sounds profound but it doesn't really mean anything. If I don't get milk, I'll drink my coffee black."

Brad shook his head. "That's sad. No wonder your life is such a mess."

"My life isn't a mess. I'm a successful lawyer with lots of money. I've got the best education money can buy and a career that makes women swoon at my feet. I've got a condo in an exclusive building and a hot car."

"Your hot car is gathering dust in the tool shed and you sleep in the barn." Big Brad shook his big head, his almond shaped eyes showing no emotion. "Part of prayer is taking time out for a reality check, something you sorely need. You aren't going to be a lawyer for too much longer. You're on the run from the police and can't even pay your way here. You have everything you want, but you don't have what you need. You worked for what you wanted, so you think that's why you've got it."

Jack took a step closer to the big man. "That's right. I worked damn hard for what I have."

Brad's eyes didn't waver. "And you've got it. That's logic, science, cause and effect. But did you enjoy it? To enjoy it, to get the good from it, you have to pray. That's why you have what you want but not what you need. You've got so much, more than a man needs to be plenty satisfied and happy. But you never saw the good in it because you didn't pray; you never realized it was a blessing. Your boss' hate was contained in everything you earned and it made you sick. You threw it away and ran. That's why a hotshot lawyer is hiding out in a barn. It was the first sane thing you have ever done." Brad put his hand on Jack's shoulder making it sag with the weight of the big man's arm. "That education you're so proud of didn't do you much good. It didn't teach you what you need to know to be a man. It taught you some tricks to game the system. The system rewarded you with toys that made you feel important but the system can't give you anything real. Real things may not make you happy, but they make your life worth living. You can't wash your own clothes, or cook your own food, and you don't know enough to wash your own plate when you're finished eating. You know all about sex but don't have a clue about love or how to be with a woman for more than ten minutes. You had a dad but the system made you forget how to be a father. Theo's smarter than you and they kicked him out of school last year when he was twelve."

Jack bristled. Big Brad had struck a nerve. He felt his anger rise. Anger was a lawyer's trained attack dog and most lawyers let it run loose to keep it in shape. Paralegals and secretaries got used to it or quit. Waiters and other service staff put up with it because lawyers tipped well, mostly to show off. Most people assumed the lawyer was busy and important so they grudgingly respected the anger. In the middle of a field, smelling of cow poop, Jack realized that anger was getting in the way of finding out what he wanted to know. Anger might also get him killed by an out-of-control Indian looking to take back Manhattan from the yuppies. He took a few deep breaths. "Okay. Maybe you are right. I've made a few mistakes, and Theo does seem like a smart kid, even if he is strange. The books he left in the hay loft for me to read are pretty heavy and they look like they've been gone through several times. How did a kid like that get kicked out of school?"

"School can't teach you to want to learn. Most of the time, they kill that. A curious kid gets in the way of their agenda. Theo learned a lot from his dad. He learned to listen the first time something was said and to think twice before speaking once. He learned about the world he lived in; how to fix a car that he was going to need to drive, how to wash dishes, how to do laundry, how to cook. He learned how to learn. The system wants you to master the system, but stay helpless. They want to keep you inside a box and help build boxes for other men. You make enough money to buy machines that clean and cook for you but it doesn't really do you any good. It feeds the system, keeping other guys in the system as well. If you need something, you go out and buy it and the system gets bigger. If Theo needs something, it's an opportunity for him to learn something new and he gets bigger. You can't take care of yourself. You wear pretty shoes that can only walk where the system has already paved the way. Theo learned to take care of himself and how to help others. He learned to listen to the voice inside that tells him what questions he needs to ask and where he needs to go to find the answers." Brad paused. "And he learned how to pray."

"Hanna said you don't talk much and you especially don't talk about prayer. You talk plenty once you get started."

Brad grinned mischievously. "She only got it partly right. I don't talk to her much and I surely wouldn't teach her about prayer. That girl prays every time she takes a breath. I'll teach you since it seems like your dad forgot to teach you anything worthwhile before he sent you off to all those expensive schools."

"My father died while I was in high school. He had a heart attack."

Big Brad stopped short, a look of sadness wrinkling his smooth brown face. He put his hand on Jack's arm. "I'm truly sorry to hear that, friend. What was his name?"

"Why do you want to know that?"

"You need to know that if you want to pray. You also need to know your mother's name, but that is a different kind of prayer. There is a reason why religion is a family thing. God is everywhere, but you have to know who you are, how you came into the world, in order to connect to the Creator. Your parents were the way God chose to bring you here. It's a good thing to remind Him of that before you start asking for stuff."

"Is that what you were doing? Praying to your Indian ancestors?"

Brad punched him lightly on the chest, a tap that sent him back a few steps and made him cough. "Stop calling me Indian."

Jack rubbed his chest. "I'm sorry. What do you guys like to be called? The tribes? Apache? Navajo?"

"You can call me Big Brad. Or you can call me Oogrooq, my Inuit name. It means 'bearded seal' or 'one who has long life.'"

Jack stood looking at him in shock. "Inuit? You're an Eskimo?"

Big Brad nodded slowly, his black eyes still emotionless. "I guess that fancy education wasn't totally worthless. At least you know who the Inuit are."

"So what are you doing here? Looking for a hopelessly lost herd of caribou?"

"Nope. I'm milking cows, just like you. A stranger in a strange land."

"How did you end up here?"

"The oil company stole my land. As a lawyer, you might not agree, but if someone takes something from you, even if they give you money, it can still be stealing. If you don't want to sell and if they are the ones setting the price, it's stealing. The courts pushed it through because there was a lot of money to be made. On paper, it looked like we were getting a lot. But by the time the lawyers got done with it, none of us walked away with much. It was all perfectly legal but none of it could stand for one second in God's eyes or a man's heart. The money only meant something if we stopped being Inuit and became like the white man. When the lawyers went away, we had enough money to do anything we wanted for a while, but what it really meant was that we would never be Inuit again. The problem is, that's exactly what most of us wanted. I tried working the oilrigs, but it seemed wrong to help them kill what should have been mine. I worked the fishing boats but pulling that much from the ocean seemed like a sickness. I had to get away. It hurt too much, seeing the ice and not going out to hunt like my grandfather."

"I'm sorry."

Big Brad's eyes remained the same, giving nothing away. "I'm telling you this because it is another part of prayer and who you

58

are. A man needs to know who his people are and where his land is."

Jack shrugged. "Well, I guess I'm out of luck there. The closest I can come to belonging to a people is the New York Bar Association and they are about to give me the boot. My land is an overpriced condo on the Upper West Side overlooking Central Park."

"If you don't like it, then why are you a lawyer?"

"Being a lawyer is a great job. How else am I going to get paid six figures for being a nasty jerk?"

"Is that what you want? To be a jerk?"

Jack sobered. "No. My dad passed away and left me enough to get a top-notch education. He was a lawyer so I guess I wanted to be a lawyer as a tribute to him."

"Being a high priced jerk isn't much of a tribute. Is that what your dad was?"

Jack searched those deep black eyes for a sign of mocking but saw that the big man was serious. "No. My dad wasn't a high priced jerk. My dad was an awesome lawyer. He was respected in the courtroom. He wasn't in it for the money. He took cases he believed in and fought them tooth and nail. My dad was a fighter. I'm more of a wheeler-dealer. I make things happen in the back room so that they never have to see a courtroom."

"So you've erased your father's memory, as a lawyer and as a man."

Jack was speechless.

Big Brad nodded and continued. "Why was your dad so tough? He didn't pass it on to you. You are a little guy with not much fight in you."

Jack laughed. "Maybe you're right about me, but my dad got it from his dad. The Nazis chased my grandfather through the forest. When Grandpa was ten years old, he was in the underground, running ammunition to the Partisans. When they got caught, the Partisans were shot. Bullets were too good to be wasted on Jews so my grandfather got put into a camp. He survived the war and came to America alone, at the age of thirteen. He was small but tough. After the war, many of the boxers were Jewish immigrants from Europe."

"Grandpa paid for my dad's schooling with sweat and blood. He taught my dad to box. He even gave him a scar over his right eye. My dad learned to fight and he won some important cases that other people had given up on."

"What would your dad do to Mr. Jonas?"

Jack turned, surprised to see Theo. "I thought you went to town."

Theo shook his head. "I'm here. What would your dad do to Mr. Jonas? Would your dad be milking cows, hiding from the police?"

Jack looked at the boy. "No. My dad was a fighter. That's the kind of man he was and that's the kind of lawyer he was."

Theo and Big Brad exchanged a glance. Theo continued. "So if you went to all that trouble to honor your dad by being a lawyer, isn't now the time to be that lawyer? Especially since you haven't been honoring his memory until now. You did what Mr. Jonas told you to do, not what your father would have done. And look where it's got you. I think you need to talk to your dad, ask him to help get you out of this mess. And your grandfather too."

"But the police . . ." The words died on his lips. A police car was driving slowly along the main road. It stopped at the farm's driveway.

Brad nodded and spoke gently. "When you are out in a sealskin kayak, surrounded by ice, and you see an orca swimming underneath you, you understand how the seal feels when the spear is about to fly. It isn't the orca that kills and it isn't the spear that kills. When fear faces courage, fear will succumb. Fear kills speed. Fear makes the brain stupid. Your courage must be bigger than your fear. An enemy that is bigger than you doesn't make you weaker. It makes your courage stronger. That is the gift a stronger foe brings, the real prize. Asking your Creator for help makes survival a connection between you and your Creator. It makes your life as big as the universe."

In almost the same tone, a gentle echo of Brad's deep voice, Theo said, "Justice isn't for the strong. The strong can take what they want. Justice is for the weak, those that need help for their voices to be heard. Isn't that what your father would have taught you? Isn't that what his father brought out of the forest and the camps to tell him?"

Jack's legs grew weak. He fell forward onto his knees. "I need to think about this for a while." The air over the cow pasture seemed suddenly clear, making the police car look impossibly close. The trooper was talking on the radio, his broad hat on the dashboard.

Big Brad walked away but Theo hesitated. "Ask. What have you got to lose? The worst that could happen is you don't get what you want. If you get what you need, then it's better if you asked first. It's nicer to receive than to take. Grabbing is empty, helping you through the moment but leaving you hollow and alone. Receiving creates connections, creates the other. Even if it is fantasy, it's good for you, a healthy change." Theo walked away.

Jack sat in the open field, feeling too scared and tired to move. The field had been recently harvested and Jack was the only thing in it higher than a furrow. He didn't know why the police were here and he didn't want them to find him. The trooper seemed not to see him, although it didn't make sense. He felt like a field mouse cowering under the gaze of a soaring hawk, only this hawk wore mirrored sunglasses, a uniform, and carried a gun. Standing up and running away would surely draw the trooper's attention. Jack tried to figure out how they tracked him. He was quickly running out of all the arguments he could use in his own defense because they all sounded hollow and useless. The trooper got out of the car and stared across the field, looking right at Jack. Jack lowered his head; tears fell down onto his dirty work pants. At first, the only thing Jack could concentrate on was the mantra, 'Oh shit, oh shit, oh shit . . .' his thoughts constantly interrupted by staccato bursts of static from the police radio, the trooper's low voice too distant to be understood.

All at once, his nostrils filled with the smell of the freshly cut hay, and a memory hit him, heavy with associations, accompanied by a pang of sadness that something so sweet could have been forgotten so easily. He was running across a wide lawn, breathing in the scent of freshly mown grass. He had cut the lawn by himself for the first time, repressing his fear of the noisy engine and blades spinning inches from his sneakers. His father had surprised him, coming home in the early afternoon. At first he feared the worst: his mother had died, he was in for a whupping, or they were putting him up for adoption. In the end, everyone was healthy, he was still part of the family, and he was very much loved. His mother had called his dad at the office to tell him of Jack's gardening endeavors. His father left the office and hurried home, stopping off to buy a first baseman's mitt, a Louisville Slugger, and a real horsehide ball. His dad dug an ancient mitt out of a dusty cedar chest in the basement, took off his coat and tie, and rolled up his sleeves. They spent the afternoon playing ball and sliding around in the grass. Not long after that, his dad took him to his first game. In a few short years his dad was gone.

Jack sat up straighter. "I was important to my dad; he left a part of himself in me. I can't give up and go down easy. I can't be what Mr. Jonas wanted me to be because he wants me to fail. My father and grandfather didn't teach me that," he thought.

He knelt on the damp earth, eyes closed, moving his lips. He talked to his father, each word rambling one half step behind his thoughts. Images began to flow. His thoughts rambled back and forth through his childhood, always returning to his father.

Twenty minutes later, his tears stopped. He heard a car drive past and looked up to see the police car disappearing down the road.

Jack was achy and tired. The days were long, but when he lay down on the hay at night, he was surprised at how many of them had passed since he arrived. He used to enjoy a nightcap before going to sleep, something to take the edge off, calm him down, and help him to forget the stress of the day. He briefly considered asking Theo to get him some liquor, but asking an underage kid for booze was out of the question. After a few nights, he didn't miss the nightcap. Farm work left him physically drained, ready for sleep, and a strange feeling of contentment made it easy for him to fall asleep on his straw mattress. Each night he lay down and waited, his eyes half-closed, and every night Hanna came to read to him like a prelude to the dreams he could never remember. He heard her boots slide through the straw and climb the ladder. He took the key out from under his pillow and placed it on his hay bale night table; it waited for her, glinting in the moonlight. The loft was so quiet he could hear the pen on the paper, moving fast to expel words that had been bottled up inside her all day. The furious writing went on for ten minutes until she stopped, pausing for a moment before beginning to read. Her voice began as a whisper that he barely heard, but grew stronger as she read.

"Thoughts come alive through writing. As I write I begin to see myself more clearly. It is a mistake to think I will write the same thing tonight that I would have written yesterday or tomorrow. But for now these words on the page are as real and as true as they could possibly be. Writing has forced me to think, perhaps for the first time, about the expectations I have for myself; I realize that my dreams are possible because it is in my power to make them happen. The dreams I had as a young child were snuffed out the way a small flame is extinguished by a cold heavy wind. Writing is helping me to rekindle that flame, and to use it as a beacon in the dark. This flame is leading me in a new and wondrous direction of self-discovery, strength, and ultimate fulfillment. Somewhere on that journey I will find the one, the lover who will give me strength and courage."

"Before I sleep the sleep of death, I must dream the dream of life. But I can no longer dream alone. As I grow weaker, my dreams become smaller. Like a winter apple left too long on the tree, they have been bitten by frost until one small bite contains an entire year of sweetness, too much for one person to bear. And like these apples, they shall fall when winter arrives."

"These words may be the only life my dreams will ever have. But I won't accept this. I would see my seeds sprout and reach for the sun, even in the winter of my existence. I fight with God, demanding more than justice. I demand love and life and everything that goes with it. I demand it because I can and I demand it because I must. If I accept my illness and death, if I allow my dreams to fade and die, then I will be less than God created me. The pain grows daily, but as it does, my strength to fight for my dreams also grows. I am weaker but my will grows stronger with my need."

Jack closed his eyes, pretending to be asleep. He heard the book close and the rustle of Hanna's skirt as she moved to the ladder.

Her words were barely audible even in the silence of the country night. "Goodnight, Jack."

As he drifted off to sleep, he heard her climb down the ladder and walk out of the barn.

"Goodnight, Hanna." He whispered so softly that he wasn't even sure he had spoken. A minute later he was asleep.

Jack woke up well before dawn, awakened by the cows' bellows to be milked. Brad was his usual silent self but the walking mountain no longer intimidated Jack. He even caught Brad smiling at him when he greeted the duchess with a pat on the udder and a handful of oats. When they returned to the house, Jack was hungry from work, eager to get to the serious business of breakfast. He slurped down his first cup of coffee and poured another right away. Brad's chuckle was like gravel sliding down a dark slope. "You sure do like your coffee. A young guy like you shouldn't need so much caffeine to motivate himself."

Jack smiled, slightly less intimidated by a friendly Eskimo than an angry Cherokee. "Lawyers run on coffee. That and an obscenely well-developed level of greed cheered on by an ego that's been fed steroids since kindergarten."

Mr. Meyer cleared his throat. "You said you work in bio-engineering? Maybe you'd like to hear a story." He didn't wait for an answer to his rhetorical question but Jack could see everyone settle into their chairs, as if what was to follow was part of a daily ritual. "Some bio-engineering folks showed up here once. They had an idea they wanted me to work on. Some marketing genius had come up with the idea for caffeinated milk. They thought they could make millions selling it to people who wanted to put milk in their coffee but didn't want to dilute the caffeine."

Jack nodded. "It sounds like a great idea. I'd buy it. Did you do it?"

Mr. Meyer nodded slowly, taking a sip from his coffee cup. "Sure did. It wasn't really a big deal. I just found a cow that liked the taste of coffee and made sure she had plenty on hand. There was this one cow that was always trying to take a slurp out of Brad's cup when he wasn't looking. She got the job."

"How did it work out?"

Mr. Meyer shook his head. "It didn't work out the way those marketing whiz kids thought and the bio-tech company ended up pretty disappointed, though I guess it didn't cost them too much money. They didn't need an expensive laboratory or scientists. It only cost them in coffee, though that heifer was up to five gallons a day."

"What was the problem? Did the coffee mess up the milk?"

"I wouldn't know. You see, after she drank her first bucket of coffee in the morning, we couldn't get her to stand still long enough to get any milk out of her. But it wasn't so bad. It softened the blow for the cigarette people who came by after that to cut down the trees that grew next to the road. They wanted to use them to make rolling paper with tar already in it."

Jack's jaw dropped. "Are you serious? That's . . . " One quick look around the table confirmed that Jack had been served for dessert. Brad was beginning to snort and Hanna was breaking out in giggles.

Mr. Meyer chuckled. "Mother, why don't you give this young man a nice stack of flapjacks? My guess is that hotshot lawyers aren't so smart on an empty stomach."

Theo handed him his plate piled with a hearty breakfast, and for the first time, he felt like he truly earned his meal.

Jack lay in the straw waiting for Hanna. It was a treat he found himself enjoying more and more. He closed his eyes listening to the sound of her voice that was sometimes a melody without words. Often she wrote about death and her anger about having to die. Jack assumed she was speaking in a metaphoric sense because she seemed stronger every day, and watching her at work he often wished he had her stamina. She no longer had the pale color he noticed the first time he met her, and now she actually had rosy cheeks. While Jack suspected she'd beat him if they arm wrestled, her femininity was obvious even though it was hidden under work boots and faded coveralls. Neither of them could deny the growing chemistry between them, even if nothing was said.

All in all, life on the farm was a pleasant routine. Cows were creatures of habit. People who spent their days and nights with cows followed suit, moving to the rhythm of nature. Jack had been on the farm two weeks but it felt like years. His cell phone was under his expensive suit, piled carelessly on a hay bale. Its silence sealed him off from the outside world, a condition that he found strangely acceptable. He woke before dawn to milk the cows with Brad, joining him in the field for prayer before breakfast. Police cars passed by less frequently, though the first few days had been intense. They drove up and down the road, cruising slowly but passing the farm as if it were invisible.

Daytime was filled with chores that kept him moving and worked muscles apparently overlooked by the fitness equipment at the gym. He took a nice afternoon nap in the shade of a tree behind the barn, catching up on his sleep so that he could later enjoy a bedtime story from Hanna. Every time he saw her his spirits lifted, and though he looked forward to seeing her, he didn't know how to move the relationship along. Normally he would have invited her out to an impressive restaurant, making sure the maître d' recognized him, followed that with a quick drive around the park in his sports car, and then a nightcap in his fancy uptown apartment. None of that applied now. He couldn't even take her for a ride in his car without risking arrest. His apartment was on another planet and he didn't need to invite her up to the hayloft because she had a nightly appointment. He considered himself a ladies' man and hadn't been shy about making physical advances since high school. Even so, being around Hanna made him nervous and shy in a way that reminded him of being a teenager. He smiled as he heard her open the barn doors. Hanna stumbled as she climbed the ladder. She clambered over the last few rungs and fell onto the hay-covered floor, laughing.

"Climbing a ladder in a skirt is for the birds."

He watched her rolling around in the hay, laughing. "Are you okay?"

"I'm better than okay. I'm drunk." She held up a bottle, its half emptiness evident in the moonlight. "Wanna drunk?"

Jack took the bottle from her. "Can you write when you are this drunk?"

She shook her head. "I didn't bring my journal. I don't feel like writing." She reached out and began stroking his hair. "You're kind of cute. Did you know that?"

"Yes, I've heard that." Jack was confused, faced with a dilemma his previous life never prepared him for. The situation was familiar but his feelings were not. Jack was used to intoxicated women expressing their affections. The next step was a dance routine he knew well. He told himself that this was far better than all of the previous women. He truly liked Hanna. He didn't understand his own reluctance. Common sense told him that he should be running into her arms, happy to make love to a woman he cared about for a change. His head and hormones were ready but something held him back. Hanna continued playing with his hair and being close to her was starting to have an effect on him. He picked up the bottle and took a long drink. The wine was cheap and sweet but the liquor went right to his head. He laughed and began to play with her long, dark hair. He took another long pull at the bottle before letting it drop, almost empty, to the straw-covered floor. As the kiss began to heat up, his instincts took over. She pushed him away, smiling nervously, something he wasn't used to and found a little unsettling. He would have preferred her unbridled enthusiasm. It would have quieted the voices that were trying to tell him that something was wrong. She started to fuss with the mattress and sheets. He knelt down trying to help, but she pushed his hands away. She finished arranging the bed and turned to lean in for another kiss. He pulled back.

"Did you take care of things?"

She looked confused. "What things?"

He hesitated. "You know. Things."

She stepped back. "What are you talking about?"

He came towards her but she held up her hand. "What things?"

"I'm just trying to be responsible. We're both adults. I don't want any unwanted complications or consequences. It wouldn't be good for either of us."

She hesitated before stepping forward, trying to kiss him. "I took care of it."

He stepped back. This was turning into a strange dance he didn't understand.

"How?"

He felt her body stiffen. "You know how. I took something."

Buzzers went off in his head. "You're lying."

She grabbed him, trying to pull him close. "What do you care? If I get pregnant it's my problem."

He shook his head. "I don't want to be a father."

She stepped back and turned away from him looking out at the empty field. Sitting down in the window, she let her legs dangle outside, her boots banging against wood. She went from steamy hot to cold and distant faster than his car could do zero to sixty. "Don't worry. I won't get pregnant." He sat down, putting his hand on her shoulder but she shook it off. "You are a stupid idiot. Those pills I take every day aren't vitamins. What do you think I'm sick with? The flu?"

He stepped back. "I don't understand. You wrote about being sick but that was a long time ago. I figured you were over it by now. You seem healthy enough."

"For your purposes that means I have a pulse." She laughed bitterly. "Don't worry. It's not a social disease or anything communicable. It's an anti-social disease."

"I don't want to pry into your personal life."

"A typical jerk. You don't want to pry into my personal life but a minute ago you were about to jump into bed with me. I don't know what planet you're from but between humans, sex is personal."

She took a deep breath and struggled to calm down. "I've got ovarian cancer. The doctors told me it is physically impossible for me to get pregnant. You've got nothing to worry about. They also told me I had six months to live. That was a year ago. Even a super stud like you has nothing to worry about. No babies and no long 'good-byes.'"

He put his hand on her shoulder but she shook it off again. "Get away. You disgust me. I never wanted kids until all of a sudden I couldn't. Now I would give whatever life I have left just to hold my baby for one minute."

Jack, standing behind her, put his hand on her shoulder again. "I'm sorry. I didn't know. But it still doesn't change the fact that

I don't want children, especially not now. In my real life, I work eighty hours a week at a very high-pressure job that doesn't leave me time or energy to deal with a family. It wouldn't be fair to my wife or children."

She shook his hand off, jumping to her feet to face him. "Those are very noble words to be coming from someone like you. This incredibly high-minded consideration never stopped you from romance and la-di-da before."

Jack looked at her, confused. "La-di-da?"

She let out a strangled cry. "La-di-da, or whatever you want to call it. For you it means candlelight and a quick testosterone rush."

"And for you it means paying for one night of fun with a lifetime of commitment and regret with a woman who used to be pretty."

This time her yell was unrestrained, causing some cows in the next field to wake up and bellow. "You would see it that way. I see it as a lot more than that, but you wouldn't be able to understand. I see it as two people coming together in the promise of love that goes beyond their own lives. Romance is good for a day or two. I might not even have that so I need more. I need a lifetime of love and commitment. I need a friend, someone who cares enough to hold my hand while I vomit my guts out after chemo. I need a baby but the doctors say I can't have any."

Jack shook his head. "Listen, Hanna. I like you but—"

A feminine fist making sudden and effective contact with his solar plexus stopped him in mid-sentence. "Don't try to be a nice guy. You can't play it convincingly. Maybe those stupid bimbos in skimpy skirts bought it but it was probably just for a quick ride in your fancy sports car. You are such an idiot. I didn't want you for anything except to be the father for the first ten minutes. Even that would be too long but simple biology doesn't give me any other choice. You are so full of yourself that you don't realize that you

71

aren't really much of anything. You think you are a hotshot lawyer but the next time you stand in front of a jury it will be for your own sentencing. You think you are intelligent and popular but your friends, your co-workers, and your boss all sold you out so they can keep on making big money. You think you are such a great lover but all your lines come from sleazy movies that don't have anything to do with love. The thing I don't understand is why you still want to go back to that world. You talk about your real world even now when this world is the only world you have. What will it take for you to wake up? You are so hopeless." She turned her back on him and stood in the open doorway, looking out at the moonlit farm. "The real pity is that you forgot who you were supposed be and that was someone really special." She jumped forward, falling fifteen feet to the pile of straw under the barn window, stumbling before running away into the dark. He ran for the ladder, ready to chase after her. Suddenly he heard his cell phone ringing, instinct forcing him to stop and pay heed. He flipped open the phone, the bright display blinding him for a moment. The twangy voice, annoyingly upbeat as a banjo, began speaking even before he put the phone to his ear.

"Hello, Mr. Nathan. This is Candace from The Baby Shop. We got your message asking us to go ahead and send out your order. We made the changes you requested and everything is ready to go. Your baby will certainly have everything he needs. We just need the address you want it sent to. Your message said that you recently moved."

Jack gritted his teeth but the worst slipped through anyway. "Listen to me, you ignorant minimum-wage bumpkin. Babies disgust me. They are tiny little anchors that keep a person from doing anything worthwhile in his life. I'm sure you have ten. The only reason I would ever have a child is if it was a mistake, which is why ninety percent of the people in the world breed. They are too stupid to read the instructions for contraception. I want you to take all of that baby stuff, all the cute toys, all the frilly furniture, all the paraphernalia to deal with uncontrolled pooping and puking, and I want you to put it all back on the shelf where some misguided overly fertile idiot can find it. If there were any words I used that were beyond your fourth grade vocabulary, write them down and ask your supervisor. Oh, and one last thing. Any attempt by your company to use my credit card for any purchase will result in a lawsuit that will leave your bosses dirt poor for generations to come. Have I been clear?"

The voice lost its twang and it was difficult for Candace to be chirpy when speaking through clenched teeth. "I understand." Saying the next four words cost her dearly, leaving Candace feeling ill enough to ask for the rest of the night off and gulp down two glasses of white wine as soon as she got home. "Have a nice day."

Jack punched the "off" button with his finger, but the phone was already dead, the battery drained.

He looked out the window but the field was dark and empty. Jack lay down, struggling to relax enough to sleep. After half an hour, physical fatigue forced his eyes closed. When his breathing became deep and he began to snore, Hanna stood up, stepping away from the tree that stood outside Jack's window. She began to walk across the field towards the main road. Her cheeks were dry but the dust at the base of the tree was still wet with her tears.

The next morning, Jack worked with Brad. The big Eskimo seemed more quiet than usual, even by Arctic standards, where barkless huskies were raised as a survival tactic to prevent avalanches. Breakfast, usually the most gabby, social part of the day, was an uncomfortable affair. Hanna raged silently, like a nuclear reactor moments before meltdown. Mr. Meyer tried to break the ice a few times but a silent cue from his wife quickly ended that. Mrs. Meyer's intuition had filled in the blanks and he got the message during a hushed conversation between them at the sink while washing the dishes. Hanna pushed her half-finished plate away and was hurrying out the back door when Mr. Meyer stopped her.

"I think we've been working too much lately. You guys have been slacking off and I think everyone needs a diversion to get their sorts back in place. There's enough anger in this room to curdle all the milk in the tank. It's springtime and I feel like a game of baseball. Who else wants to play?"

His glance around the room was met with a look that was something between incomprehension and open hostility. Theo stepped into the middle of the emotional maelstrom raging silently around the kitchen. "Sounds great. I'll get my glove." Mrs. Meyer led Hanna away, warbling like a mother hen preening a grumpy adolescent falcon. Ten minutes later, they were all out in the cow pasture watching Mr. Meyer trot around, setting up the field. Mrs. Meyer equipped herself and Hanna with a pair of decidedly non-regulation oven mitts. Hanna tucked her dress up into her belt and her long hair was hidden out of the way under a floppy fishing hat. Theo brought his glove and a spare one he had found. Mr. Meyer carried the bat and a lopsided softball.

"This mud patch is home plate. That cow patty over there is first base."

Brad growled. "Kind of makes sliding a tough decision."

Jack laughed. "You don't slide into first base. But you are right. Any time you make it on base, you'll be dragging one shoe full of cow poop behind for the rest of the game."

Brad shrugged. "I never played baseball. There's not much organized sports where I grew up."

Jack slapped him on the back. "It's a pity. You would have been a natural at football. I was a walk-on and made my college baseball team. I wanted to play in the major leagues but I was never more than an enthusiastic amateur with a little talent. My pop taught me when I was a kid and he never did anything halfway."

Mr. Meyer continued trotting, marking out a lopsided diamond. "The salt lick is second. That dead crab-apple tree is third. If the ball makes it to the creek, on the fly or on a roll, it's a home run. The ball floats but you better hustle before it gets washed downstream. Any batter who hits a cow gets an automatic out. If a fielder hits a cow with a throw, the runner gets two bases." He returned to the mud patch where the others stood. "Let's choose up teams."

Theo's stating simply, "odds and evens", cut off Hanna's protest. They formed a circle with Theo counting off. On the count of three, six fists shot out, displaying digits of varying sizes and cleanliness. Brad, Jack, and Mr. Meyer each stuck out one finger while Mrs. Meyer, Hanna, and Theo each put out two.

Jack smirked. "Not very fair, is it?"

Hanna glared at him. "Why? Two men and a worm against the three of us sounds pretty fair to me."

Jack snapped back. "And your team is made up of a boy, a woman, and a . . ."

"No name calling. It upsets the cows and curdles the milk." Mr. Meyer stepped in the middle, handing the bat to Hanna. "Your team will bat first. You can use this on the ball or you can use this on Jack. At this point, I don't really care. I figure he probably deserves what he gets. But I think Theo wants to play."

Jack's team took the field, Mr. Meyer as a modified shortstop and Brad an immobile hulk near the first base slab of poop. Theo squatted behind home plate, filling in as catcher. Jack worked Theo's mitt onto his hand. It was too small for him but it was better than an oven mitt. He watched Hanna step up to the plate. She glared at Jack as he began his windup. Mr. Meyer yelled out, "Ease up on the pitching, slick. We play slow ball around here." Jack stopped awkwardly and took a step back. He began a slow windup to pitch underhand and watched as the ball drifted towards Hanna. As she began her swing, Jack realized that he had made allowances for her being a girl when she didn't need any. She swung like a pro, hard and level, the drive sizzling just over Mr. Meyer's reach. The ball scattered a small crowd of cows that had gathered to watch. Jack looked to first base and saw that Brad was watching the action with a bewildered look on his face. As Mr. Meyer reached the lump of grass hiding the ball, Hanna rounded first and headed for second base, her loose skirt flying, her boots slapping the back of her thighs. Jack ran to cover the base. The ball slid into the mitt's undersized pocket just as Jack's foot hit the saltlick. Jack turned with a grin and was sent flying as Hanna plowed into him, not slowing for impact, elbows pointed forward for effect. His teeth rattled and he hit the ground hard. The ball dribbled out of his mitt. Hanna bent over his ear and yelled, "Safe, from worms like you!"

Mr. Meyer picked up the ball and tagged her. "You never touched the base."

She smirked. "I wasn't aiming for the base." She strode away, sitting on a hay bale behind home plate. Jack sat gasping until Brad picked him up and held him in the air, while he got his feet under him. He walked to the pitcher's mound, a bit wobbly but trying hard not to show it. Mrs. Meyer stood at the mud patch, crouched over, the bat resting on her shoulder. Mr. Meyer tapped Jack on the shoulder.

"I'll pitch this one, if you don't mind. After twenty years of marriage, we're pretty good at throwing things at each other." Jack handed him the ball and took his place at shortstop. Mr. Meyer moved even closer to the plate and tossed a ball that drifted over the plate. The bat left Mrs. Meyer's shoulder just as the ball slapped into Theo's glove. Jack couldn't figure out how, but the second pitch was even slower, defying the law of gravity and hanging in the air, waiting politely over the plate. She managed to hit the ball a glancing blow that sent it dribbling through the grass, stopping halfway towards Jack. Jack ran in but was pushed out of the way as Mr. Meyer snatched up the ball, tumbling dramatically before bumbling it and then tossing it underhand to Brad. The ball bounced off Brad's chest just as Mrs. Meyer stomped on the cow patty. Brad looked down at the ball. "Was I supposed to catch that?"

Mr. Meyer patted him on the back. "You did just fine."

Mr. Meyer told Jack to pitch but hesitated before handing him the ball. They were standing on the mound, their heads close, speaking in whispers, just like the big leaguers did. "Jack, you should know that Theo hits worse than his mom. It's been an embarrassment to me, especially since I used to coach in peewee league. Try to pitch one he can hit. Maybe we should have painted the ball Day-Glo orange or something."

Theo was in his batting stance, looking grim. Hanna squatted behind him playing catcher, her oven mitt set up as a target, flashing obscene fingers at Jack instead of the normal catcher's signs. Jack lobbed the ball at Theo, but the boy seemed to hesitate, his swing starting and stopping several times before the ball floated past. Mr. Meyer called out, "Strike one!" Hanna shot the ball back at the pitcher harder than she needed to, stinging Jack's hand through the thin leather. Mr. Meyer reprimanded her. "Let's keep this a friendly game. The sight of blood upsets the cows."

The same thing happened again, Theo's swing ending after the ball was resting in Hanna's oven mitt. "Strike two!" a note of desperation in Mr. Meyer's voice.

Jack wound up in slow motion, but as the ball left his hand, he thought he saw Theo's hands shift. A flash of light flowed up the bat, as if Theo were performing a magician's trick, making a new baseball bat grow from his hands, overlaying the bat already in his grip. Jack tried to focus his eyes, but the scenery around Theo became cloudy and the only thing he could concentrate on were Theo's eyes staring at him. The bat seemed more clear and solid than it had before. Theo's hands looked suddenly larger. Jack watched the ball as it moved in slow motion towards the plate. In a sudden blur, the bat stopped in mid-arc, meeting the ball just over the plate. Jack expected the ball to thud to the ground. Instead, the ball took off like a bullet, straight back at the mound. Jack brought his glove up sluggishly as if the air were thick as molasses, his muscles debating whether to follow his brain's desperate commands. He could see every detail on the ball: a small smudge, a hole in the leather cover. The ball wasn't spinning. This defied the basic principle of physics that every ten-year-old boy learned in grassy fields across America. Then the ball crashed into his temple and the earth tilted at a crazy angle as the ground met his head.

Instantly his vision was gone, and he was traveling backwards down a tunnel, a circle of light getting smaller until it disappeared. Jack felt someone grab his arm and pull. Suddenly he was on his feet and looking up at Theo. The boy looked concerned, almost ready to cry. Jack laughed. "Your dad said you couldn't hit but you really popped me one. I thought for sure I was down for the count." Jack felt giddy and Theo kept staring at him in a strange way.

Brad appeared next to Theo, his gravelly voice cutting off Jack's chattiness. "We don't have much time. The longer we wait, the more difficult it gets."

Jack was confused. "What are you talking about? I feel fine."

Brad pointed to something behind Jack. Jack turned and a cold wave filled his body. On the ground, a few feet behind him, he saw himself lying on his back in the grass, his arms and legs askew, a black patch of blood wetting the hair on the right side of his head. Hanna, caught in mid-stride, a three-dimensional photo of a beautiful woman running towards him. A twin Theo, frozen at home plate, the bat dangling from the tips of two fingers, waiting to complete its fall to the ground. Mr. Meyer, crouched, a concerned look frozen on his face. Jack jumped when he glanced over at first base. The frozen image of Brad stared right at him, the only one of the group paying attention to him and ignoring his inert body.

Jack turned to Theo, needing answers but too afraid to let the words leave his lips. Theo answered a different question. "I'm sorry but it was the only way. You needed to be fixed."

"What are you talking about?"

Brad stood behind Jack, pressing down on his shoulders until his knees gave way and he was kneeling in the grass. Pressure began to build up in Jack's chest and he began to scream. The next second, the pain was gone and everything went black.

When he opened his eyes, he was staring up at Hanna, his head resting in her lap. Her tears dropped onto his face. Mr. Meyer appeared, gently touching the side of Jack's head. "Slide over, girl. I was a medic in the army." Hanna reluctantly changed places with him as he slid Jack's head off her lap. He rolled up his jacket under Jack's neck and pulled his eyes open one at a time, checking the pupils for dilation. Mrs. Meyer's appeared, motherly concern distorting her features. Mr. Meyer finished checking Jack's head and sat back on his knees. "Boy, can you hear me?"

Jack sat up, pushing away hands that tried to hold him down. "I'm fine."

Mr. Meyer shook his head. "I don't get it. That ball hit him like a bullet. I saw him drop and I was sure this boy was gone. His eyes were rolled back in his head. I for sure saw the side of his head busted open and crooked. There's blood but I can't find a scratch on him. He doesn't even have a bump on his head where the ball hit him." He shook his head in disbelief. "Even so, he took quite a hit to the head. Brad, run to the house and call an ambulance."

Brad, standing off to the side with his arm around Theo, was pale and shivering, looking like he was about to fall over. Jack shook his head and struggled to his feet. "I'd rather recuperate here, lying on a bale of hay with Hanna throwing rocks at me than in a nice soft hospital bed handcuffed to some ugly cop."

Mr. Meyer considered for a few moments. "You go lie down. I'll send Theo to check in on you later."

Jack sat in the hayloft, grateful for the time alone to think about what had happened. He had seen himself in a parallel universe. He might have even been witness to his own death. These were the simplest explanations, possibly the only explanations, but Jack was entirely unwilling to accept them. Theo appeared with a steaming bowl of chicken soup. He watched Jack eat, waiting until he was halfway through the soup before speaking. "Hanna's gone."

Jack stopped eating. "She'll be back. She's got to write in her journal." As soon as the words were out of his mouth, Jack realized that they made no sense. But Theo was nodding his head, as if in total agreement.

"Maybe yes, maybe no. In any case, it depends more on you than on me now."

Jack felt a throbbing at his temple, a painful memory of the hit. "I've got enough to worry about without chasing after wayward milkmaids. The cops are looking for me and my hard-earned career is about to implode. I've got a fancy car and a lifestyle that milking cows won't support."

Theo twirled a piece of straw in his hands. "I thought that was all taken care of. You walked away from all that."

"Listen, kid. You don't understand. You may think you have it good out here on the farm, but this isn't the real world. I'm the one coping with the real world and all the awful stuff in it. Right now I'm living in Oz. Someday, real soon, I'm going to have to go back and face the music. And try to put the pieces of my life back together."

Jack found himself staring into Theo's eyes. They seemed to glow red until it was all Jack could see in the dark hayloft. "No. You don't live in the real world. None of us do. You got a glimpse of the real world and it nearly killed you."

"Are you talking about what happened after I got in the head hit by that ball? That was a dream, a hallucination. I'm not going to change my life because of that."

"You still refuse to understand. You don't know how the real world works or how it affects us. If you did, you wouldn't be talking like this. None of those things you mentioned are the real problem. None of those things work the way you think. The real problem is that you were alone. Your soul was sick. We fixed it but you could still die from it. That world was killing you. Do you really want to go back?" Jack opened his mouth to answer but no words came out. "You got a free ticket this time. Brad and I did the impossible in order to fix what was wrong inside of you. You just had to lie there and die for a few minutes. The rest of your life is up to you. And it's a lot of work. Death is easy. Life

81

is hard. Living alone and dying alone is easy but it is a sickness. Joining, creating life, being alive, that is what you need to do. In any case, I'm tired." Theo stared at Jack until the glow in his eyes subsided; he left, his tired feet dragging trails through the straw. The rest of his dinner sat untouched while Jack lay in the dark shivering, wide awake, wishing his eyes would close so he could lose himself in sleep.

Just as he was starting to nod off, he heard someone climbing up the ladder. His heart skipped a beat, hoping it was Hanna coming for her nightly journal visit. He was surprised when it turned out to be Mr. Meyer. He struggled up the ladder with a thermos in one hand. He settled down onto a hay bale and pulled two ceramic mugs from the oversized pocket in the bib of his overalls. He poured two cups of creamy coffee, generously topping them off from a hip flask he produced from a back pocket.

"Mother's cure for everything is chicken soup and sleep. I believe in greasing the wheels to help you feel a little better along the way."

Jack sipped the coffee, wincing at the strong alcohol. "By the way, I appreciate all the soy milk you've been getting for my coffee."

Mr. Meyer looked at him over the rim of his cup, his eyes crinkling at the edges from his hidden smile. He paused after putting his cup down. "Like I said, soy milk comes from tofu cows. And we don't have those kind. You've drunk a couple buckets of real cow juice since you got here."

Jack stared at his half-empty cup. "But that isn't right. Ever since I was in high-school, milk gave me acid heartburn and it would come shooting up like Old Faithful."

"It might not be the milk that was bothering you but all the other stuff they did to it. Sometimes new and improved isn't. Nature was getting along just fine before we showed up."

Jack let that sink in. "I have to tell you something. The company I was working for is called Herdsman. They make a product called Bo Plus. It helps dairy farmers produce more milk. I got in trouble trying to push it into production."

Mr. Meyer nodded. "I know all about Bo Plus. You weren't trying to help the dairy farmers. You were trying to make your bosses rich enough to pay you a fat paycheck. And believe me, they are rich enough already. A lot richer than the dairy farmers they claim to be helping."

"I don't think you understand. We tested it thoroughly."

Mr. Meyer grinned. "Oh, I 'spect I knows a tiddle bit abouts dem Bo Plusses. I's gots me a Masters Degree in Dairy Science from Texas A&M."

"This is cutting edge, totally new."

Mr. Meyer's grin got wider. "Weeeellll, I sure wouldn't understand none of dat. Not like if'n I gots me a law degree. Fust semester they taught me to quit draggin' my knuckles through the straw when I walked around the barn. Second semester they taught me to stop askin' the cows out on dates. Grad school was all about larnin' which end the food went in and which end the milk came out. Dat got confusing. You see, cows don't jes give milk. Dey poops a lot, too."

Jack lowered his head and tried hard not to laugh. "Okay. So maybe you do know about it. It's a good product that really helps dairy farmers."

Mr. Meyer shook his head. "I wrote a paper in grad school comparing meat production in America and Argentina. American cattlemen had production figures that blew Argentina away. They were using antibiotics like candy and hormones like you wouldn't believe. The Argentineans would put the cattle out in the field, inoculate them once, and supply them with salt licks. The figures made it look like the U.S. cattlemen were on to something. But after a little investigation, I found that the Argentineans were earning more money. They didn't have a whole agri-business on their back to support. And the problem with the hormones and the antibiotics is that once you start, you are committed and can't stop. What you've got are sick cattle that don't have any natural immune system anymore. And guess who ends up with all those hormones and antibiotics as the last ones on the food chain? We do. Kids today, especially the ones whose parents can't afford organic milk, have a higher maturation rate in addition to other problems.

"It's hard to make a living milking cows. Hell, it's hard to make a living at just about anything today. I can understand a desperate farmer using your product to try and squeeze out a few more gallons of milk from his herd. But that doesn't mean it's better for the farmer. It's certainly not good for the people who drink the milk. The problem begins when chemists and biologists start thinking of cows as milk-making machines with a funnel at one end and a faucet at the other. Cows are animals, and like everything else, part of a complex ecosystem. Then they start thinking about people like they were machines where merchandise goes in one end and money comes out the other. We're part of an ecosystem violated by corporate greed that totally disregards the consequences."

"We tested it thoroughly and it's totally safe."

Mr. Meyer looked Jack right in the eye. "I guess that explains why you are hiding out in my barn. The worst mistake a snake oil salesman can make is to take his own medicine."

"There are laws to protect people from unsafe products."

"That car you've got parked out in the tool shed is the number one killer around and they built it to go faster than the speed limit. How could the law allow that?" Jack started to object but Mr. Meyer just laughed. "If you stay around much longer I might have to go out and buy one of those tofu cows. If all these new agri-products are so safe, how come Americans are allergic to damn near everything that they have to eat? Why don't you think on that for a bit?" Mr. Meyer left and the spiked coffee took effect. Jack fell asleep almost as soon as he heard the barn door close.

The next day was a nightmare. Jack had a dull headache, either from the liquor or the knock on the head. Hanna had disappeared; her chair at the breakfast table stood empty, and the kitchen, usually full of breakfast banter, was strangely silent. The display of pills on her plate bore mute witness to the gravity of her absence. Jack was assigned to fill in for her as penance and do two milkings. The unspoken understanding was that Hanna's flight was Jack's fault. Jack pushed the breakfast around his plate with little appetite for food and even less for conversation. To fill the silence, Mr. Meyer launched into one of his folksy wise tales, his voice taking on the sleepy cadence and bumpkin dialect.

"This reminds me of the morning we were stringing a wire fence down in the south pasture."

Jack pushed his chair back and began to stand. "I've got a lot to do." One of his shoulders dipped as Brad rested his hand on it.

"We are behind in compost. There's a heaping pile of manure that needs turning, but I've never seen anybody in such a rush to spend a day with cow poop before. Except maybe Hanna on her way to see you. Until last night, that is. My guess is you want to hear the story."

Jack winced as the grip on his collarbone tightened. "Given the choice between tying my shoes one handed for the rest of my life and hearing the story, I guess I would prefer to shut up and listen."

Brad nodded. "It's a wise man that avoids pain and permanent disfigurement when there is nothing to gain."

Mr. Meyer continued as if the interruption had never occurred. "We were taking a group of yearlings down to graze the south field so first we had to set up a wire fence. It was a bit much for Brad and me alone so I called in an extra hand. I've known Rock since he was twelve years old. We met when I had to help him down out of a tree after being chased by my bull. He'd been teasing the bull for years from outside the fence and when the bull caught him on the inside, he decided to even the score some. Rock wasn't God's best attempt at intelligence, but he also wasn't totally stupid, so we figured he could help us out on a simple job. It was a half a day of hard, sweaty work, with two lungfuls of dust thrown in. It's the kind of job that makes me look forward to sitting back, with my feet up while enjoying a couple of beers. Not enough to get loopy or stupid, but just enough to make the sweat seem worthwhile. We were kicked back, watching the cows watch us, when I guess Brad got a little bored. Rocky had been teasing Brad like he used to tease the bull, and how I saw things, it wasn't much different—except Brad might have let him down outta that tree without breaking both his legs."

"So Brad stepped off to the side to pass water due to uncomfortable levels of beerage and decided a bet might help pass the time. He pointed at the steel wire we just finished setting up and said, 'I bet ain't no man can step back four feet from that wire and hit it while pissing, and hold it for a slow five count.' Well, Rocky, being more rooster than man, must of figured that the ability to piss like a sharpshooter was a sign of manhood 'cause he took that bet. Brad and Rocky each pulled out a five-dollar bill and stuck it under a rock for safekeeping. Rock had drunk more beer than he was used to, I guess, figuring it was another sign of his not-so-evident manhood, so when he stepped up to the line his pumps were primed and ready. Now any fool could see that all you really needed was a full tank and a steady hand to win that bet and since Brad didn't piss his money away, as the saying goes, there had to be a catch. But Rocky didn't think about that. And while he was busy not thinking about that, there were a couple of other things Rocky forgot to think about. You see, we'd spent all day stringing wire to keep the cows in and even though he was right there with us, Rocky didn't notice that it wasn't the wire keeping the cows from being tourists. It was hooking the wire up to two fully juiced truck batteries that convinced them to stay put. The second thing Rocky didn't think about was how a good solid stream of salty piss will pass a current just about as good as copper wire.

"Now, watching Rocky stand there counting to five with his pecker plugged into a socket was just about the funniest thing we'd seen since that city boy from the Department of Agriculture tried to demonstrate modern milking techniques on our stud bull. I had to give Rocky his due. He held it for the full five count and then some. His hands were shaking something fierce when he pulled the ten dollars from under that rock and he couldn't straighten up enough to pull out his wallet. His face was gray and sweaty but he was smiling like he'd just won the lottery. Brad and me were having trouble getting up off the grass we were laughing so hard. Rocky said, 'My momma didn't raise no fools or fairies.' He snapped each five-dollar bill in our faces and strutted around about as much as his fried pecker would let him. When Brad finally stopped laughing, he explained it to poor Rocky."

"Look", he said, "These days a Sunday matinee will cost eight dollars, without popcorn or soda pop. If I'd offered you twenty dollars to electrify your swizzle stick jes' so I could hoot an' holler, you would've told me to jump-start a sheep. But as soon as I made a bet out of it, hell, you stepped right up to the plate like Mickey

Mantle with the bases loaded. I ain't laughed that hard in a dog's age and it was worth every penny. The only one betting money was you. And Rocky, when someone invites you for lunch, make sure your name is on the guest list and not the menu."

Jack sat there fuming. "It's a nice story but I think Brad still expects me to scoop the poop."

Mr. Meyer considered for a moment. "So I guess you really don't get the message. I'll say it straight out. For all your brains, you're still a lot dumber than Rocky. He only fried his pecker and at least he got five dollars for it. Your boss turned you in to the law for something he did just to save his own tail. He may be paying you a bundle but I'll bet that if you cashed it all in and paid off all your bills, you'd still end up with less spare change than Rocky." He looked at Jack for a few moments before touching his own chin and then pointing at Jack's. "Shut your jaw before it fills up with mosquitoes. From what Theo told me, Hanna offered you the best prize in the world: a son. Why she would want to hook herself up with a man like you is a mystery to me, but turning her down was just plain dumb. Your boss sold you out, lied to the cops, and ruined your life. Even so, you still want to go running back to him and leave a woman behind who wants to give you everything she's got for as long as she's got to give. You and Rocky have got the same idea of what makes a man, and the two of you together don't have enough brains to light a match without reading the instructions on the back of the box."

Jack spent the next couple of hours turning compost, wondering why the flies preferred him to processed poop. He had a sinking feeling that Brad would have an obvious answer to that question.

He came back for lunch smelling so bad they made him eat on the back porch. Theo left after lunch, mumbling something to his father about finding Hanna before she made a mistake. Jack came back to his hayloft bed later than usual, especially sore from a double dose of farm work. He fell right to sleep, pricked awake every ten minutes when his tossing and turning rolled him off the mattress and onto the wood floor. Around midnight, he spread his blanket on the floor on a thin bed of straw and managed to sleep uninterrupted.

He woke up to a strange sound. The moon had already set. He suddenly realized the sound that awakened him was his cell phone, lying under his neatly folded suit on a bale of hay in the far corner of the loft. He had heard it dozens of times a day when he was working in the city but now the sound grated on his ears, too loud and artificial, even muffled by the clothes. It hadn't come near a charger in two weeks and shouldn't have made any sounds unless thrown against musical instruments with great force. Jack dug through the clothes. As he picked up the phone, something fell out of the pile. It was a piece of cardboard, impossible to read in the dark. The phone rang, its light blinking furiously in the darkness. He flipped it open and the glow of the screen hurt his eyes. He stared at it, confused and unsure. The phone number was his personal office extension. He hesitated, but the image of Hanna bowing her head in prayer flashed through his mind. He pressed the phone to his ear, the small device feeling strange in his hand.

"Hello?" He heard his own voice as if for the first time, hearing the powerful question implied in this unexpected moment.

"Hello, Mr. Nathan. I'm glad you answered. My name is Brian Rand. I am the assistant DA assigned to your case. They told me your cell phone wasn't working but I had to speak to you. I apologize for calling at such a crazy hour but I've been working night and day on this case and just came across something you need to hear. Considering its gravity, I thought you wouldn't mind being awakened."

Jack rubbed the sleep from his eyes. "It's okay. I had to wake up soon to milk the cows."

The eager voice on the phone turned hesitant and unsure. "Excuse me?"

"It's nothing. Just a momentary glimpse into an alternate reality. You should try it sometime. It's cheaper than cable television and way more educational."

There was a pause before the other man spoke. "I should preface this by saying that I've been on your side since the investigation began. I've done a lot of digging into your past and you seemed like a straight shooter. Also, I've dealt with your firm before. To be honest, I don't like the way they do business. I believed that the firm was more to blame than you were but until now, I couldn't prove it. They represented the parent company, Creves, in a few very shady cases."

"Mr. Jonas never mentioned that."

"Of course not. Anything with Creves' name attached comes under special scrutiny. Mr. Jonas was always Creves' attorney of choice. He is expensive, unethical, and willing to do anything to make sure his clients can pay his exorbitant fees. If Mr. Jonas had represented Herdsman, it would have raised too many red flags and our office would have started an investigation. By sending an underqualified attorney, not even a junior partner, it made Herdsman look like a small account not worth investigating. After we got the report, we started digging and found the connection between Herdsman and Creves. It also meant that if things went wrong, you were expendable. Things looked pretty grim. The DA was looking for someone to blame, a name he could give the press as the great villain. He wanted to set a precedent for future standards in the biotech industry, before things got out of hand. You were convenient and your colleagues were feeding us fuel to make it happen. I was going through the files and everything you did seemed consistent for an aggressive but honest attorney. Reading your files on the case, I didn't see you step out of bounds. I have to admit, I didn't exactly respect what I saw. You were pushing the limits so that your client could make more money. And your client is no angel. I figured you were greedy but honest, like most of the slimy lawyers in town."

Jack felt like crawling back to his compost heap. "Thanks for the compliment. I try to keep the slime build-up under control."

The expected friendly laughter didn't happen and Jack realized the man on the other end of the conversation was dead serious and held his life in his hands. "Like I said, slimy but honest. That last bit of maneuvering didn't seem consistent. The phony test results didn't make sense. You weren't making enough money representing Herdsman to risk being disbarred. I couldn't figure it out until I saw the transcripts of your consultation with Mr. Jonas. That made it all coherent and cohesive. He was probably going to get a sizable bonus from Creves when Bo Plus got FDA certification. He would have thrown you a few perks but he probably never would have told you about the real money the firm was making from Creves. My guess is that you didn't know half of what was going on. I'd like to sit down with you and get your side of the story. It won't get you off the hook entirely but with his tail on fire, I think Jonas will come around. You'll still get some heat, but not all of it."

Jack chewed on a piece of straw while he tried to figure out what he had just been told. The sharp lawyer in him understood perfectly. The tired young man standing in borrowed long johns in a hayloft listening to a cell phone that shouldn't be working realized that even the lawyer part of him was confused. "What transcripts?"

"The transcripts of your advisement with Jonas when he told you to get even more aggressive and manipulate the lab reports. The plan he outlined for you was fairly simple; aggressive, shrewd, and clearly illegal. Essentially, he advised you to break the law. His secretary typed up the transcripts. We subpoenaed all his files pertinent to this case, but he didn't turn these transcripts over so we didn't know about them. It turns out that his secretary sent you a copy of the recording and a copy of the transcript. I was going through your office and found it misfiled. It was with the files for the fertility lab you represented. To be honest, I am a bit confused as to why he recorded the meeting and even more confused as to why he sent you a copy. It doesn't really matter. What does matter is that we have it in our hands. With this in mind, I would like to advise you to come forward and testify. We can come to some sort of agreement."

A cool breeze blew through the open doors. Jack shivered. The meeting with Mr. Jonas ran through his mind like a rerun of a bad movie. They had met at Mr. Jonas' health club. They were doing laps around the indoor track, power striding in sweat pants and tee shirts. After that, they sat in the Jacuzzi drinking gin and tonics. If the secretary had been taking notes, she would have needed scuba gear and waterproof ink. And he had never represented any fertility lab.

He became aware of the piece of cardboard he was holding. Looking down, he saw it was the baseball card Theo had given him. In the soft moonlight, it looked new and the pitcher looked young and alive. The sweet smells of the farm made his head swim. The lawyer inside of him was finally awake but distant, like a character in a book he once read. A younger, more alive man, one who was more real, was whispering instructions in his ear, telling him what to say.

"I appreciate your calling to tell me this. I knew it would all work out. I totally agree with you. Now, if you don't mind, these are my conditions for cooperating with the District Attorney." Jack spoke uninterrupted for ten minutes while the stranger on the other side of the phone listened in shocked silence. Jack listed his demands as though he was reading from a legal brief, but he was actually studying the stats on the back of the card, rediscovering what he once knew by heart. He shut off his phone and put it in the pocket of his work jeans before lying down. He lay thinking, too excited to sleep.

He was still awake half an hour later when he heard Hanna open the barn door and climb the ladder. She was trying to be quiet but work boots were not designed for stealthy approaches. The windows were wide open and the moon had disappeared behind clouds. She sat on the floor, watching him.

They sat in silence for a long time, long enough for the moon to come out to show she had been crying.

Jack finally broke the silence, almost whispering. "Welcome back."

Her response was even lower, but the cold anger behind it cut as if she had shouted it out. "You're leaving."

"How do you know that?"

"Because you are a jerk and that's the only thing a jerk is good for."

"You're right but I'm surprised you know already."

She growled. "I've known you were a jerk for a while."

"No. My leaving. I just made that decision."

"Theo told me."

"About me being a jerk."

She almost smiled. "No. About your plans to leave."

Jack nodded. That made sense. "I'm leaving tomorrow." The space between them disappeared as she flew across the room, a rolling ball of anger. A small fist caught him on the mouth, splitting his lip, before he could catch both wrists and hold her back.

She struggled for a minute before standing firm. He took a deep breath, preparing to explain himself. A black boot swung back and then forward like a kamikaze pendulum, catching him between the legs. He went down, thrashing around in the loose straw, struggling to breathe. She ran to the open window, reached out, and broke off a thick branch from the old tree. She held it over her head, taking a moment to contemplate what she was about to do. He gasped out a few words, spitting out straw while he spoke.

She looked at him. "What did you say?"

"I . . . want . . . you . . . to . . . come . . . with . . . me."

The branch stayed poised and ready. "I'm not a floozy, if you haven't noticed."

He shook his head and took a few deep breaths. "I'm driving to New York. I want you to come with me."

"What for?"

He pulled himself up and sat on a bale of hay. "I just spoke to the assistant District Attorney. He uncovered some new evidence that helps my case, so we made a deal. I get a one-year suspended sentence for a few misdemeanors. No felony charges will be brought. I'll do some community service, most of it pro bono legal advising. My license to practice is suspended for one year at the end of which I will be put on review."

The branch stayed where it was. "That's a pretty sweet deal. How did you get him to go for it?"

"I convinced him that it was better for him to work with me than to put me away. My pro bono work is going to be advising a council on the legal ramifications of the new gene technology. I have a lot of inside knowledge and experience."

She reached back, ready to swing. "Sorry. I don't care about the new directions your career in law is taking. I hope your health insurance is paid for."

He scrambled back, falling off the hay bale. "Wait! That's not all."

"Talk fast. This branch is getting heavy and your head is looking like a convenient place to put it."

"We're driving in but taking a bus back. I'm selling my car and moving out of my apartment."

She waved the branch. "So?"

He started to stand but sat back down on the floor when he heard her growl. He gulped. "I need you," he blurted out.

"What for? Was I part of the deal with the District Attorney? You want to show him your latest pity case?"

"No! I'm going to visit my mother."

"I hope she knows first aid!" She swung hard but the branch met thin air where his head had been. The swing spun her off balance until she fell. He stood over her wondering how she could have missed and how he was suddenly standing.

"I want you to meet her. One of my conditions is that I would be living here. I won't have a job so without any income; I won't be able to make the car payments or the high rent. I guess I will be milking cows to put food in my mouth and a roof over my head."

"So what do you want me to tell your mom? That milking cows is better than being a lawyer? It is, but she won't buy it."

"No." He began to sputter, at a loss for words. "Well, I . . . I mean . . . I thought . . . umm . . . we're getting married, aren't we?"

She looked up at him in the fading moonlight. He could see enough to know that she wasn't about to cry. Her anger was quickly rising. "You're an idiot. Didn't anyone ever tell you that you're supposed to ask?"

"So? I'm asking."

"The answer is no. The doctors are sure I'll be dead before we celebrate out first anniversary."

He reached out for her hand but she pulled it away quickly. "I'll take it. I'll take the year if that's all I can get. And we'll pray for more."

"The answer is still 'no.' I want kids and you don't want to be a father."

He opened his mouth but his cell phone rang. "I have to answer. It may be the DA." A young woman with a rapid-fire southern accent spoke. "Hello Mr. Nathan. Gosh, you are a difficult person to get in touch with. We received a message on our answering machine saying that you changed your mind and still wanted the order. We need the shipping address."

He looked down at Hanna. "What is the address here?"

She looked at him with a puzzled expression. "Is that the DA?"

He smiled and nodded. "Yes. He wants to know where I will be for the next year."

Her mouth dropped open and she stared at him before answering. He repeated the address, and the woman on the phone repeated it back. "We need one more detail. You didn't specify what color sheets. You know; pink for a girl, blue for a boy. We could make them white or yellow but I thought you might have a preference."

He looked down at Hanna. She didn't look angry and the stick was nowhere in sight. "Boy or girl?"

Hanna's mouth dropped open again. "What?"

"The baby you've been praying for. Is it a boy or girl?"

"Why does the DA want to know that? Who are you talking to?"

He shook his head. "If we are going to be spending time together, you need to learn how to answer a straight question with a straight answer. If you promise to do that, I'll promise to stop lying."

She hesitated. "A boy."

He nodded and spoke into the phone. "Blue."

"Who is that?"

He grinned even wider. "The Baby Shop. They want to know what color sheets we want for the baby."

She held out her hand and he helped her up, feeling tough muscles under her soft skin. "And if we are going to be spending time together you'd better stop hiding the truth and start asking me straight questions. One day, I might find myself lying in a hospital room surrounded by idiot doctors and you'll be the only friend in sight. I'll need you to be honest with me."

He looked into her eyes and nodded grimly. "Okay. I promise."

She held out her hand. "Give me the phone."

"Make them purple. None of this 'blue is for boys' stupidity. And did my . . . fiancée . . . order a pump? I'm going to breast-feed. He did?" She looked up at Jack. "Yes, I agree. I think he is going to be a fine father after we iron out few rough spots. It's something he's wanted his whole life." She paused and looked up at Jack. "When?" He shrugged. "There's no rush." She paused. "Yes, that will be fine." She handed back the phone. "Jack, you are slightly more than a little crazy."

He nodded. "That's what it takes."

"I guess it does. Don't think that because we are engaged and wanting to be expecting a baby that you can take liberties."

He shook his head. "Not at all. You haven't met my mother yet. And it may sound strange, but I also want to take you to my dad's grave." His eyes dropped and he blushed. "Hannah, I'd like to do something I've never done before."

"Careful. I can always grab another stick if you start getting fresh."

"Can I hold your hand?"

She blushed and stammered. "You've never held a girl's hand before? Is this just a way of stopping me from punching you again?"

He shook his head. "I've never asked before. I have a feeling that receiving is going to be so much nicer than taking."

Tears welled up in her eyes. "No one's ever asked before. For anything." She held out her hand. Their hands intertwined but they were afraid to look at each other. She led him to the open window and they sat down, still connected.

Jack turned his head but Hanna's chin dipped forward, her hair hiding her face. Her voice shook. "There's something you should know. The bar Theo found me at . . . I wasn't just drinking there. I was working."

Jack tried to turn her head but she slapped his hand away. "You don't have to . . ."

"Yes I do! After I was diagnosed, I lost all hope. I was juiced up most of every day, feeling no pain. And believe me, I had lots of pain that needed juicing. I did a lot of things there I don't remember and a lot more that that I wish I could forget. I ended up with a job dancing at a bar. One night, I was dancing on the stage, swaying to music only I could hear, trying to figure out which loser sitting at the bar was sleazy enough to take me one rung closer to hell. It was almost closing time so it must have been around three in the morning.

"The door opens up and in walks this kid. I stopped dancing and just stood there on the stage, buck naked, staring at him. I couldn't figure out why Jake, the bouncer, let him in. He sat down right in front of me, pulled out a journal, and started writing. I couldn't stand it so I got off the stage, put on a robe, and sat down next to him. I asked him what he was writing. He started reading to me. I don't remember a word of what he said, but I know I cried from beginning to end. When he finished, he handed me the journal and I flipped through the pages. The pages were all blank. He told me that writing in the journal would heal me, and that he was reading to me what I was going to write. I looked around and the bar was empty. Even the bartender was gone. I couldn't figure out why Jake hadn't interrupted to give me a few slaps to get me back on stage. Theo took me outside where Brad was waiting with the tractor. They brought me to the farm. I slept for a week straight, waking up a couple of times a day to eat some soup. And once every night to write in the journal."

Jack put his hand on her chin, forcing her to look at him. Her painful expression didn't surprise him, but he couldn't understand why she was shaking with fear. "I don't care about your past. It made you who you are and I love you."

Hanna's face twisted in pain. "Try not to be a jerk, spouting stupid love songs. That's not the problem. It's not my past I'm afraid of." She took a few deep breaths and closed her eyes. "That first night we met, when I came up into the loft for my journal . . ." Her eyes opened and Jack could see her face twitching with real terror. "That was my last entry in the journal. No blank pages left. Writing in the journal kept me alive, one page at a time. The doctors acted like a bunch of idiots, trying to figure out why I wasn't dead already. The problem is now the journal is finished and Theo won't give me another one. Jack, I'm scared!"

Jack held her hand tightly. "I'll be your journal."

A small sob escaped and she grinned. "You are such a jerk. That is the stupidest thing . . ."

He touched her lips. "No, really. I sat through years of college and law school, memorizing anything they said was important. This," he reached over and put his hand on her heart, "This is the most important thing to me. I will memorize every word you say. I will treasure every tear that falls from your beautiful eyes. And when we are old and gray, I will read them back to you. But remember, the words are yours, but the key to this journal is mine."

She lifted his hand to her face, to brush away the tears. "Gee, you don't sound like a jerk at all. Not even a little bit. Maybe I will let you stay around."

They watched the sky change gradually from black to deep purple and the pale pink of dawn. The sounds of the cows waking up made them laugh but also reminded them that the day was starting. Jack broke the long silence. "I have to go. I'm milking with Brad this morning."

She smiled, nodded, and stepped onto the ladder. She was standing on the top rung, ready to climb down, when she stopped. "What was his name?"

"Who?"

"Your father."

"Why?"

"Answer the question."

"His name was Benjamin."

She smiled and nodded, disappearing down the ladder.

LANCE

By the time Jack arrived at the milking parlor, Brad had already brought the cows to the showers and was sitting in the office reading a paperback. He grunted once, putting his book on the shelf. The cows, standing in their places, waited patiently. Hanna walked in. Big Brad frowned and mumbled something inaudible to Jack. Hanna smiled at Jack and said, "I couldn't sleep so I figured I'd come and give you a hand milking. It will help us get an early start." They worked side by side without speaking, nothing but silly grins on their faces as the work went by quickly. Jack hurried back to the barn to pack. His suit was full of dust, but he didn't have time to stop off at his apartment in the city to change clothes. He'd meet with the DA in borrowed work clothes that smelled of hay, but at least they were clean.

He arrived at breakfast late, walking into a kitchen full of eyes staring at him. Theo's parents sat at the table but Brad stood by the door, blocking Jack's entrance. The room was silent for a moment until Jack suddenly felt himself lifted up in a grip that threatened to crack his ribs. Brad jumped up and down, nerely bouncing Jack's head on the ceiling, whooping in a yell that made the china rattle on the shelves. Theo's father calmly called out, telling Brad to put him down. Jack was just starting to breathe again when an oversized Eskimo paw slammed him on the back.

"Congratulations, brother. When's the wedding?"

Jack was about to ask how they knew when he saw Theo sitting at the table, a big grin on his face. "Wedding date? I don't know. Ask Theo. He seems to have all the right answers."

"Maybe I do and maybe I don't, but I sure want to hear what you've got to say."

The Mercedes looked strange, shiny and sleek, like a flying saucer that had landed in front of the barn. Jack's only luggage was a very dusty, wrinkled Italian silk suit stuffed into a plastic bag with a few stalks of hay. Hanna was waiting for him in front of the house with a canvas overnight bag.

He smiled at her. "You travel light."

She smiled back. "We're only going for one night, silly."

"You must really trust me."

"If we stay one day longer, you'll have to take me shopping. And I'm warning you, I have expensive taste."

Jack laughed as he turned the key. The starter remained stubbornly silent, but he calmly took the key out of the ignition and sat back, humming a nameless tune. He couldn't help reflecting that a lifetime ago his response would have been a string of expletives. Hanna looked at him with a frown. "What's the matter? Should I get Brad to help us fix the car?"

Jack shook his head. "No. I am learning to listen to my inner voice before making decisions and acting. Right now I'm praying for the motor to start."

She seemed about to say something but thought better of it and sat back in the leather seat. Theo came out of the house carrying a small backpack and opened the car door. Jack tilted his seat forward, allowing Theo to wriggle into the tight back seat. Jack turned the key again and the car started. Hanna turned in her seat, watching Theo search for the seat belt.

"Where are you going?"

Theo snapped the seat belt shut. "Same place you are."

"Why do you need to go to New York? Did you just want to come for the ride?"

Theo shook his head grimly. "No. You'll be coming back tomorrow but I'll be staying. I need to set up shop there."

The car was headed down the lane, and Hannah yanked on the hand brake, stopping the car with a jerk. Jack put it in neutral. "Is there a problem? Did you forget your toothbrush?"

"This is crazy. Theo can't just leave his house and open a store in New York City. He's just a kid."

"I'm sorry, but the last two weeks have been such total insanity I guess I didn't notice when things settled down into merely crazy." He looked at Theo in the rear view mirror. "Did you tell your folks? I'm hoping to stay here for a while and I wouldn't want them to hold a grudge against me."

Theo nodded and Hanna suddenly noticed that his eyes were red from crying. "They agreed?"

Theo nodded, tears beginning to slowly reappear. "They've known for a year that I'd be leaving so there wasn't too much to say. I told them so they would be prepared. After waiting for it to happen, I think it finally came as a relief."

Hanna looked at Jack with alarm. "Are you going to facilitate this? He's just a kid. I'm sure his parents don't want him to go."

Jack put his hand on hers, lifting it gently to contemplate the hidden secrets of her palm. "You taught me that there is a reason to fight with all your strength to hold onto life. One day, I may need that. Until I met you, I wouldn't have believed it. I thought arguing was only a way to make money. But there is a reason why we are together. We are different. When it is time to let go, sometimes you don't fight. Sometimes you need to move forward and change, even if it hurts or if it isn't what you would choose. I think Theo's parents understand that, each in their own way. You don't raise a son like Theo and then get upset because things don't work out the way you planned, the normal way."

Hanna looked at her hand resting in Jack's. "You learned that here?"

He nodded. "I had to. Because someday I may need to teach it to you. Or to our son."

Hanna looked down for a few seconds and when she looked up, she said, "I'll write you a whole long list of things you need to teach Ben."

"Who is Ben?" Theo asked from the back seat.

Hanna looked back at Theo. "He is the son we haven't had yet, named after Jack's father."

Theo smiled. "I like that name. I wish I had a friend named Ben. Maybe someday I will."

Jack drove away from the farm slowly, suddenly afraid to hurry towards the city and the problems awaiting him. He drove with the radio off, wanting to use the time to think. He kept glancing over at Hanna. His thoughts were all about their future together instead of the legal tangle ahead of him. Hanna was trying to imagine Jack's mother and hoping they would like each other. Theo was curled up in the back seat, looking out the window. The on-ramp to the highway was on the other side of town. Theo tapped Jack on the shoulder as they approached the town.

"You need to stop for gas."

Jack shook his head. "I've got half a tank. That will get us most of the way there."

"You need to stop for gas."

Jack glanced down at the gas gauge and saw it bouncing wildly from side to side, 'E' to 'F'. He took a deep breath. Having Theo around was a special experience that could drive a person crazy, though Jack was well aware that he had benefitted beyond measure from Theo's strange gifts. He pulled into the gas station and waited while Lance ambled slowly towards his car.

Lance looked at the luxury sports car, a sour look on his face. "Wern't ya in here while back?"

Jack nodded. "I stayed a while. Now I'm leaving."

Lance put his greasy hand on the dusty hood. "Da cops was in here lookin' fer a car jes like dis."

Jack nodded. "They found me. I'm on my way to turn myself in. I need gas to get there."

Lance spit brown. "Ah woudna tol dem anyways bein' as I don' like cops. Dey always be stickin der nose in udder people's business. How much ya be needin', Slick?"

Jack shrugged. "I'm not sure."

Lance looked up at him sharply. "I ast ya a question. You be gettin' smart wit me?"

Jack took a deep breath. He decided to humble himself rather than confront the angry man. "No. I'm just not very good at these mechanical things. Please just fill it up with hi-test."

Lance gave him a suspicious look before pumping the gas. He was watching the meter on the pump when he heard the car door open. He looked back and saw Theo shimmying out of the tight back seat. Theo stood there for a moment, looking around. Lance straightened out of his slouch, a wicked grin making his teeth shine yellow.

"Hey, boy! Ya wait rite here. I got sometin for ya." Lance jogged across the driveway, disappearing behind the garage. He reappeared, dragging the wood crate that had been Theo's roadside stand. In his hand was a tire iron. Lance stopped in the middle of the garage entrance. "Hey, guess what today iz. Ah give ya a hint." He kicked the box, toppling it over. The door flopped open, spilling the contents onto the asphalt. "It ain't yer birfday." He swung the iron, cracking the crate in half. "Nope. It sho ain't. It ain't New Years." He brought the tire iron down again, splintering more wood. "Uh-uh. That wouda bin a bad guess." He brought the tire iron down twice, and the wood gave way. The crate lay broken, its contents exposed. "It sho'ly ain't Christmas. It ain't even code out. It might be Thanksgivin' but I'm not smell no turkey cookin'." He lifted up his greasy work boot and held it over the pile. Theo watched with a sad expression on his face. "Since ya cain't guess, I'll tell you. Dis the day after yer lease expahred." With a shout of joy, the greasy man brought down his boot, shouting again as a broken piece of something skittered away. He began stomping on the pile, laughing as glass and plastic pieces cracked and broke. He continued for several minutes until the pile was flat and everything that could be broken had received individual attention from the tire iron. He stepped back to admire his handiwork. Theo slowly approached the remains of his former roadside stand. He pulled a torn comic book from the mess, shaking off bits of broken glass. He turned a few pages, not looking up at the man. Jack clenched his fist and took one step forward. Lance had pushed his buttons and he was aching to smack his nasty face. He felt someone grab his hand and he realized that Hanna had gotten out of the car. He looked at her but she shook her head, giving his hand a reassuring squeeze.

Theo's voice was gentle and soft. "Do you want this comic book, Mr. Higginbottom? I could sell it to you cheap. Kind of a 'going out of business' sale."

"I don't want nuttin from ya but to see yer backside walkin' away."

Theo kept his gaze on the pages of the comic book. "You have way too much anger for one man. Someone must have given you theirs. Who gave you all that extra anger?"

Lance tapped the tire iron on his open palm. "Nope. I ain't angry. Right now, I'm happy. Dis is sometin' I been meanin' to do fer a while."

Theo stared at the pages, speaking slowly as if he was reading out loud. "Anger is a gift. Someone gave it to you. They probably told you it was for your own good, because they loved you. It's natural, a human thing, to love. You want to show your love but all you know about love, all he taught you, is that it looks like anger. What is amazing is that you want to show your love to everyone you meet."

The grin on Lance's face wavered for a second but instantly reappeared. "Boy, you crazy. I don' even likes you a little bit. Now ya bes be cleanin up yer garbage and git."

Theo continued reading from the comic book. "But he gave you something else. It was his last little bit of real love. What was it? What happened to it?" Theo turned the page.

Lance raised the tire iron but Theo didn't even look up to acknowledge the threat. "Ya be talkin' nonsense boy."

"Your daddy gave it to you on your tenth birthday. It was the year after your momma died. You were old enough to still remember what it sounded like when your mother and father laughed together, but you were too young to hold on to that when the hard times came along." Theo turned the page as Lance took a step closer, now shaking with rage. "It came in a box with a red ribbon. You didn't wait because you could hear it moving around and whining even before you opened the box."

The tire iron rang as it hit the asphalt. It slipped from Lance's numb fingers. He stepped quickly forward, grabbing Theo, lifting him up off the ground. He began shouting, his face inches from Theo's. "Where'd ya hear 'bout dat? People in dis damn town be talkin' too much. My pa was a good man. They all be fergettin' about what he was like fore he started drinkin', before momma got sick an' da good Lawd took her away." Jack started forward, tearing his arm out of Hanna's grip. Theo looked deep into Lance's eyes, and Lance felt a lump in his throat so big he could barely breath. Lance's eyes glanced aside for a moment, seeing something behind Theo. He roared and threw Theo to the ground. The boy landed hard, groaning in pain. Lance ran past him, his heavy boots pounding the pavement. And suddenly he was gone, running into the street, a car honked and swerved to avoid the lumbering figure. Lance went down to his knees, huddling in the middle of the intersection. Traffic came to a halt, cars beeping and braking. He stood up, shaking visibly, something cradled in his arms. Jack helped Theo to his feet and they watched the figure in greasy coveralls walk back, ignoring the shouts of the angry motorists. When he got closer, they saw that Lance was holding a trembling black and white puppy. Lance stroked him with big greasy hands, cooing softly.

"You shouldna ougther dun dat. De street ain't no place fer little guys like ya. Dose people don't care. All dey care bout is runnin' roun' from place to place. Dey won't even be takin' a second to look if maybe a little guy like you might be lost and scaid in da middle of da street."

Theo limped over to pet the tiny dog. "This is a special little guy. Do you see the heart shape on his forehead? I've never seen that before."

Lance's fingers gently touched the strange white mark. "I seen it afore. But I guess ya right. It don't happen much."

Jack stepped up behind Theo. The white splotch on the puppy's forehead didn't exactly look heart-shaped but it was unusual. Theo looked up at Jack and smiled. The boy was clearly tired and small wrinkle lines were visible at the edges of his eyes. Jack had noticed that phenomenon before in other situations, as if some extraordinary exertion aged Theo way beyond his actual years.

Theo looked at Lance petting the dog. "Are you going to take care of him?"

Lance stopped petting the puppy. His voice became strained. "Cain't do dat. Gas station ain't no place fer a puppy. Cars comin' in an' out, somethin' awful boun' to happen to him."

The puppy began to lick Lance's greasy hand and Theo laughed. "He likes the taste of motor oil. I think a gas station suits him fine. You saved him once. I think he trusts you to take care of him."

Lance hesitated but the puppy began to cuddle and rub his ears against his hand. Lance's fingers instinctively stroked the puppy. "I guess I could take him in fer a bit. Till he gits ode enough to take care a hisself."

"What are you going to feed him? Do you have any dog food? You should run to the store and get some." Lance hesitated until Jack added, "We'll watch the gas station until you get back. But don't take too long, I've got an important appointment."

Lance gave Jack a sharp look. "As ah recollect, you was singing dat song fuhst time we met. Mus not be dat important if ya could put it off fer almos' tree weeks."

109

Jack shrugged. "I thought that one was important but I was wrong. This one is way more important. This one is about a woman."

Theo looked at Lance. "Maybe you should get the food now. We'll wait until you get back."

Lance hesitated. "I don' go to dat store. I ain't been dere in tree years."

"But the little guy is hungry." The puppy began to whine as if on cue.

"Last time I were dere, dat uppity Mrs. Danzinger tole me to wash my face an hands. I tole her it weren't none of her business. I ain't been back dere since. I do all m'shopping over in Weaverville. Cheaper, anyway."

Theo nodded. "Maybe you could do it just this once. For the puppy's sake. He sounds awfully hungry."

Lance handed the puppy to Theo and walked towards the store. Theo called out. "Hey Lance. Maybe you want to wash your face and hands. For the puppy's sake." Lance grimaced but walked to the restroom to scrub up.

Lance even removed his coveralls, hoping that he would be less recognizable in street clothes. He tried to slip into the small market unnoticed, heading quickly for the pet food. There were two other people in the store and Lance decided to wait a few minutes to allow a few more customers to come in. Instead, the other customers left, leaving him alone in the store with Mrs. Danzinger who was reading a magazine behind the cash register. Lance had no choice so, with the bag of puppy food clutched in sweaty hands, he approached the checkout counter. Mrs. Danzinger looked up with a smile and Lance breathed a sigh of relief. She probably forgot their last encounter.

"Hello, Lance. It's been quite a while."

Lance froze, his hand reaching for his wallet. "Hey, Mrs. Danzinger. Yeah, guess it has been."

"Do you have a dog?"

Lance wanted to grab the bag and run, but her straightforward friendliness caught him off guard. "Well, um, yes. Dat's why I had to stop in an get dis puppy food. It's a puppy and mighty hungered."

She nodded, with a friendly smile. "I entirely understand. I have puppies too and I know how demanding they can be. When did you get him?"

Lance shifted uncomfortably. "Jes dis mornin. I kinda foun him in the middle of da street. He was gunna bouta become road pavement. Same place a dog got runned over when it were my paw's station. I left im at de station one day and my poppy forgot to tie im up. He was sad on count of my ma passin' away so he drank some. I be guessin' he din' pay so much attention as he shoulda."

"Oh my! How awful. What kind of dog is he?"

Lance had reached his limit of friendliness. He picked up his bag and stepped towards the door. "Jes a mutt. A little black an white with a heart shape on 'is head."

"Why, that is one of mine! My Jackie gave birth two weeks ago in the storeroom. I've been looking for homes for them but that one was nippy so no one wanted him. I didn't understand because he was my favorite and loved cuddling with me. But he would bite anyone else who tried to pick him up."

Lance hesitated in the doorway, suddenly afraid she would demand her dog back. "He din't bite me. We git along good. I'm gonna take good care of 'im."

"I'm sure you will." Lance relaxed and turned to leave. "Why don't you bring him by on Sunday so he can visit with his momma?" Lance froze, one foot outside the store. "I'm sure the puppy would like that. And Jackie is sad, now that she is alone. It must be hard for a momma to be alone after her babies leave. Even if she is just a dog."

Lance closed his eyes. He wanted to yell but she hadn't said anything to offend. "I don't think I can come by on Sunday."

"Your gas station is closed on Sunday. I've got a big yard. Bring the puppy. It will be good for him to play in my yard. And to see his momma one more time. They might not have had time to say a proper goodbye before he snuck out and ran into the road."

Lance hesitated but still did not turn around. "Okay. Maybe a short visit."

"Oh, and Lance, I do appreciate that you washed your hands and face but three years is a long time to spend in the washroom." He spun around in anger, ready to lash out, but her twinkling eyes and smile stopped him short. "When you come on Sunday, comb your hair. I do believe that underneath that tangle of hair is a fine looking man that I would like to get to know better. Excuse me for being so forward, but I don't want to have to wait another three years to make my intentions clear."

Lance looked around the store. "Where's Mr. Danzinger? I 'member him from when he used to buy gas."

"Fred passed away four years ago. I don't drive so I sold the car. I live right around the corner and don't go out much. I'm a home-body with an empty home." Lance nodded, not knowing how to respond. She seemed to understand, nodding back. "I'll see you on Sunday."

Lance was deep in his own thoughts and didn't notice as the three drove away. Theo curled up and went to sleep on the back seat. Hanna reached back to pick up the comic book that had dropped onto the floor. It was torn and a few pages were missing. She leafed through the pages. The artwork was bad but the story line caught her attention. An illustration of a child's birthday party compelled her to turn back to the beginning of the story. She shuddered at the pictures of a woman in a hospital bed and the next frame showing a man and boy at a gravesite. She shivered at the images of childhood. The next frame showed the man slouched in a chair, an empty bottle fallen from his hand, 'x's for eyes to show he was drunk. She flipped the pages and laughed out loud at the comic scenes of an angry gas station attendant yelling at customers. She looked back at Theo snoring away. She turned the page. A cartoon sports car pulled into the gas station. A crude depiction of herself in a dress and black boots made her wince. The next page showed a couple getting married. The facing page had another hospital scene, black boots at the foot of a hospital bed, a doctor explaining to the handsome young man that his wife had only a small chance of survival. The young man asked if the baby might survive. Her fingers itched to turn the page, to flip forward to the end of the story. She closed her eyes as her lips moved in silent prayer. On a sudden impulse, she threw the magazine out the open car window.

Jack looked over. "What was that?"

She smiled at him and reached over to hold his hand. "Nothing. I'll tell you about it later."

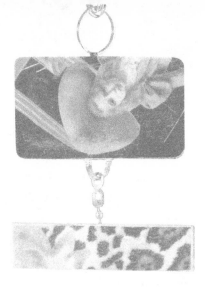

THE HOPE
MERCHANT

The weather was a gift, sunny and warm, so Jack decided to take a one-day vacation from his heavy schedule. It hadn't really been his idea. Without consulting him, his boss, the DA, called Hanna and told her to take Jack out of the office for some badly needed downtime. When Hanna showed up at the office with a picnic basket, Jack protested. The DA, a quiet family man ten years Jack's senior, smiled and called in two burly marshals. Each taking an arm, they ferried a mildly protesting Jack out of the building. Hanna handed him the basket and pulled his arm around her so he could feel the baby kick.

As they strolled through Central Park, Jack considered how his career had transformed into something entirely unexpected. A year ago, as a high-powered attorney at a prestigious firm, he thought he was working hard. The deal with the District Attorney had done for him what the high-power legal firm could not. He was calling the shots in a new branch of law, one with serious moral implications and lots of money at stake. Other people were making the money, but that didn't bother him. His new career had its own perks. He was working harder than he ever worked before but with a zest and energy unlike anything he had in his previous legal incarnation.

Working for the District Attorney involved the same long hours and the same pressure, but he finished the day feeling fresh and energized. He didn't need or miss the expensive perks. His weekends on the farm were better for his health than the fancy health club. And if he did get tired, thinking of Hanna revived him. He was still technically on parole with one foot in jail, yet he was practicing law the way his father did, the way he had always dreamed it would be. His former colleagues would have thought he had totally lost his mind, but Jack was happier about his law career than he had ever been. Job satisfaction was high but the paycheck was best not thought about. He would have starved but the District Attorney kindly arranged a stipend for him, small but sufficient for setting up house with his bride. After a lot of hard bargaining, he managed to cash in all of his possessions to eliminate his debts. The only remnant of four years of high-pressure legal practice was a closet full of expensive suits that he rarely wore.

It had been a year since he met Hanna on the farm. The three weeks he spent milking cows changed him forever. He had come back to the city with her, but the city seemed different to him. He used to love driving fast but with Hanna sitting next to him, the drivers passing him on the highway seemed reckless. They took the bus for the trips to the farm. His city apartment made him feel claustrophobic, and he missed the smell of the cows. To his surprise, his uptown mother loved Hanna and they bonded almost immediately. He watched them chat away on the sofa in his mother's posh penthouse like two sorority sisters. Despite Hanna's protestations, he looked for a large and luxurious wedding hall, but they were all booked at least six months in advance. Under normal circumstances, that would have been a reasonable amount of time, but despite Hanna's healthy appearance and their joint optimism, waiting was not an option. It also became clear that in his new socio-economic circumstances, he didn't have enough friends left to half-fill even the smallest hall. They got married on the farm, the cows looking on with great interest. The entire town, all three hundred and fifty-eight residents, showed up, bearing pots and Tupperware. Hanna was a beautiful bride. Everyone spoke of the wedding for months, how a special aura of joy had descended on the crowd. The assistant DA showed up as a surprise guest, and Jack found out that his new boss had been raised on a farm. After the ceremony, he whooped it up, tearing around on the tractor but making up for it by helping with the milking. Theo's absence was sorely felt and his parents made it clear they didn't want to discuss it. Brad surprised them with a wedding present. He had converted the shed that once housed Jack's sports car into a small but lovely cottage for their weekends on the farm.

Six weeks after the ceremony, as he lay beside her, she whispered in his ear that she was pregnant. They went to the hospital to confirm it. While she was in with the gynecologist, her doctor took Jack aside and told him that she was certainly fooling herself, the symptoms a result of her cancer treatment. Her cancer was probably making a comeback, and they should prepare for the worst. It was virtually impossible for her to conceive, he assured Jack. It was certainly no simple matter and would take years of special treatment, years she didn't have. An hour later, the doctor was raging at Hanna's irresponsibility, getting pregnant when she was probably going to die before the child could be born. Jack surprised himself at his own equanimity. He had seen through the lies and posturing of his own profession, and other professionals were no less immune to the intoxicating feel of power. He realized the doctor was angry at his own ignorance. They found another doctor, an older man with pictures of his grandchildren lining his office. He ran some tests that hadn't been done since the beginning of her treatment and discovered the cancer was a wispy shadow where there had once been raging storm clouds. He showed up unexpectedly to cry with them in joy when they saw the first ultra-sound.

One year after buying a baseball card from Theo, Jack found himself in the most improbable circumstances, happily married to a woman who would rather drive a tractor than a Mercedes, and expecting a baby. As he walked through the park, his arm rubbing against Hanna's swollen belly, he realized that the original plan was the root of his problem. He had been a bright teenager with a clear sense of direction and purpose. He wanted to be a lawyer so he picked the best school and set out achieving everything he needed to do to get accepted. He had always looked to his peers, who shared the same goals, for the definition of success. He had rented an apartment in the most desirable part of town. People watched as he drove past in his eye-catching car. Every aspect of his life spelled success.

And yet, looking back on his life as he walked next to Hanna, he could see that as the years passed, he had become angrier and enjoyed his life less. Intuitively, he knew that following Mr. Jonas' orders would end in disaster, and yet he followed those orders. Jack now realized that this direction represented an unconscious attempt to self-destruct. It was the only way to put an end to his lifelong plan for success, the plan that was making him, against all conventional wisdom, completely miserable. He thought of Mr. Jonas, trapped in his own luxury castle, alone and afraid of stepping out from the spotlight of success that was killing him. Jack pulled

Hanna closer as they walked through the park. He mused about searching eBay to find out how much a stroll through the park on a beautiful spring day with the woman you love was worth.

He wondered about Theo. Despite his initial feelings about self-determination, in the final analysis Jack felt guilty for taking away the Meyer's son. He had agreed to take Theo on impulse, feeling confident the boy would change his mind the moment he was faced with the reality of being alone in the big city. The weather had been so lovely that they stopped off for a picnic before arriving in Manhattan. Realizing it would probably be his last road trip in the fancy sports car, Jack popped open the roof and treated Hanna and Theo to the full sports convertible experience. Hanna laughed as her long hair flew around, but Theo just sat silently in the back seat until they entered the city. They came out of the Midtown Tunnel and landed in the middle of a rush hour traffic jam. Without any warning, Theo jumped out of the back seat and slid off the dusty trunk, leaving a trail before his canvas sneakers hit the asphalt. He took off running, weaving in and out of the stalled traffic. His denim jacket flapping as he ran away was the last Jack saw of him. Jack, familiar with the horror stories about young runaways in the city, felt more than a little uncomfortable about his irresponsibility in allowing Theo to just disappear.

Abruptly, Hanna stopped short. Ten feet in front of them a homeless man, with a shopping cart full of junk, was staring at them. He was in his mid-twenties, though life on the street had made him look older. His long hair was tangled in thick dreadlocks and he wore a long trench coat despite the heat. The cart was piled high with cast-off rags and empty bottles. Perched on top was a boom box held together by duct tape. Jack didn't understand why the man was looking at them so intensely until he pointed at them and shouted.

"You took my bottle. Give it back!"

Hanna took a step back and Jack instinctively stepped in front of her. The man dug through his cart, pulling out several empty bottles until he found one half full of brown liquid. He held it up to the light before taking a long drink, some of the liquor dribbling past his lips and down his chin. He slid the bottle into his baggy coat pocket. Pointing his finger accusingly at Jack, he screamed loud enough to attract the attention of the few dozen people around them. "You drank it. Now I only have half." A crowd was forming, curiously watching but keeping a safe distance. The man reached into his coat and suddenly he was pointing at Jack with a small, very shiny, silver sword.

"He's got a knife!" someone shouted. Those near enough to be in danger were moving back. Jack looked at the long blade and wondered how strange it was for a dirty homeless man to have such a long and shiny knife. Homeless men typically carried short, nasty knives, or rust-covered razors. He became angry with himself for focusing on the man's choice of weapon when he should be dealing sensibly with the situation. Still, he stood rigid with fright, praying that he would be able to react when the man finally made his move. The man reached into his baggy coat and pulled out two more swords identical to the first. Jack's jaw dropped. For some reason, one sword was scary, two even more so, but three swords were so absurd that it made any reaction seem pointless, defense utterly impossible. Jack watched helplessly as the man moved quickly, swinging his arms. He brought the swords together, the ringing clash startling the crowd. The man slumped, and then lifted his head. Suddenly the swords were in the air. The swords flew high and began to arc downward. Jack was so intent on watching the blades that it took several rounds before he realized the swords weren't flying towards him. The man began to twirl and spin, dancing as he juggled the swords. Between the flying blades, he reached out and punched the button on the battered stereo and electro pop started pumping, matching the rhythm of his dance. The swords flew, glittering in the sun, flying higher until they almost touched the branches overhead. The man reached into his pocket and pulled out the half-full bottle, taking a quick swig before tossing it up to follow the swords in their flight. Every time the bottle came around, the man took another quick swig. He began to stagger, acting drunk, swinging his arms wildly, and catching the sharp swords at the last possible moment. Jack was stupefied, unable to move, watching the swords with his mouth open. The routine went on for an action-packed fifteen minutes, the man pulling a crazy assortment of articles from his cart to display their flight properties to the growing crowd. The grand finale was juggling an assortment of dolls, each displaying a different emotion. When a doll landed in his hand, he stared at it and mimicked its emotion. As the dolls flew, he rotated through fear, laughter, anger, surprise, and boredom. As the dolls flew faster, he switched from one emotion to another in sync with the speed of the dolls until one emotion became another with lightning speed. He had his audience cheering and laughing until their response reached one long crescendo of applause. The performer ended his act by lining up his dolls in front of him. Spare change filled the air as he took his bows and people approached him to shake his hand, depositing crumpled bills in his palm, asking the same questions over and over. 'Where are you from? Where did you learn to do this? Is this what you do for a living? Do you have a job?'

Jack was surprised when a stranger from the audience stepped forward and slapped him on the back, congratulating him for his part in the performance. He turned to see others nodding and smiling, assuming that Jack was the juggler's assistant. A hand grasped his shoulder. He turned to see the street performer grinning at him.

His white teeth glowed, surrounded by dark makeup imitating street grime. The young man reached up and pulled off a heavy wig, revealing close cropped blonde hair.

The juggler shook Jack's hand. "I'm sorry for scaring you but it was a great way to gather an audience."

"Sure. But don't expect me to pull them in for your encore. I don't particularly like having knives pointed at me by men I don't know."

The man gave Jack a strange look before looking away. "I'm sorry about that. It won't happen again. It only works with an unsuspecting victim. I need an innocent bystander because most people can't act well enough to pull it off. But you saw the results. I can retire from juggling for at least two days on what I earned today. They were a great crowd."

Jack smirked. "Sure. Everyone wanted to get a good seat to watch me get killed."

The young man laughed. "That's an unfortunate side of human nature that jugglers have learned to use to our advantage. Juggling dolls is harder than juggling swords but people won't pay for flying dolls. The swords are the big draw. The audience wants to count my fingers at the end of the show." He held out the bottle. "Do you want a drink? You earned it."

Jack shook his head. "No thanks. We were on our way to a picnic."

The man smiled and took a long pull from the bottle. "The best iced tea I've ever had." His smile twisted into something Jack couldn't identify. "Can I join you for lunch?"

Jack felt Hanna pulling his arm. "I thank you for the show but we were planning a special picnic, just the two of us. Once the baby is born, we won't have a lot of alone time together so we really don't want a guest today. I'm sorry." Hanna was pulling hard on Jack's arm and they began to walk away.

The young man called after them. "C'mon. I'm hungry. How can you say no to someone asking for food?" Jack glanced over at Hanna but she shook her head, pulling him away. The young man shouted louder as they got further away. His tone turned mocking. "That's not very nice. Can't you spare a peanut butter sandwich for an old friend, Jack?"

Jack stopped short before turning slowly to face the stranger. "How did you know my name?"

The man stood looking at them from across a small patch of grass. Hanna gasped. Jack turned, shocked to see her face grow suddenly pale. He walked back to face the stranger, leaving Hanna behind. Approaching the man, Jack tried to fit a name to the face but drew a blank. He came within a foot of the man, close enough to smell his clean sweat. Juggling was hard work and his clothes were dark and wet and stuck to his lanky, muscular body. His legal training had made Jack more comfortable with direct confrontation than subtle diplomacy as a means of dealing with an unknown threat. "Who are you?"

The young man returned Jack's gaze without blinking. "If I told you, you wouldn't believe me."

"Try me."

The young man smirked for a moment before breaking into laughter. His smile was wide and friendly. "Theo."

Jack squinted, wondering what kind of scam this was. He inspected the stranger's face, walking around him slowly to examine him from all angles. "The last time I saw Theo was a year ago. He was fourteen years old. You have to be at least twenty-five." Jack took a deep breath. "My ability to believe the impossible has improved greatly in the last year. If you are Theo, you owe me an explanation."

The man who called himself Theo nodded. "I'll be happy to give you that explanation. But it will cost you." Jack gave him a questioning glance but the man shook his head. "Don't worry. Your cell phone is safe. I really am hungry. What did Hanna pack for lunch?" They walked across the field to Hanna, the performer pushing his cart. Hanna waited, the basket of food on the ground next to her. They stood facing each other for a few moments. Jack didn't know what to say. It seemed absurd to introduce the juggler as Theo. Hanna surprised the men by speaking first.

"You remind me of someone I used to know."

Jack was startled. "He says that he is Theo."

Hanna nodded. "Good. You can join us for lunch. Your mother would never forgive me if I let you go away hungry."

Jack put his hand on her arm, stopping her as she began to spread out the blanket. "Doesn't he seem a bit old to be Theo?"

Hanna gently removed Jack's hand. "You forget. I've been living with miracles a lot longer than you have. He'll explain himself."

Hanna had brought a bottle of Beaujolais for Jack and iced tea for herself. She set out the glasses and Theo pulled the cork. Jack filled the glasses but Hanna took the stranger's glass from him as he lifted it to his lips. She shook her head. "You're too young to drink."

The man laughed and turned to Jack. "Hanna believes me."

Jack nodded solemnly. "I believe you too. But I still want an explanation."

Theo filled his glass with iced tea, twirling the stem between calloused fingers. "Business was a little shaky at first but I wasn't depending on a lot of business in the beginning. I still have a lot to learn. I'm not nearly as good as I should be, but there isn't any competition. I'm busy night and day."

"That's not much of an explanation, but I guess it proves you are Theo." Jack sipped his wine, hoping it would help him make sense of the situation. "What is it that you do?"

Theo looked into Jack's eyes for a few seconds. "You've seen my work first hand. What would you call it?" Jack's mouth opened, ready to make a sarcastic comment. Nothing came to mind so he backed down. Theo laughed. "The sign on the door says The Hope Merchant."

Jack raised an eyebrow. "You have an actual store?"

Theo nodded. "I have several stores in different towns. Like I said, there is a huge need and I am the sole provider. Sometimes I even make house calls."

"A franchise? I haven't heard of it. I must have missed your ads."

Theo smiled. "I provide special, personalized service, custom tailored for each individual. There are people I can't help and others I won't help. People who need my services hear about me eventually."

Jack smiled. "Advertising on a need-to-know basis. That is a unique approach to marketing. But you still haven't explained how you got older so fast."

"The first question is why I needed to get older. So many of the customers I needed to help refused to listen to a boy. I needed to be older so they would listen to me."

"Okay. I'll believe that for six minutes. So now tell me how you got old."

"It's not really a big deal."

"So how do you do it?"

Theo poured more iced tea from the whiskey bottle into his wine glass. "I don't know," he said calmly. "I just know that some days I'll wake up and my hair will be a different color or my eyes will change shape. Sometimes I'm Asian, sometimes black, and sometimes Caucasian. I get older or younger. It doesn't happen all it once. Usually it takes a couple of days. Sometimes it's a lot faster than that. I don't control it."

"Why does it happen?"

"Usually it becomes clear after a few days. I'll meet somebody, someone comes into the store, or I meet them on the street. I do some business with them and then the process reverses itself. I think it's because they needed me to be a certain way. A few days later I'm back to looking like my old self."

"You mean younger self."

Theo laughed. "I can't tell anymore which is which."

"What kind of business?"

Theo looked into Jack's eyes for a few moments before answering. "You know, the same kind of business I did with you and Hanna."

"Why do you have to change? You did fine with me and Hanna looking like a kid."

Theo shrugged. "Different people need different things. I had more time with you. After a couple of weeks, you were willing to listen to a kid. Hanna was on the edge so any little thing could have pushed her either way." A smile flashed across his face and for a fleeting moment Jack recognized the boy behind this stranger's face. "I think I was still in training. I don't have that much time anymore. I'm usually working on a couple of projects at once. Sometimes they overlap. Sometimes I'll have two customers who need to come together and I just happen to be the way for that to happen. I can barely keep track of all my customers and their individual needs. That's why I have stores all over. I don't have time to set up shop for each deal. I run from place to place, from store to store, usually getting there just in time to greet the customer."

"You want to tell me that you don't make appointments. People just show up and you happen to be there with exactly what they want." Theo nodded. Jack was irritated. "I don't believe it."

Theo ducked his head and smiled. "Isn't that how we first met, Jack? Isn't that what happened to us today? How often do you come to the park?"

Jack shook his head. "I sometimes walk through the park but I don't come here to hang out. It looks like you are a regular. I was bound to bump into you whenever I did come to the park."

Theo shook his head. "This is the first time for me, too."

"I don't believe you."

"Did you ever see me juggle on the farm? I didn't know I could juggle until I saw you."

"And you just happened to have a bunch of knives in your coat."

Theo nodded. "I had a feeling when I left my shop that I would need them so I stuck them in my pocket. I didn't know why until I pulled them out and started the act. When I put them in my coat this morning, I was scared of what was going to happen. I didn't know what to expect. I'm glad it was for juggling and not fighting."

"So if you pull out the knives now you wouldn't know how to juggle?"

"I'd be afraid to try."

They sat in silence for several minutes letting Theo's words sink in. "I still want to know how you got old."

Theo shrugged. "I don't actually do anything. It just happens to me. When I try to force it or stop it, it goes away. I think I understand it a little. It's pretty simple and also complicated." Theo took a deep breath. "This idea of the individual person is relatively new in human history. In ancient times everyone knew they were all part of the big 'one'. When I first started learning about that, it really resonated with me."

"That's ridiculous. The individual is not a social concept. It's a fact. And what does this have to do with your getting older?"

"I'll get to that. Facts change with time. I'm starting to think that when men thought the sun revolved around the Earth, it was true. When Galileo decided that the earth revolved around the sun, the sun stopped moving and the Earth kicked in."

Jack looked at him to see if he was serious. Theo looked totally matter-of-fact. "That's crazy. There is no way that can be true."

Theo shook his head. "There is no way you can prove me wrong. Not only that, before Galileo, it was true and a fact that the sun revolved around the earth. It was crazy to think otherwise. You believe that the individual is an unchanging fact. The individual is actually a social concept due to change as a result of group consciousness. The individual barely exists outside of being a conglomeration of connections. A person changes as he or she makes new connections." Theo smiled and ducked his head coyly. "You're not the same now that you are a husband."

Jack shook his head. "I've learned and changed. I have a wife so I can't be the same way I was. That doesn't mean I've stopped being 'me'. I am still a white male almost thirty years old."

Theo looked at Hanna and then back to Jack. "No. You have a wife but, more importantly, you have become a husband. Your connection has created a new you. You will have a baby and then become a father. A new 'you' is created by that new connection."

"This still doesn't answer my question."

"When someone needs something, if I am connected to them deeply enough, I change in order to help them. It's not conscious. It's just that my connection to them creates a new Theo. I guess I can do that because my attachment to myself is so loose and my desire to connect to another person and help him is so strong. I am not so stuck in being a certain age, race, or having a particular physical appearance. My connection to them is stronger than my connection to myself. I've never been a woman so I am probably strongly attached to that as part of 'me'. I've spent a lot of my time being an old man. I think a lot of people today need a sage, a wise man. There's so much emphasis on 'new and improved' that people don't know where to look for wisdom and experience anymore."

"So how come you look twenty five years old today? If you were really connected to us, you would look like what we recognize as Theo."

Theo shrugged. "I guess you were worried and needed to know that I was doing well and taking care of myself. That would be more convincing coming from a twenty five year old street performer than from a fifteen year old farm boy living alone in the city."

Hanna burst out laughing. "And a seventy year old Theo would have been too much for us to believe."

Theo smiled and nodded. Jack looked at her. "You believe this?"

Hanna smiled and reached out to ruffle the young man's hair. "Sure. I spent a lot of time reading to Theo at night. I stopped thinking of him as a young boy a long time ago. And . . . " She patted her swollen belly, "I've had a lot more time to realize that 'impossible' and 'miracle' are only words to describe things that don't make sense on one level but make a lot of sense on a much deeper level."

Jack's mouth opened but it was impossible to say all five things he wanted to say at the same time. His mouth closed when he realized he didn't have anything to say. Hanna slipped her hand into his and spoke for him. "It was nice to see you, even if you don't look like Theo. I guess this explains why you haven't been home to see your parents."

"Actually, I had a reason for coming to see you now. One of my clients needs something I can't provide. I need your help."

Jack raised an eyebrow. "Do I have to change into someone else?"

Theo shrugged. "Only if you want to. It's more like an introduction. One of my clients needs to meet an old friend of yours. To be honest, he needs a job."

"Your magic doesn't cover that?"

Theo shook his head. "This time, I guess it doesn't. Sometimes, magic gets stronger if there are more people involved." A cloud seemed to suddenly pass over the park and Theo's smile disappeared. "How's Brad?"

Hanna shook her head. "He's more silent than ever. I don't think he says ten words in a day. Now that I'm expecting and you're gone, Brad has to work twenty hours a day. He doesn't complain and he never gets tired, but he just keeps sinking deeper and deeper into himself."

Theo grimaced, mumbling something before looking up. "He's due for a change."

Hanna shrugged. "I can't imagine him leaving."

Theo winced. "I didn't mean that. He was the one who taught me how to change. It's an Inuit thing. Their shamans change shape. Brad taught me how."

"Brad is a shaman?" said Jack.

Theo nodded. "Something like that."

"How did he teach you?"

"He didn't really teach me. First he showed me. He scared me out of my skin with what he did that night. I'm not going to tell you about it. I don't even want to think about it. Then, he tricked me into doing it. After that one time, it just kept happening. He said that the solitude of the far north allows a man to realize how much he isn't. Once you realize all the things you aren't, becoming something else is just natural, almost easier than staying the same."

"What did he do?"

A grimace of pain crossed his face. Hanna and Jack sat staring at the young man who called himself Theo as he fought an inner battle they couldn't understand. His face seemed to change, grow older, as they watched. For an instant he looked young, and a smile flickered across his face. The dirty overcoat hung loose on him, oversized, like a costume. He was Theo for just a second before his face settled back into the older stranger. He took a deep breath and stood up. "I've got to go."

Hanna reached over and held Jack's hand as they watched him walk away. It had been a strange reunion, but they were happy to have seen Theo. It was enough for them to know that their union was a testimony to the fact that in his strange and special way, Theo was doing good in the world.

They could just barely see the face of the street beggar as he strode through the park. His face was twisted and scarred from some horrible accident, and covered with a thick layer of dirt. Fresh scabs, red and glistening, forced the holiday crowd to look away as he pushed his way down the center of the path. Those who caught a glimpse of him were shocked at this pitiful human being whom God seemed to have abandoned.

The inside of the store was quiet and dark, cool like a forest cave. Dim sunlight found a way through a small grimy casement window into the store below street level. Traffic was a muffled whisper barely heard from a hundred yards away. The urban cave that became the shop had stood abandoned for years in an alley, ignored even by the homeless. Even now, with its new occupant, it was easy to overlook. A shadow passed across the stucco façade as a key rattled in the ancient brass lock. The shopkeeper stepped inside, leaving the front door open. He was middle aged with long but thinning hair, bifocals perched at the end of a prominent nose. He shrugged off the dirty overcoat, hung it on a hook, and slipped on a baggy sweater with suede elbow patches. He reached behind the counter and picked up a large duster made from ostrich feathers. He wandered around the store dusting the merchandise, favoring his left leg with a limp that seemed to come more from habit than disability. He mumbled as he dusted, sometimes stopping to stroke an object or just to stare at it.

A figure descended the cracked concrete stairs and entered the store. The old woman, wide as she was high and loaded down with packages, filled the doorway. She was grotesquely ugly, made worse by too much powder and lipstick. A few thick whiskers sprouted from her chin making it all but impossible to look away from her.

"Is this your place?" Her voice was gravelly and low, almost as unpleasant as her face.

The shopkeeper paused, a heavy clock in his hands, before looking at his new customer. His glance lingered for a moment before returning to the piece in his hands. It was an antique but too absurdly kitsch to be collected. Two full size bowling pins stood guard over a wind up clock, its face adorned with Roman numerals written in tiny painted pins. "This might interest you."

The old lady snorted, her nostrils flaring. "What would I do with that ugly thing?"

The shopkeeper sighed as he replaced the clock on the shelf, and took up his duster again. "Its alarm is unusually loud. It would help you wake up for the morning milking. I heard that you've been working too hard lately."

The old lady hesitated before putting down her packages. "It's not so bad. It's awful when your father tries to help. His heart's not in it anymore. He's not very good at missing you. Your mom is worse."

The feather duster paused. "I didn't expect you to bring that up."

The old lady went over to the shelf and picked up the bowling clock. "I was wondering if seeing Jack and Hanna would inspire any regrets. The farm is a nice place and your parents are fine people. Jack and Hanna are helping your folks deal with missing you." The old woman hefted the large clock, flexing stocky arms. "I think I'll take this. I've become a little too indifferent to time lately. This would be an unignorable reminder."

"'Unignorable' is not a word."

"I'll take a dictionary also, if you have one."

The feather duster twitched as the shopkeeper tried to hold back his laughter. They broke down at the same time, the man's laughter a higher pitched giggle. The euphoria, propelled by nervous energy, lasted longer than the joke justified. A smile lingered on the man's face as he turned to look at his customer. "It's good to see you. Even if it doesn't look like you." He tilted his head back to stare at her through the small lenses of the bifocals. "Actually, there is quite a resemblance."

The woman held up a square fist. "I'll show you the resemblance. I am a handsome Inuit buck. It pains me to think of myself as this fat overstuffed sausage."

The old man paused before answering. "I know better than to believe you. You taught me well. If it pained you to think of it, it wouldn't be possible."

The fist dropped. "Maybe I taught you too well. Do you forgive me?"

A look of pain passed over the man's face. "Not yet, but soon. I will come to tell you when my pain is forgotten. Where will you be? Don't you want to go back to the ice one last time?"

The old lady shook her head, thick jowls wobbling under her hairy chin. "It would be good to hunt again but the ice is gone. That is why I had to teach you the way I did. It might have been easier to take you north but the ice can be a cruel teacher, crueler even than I was. The world has lost a great thing by taming the North." She walked to stand next to the man, stretching to put the heavy clock back on the shelf. She stepped back and pointed to the inaccessible top shelf. The man sighted along her stubby finger, and nodded. He disappeared into a back room, returning with a wooden stool upon which he climbed, dragging his bad leg behind. He struggled to retrieve the heavy, and impossibly thick, leather-bound book with a strap struggling to keep it closed. The pages were from a different era when paper more closely resembled the trees they were made from. The man grunted with effort as he handed it over, but the woman held it as if it weighed nothing. She smiled as she opened it and caressed the rough pages. "I believe I shall sit quietly and write for a while."

The old man held out a fountain pen, an antique of real value, its black lacquer deeply polished. "I believe you will." The old woman rested the book on a shelf and opened the pen, the wide gold nib flashing even in the dim light. She seemed about to say something, but snatched the heavy book from the shelf and hurried to the door.

The man called after her. "Your packages."

The woman barely twisted her head around on her thick neck, yelling over her shoulder. "I don't want them. Keep them. It's more useless stuff for you to sell. Put it next to that ugly clock." The door closed behind her as if sucked in by the gale she created in passing. The man limped over to the pile of bags, struggling to lift them onto the counter. He spent the next hour unwrapping small packages, sometimes laughing, occasionally crying. When the objects all lay before him spread out on the counter, they seemed to speak to him, whispering a message he almost understood. He stood without moving for several hours, staring at the display of objects.

The pale glow of moonlight filtering through on the counter coincided with the understanding that he could no longer ignore the emptiness he felt. He missed his friend, but now for the first time, he missed his family and the childhood he left behind. The objects were all reminders of his home: a plastic cow with impossibly large udders, a metal tractor that would be a treasure for any nine-year old, a worn and tattered copy of Khalil Gibran, each item carefully chosen to strike a chord. Brad had come to teach him one more time. It left him healed in one part of his heart but broken and hurting in another. The sun set on a tired old man but when it rose, it struggled through the half-hidden windows to shine on a young boy, alone and lonely, who lay weeping on the dusty floor.

THE
BOOK
OF
LOVE

KAREN

Liza stood in the familiar elevator, taking in the shiny faux mahogany panels and posh interior. She hesitated before pressing the button. The only other occupant was a young woman with a ponytail who smiled sweetly at her from above a stack of manuscripts. Liza suddenly remembered being a starry-eyed editorial intern armed with her honors degree in English Lit, glowing recommendations and a determination fostered by a mom who preached that Liza could achieve whatever she put her mind to. For five years it was that determination that helped her learn how to fight tooth and nail to earn an enviable position in the do-or-die publishing business.

In time, she had become the sophisticated, savvy Liza who pushed the up button in this elevator for what she thought would be the last time. Liza was now coming from a different world. She was about to meet her old friend with whom she had eventually and unfortunately developed an adversarial relationship when they became competitors rather than colleagues. Liza fought a sudden urge to stay on the elevator, wait until the doors closed, and leave the building rather than face Karen, her old nemesis. She would not have returned, risking Karen's probable disapproval and ridicule, but she felt the old man like an unseen presence in her mind, gently forcing her to complete this bizarre mission. She hated to admit she felt threatened, but after coming this far, making the appointment, fortifying herself with a good breakfast and positive thinking, and taking the trip to the city, she was not about to turn back. She felt a sudden urge to run first to the bathroom but knew she would risk being late for the dreaded meeting. Gravity shifted as the elevator slowed, lightening the pressure on her bladder. The urgency passed but her nervousness grew.

She turned in the direction of the voice, and faced the young woman. She was somewhat older than when Liza last saw her but still the epitome of Madison Avenue chic. "Liza? Oh my god! Is that you? In a dress? How incredibly and unexpectedly gender correct!"

Liza took a deep breath, surrendering her impulse to counter what was clearly a backhanded compliment. Seemingly unperturbed, she smiled and turned toward her old friend, sparring partner, and sometimes enemy. "Well, you know how it is with me. Always expect the unexpected."

"You certainly have perfected surprise as an art form. My ribs still hurt from that time I took you to my martial arts class. You had me snowed. I totally believed you when you said you had never been in a dojo before."

"I didn't lie. That was the first time I ever threw a punch."

"Riiiiiight! Tell that to someone from Jersey. They might believe you. I never even saw you move and suddenly, there I was, lying on the floor gasping for breath."

"My sensei says I'm a natural."

"That's what mine says every time I think of switching to aerobics. How about stopping by my health club after work today and giving me a shot at payback?"

Liza's smile faltered for a split second, before she shook her head. "I've taken a break from kick boxing. But if you want, I can probably whip your butt at low impact yoga."

Karen looked confused for a moment, her perfectly manicured eyebrows forming twin question marks. "Yoga? How very New Age of you. You are the queen of surprises today. Why don't you step into my office and surprise me some more. You said you have a new project to show me but you were so mysterious over the phone. You know that I play hardball even for great stuff. Don't expect any breaks, no matter how good it is."

Liza hesitated so visibly that Karen didn't have to strain her fine-tuned business radar to pick it up. They stepped into Karen's office, the scene of battles more fierce than either of their sensei's had ever witnessed. Some blood might spill at the dojo, but Karen's office was a virtual war-zone where book deals were made or crushed.

Karen settled in behind her desk, a conspicuously expensive Louis XIV original. Her office decor was part of her arsenal. By the time the supplicant settled into the hand-stitched cushions of the Renaissance Revival parlor chair, letting her feet sink into the authentic Persian rug, while being bowled over by the signed and numbered lithographs covering the wall behind her, Karen had already won the first three points on the contract she intended to argue. Anyone who understood the value of the furniture and artwork was immediately intimidated. Anyone who couldn't appreciate the trappings was in the wrong place, outclassed, and in for a painful lesson. Karen published books but money was what the business was really about. And anyone who doubted that

Karen was absolutely the best at making money from books was quickly dispatched to the tastefully, albeit less elaborately decorated lobby.

"Well, I must say that despite that hopelessly feminine dress, life on a different planet does seem to suit you. What do you call that place you moved to?"

"I only moved two hours out of town. You should try it. I actually get to breathe air instead of exhaust fumes and drink water from the tap instead of plastic bottles. And at night I re-discovered these beautiful celestial objects called 'stars'. It's an extra ten dollars a month on our municipal taxes but it's worth it."

"I know about stars. They are solar powered night-lights. I was going to order a set online." Karen put on her tiny reading glasses, another tool in her arsenal. No contract was ever agreed upon unless every word passed through those fourteen karat gold frames. She peered at Liza over the lenses. "The rosy cheeks are a nice touch and the few extra pounds seem to suit you. I would be careful though. Take it too far and you'll end up looking like a Cossack peasant woman. I didn't think David was exactly your type, despite his wealth and successes. He is such an intellectual nerd. I gave the relationship two months max. But here you sit, a blooming flower of femininity, proving all my expectations wrong."

"I used to think the same thing. I got married thinking I could change him, but instead he changed me. I think he smoothed out my rough edges."

"I should say so. Here we are chatting away like giggly girlfriends sharing confidences. In the old days, we always had the meter running. Five minutes into a meeting one of us would have drawn first blood, and it was usually you." Karen paused but Liza ignored the cue, breaking eye contact and looking down, her anxiety mounting as she noticed Karen's reflection in the glossy wood of the desk. Karen jumped into the gap. "I'd offer you a cigarette but all these sweet children wandering the halls, taking over the business, tell me that nicotine is only slightly less evil than child porn and more deadly than the bubonic plague. I've been forced to revert to my adolescence, smoking in the stairwells, even though it occasionally sets off the sprinklers."

Liza felt claustrophobic as she listened to Karen's full volume staccato echoing off the sealed walls of her office. Perched on a top floor of this huge steel and glass building where she used to feel at home, Liza longed for the natural environment. She reminded herself that the nearest tree was in the park ten blocks away. "I quit smoking," she blurted out.

"I'm sure that is another of David's eco-correct personal improvements. You used to laugh at people who . . ."

"I'm pregnant."

Karen's mouth hung open. She took off her glasses and leaned over the desk for a closer look. "My god! I thought you couldn't. That's what you told me before you left. You said a change of scenery might help you out. But after five years I assumed the old-fashioned biological method wasn't going to work."

"I couldn't. At least that is what all of the doctors said. And we didn't want to adopt. It just didn't seem right. I mean, I think it's great, maybe for other people. But David seemed so disappointed. He was very close with his dad and family means something different to him, especially as an only child."

Karen leaned back in her chair, polishing her glasses before putting them back on. "So is that why you are here? You wrote a book about your miracle pregnancy? We don't publish that kind of fiction, unless you can convince me that we can move a half a million copies. And if you think that's the case, you had better stop right now because you can't convince me."

Liza longed for a cigarette, something to keep her sweaty hands busy and take the edge off her discomfort. She remembered how she retched the last time she had puffed, the first sign that her period, always so regular, wasn't just late but missing in action. She rubbed her palms on the hand-stitched upholstery, not caring that Karen noticed she was nervous.

"It's not that simple. I wish it were. Then I could yell and scream and force you to see it my way. But this is different, very different. I don't know who publishes this kind of story. I'm not sure there ever was a story like this." Karen stared at her over her glasses, impatient with her vague and unconvincing argument and assumed the expression of a disapproving mother about to ground her daughter. On the verge of crying, Liza wanted to run out of the room, afraid she might cry in front of this woman who knew a different Liza, a hard-hearted businesswoman incapable of tears. There was a time when she would have stood toe-to-toe with her, both fighting, neither of them willing to back down, concede, or even compromise.

Liza, fumbling through her purse, was shocked when Karen condescendingly slid a package of tissues across the desk. Karen waited while Liza dried her eyes, noting that Liza had no eye makeup to smear.

"What is the book about?"

Liza shrugged. "It's just a story. Don't get me wrong, a really good story that would probably make a great movie. The writing is good. This guy is no Hemingway, but then again, even Hemingway would not have been as good without Maxwell Perkin editing. But this book has something special. The author said . . . " Liza stopped short, realizing that she was babbling, barely making sense, and on the verge of sounding like a lunatic driven crazy by hormones.

Karen stared and waited until she realized that Liza was too afraid to say anything more. She pulled out a new pack of cigarettes and offered one to Liza. Her gold-framed eyes were fixed on Liza. "That was absolutely the worst pitch I have ever heard from an agent in all my years of publishing. I'm not sure if you deserve a prize or a kick in the pants. Couldn't you at least lie and tell me the book is a knockout, a bestseller, and that I would be a world class idiot for passing on it?"

"It will sell a lot, way more than you or I expect. But that isn't why you should publish it."

"Oh, really. Next thing you'll tell me that little fairies came to you in the middle of the night, whispering in your ear."

Liza fumed. "Almost, but not quite. The author said so. And then I didn't have a choice. He made me promise."

"This Hemingway-wannabe of yours made you promise? Was it an unbreakable pinky promise that if you break it all the kids in the playground will call you names?" Karen pointed a finger at Liza, the nail sharp and shiny and bright red from silk-wraps and manicures. "You may have been gone for a while, living in some hi-tech hillbilly's dream cabin but let me tell you something, girlfriend. Birds still fly, bears still chase salmon upriver, fat girls dream of Twinkies, and I publish best sellers. Those are the unchanging laws of nature. I make sure starving artists don't quite starve all the way. I make sure agents get their unfair cut. But I especially make sure my profits stay on the high side of obscene. If I want to give charity, I'll buy a token and go down into the subway to throw quarters at the homeless."

"They haven't used tokens for years."

"Let's just say the charitable urge hasn't hit for quite some time." She snatched the cigarette off her desk, pressing it into the corner of her mouth with one swift movement. She held the lighter close to the cigarette tip, pausing before lighting. The tip of the cigarette danced wildly as she spoke, the lighter's flame reflected in cold eyes that focused on Liza like twin lasers of fury, but her words were measured and calm. "I can't remember the last time I was this pissed off, and I can't figure out why. You wasted my time but that isn't it. You come strutting in here, waving out of date credentials, expecting favors for free. Maybe you want one last fling before the gates of domesticity slam shut, something to tell your fat hick friends about while you fold laundry. You'll tell them how you once were a top literary agent and could still pull it off if you really wanted. That isn't the way the game is played. You think touchy-feely has any juice in this business? Get real!"

Karen's tirade was brutal, even for her. Liza felt like an idiot, unable to speak and at a loss to defend herself. She felt dangerously close to being demolished by a wave of hopelessness. Any self-confidence she had was gone, packed up in cardboard boxes when she closed up shop and left her office and career behind. But in the final moment she had an insight, understanding the source of Karen's rage. Liza had rejected the world of the self-sufficient, self-possessed, single, thirty-something businesswoman, declaring it second-rate, while Karen was trapped in her world of superficial glitter. Karen placed all her chips on the square labeled 'Career' and Liza's obvious contentment with housewifery and impending motherhood was an affront and personal challenge.

Liza understood all this in a flash, but she also saw that Karen only partially understood. She knew that Karen looked down on her, assuming she had given up the fight and taken the easy way out. Karen didn't understand the struggle and pain that choice entailed. Liza had been so much like Karen, successful in her career and working hard at personifying a lifestyle. Just in time, for reasons she barely understood, she made a final, desperate leap, grasping at what Karen would denigrate as a silly dream, far too provincial and naïve for someone as cosmopolitan and successful as Karen. This was the woman Liza once was, and the bond between them, regardless of the battles, was based on the implicit agreement that they both subscribed without any question to these values. Liza's sudden and unexplained longing for a child had provided the perspective on her previous life that she needed in order to realize how empty it had actually been. Miraculously, the proverbial gold ring that was beyond her grasp for five years had fallen into her hands after she was sure it had passed her by. Karen was jealous, bitterly jealous. And Karen was angry because she was locked in an impeccably decorated prison of her own making. This wasn't business. This was deeply personal. Liza wanted to smack Karen in the face and shout that the smoke was bad for the baby. But she sat with her mouth hanging open, fighting to hold back tears that were already flowing down her cheeks, her hands twisting the damp tissue.

The heavy oak door swung open, smacking into the doorstop with a sudden, startling noise. A heavy toolbox flew into the room, landing with a loud thump on the Persian rug. The end of a ladder appeared, hovering in the air like the opening for a magic act. An older man in jeans and a gray work shirt finally appeared at the other end of the ladder. He was grinning, his round face surrounded by a salt and pepper beard. He was unusually quick and agile for a roly-poly old man, his grey-white hair waving around the sides of his head like a halo.

"Sorry to bother you ladies. The management sent me up to install a smoke alarm. The building codes keep changing all the time and it gets kind of crazy, trying to keep up." He looked up and pointed at Karen's cigarette. "It looks like I got here just in time."

Karen yelped, dropping her lighter as it burned her thumb. She cursed silently as the man set up his ladder, climbing up with a surprisingly youthful energy. He worked quickly and the installation took less than two minutes, the women watching in silence. As he was twisting in the final screw, he asked, "What do you do here?"

For a second Liza thought he was speaking to her and was tempted to answer, "I came here to be abused." But Karen answered, her voice almost shaking with anger. "Publishing!"

He stepped down from the ladder and began to put his tools away, moving slowly and with great care. "That would be books, right?"

"Yes." Karen answered, drawing out the 's'. Liza, expecting her to throw in 'you idiot', was impressed by her restraint.

"That's a glorious profession. Books can be magical things." The man straightened up, rubbing his lower back. "These old bones have a lot to say, these days. Mostly they just complain about the weather." He looked at Liza. "Why, isn't that nice? So many people running around single these days, it's nice to see someone building a family."

Liza felt her face grow hot. "I'm not really showing yet. I'm only eight weeks. We only found out last week."

He smiled and Liza who was thinking; 'People with bad teeth shouldn't smile so much.' Though a voice echoed in her head, 'Unless they are really good at being happy.'

"In my day, people were proud of their kids. Pregnancy wasn't something to be ashamed of. So we weren't afraid to ask and women weren't afraid to tell. The only kind of child that was unwanted was the kind that sassed his parents. A couple of swats on the tush and he got back to being a wanted child right quick."

Liza smoothed out her dress. "Is my belly that big?"

The man chuckled. "No. And don't go fretting about being fat. I seen the way pregnant women go running off in skintight leotards to do aerobobics. That's just silly. You ain't fat. And a husband that complains about his wife's belly don't deserve to be a daddy. But I don't figure you'd marry that kind of fellow. He looks at your round belly and thinks about the beautiful baby you're bringing into the world. As pretty as the moon at night."

"So how did you know?"

"It's showing on your face. First thing the hormones do is start changing your face, padding it up."

Liza blushed. "Making me look fat."

"Making you look soft, like the kind of mother a baby can trust."

Karen snorted. "What a crock of nonsense."

The man eyed her for a moment. "I look at magazines and see angry women starved most to death. They don't look pretty to me. They look like they'd be ornery and mean, having to go through so much starvation and wearing those uncomfortable shoes and clothes, just to attract some man that don't care about how they feel or if they had a good supper. I like it when my wife looks healthy. It means I'm taking care of her. If she gets too skinny, it means I don't love her enough to feed her. Is that the kind of women you put in your magazine?"

"I publish books, not magazines. And I don't need a man to feed me."

"No woman truly does. But it's just one of the things you do to show someone that you love them and to make it real." Liza could hear Karen's teeth grinding. "And books today don't impress me much. Most of them are like magazines without the pictures. It used to be buying a book was something special. It was like making a new friend. Nowadays, they expect you to buy books just to look pretty on the shelf or to impress other people. That's not why I make friends and that's not why I would spend a bunch of hours reading a book. A good book makes you want to come back and read it again, just like you don't mind sitting down and hearing your old friend telling the same stories again. Problem is, if I keep reading the books I bought last year, your company won't be able to sell me more books this year. So instead, you make sure to sell something that ain't worth reading twice." It was the first time Liza ever saw Karen speechless and without a razor sharp response. The man didn't seem to notice the amazing effect he had produced. He turned to Liza. "Boy or girl?"

Liza blushed. "We don't know yet. We'll be happy either way."

Karen was so livid her face turned red. "Listen, whoever the hell you are, I want you out of here before I call security."

The man shook his head. "Sure you care. I bet your husband cares. He probably wants a son to name after his father. Every man wants that. Don't get me wrong. I love my girls and that's for real. Let me show you something." He reached into his collar and pulled out a silver locket dangling at the end of a silver chain. "My daddy gave me this. He was keeping it for me. It belonged to his dad, who I'm named after. He died before I was born. His granddaddy gave it to him since he was named for him. We were all named Aaron. I imagine it goes back a ways further. But I don't know about that. See this necklace? It's got the letter 'A' on it. One side it goes in and the other side it's pushed out."

"This belonged to your grandfather's grandfather?" In spite of herself, Karen leaned over the desk to get a closer look.

"Yup. Maybe further back than that. And we were all named Aaron. But the special thing is the metal it's made from. The chain is regular silver. I bought that on Fiftieth Street for twenty bucks but the original piece is different. The silver was made different

147

back then. It's more sensitive. If you breathe on it hard, it'll fog up. But if you got a girl baby inside of you, it fogs up on both sides. Girls are hotter blooded than men."

Karen practically shouted, "That's ridiculous. Get yourself and your stuff out of here and I mean now!" The man looked at Karen for a moment before calmly shaking his head. "I've been in my share of bar room brawls. A man generally needs a lot of pushing before he takes a swipe at you. Unless someone was pushing him hard before he came your way. And he don't lash out until he feels his back up against the wall and nowhere to go. I have a few scars to show that I know what I am talking about. But a woman . . ." He shook his head. "Those scars run deeper. And a woman will take you out of the world in a heartbeat if she thinks it's something that's gotta be done. Yup, women are hotter. Here, let me show you." He held the chain in front of Liza, letting the amulet spin slowly at her eye level. "Breathe on it, like you were warming up your hands after throwing snowballs."

Karen's sharp voice cut in. "Stop this nonsense. Let's get rid of this old lunatic and finish our business."

Liza watched the silver necklace spin. The silver was a strange shade she had never seen before. She imagined it passing through the generations of this family, bequeathed from father to son. She wondered if the deep silver color was a patina resulting from decades of absorbed sweat. She wanted to ask if there was another Aaron waiting his turn. She thought she felt a tiny movement in her belly. Closing her eyes, she concentrated and was rewarded with another, this one strong and undeniable. She knew that it was too early to feel the baby but she had never felt anything like this before. With her eyes closed, she breathed out hard. When she opened her eyes, the amulet swung just below her eyes, unmistakable drops of moisture clinging to one side. "In five generations, it ain't never been wrong.

Not once. That would be a little baby boy in there. You be sure and tell your husband. I think he'll be pleased."

The man picked up his tool-chest and ladder and stepped out of the room. Karen glared at the newly installed smoke detector for several angry seconds. She picked up the cigarettes and lighter. "What a crock of horse manure. That guy is totally insane."

Liza shrugged lightly, wanting to laugh. "Maybe. But I'm beginning to like the idea of a baby boy."

"And what if it's a girl?"

"I'll say he was just a crazy old man. But if it's a boy, you'll still be calling him a crazy old man. You'll say he had a fifty-fifty chance of being right and totally deny what you saw with your own eyes. The amulet has never been wrong. Not once."

"Believe whatever you want. He was crazy and you're hormonal." She put the cigarettes and lighter away. "It's been nice seeing you, almost like old times. I'd love to chit chat some more but I've got a full morning."

Liza sat back down in her chair, shaking her head. She was in charge, riding a wave, and it felt good. "I'm not leaving without a signed contract."

Karen leaned back in her chair. "The way things are going, it will be written and signed in crayons, and we'll make a toast over milk and cookies."

Liza shook her head. She knew this tiger and exactly how to tweak its tail to get it to jump through hoops. Her fear was gone. She was still the same old Liza, strong and experienced, but now she was even stronger. She had David's unseen presence holding her hand and the baby cheering her on. "I can't leave. He said it would get published."

"Who? The author? What do authors know about the book business? Authors are a necessary evil, only semi-relevant to publishing. Go back and tell him you gave it your best shot. Tell him that I was an unreasonable witch. That will spare his precious artist's ego."

Liza leaned forward, her eyes shooting out Flash Gordon death rays. The old business beast was waking up. "You don't understand. He said that if I got pregnant, the book would get published. It's not a promise. It's cause and effect. It's a done deal."

Karen tried to ignore the beads of sweat that appeared on her forehead. Liza's persistence was having an effect on her. "Let's bring this discussion back to earth. What is the genre? The target audience?"

"It's a totally new genre. It's never been done before."

Karen waved her hand, as if to dispel a bad odor. "In other words there is no audience."

Liza pointed her finger at Karen. "Which means the people who want to read this book are hungry for it. They need it and you have never even come close to giving it to them."

"Okay. This conversation is coming close to familiar ground. What's your pitch?"

Liza shook her head. "No pitch." She pulled a sheaf of papers from her bag and dropped it on the desk. "Here is the book. Read it."

"That's not the way things are done, girlfriend, and you know it. You could have Hamlet part two in your hands and all it means to me is that you have a room full of monkeys pecking away at word processors, waiting for me to cough up some bananas. In this business, I can't afford to read anything that doesn't tell me how much money I'm going to make. Great authors are a dime a dozen and they are all starving. I don't print good books. I publish books that sell. So I won't read it because I don't care."

Liza held up her hand, cutting Karen's tirade short. She looked into Karen's eyes and remembered another Karen with ideals and values. "Read it. And then do whatever you want. I could have taken it to any publisher in town. It wouldn't have been as much fun sparring with them and there would have been less blood on the floor, but I know a different you, someone with talent and integrity. Don't tell me you don't care because that is only part of the truth. I remember a young acquisitions editor who refused to print junk. You loved curling up on a ratty old sofa with a pot of tea and a good book, discovering a gem in the wasteland of superficial, grammatically challenged pop-fiction, schlock, and pseudo-intellectual, academic writing. I want to give that back to you just one more time, a gift with no strings attached. I am giving this to the Karen I knew and respected. More than anyone in the field she has the intuition and courage, above and beyond financial considerations, to push the kind of book that will make a difference in this world." Liza had more to say but she knew well enough to realize that her words had already struck the right chord. She patted the manuscript once and walked out of the office.

Karen stared at the closed door for a minute. She walked to the bookshelf, cursing silently. Despite their acrimonious interchange, the meeting reminded her how much she missed her sparring partner. Two young interns, the lowest on the totem pole, they had arrived together and it was their friendship and shared experiences in those early years that had kept this business and the whole New York scene from being altogether intimidating. Kicking off her high heels, she climbed the stool, her suit jacket riding up her shirt as she reached for the top shelf. The tea set gently rattling, she carefully lowered a porcelain tray. There had been two cups and saucers back when Liza gave her the present after their first successful deal. One of the tiny cups had broken and sets like this were out of fashion and almost impossible to replace. She vaguely remembered trying to glue the broken pieces together before putting them into a plastic bag in the drawer of her old desk.

The receptionist was shocked to see her fire-breathing boss walk past in her stocking feet to make her own tea. It would make good office gossip to add to the usual scuttlebutt about Karen who was universally feared and disliked. Loneliness was the price Karen paid for respect. She poured a cup of sweet tea and hesitated before the stack of pages in front of her. Sighing and feeling slightly foolish, she picked up the manuscript and crossed the room. Seating herself in the loveseat, she assumed a pose that was so out of character that anyone in the office would have sworn that this could not have been Karen sitting there, tea cup in hand, feet tucked under her, and looking thoroughly relaxed.

DAVID

L iza was out on the street, not only relieved the confrontation was over but confident that she had pierced Karen's armor and achieved her goal. In search of a bench in the park, she walked away from the building that had once been her second home.

Liza couldn't remember when she had begun to think about settling down. It was a gradual process starting with the realization that she had reached her professional goals. She wanted someone to hug her when she walked through the door, who was eager to hear about her day, and who would wrap her in his arms at night. None of the men she was meeting even knew what a relationship meant. They thought the sum total of a relationship consisted of sharing a financial adviser and splitting the maintenance cost on a co-op.

She would never have considered dating someone like David. Since first arriving in the city, she was attracted to driven men, movers and shakers with egos to match. Fiery passion attracted her like a campfire attracts moths, but this bred relationships that were doomed from the outset. Gradually, the great and gifted began to lose their attraction for her. It began to look too much like a game played by clever children, with shiny toys for prizes. During this time, as she became less and less enamored of the glamorous life, Karen was evolving into the epitome of a New York publishing icon in love with expensive acquisitions and easy entry into the social life of the rich and famous.

Ironically, Liza met David because of Karen. David was at least as intelligent as the artists and empire builders she had dated before, but his brilliance was more gentle and introspective. He was a genius in cinema, the mind that beautiful faces listened to. The co-author of a book about the history of animation, he walked into Karen's office just as Liza was leaving. Karen made hurried introductions, and Liza never gave him a second thought until he called her that evening. He hadn't made much of an impression and it took a few embarrassing seconds to remember having met him. She only consented to another meeting when he used the guise of seeking her editorial advice.

David was a total nerd, but when it came to digital animation, he was a genius. Underneath the suburban geek lay a twenty-first century techno-cowboy. Despite working with the biggest names in Hollywood, he was still a down-to-earth guy. Their first date was ice cream in the park and he insisted she have a double scoop with chocolate sprinkles. Liza was a bit shocked, unsure of how to react. She was used to nouvelle cuisine with expensive wine and portions too small to satisfy anything larger than a medium-sized hamster. She wasn't sure what to think of him. She had to admit that it was very endearing when he confessed that her editorial advice was a guise for getting her to meet him. When she listed the pros, he was prime matrimonial material; he was rich, intelligent, a creative and innovative thinker in an exciting field connected with the arts, and she couldn't deny the chemistry between them. But after dating sharks for so long who could only prove their masculinity by getting her into bed, David seemed too nice. She agreed to a second date, promising herself she would turn down any request for a third. He showed up with flowers for the second date, explaining they were going to see a movie. She ducked back into her bedroom to change out of her dress and pull on an old pair of jeans.

The movie turned out to be a closed post-production viewing of David's latest project at the director's downtown loft. Liza was caught speechless, somewhere between embarrassed at her drab attire and star struck, when the leading heartthrob of the film begged David for a mini-lecture on the latest developments in 3-D imaging. David seemed not to notice the small crowd of big names surrounding him while he spoke. Okay, so he wasn't quite the nerd she thought he was, but she still wasn't interested. Now she found herself looking for excuses to turn him away. He was proving to be more aggravation than she could handle. Her tried and true methods of dissuasion were being dutifully ignored. Even scarier was the dawning realization that her efforts to push him away might only be half-hearted. He simply did not fit into her vision of what her future should be. During the cab ride back to her apartment, Liza argued with herself, trying to find the nicest way to say 'no' to a goodnight kiss. At the door to her apartment she turned, one hand raised to push him away. She was shocked into silence when he shook her outstretched hand, saying, "Thank you for a great evening. I am sorry we didn't have time to talk, just the two of us."

"I'm a little angry at you. You didn't tell me who was going to be there. I dressed like I was going to the college pub."

"Most of the people there were dressed casual. They only dress up if they expect paparazzi. And it didn't matter. You were the prettiest girl there."

Liza bristled. "Don't call me a 'girl'. And I am not sure how I feel about you thinking I am pretty."

He looked directly into her eyes and Liza became aware that he was still holding her hand. She realized she had underestimated him. Underneath the fuzzy, nerdy appearance was a man, successful and so sure of himself that he didn't need to act a part that he already owned. "I will call you 'girl' because I want you to be my girl. And I think I actually know how you really feel about that. And, if you don't know yet, it will be my very pleasant job to remind you in the sweetest ways possible." Without another word, he turned and left. Liza was mystified, and even a bit disappointed that he had deprived her of the satisfaction of fighting him off.

The next night he called and asked her out to dinner. Liza already decided that she would never see this man again, yet after hanging up the phone, she realized she had said 'yes'. If she had paused to look in the mirror she would have been more surprised at the big smile across her face. A week and two dates later, he took her for a day trip. They drove north into farmland and stopped at a deserted campground overlooking the valley. The leaves were changing color in the brisk autumn air and it was such a picture postcard day that Liza wondered if the entire year was a dress rehearsal for this one afternoon. A little voice inside her head asked her if the day wouldn't be even better if there were a dream-man to spend it with. She was about to concede when another voice surprised her, answering that David might be a very good facsimile. Certainly he was far better than any man she had gone out with before in the gentle-and-caring department.

He took out a bottle and pulled the cork, announcing, "Organic champagne." As she took her first sip, he placed a small box between them.

She froze, dreading what she knew was in the box. "If that is what I think it is, then the answer is 'no.'"

He nodded, seeming to agree, but Liza felt her resolve melting. "I want you to think about it."

Her eyes darted away from his. "That's what I've been doing since we met, thinking about how to say 'no' to you when you asked." She looked up to meet his gaze.

He reached out and took her hand. "Of course you've been thinking about it. That's because ever since we met, I've wanted to ask. Now, I'd like you to think about whether saying 'no' is what you really want. Also, think about saying 'yes' for a while. I won't bother you or try to persuade you. I trust you. I have to. If you say yes, then you will be my soul mate, constant companion, and the mother of our children. I trust you to tell me if I am doing the right thing here. Think about it. In one week, give me your answer."

"This is ridiculous! We've never even kissed." Blushing bright red she added, "That wasn't an invitation."

"I know. When you think about it, keep in mind one thing. I offered you this ring but it is worthless unless you accept it. The same for all of my love. I want to learn how to love you. You need to accept that love. Until you do, I don't know how to love you." They drove home in silence, Liza weighed down with questions she didn't know how to ask. She was sure she would say "no," sure he was out of his mind. She was used to suave and sophisticated. David was overwhelming her with sincerity. Instead of Don Juan, this guy was a cross between Gary Cooper and the Lone Ranger. She spent the night tossing and turning with the ring on her night table. By the end of the week, she was ready to say "no," but felt a deep, illogical, dread that David had changed his mind. At the end of the week, while she was still terribly conflicted, they met in the park. She had composed a dozen scripts, all of them ending in "no." They climbed wordlessly to the top of a hill, finding a spot to be alone. Silently, she handed him the box, hoping this would suffice for an answer. He put the small box on the grass between them and opened it, as they both stared at the facets of the diamond glittering in the sun.

"I really can't marry you. You aren't what I was looking for." This was her rehearsed answer but she wished for something that sounded more genuine and less like a pathetic cliché.

David nodded his head, his calm acceptance making her angry.

"That can't be true. You haven't found what you were looking for because you were looking for me." Lisa resented his self-assurance.

"Aren't you being presumptuous? I am looking for a nice, normal, man with a decent career and the emotional development that's more advanced than a post-adolescent orangutan."

David smiled. "I think I can easily fit that description and maybe even surpass it. I think that I'm nice, fairly normal with a decent career, and only slightly resemble an orangutan if I am supplied with a strong cup of coffee right after waking up." Though she tried her best not to, Liza had to laugh as he growled and scratched his chest. "And besides all that, I'm a favorite with mothers."

Taking a good look at him, Liza knew her very sensible mother, who had always pushed "nice and normal" would probably have approved. She would have seen the nerdiness as a plus. "Okay, now that we've settled that, do you have any other expectations?"

"You're too, too . . ." David, with a small wave of his hand, did what so many screaming editors had failed to do. Liza stopped talking and listened, changing her mind along the way. "I am sure that a brilliant and beautiful woman like you has been wooed and pursued by many brilliant and successful men. Many of them were probably very handsome; some of them probably struck you as prime matrimonial candidates. And yet you never got married. That is because, very simply, your soul didn't recognize any of them as your husband. I may not be the best, brightest, wealthiest, or handsomest man you have met. That's what you've been looking for, and you haven't found it. Or when you do, it's only good until a better one comes along. And he's only happy as long as you are the best. But I am the one who will become your husband when you become my wife. We aren't signing a contract that will become null and void if one of the partners fails to hold up his end of the bargain or if a better proposition comes along. This is different. I am the only one like me and I need you, because you are the only one there is. I am asking you to be my wife because it is the only way to become your husband, and no one else can do that for me except you. And your husband is the person I want to be for the rest of my life. Like I said, your husband doesn't exist . . . yet. I am not that man yet, and that is why you aren't sure of your answer. But I want to become that man if you'll let me. And how do I know this? I like to think of it as a gift, this intuition I have about the really important things in my life. I feel compelled to follow through, and so far this intuition has never failed me. When I first saw you, it was clear you were my soul mate. Now, how in the world could I possibly disregard this totally compelling insight?"

Liza was still thinking about what he just said when he gently took her hand and started to slip the ring onto her finger. She wanted to stop him, discuss what he had said, but in the very core of her being, the matter was already settled. She realized that she agreed with him and though she had never verbalized this to herself, all this time she had been waiting for the man who knew this special thing about marriage. She had been living in a world of cutthroat bargaining and bitterly won contracts. It was a game and she was good at it, but all along, she knew that marriage was something different. It wasn't about having, getting, achieving, or owning. It was about being, and being meant being together. The birds seemed loud enough to drown out all thought. She looked up at David and was startled, somehow he looked very different. It might have been his smile, large and full, and so warm. It was different than any smile she had seen on his face before. Then she realized why he was smiling. She looked down, tilting her hand to let the diamond sparkle in the sun.

Liza approached her wedding with determination to prepare for every detail, the decisions and planning bringing her closer and closer to the reality. Her occasional bouts of panic were met with David's simple smile, a surprisingly effective solution. The weekly sessions with her therapist became strangely silent. She realized, in the middle of one session, that all she ever needed was someone to listen to her and that David's smile was far more soothing than her therapists omniscient pronouncements. She who had always been in charge resigned herself to being carried along by the relationship that became deeper and more fulfilling each day. Liza who was never much of a believer felt that she had been blessed. It might not have been enough to make her believe in God, though maybe a guardian angel. Her only regret was that her parents, and especially her mother who had always been her staunch advocate, wouldn't be there to see her marry a man who would surely have endeared himself to them.

The event itself, held in a large white tent on a country club's manicured lawn, proceeded without a single problem, and the weather was superb, warm and sunny for mid-October. The wedding was memorable in every way, even providing a spectacular setting for business networking. Her literary associates wooed David's movie friends and vice-versa. All this frantic glamour was fueled by caviar and organic champagne. The guests, Karen among them, were busy entering phone numbers and e-mail addresses into their iPhones and BlackBerrys. At one point Liza caught Karen looking at her with a somewhat wistful expression when she wasn't in a huddle with the guests. Liza and David were so oblivious to everything but each other that they couldn't remember whether they had eaten anything besides a slice of wedding cake. Later they would laugh about how many contracts were consummated on their wedding day.

Liza was not surprised that David was pretty conventional in his ideas about married life, but what did surprise her was how much she liked it. He preferred home-cooked meals and though Liza had never made anything from scratch except an occasional salad, she found she enjoyed cooking. At first she was frustrated by the idea of only buying organic ingredients to satisfy what she felt was an unreasonable obsession, but when David had her do a blind taste test between regular and organic carrots, she became a convert, and a regular at the local farmer's market. She appreciated having her mother's cookbook and read the inscription for the first time: "The way to a man's heart is through his stomach so consider the enclosed your road map. Much love, Mom."

They discussed the issue of children from every possible angle and decided that they wanted to get pregnant as soon as possible. Realizing that her working days would be over, Liza had taken a sabbatical soon after the wedding, expecting to become pregnant in short order. When nature didn't comply, she was left in the unfamiliar situation of having time on her hands and a growing fixation with the calendar. Although David was more positive about wanting to be a parent, Liza felt disappointed that she could not give him his heart's desire. For someone who always achieved what she wanted, either through talent, hard work, or a combination of both, for the first time, victory seemed beyond her grasp. Month after month she felt the same sense of failure and impotence.

They bought a ridiculously large house upstate, and checked out the local school system and available activities for children. But Liza did not become pregnant, and after many tense trips to several specialists, it began to look like she never would. The doctors didn't pull any punches. In his callous attempt at humor, one specialist said that Liza's getting pregnant would be tantamount to shooting an arrow into a tornado in Kansas and having it knock an apple off the wicked witch's forehead in downtown Oz. And you only get one shot a month. She had a bad case of twisted tubes, LA freeway instead of German Autobahn.

The house kept getting bigger and emptier. To fill up the too-quiet Sundays and the spare bedrooms, they made the rounds of all the garage sales and flea markets within a radius of fifty miles. That part of the state hadn't been entirely gentrified and many of the farms were still working. The scores of barns and attics that hadn't been opened for years were a paradise for collectors and auctioneers. Covered with spider webs, generations of junk sat gathering dust until one day, mom and pop decided to do some spring-cleaning. Liza applied the same zeal to ferreting out precious antiques as she had to finding the one gem in the pile of manuscripts late at night in her previous profession. Soon she had an array of what looked like junk at first glance but were actually valuable collectibles. She became an expert on old glass bottles, paperweights, hurricane lamps and various other esoteric antiques found in the dusty bins of abandoned attics. She especially enjoyed the country auctions where she could exercise her competitive spirit. She couldn't resist bidding on an old, hand-carved cradle that played 'Lullaby and Goodnight', and cried as she lugged it home wondering if it would ever be more than a decoration.

Her acquisitions lined the sunroom with bottles, the playroom with hand carved duck decoys, and the kitchen with outdated non-electric appliances. David had a genuine imitation elephant foot umbrella stand full of bamboo fly-fishing rods waiting for him to get over his aversion to fishing. The barn was full of real farm equipment that hadn't been used for several generations. They certainly weren't going to use any of it but when they bought the house, they thought the barn would make a perfect gameroom. It hurt too much to see it rotting away, empty. So they turned it into an ad hoc farm museum.

Liza became tense and took up smoking again, sneaking out after David fell asleep. Boredom chafed at her and she frequently snapped at David when his smiling face emerged from his office. His patience angered her all the more because she felt she had let him down. Their marriage was suffering, challenging David's patience and her determination. Thoughts of a flea market could cheer Liza up, imagining the open field with hay bales at one end and tables piled with an assortment of curious items, the hick analogue of a posh Fifth Avenue shop. But one flea market Sunday, she was caught in a funk. Even this new pastime of amateur antique hunting was starting to feel old and tired. Liza couldn't think of a substitute to fill her days and the emptiness scared her. She was such a skilled vegetarian cook, she could compete on the Food Network, and she'd already been the recipient of an award for her volunteer activities in the neighborhood.

She was half-heartedly picking through a rack of dresses, considering if they were old enough to be coming back in style, when she saw David arguing with an old farmer a few stalls away. She went over to see what was making him so uncharacteristically angry. The man specialized in old books. David had begun to fill the empty spaces in the study with an odd assortment of leather bound tomes, taking joy in finding the most esoteric subjects and oddest titles. Liza glanced at the old man's selection. Most of his books could easily be dismissed as garbage, but David had found an old, leather bound book, its cover in tatters, the title no longer legible. The book was so large and heavy, it took David's two strong hands to lift it. The pages were heavily water-damaged, and those that weren't stuck together were stained with brown streaks. The page that would have shown the date of publication was missing. It seemed like an obvious discard because even if it were an antique the missing publication date made it worthless.

In any case, it was a strange book, a reference listing names and their meanings. There were even lists of famous people, long dead and mostly forgotten. It was from an age when Mervin, Hubert, and Eustace could be found out back playing stickball. Liza, struggling to separate the pages without them tearing, overheard David haggling with the vendor. David wasn't interested in the book but in the perfectly preserved map that folded out from the middle pages. He was working on a pirate comedy and he wanted the map for some of the visuals in the treasure-hunting scene. Actually, on close inspection the map was truly spectacular; the page was thick and cream-colored with the slight imperfections of handmade paper. It had the unmistakable look of authenticity that would easily catch the attention of an expert. Liza could see why David wanted it. The problem was, the man was asking twenty dollars and wouldn't sell him the map without the book.

The afternoon dragged on, dry and hot, and Liza was getting annoyed. "Why not just give him the money and throw the book into the first garbage pail on your way out?"

"I can't. Look at this book. It's been around for a hundred years. You can't just throw something like that away. And if I take it, what am I going to do with it? It's enormous, and I don't want it taking up half a shelf."

Liza was exasperated. It was one of the wonderfully frustrating traits of her husband that made him so special, so gifted, and such a bother to live with. David was an ecology freak. Everything got recycled or composted or mailed to some third world country. Liza understood the problem. The idea of buying something just to throw it away offended David's principles. A long time ago this book might have been someone's life's work. He couldn't throw it away, no matter how much he wanted the map. When Liza showed up, David had just offered the man a hundred bucks, and the crazy old geezer just stood there shaking his head 'no'.

Liza sighed. Their domestic tranquility in recent weeks was as fragile as eggshells. She looked at the map, knowing how much it would mean to her husband. "I'll take the book", she announced.

"Are you sure now, ma'am?" She nodded, chafed by being 'ma'am'ed. "And you ain't gonna toss it first chance you get?"

"No!" She snapped.

"You better hold onto it. You gonna need it one day."

Liza grabbed the book from the old man. "I said I would take it. Maybe one night I'll decide to name all my houseplants."

The old man nodded, "That would suit me just fine." His serious demeanor made Liza wonder if he realized she was joking.

David looked at her with a curious expression. He handed the old man a hundred dollars and was shocked when the old coot handed him back eighty in change. "A deal is a deal, and don't you

165

forget it." David began to protest but the old man ignored him, bending over to pack up his books. It took him less than a minute and David was left standing, the money still in his hand, while the old man walked away, pulling a hand wagon full of his worthless, but curious junk.

THE MAP

David couldn't take his eyes off the map. Liza drove and he sat in the back, the parchment spread out over the back seat.

Liza was feeling a bit annoyed and nervous. She thought David was acting more eccentric than usual, maybe working too much on his new film. In any case, the idea of returning to that big empty house, decorated with so much meaningless junk depressed her to tears.

"What is it, a real treasure map? South Seas, Captain Hook?"

"It seems to be a map of the local countryside. I recognize some of the road names but a lot of the major ones are missing. The thruway isn't on the map, but that makes sense if this map is really as old as it looks. There are some strange places named here. 'Poppa's Hideaway', 'First Kiss', and 'Baby Pond'. Right next to Baby Pond is a big 'X'. I guess no one explained to them that you don't get babies by fishing them out of a pond."

Liza laughed nervously. "It's probably just a really small pond."

David went back to studying the map, leaving Liza to fret silently. She composed a dialog in her mind as she drove, working herself up to let off steam by having their first marital screaming match. Despite the fact that she was still very much in love with her husband, her inability to conceive hurt too much. David yelling, "Stop the car", interrupted her internal argument. He jumped out of the back seat trading places with her, spreading out the map on the dashboard and fiddling with the GPS.

Liza decided to begin the argument immediately, rather than wait until they got home. "What are you doing?"

Oblivious to her confrontational tone, David grinned like a little boy. "We are going on a treasure hunt."

Fed up, Liza shook her head. "That map is old. Hundreds of people have probably seen it. It was probably a prank, drawn up by some Puritan delinquent. If there ever was a treasure, it is long gone."

David refused to concede. "Someone put a lot of time and energy into drawing this up. It's real. I have this nagging, powerful intuition that we will be the first. And you know better, honey, than to argue with my intuition. Besides, we have something no other treasure seeker had."

"A certificate of insanity?"

He laughed. "Modern technology." He patted the GPS and put the car in gear. Liza had never liked the gadget David played with prior to every excursion and was convinced it was just a new way for geeks to have fun getting lost. "I think I recognize some of the landmarks on the map. If I programmed the destination right, this should lead us right to the treasure." He hummed as he drove, the map folded up on the empty passenger seat. Five minutes later, the GPS beeped and a red arrow blinked on the screen. David turned left, heading into the woods.

Liza began to worry. "Where are you going?"

David had a strangely wild look in his eye and a tight, nervous smile pulling at his face, a look she had never seen before. "I'm following the map."

"There's no road here."

David struggled with the gears, grinding them while trying to rock the car through the drainage trench at the edge of the asphalt. "There is a trail."

Liza restrained herself from yelling. "I can barely see it. It's probably a trail left by half-dead deer, limping into the woods to die. It certainly isn't made for cars."

David grunted as the car began to labor up the hill. "We have a jeep."

"We have a luxury sedan that can drive through puddles in the mall's parking lot. Mud cancels out the warranty." David ignored her, clutching the wheel tighter as the grade got steeper. Liza grabbed for the shoulder strap as the car bounced from side to side. "It's getting dark. Let's come back tomorrow." He ignored her as sweat coated his brow. "David, this isn't funny. Turn the car around."

Suddenly they crested the hill and were heading down. She could feel the wheels sliding, David struggling to control their descent. She couldn't tell if he was trying to turn the car around or just trying to keep the car from flipping. Fear was rising in Liza's voice. "David, this is insane. Let's come back tomorrow."

David was straining to watch the trail in front of them, a desperate look in his eyes. "Tomorrow will be too late." Liza had no idea what he meant but was too afraid to question him. Her rock-steady, responsible husband was now possessed, making no sense, and endangering their lives for a pointless treasure hunt. Just then, the forest became dark, the last remnants of sunset hidden behind the slope at their backs. The car seemed to be on autopilot; David couldn't turn it around even if he wanted to.

The GPS suddenly flipped out, blinking and popping up city names and symbols that made no sense. She wanted to scream but afraid to make things worse, she resorted to humor. "Maybe the GPS comes with a first aid kit."

David was insistent. "No way! These things work on satellite. NASA uses them. You could drive a submarine to the moon with one of these."

Liza punched the back of his seat. David grunted but ignored the pain. She couldn't hold it back any longer and began to scream. "I don't want to go to the moon. I want to go home, now!"

The nose of the jeep dipped and suddenly they were headed straight down, the wheels sliding out of control. They hit a bump, the springs compressing and then releasing as the car leaped into the air. The headlights lit up tree trunks rushing at them. They flew past several but were thrown sideways when a large tree hit them a glancing blow. The jeep landed sideways and began to roll. Liza heard David scream her name before glass shattered, spraying the inside of the jeep with tiny shards. The jeep rolled twice more and settled, groaning, onto its tires.

The electrical system of the jeep had shorted out, leaving them in darkness. Liza sat up, waiting for pain to kick in and tell her where she was hurt. She waited in silence, listening to hot metal tick, incredulous at how well she felt. It seemed bizarre for her to be sitting in a wrecked car and not even feel a bruise where the seatbelt had held her in place. She tried to release the shoulder strap but the buckle was jammed into the seat and she couldn't find it in the dark. Worried that a blow to the head was making her confused and euphoric, she began to comb glass out of her hair. David's voice was so soft he had to call her twice before she heard him.

"Liza, are you hurt?"

"I think I got away without a scratch. How about you? Are you okay?"

His answer was almost a whisper. "Maybe."

She wrestled with fear. "What do you mean 'maybe'?"

His voice was still a whisper. "I don't think I got hurt. But I'm still afraid you are going to kill me." He groaned, making her panic.

"David, are you all right."

"Darn it! The GPS is broken."

She felt a smile come to her lips, swallowing her salty tears. Their moment of relief quickly ended with the sound of something large and heavy pushing its way through the forest, moving slowly towards them. Liza thought of all the survival tips about what to do if a bear or some other wild animal attacks you, but none of the successful scenarios began 'If you are trapped in a car wreck, and a wild animal approaches . . .' She heard David struggling with his seatbelt but his grunts made it clear they were both trapped. Whatever it was would have an easy time eating them where they were. A loud snuffle in her ear made her scream. Her window was shattered and the beast was inches from her, an enormous shape silhouetted in the darkness. It was larger than she had expected a bear to be. Suddenly, she felt something rough touch her and the side of her face was covered with slime.

David yelled. "Honey, are you okay?"

He was answered by a loud 'moo', an unmistakably bovine bellowing. Liza was confused for a brief moment, wondering why a cow, a herbivore, would try to eat her. "I'm fine, just covered in cud."

Men's voices interrupted their nervous giggles. The voices got closer and stopped, dark shapes waiting a few yards away. A voice called out, "Hello?"

David's voice was a little shaky. "We need some help. We had an accident and our car flipped over. We're okay but we can't get out." Leaves crackled and small branches snapped as heavy booted feet approached. Liza braced for more slimy slobber as a large shape appeared at her window. A massive arm reached in, a knife blade shining in the moonlight. A slight tug and she felt the seatbelt fall away. There was just enough room for her to crawl out of the car onto solid ground. The shape moved forward. David pushed the windshield out and climbed over the front of the jeep. Liza blinked in the glare of a flashlight. She kept blinking when she glanced back at what remained of their jeep. She had never seen a car so bent out of shape. It was clearly a total loss. But that was not what made her knees buckle. The jeep had spun around, its nose facing uphill, the wrecked car coming to rest next to a small stream. The rear wheels were suspended in the air, the axle hung up on a boulder at the top of a small waterfall. It was impossible to determine the height of the drop-off, but it was clear even in the dark that just another few inches would have made the tragic difference.

A young man stepped into the circle of light. "Are you sure you folks are okay?"

Liza looked at David and saw that he too understood how close they had come. His voice shook when he answered. "We seem to be okay. Thanks for getting us out."

The voice of an older man came from behind the glare of the flashlight. "I don't think we can say the same for your car. How did you folks get up here?"

"We were driving on the trail when we got lost. I guess I made a wrong turn."

The man placed the flashlight on the ground and stepped into the light. "The only people who use that trail going up the mountain are deer hunters. And they usually stop a good ways back. It looks like you just made us a new trail, coming down." He surveyed the wreck for a few moments before holding out his hand. "My name is Meyer. The big guy over there is Brad and the standard-sized fella' next to him is Jack. You got lucky. We don't usually come up here, especially after dark. You could've been stuck in your car till next winter when one of those hunters would've pulled you out, dressed you, and strapped you across his hood, like a fine pair of white-tails."

David shook his hand, more comfortable with country jargon and manners than Liza who was still trembling. "We certainly appreciate it."

The man inspected them for a few moments. "We were on our way to the water hole at the bottom of this cliff. You folks almost made it there first. I understand that you are probably in a rush to get home, but we planned on taking a dunk on the way to a wedding. It's a local custom so it's kind of important. Jack is getting hitched tonight. If you don't mind, we'll take a quick dip and then head home. It's not far. The sheriff is one of the guests and so is the tow truck operator."

David nodded. "I don't think we'll need the tow truck in such a hurry. But we may need a place to stay for the night."

Mr. Meyer smiled. "Not a problem. You can sleep in the barn. It's right pleasant on a warm night like this. It used to be Jack's room but now that he's getting married, we fixed him up with something a little nicer." He turned to Liza. "You'll have to wait here while we take our swim. We didn't bring our bathing trunks so for now, it's 'men only.'"

Liza smiled. "That's fine. I just have one question. Do you always bring a cow with you when you go swimming?"

Mr. Meyer laughed. "Not usually. But she's grown quite attached to Jack. She insisted on coming with. I'll have her wait here with you." Mr. Meyer turned to David. "How about coming with us? After what you've been through, a dip will do you good." David would have refused, but there was something compelling in the man's voice.

"Will you be okay here by yourself, honey?"

Lisa pointed at the cow. "I'm not alone. It's just us girls." They left the flashlight with her and descended, picking out the trail by moonlight.

The swimming hole was bigger than David expected. As far as he could tell in the dark, it was a medium sized lake surrounded by rock walls. The other men quickly shucked off their clothes and David followed suit. He stepped into the water but immediately jumped back. Despite the warm summer evening, the water was ice cold. The other men laughed. Mr. Meyer explained. "That little creek you nearly fell into isn't enough to fill up this pond. Most of the water comes up from the bottom. There's a spring that comes out of the cracks in the bedrock. A couple of thousand years ago, there was ice covering this whole part of the country. It got warm enough to melt the ice, but deep in the ground, it never got much warmer than that. This is just a puddle of water the glacier left behind. It'll make a man out of you, that's for sure. There are a lot of local stories about this pond to prove it."

David grimaced. He hated cold water more than anything. "I think it will make a soprano out of me."

Brad laughed. "Where I come from, a man goes out on the ice and chops a hole for his pre-wedding bath. It shows that you are a strong buck and have an unquenchable desire for your woman."

Jack slapped Brad's back. "I think it explains more about why Eskimos have a different concept of how personal hygiene relates to survival."

David shrugged. "I think I'll take a pass on the Eskimo bath. I've already had an exciting enough day." He sat on a rock and pulled on his socks.

Jack put a foot into the water and shivered, as the other men laughed. Brad gave him a tiny shove. "I won't be satisfied until I see the tiny twin moons shining back at me."

Jack laughed. "This is for my amazing very-soon-to-be wife, Hanna." He gave a whoop and splashed into the water, doing a handstand, proudly displaying his bottom to the warm and dry spectators. He flipped over and stumbled out of the water, shivering uncontrollably. "Hanna better appreciate this," he sputtered through his chattering teeth.

Brad threw him a towel. "There is a belief that ice cold baths improve your chances of having children. I've seen it work. But it has to be a special place and especially cold. And we all know how important a baby is to your beautiful bride."

Jack threw back his head and laughed. "Now it's your turn, Brad." He ran forward, slamming up against an immovable wall of flesh. Mr. Meyer joined in, laughing, the two of them trying to push the giant into the cold water. They frolicked like little boys until, suddenly, the two men collided and slipping on the rocks, they fell over each other into the water.

As Brad emerged from the water, David stood in front of him, grasping his arms, and panting. "What . . . did . . . you . . . say?"

"I said that jumping into ice cold water could help a man have a baby. But it's got to be a special place, and he's got to want it a lot. It's throwing the challenge in the face of God."

David's grip tightened and he looked up into Brad's face. "Don't you dare joke with me. You don't know me. No man has ever wanted anything as much as I want a son. I can't think of anything else. I've got a lot, but nothing I've got is worth anything without a baby. I'm going to lose my wife if she doesn't get pregnant, and that may just kill me."

Mr. Meyer stepped forward, putting a hand on David's shoulder. "Take it easy young man. You've been through a lot, maybe you should just sit down and relax until your head stops spinning."

Brad's quiet voice cut through the darkness. "Brother, this is what it takes. I see you. Your destiny is to have it all: money, love, success. But no son. If you want to change that, you have to kill that destiny. You have to kill the man that had that destiny written on his tombstone from the day he was born. You have to put him in a hole in the ground and make him stop breathing. You have to kill everything about him. When you do that, you'll come out wet and screaming, like a baby being born. Are you ready for that, brother?"

David slowly shook his head. "None of this makes any sense."

"If you don't do this, you can tell yourself that Brad wasn't anything but an ignorant savage and didn't know nearly as much as those smart doctors who took away all the hope and power you had. But if you don't do it, you'll never know. I promise you, it won't be easy and it won't be nice. You can believe me or not. You can do it or not. But I'm giving it to you now, and only now. That's all you'll get and it's your only chance."

The two men stood facing each other until a deep, wrenching, groan broke the silence. It came from David's throat but it sounded like someone else entirely. David turned and faced the lake, walking stiff-kneed into the icy, black water. Every muscle in his body was pulled tight and his breathing was a series of painful grunts. He walked out until the water was up to his chest. He began to pant like an animal running for its life, the pants growing into primal screams, until his head, disappearing under the surface, silenced them.

David stayed under. Jack stepped forward, worried the stranger had drowned. David suddenly broke the surface just as Jack stepped into the water. Sobbing, he walked out of the water and stumbled, Brad catching him at the last moment. The men helped him dress, his body trembling out of control. They held his arms, leading him up the trail. Brad stopped when they could just make out Liza in the dark.

"I hope you don't take this the wrong way, but I've got something to tell you. That whole story about jumping in ice water being an Eskimo wedding ritual . . . I lied."

David looked up at Brad, trying to see his face in the dark. "You made me go through all that for nothing?"

Brad shook his head. "Brother, that was the most awesome, the bravest thing, I have ever witnessed in my life. Just because it isn't an Eskimo tradition doesn't mean it didn't shake the heavens and the Earth. It wasn't for nothing and I wasn't trying to make you look stupid. You stepped with great courage into that water and an act that powerful never goes unanswered."

Mr. Meyer patted him on the back. "No one here is laughing at you. And I have it on good authority that Brad here is an expert on how craziness can sometimes be just what it takes to set things right."

Jack's voice came out of the dark. "I'm counting on this piece of non-Eskimo magic working at least as much as you are."

David was still confused and disoriented, but he felt that something more profound and compelling than a glitchy GPS was behind him being here. Liza was silent during the walk to the farm, sensing that her husband's experience was one he was not ready to share.

Strings of colored lights guided them on the last stretch to the farm. The festivities had begun without the groom, a glowing

Hanna seated on a throne of wildflowers. The local women happily gave their best efforts for the poor stranger they believed to be celebrating a final fling with a city slicker lawyer before wasting away and dying. The communal effort had produced a potluck buffet that could have competed with the region's finest caterer. Besides salads of various combinations and numerous bowls of appetizers, at least ten casseroles on hot plates lined the long table. Local musicians, all of them sporting colorful suspenders and cowboy hats, were playing oldies but goodies. Mr. Meyer glowed with pride as he walked Hanna down the aisle.

Jack had dressed simply in black pants and a white shirt under a simple black silk jacket he found in the back of his closet, buried behind more flashy and fashionable clothes. Years before, his mother had given him a pile of clothes belonging to his father, and Jack was delighted to imagine his father was with him on this most important day. After the vows were exchanged, a ribbon-bedecked tractor showed up pulling a flower-covered trailer with hay bale seats for the couple to ride in style to the wedding feast. The cow that had accompanied Jack attended with her calf, the music punctuated by their mooing. David and Liza sat in a corner, feeling entirely out of place, until heaping plates of food were forced into their hands and they were pulled to a table. They were famished, but they were only allowed five minutes to eat before being dragged into the circles of rowdy dancing.

Liza moved away from David, confused and frightened by the wild look in his eye as he danced in a frenzy around the bride and groom. She had expected him to call for a cab as soon as they got to the farm. He usually shied away from crowds and hated dancing, so she was totally confused watching him participate with such enthusiasm. She drifted away from the wedding party and entered the farmhouse, hoping to find a telephone. The kitchen was empty, but a pot of coffee on the stove was still hot. Liza poured a cup, aching for the cigarettes hidden behind the back seat in the wrecked jeep. Her cell phone was also lost somewhere in the wreck. The coffee was delicious, the only comfort she'd had after the crazy events that nearly killed her. She felt a growing aversion to this hick wedding and David's weird behavior. For far too long she had been a country mouse, playing the domestic, good wife, but the accident, the result of David's inexplicable and reckless behavior, topped off with cow slobber, had been a nightmare, the final straw. Besides, David was a good catch and could find another woman that would be a better baby maker than she was. She had given it her all and tomorrow, after speaking to David tonight, would be a good day to go back to her old life. Now her priority was to get out of here and then to extricate herself from this marriage.

The door opened and an older woman walked in followed by the bride.

The young bride was holding up the hem of her dress. The older woman stopped to look at it in the light. They were unaware of Liza. "All we need is a safety pin. We can fix it tomorrow or whenever. There's no rush, unless you plan on wearing this dress again a lot sooner than that." The bride laughed, blushing slightly, until she noticed they weren't alone. The older woman sensed her concern and looked up. Liza was taken aback by the shrewdness behind the blue eyes that inspected her quickly and thoroughly before smiling. "You must be the unfortunate young woman who had that car accident. My husband told me about how he found you hanging over the pond. That kind of luck would have me counting my blessings."

Liza smiled. "I guess you could say that. We are very grateful to your husband and his friends. I helped myself to some coffee and I was wondering if I could use your phone."

"I'm sorry. Brad knocked down the phone line when he was stringing the lights. The phone's been out all day. And the tow truck won't be running tonight. The truck's owner, or someone who looks just like him after a bath, shave, and haircut, just stood up and announced that he asked the widow Danzinger to marry him and she had said 'yes'. But not to worry. My husband asked me to set you up in the barn. It's already set up for sleeping since I was expecting a guest from out of town that didn't show up. Hannah can show you the way, if she still remembers." Both women broke out laughing over their inside joke, making Liza feel even more uncomfortable and alone. The older woman poured herself a cup of coffee and sat down across from Liza. "I guess you must be in a hurry to get back to your kids."

Liza shrugged. "We don't have any children, if that's what you wanted to know. I think that's partly why we had the accident. David has been out of his mind worrying about us not getting pregnant. I think it drove him a little crazy. It is very important to him."

The bride put her hand on Liza's shoulder. "You should be blessed with children."

Liza shrugged, annoyed with the gratuitous remark and attempting to move the hand away. "Thanks. We've been trying. We've seen the top specialists."

Hanna put her hand back on Liza's shoulder. "No, that's not what I meant. You should try being blessed. My mother told me that the heavens are wide open for the prayers of a new bride. We have a family tradition that brides sit on a big chair, decorated like a throne, and bestow blessings on those who need them. I didn't want to do it tonight because no one here knows that tradition. I was so hoping someone would show up to receive my blessing."

Liza wanted to jump out of the chair and run away from this gushing girl and her silly fantasies. Mrs. Meyer put her hand on

Liza's other shoulder. "Come on, honey. Give it a try. You can't refuse this young bride." Mrs. Meyer's voice carried an undertone of slyness, knowing Liza was trapped and would have to politely concede to anything the bride demanded. They locked eyes and Liza realized that she had underestimated this farmer's wife who was hard as granite beneath the country calico. Her dress was similar to those she often rummaged through at the flea market. It was only a few hours ago, but it seemed like eons. Now Liza felt there was no escape from this older woman who was pushing this weird ritual. She had no choice but to humor the young bride for whom this silly tradition was so important.

Liza sighed. "Sure. Why not?"

The younger woman pulled Liza to her feet, surprising Liza with her strength. She put her hands on the sides of Liza's head, forcing eye contact. Her gaze was so serious that Liza wanted to laugh out loud.

"May you be blessed with a child."

Liza felt silly but wanted to put an end to the ordeal. The whole ritual felt uncomfortably religious but Liza couldn't think of a polite way to leave. "Amen."

The girl continued to stare into Liza's eyes. "No. You didn't want it. A blessing has to be received."

Liza tried to pull away. "Sure I did."

The girl tightened her grip, shocking Liza. "Damn you. Don't you realize this is for a child?"

Liza tried to pull away but her grip tightened even more. "Stop it. I'm not sure I really want a child. I'm only doing it for my husband." Once the words came out Liza realized that all along she wanted this child for David and not for herself.

Hanna raised her voice until she was yelling. "No. Your son! Your baby! It may be his desire but it comes from your body. You are the one who has to make this dream real. That man will be the father of your child, and your child is a part of both of you, forever, like your love—it's forever. The two of you, the one child."

Liza pulled back but she felt Mrs. Meyer's hand on her back, pushing her closer to the shouting girl.

"Stop it!"

The girl's face, inches from Liza's, was red with anger and sweat poured down her face. "No! I need it to work for you because I need it to work for me. Your son! My son! Your baby! My baby!"

Liza screamed. "No!"

Hanna hissed at her. "Yes! Your son! My son!"

Liza felt a hand on her head. She strained to twist her head in Hanna's grip. Mrs. Meyer had one hand on her head and the other rested on Hanna's head. "My son" she said calmly. "He's lost out there in the world. He needs your blessing too. Your prayer for your son. My prayer for my son."

Liza gasped for breath as she felt something happen inside her chest. She was aware of the two women pulling her into an embrace, holding her up as her legs gave way. Liza closed her eyes and struggled to speak, to say something that would get her away from these women. "I don't want . . ." Pain burned across her chest. She gathered her strength. "I don't want . . ." The pain raced through her, making her head spin. "I don't . . ." She stopped herself before the pain could start again. Tears were flowing through her tightly closed eyes. A scream surfaced, filling the kitchen and echoing into the night. With a shock she realized it was the same scream she had heard from the lake where the men had been swimming.

"I want my baby! I want my baby!"

She wailed and sobbed over and over, held up by the two women hugging her, until she had no more tears, no voice, no strength.

An hour later, after sitting quietly over a pot of tea with the sounds of the wedding nearby, Liza was still drained of energy. The sensation was pleasing and she felt she had experienced a total cleansing of her soul. The older woman returned and led Liza to the barn. She climbed the ladder and found David sitting in the big window, staring out at the dark field. She sat down next to him and they sat in the dark, listening to the wedding celebration die down.

His voice drifted to her, soft enough to be ignored if she didn't feel like talking. "Are you angry?"

She shrugged, not caring whether he could see it or not. "For wrecking the car and almost killing us in a painfully horrific manner? Nah. We've been married long enough. If I can put up with your dirty socks and reading in the bathroom, what's a life threatening car accident? But, I'm warning you, if you use my toothbrush one more time, I'll kill you with my bare hands."

He laughed and they felt their love filling the distance between them. She flipped her hand over, palm up, on her lap. He reached over to take her hand. "I'm sorry. I've been feeling a craziness growing inside of me. I couldn't stand it and I didn't know how to deal with it. I've never done anything crazy in my life." His voice caught and she realized he was crying. "I want a kid so much, but if it doesn't happen, it won't affect the way I feel about you."

She patted his hand. "I know. Me too."

He looked up, staring at her in surprise. "Really? That's the first time you've ever said that. All this time, I felt like I was alone, like I was pushing you into something you didn't want."

She nodded. "That's why it didn't work. It takes two to make a baby. Didn't your daddy tell you that when you turned thirteen?" He laughed and Liza realized how much she liked that sound and how she wanted to spend the rest of her life listening to it. "I didn't want a baby. I was going along with what you wanted. But I forgot what it meant to be married to you. I am your wife. I am not the same 'Liza' that I used to be. David's wife wants a baby. I'm finally ready to be David's wife."

They went to bed on a quilt spread over a layer of straw. The pleasant summer night air, together with their gentle hugs, provided more than enough warmth to leave the window wide open to more stars than either of them had ever seen before.

Mr. Meyer sipped a large cup of coffee while he watched his neighbors clean up from the celebration. He was pleased with how the wedding turned out. He had walked Jack through his jitters and Mrs. Meyer had done the same for Hanna. The neighbors all chipped in, pulling together a potluck feast that put any catered affair to shame. He couldn't have done better for his own kin.

He was watching Lance and Mrs. Higginbottom pretend at cleaning up, folding tablecloths as an excuse to get close, their hands lingering a bit too long, their fingers getting tangled together in the middle. He noticed Willard walking towards him. Willard looked like he had something on his mind. Mr. Meyer scooted over to make room so they wouldn't have to sit across the table from each other and holler.

"I noticed you were dancing up a storm, Willard."

"I haven't cut a rug since my daddy died. That's been almost two years. It feels good to dance at a wedding. I noticed you weren't."

Mr. Meyer shrugged. "I haven't felt much like dancing and it might be a while before I do."

"Theo?" Mr. Meyer nodded, a lump in his throat choking off his response. "It's still pretty fresh so I guess I can understand. But be careful with that. Don't go mourning the living."

Mr. Meyer sipped his coffee to clear his throat. "I don't know where he is. I miss him. Mother doesn't say anything but I know it's even worse for her."

"He's fine. You shouldn't worry about him."

Mr. Meyer looked up, searching Willard's face for clues. "You know something?"

Willard reluctantly nodded. "I can't say more than that he is fine."

Mr. Meyer stared into his coffee. "I'd beat you up if I thought I could get more out of you, but you are stubborn as a mule. Just like your father was."

"He used to say the same thing about you."

"You know we served in the army together. You see the real man when you go through what we did. And he was one of the good ones. He was stubborn when he had to be and no one could yell loud enough or threaten bad enough to make him budge. Maybe a little of that rubbed off on me. It sure rubbed off on you. He was a good friend."

"He said that about you too."

"We haven't seen you around here for a while. All those little calves you bottle-fed are full grown now."

"After my daddy died, I didn't feel sociable. I quit working and took odd jobs to get by. I didn't go out or talk to anybody for a while. Most of my friends understood and the ones who didn't, well, I guess they're afraid of feeling things too deeply."

"Why don't you come stay at the farm for a bit? We are short handed and you know the work."

Willard shook his head. "It's too close. It would be too easy for me to put you in place of my daddy and for you to put me in place of Theo. We both have a lot of healing to do and lying to ourselves won't help that along."

Mr. Meyer nodded. "That sounds like something I should have said. So if you didn't come to milk cows, what did you come for? It's a long way to travel to dance at a wedding where you don't know the bride and groom."

Willard reached into his shirt pocket and pulled out a small envelope. "I'm doing a favor for a friend. He asked me to deliver this to the groom."

"Well, that will have to wait until morning. It is their wedding night." They both laughed and Mr. Meyer got suddenly serious, staring at the envelope lying on the table between them. His voice shook just a little as he spoke. "Do I know this friend?"

Willard pushed the envelope a little closer to Mr. Meyer. "Yes and no. It's from Theo. He asked me to tell you something. He said you once told him a story about a farmer who found some eggs that fell out of an eagle's nest after a hunter killed the mother. He gave the eggs to his goose to set on. It was a crazy sight to watch those furry little eaglets waddling after the mother goose. They even tried to follow her into the pond but ended up stuck on the beach, chirping for their surrogate mother to come back. But the saddest sight was the mother goose honking and crying as she watched her adopted babies soar away over the mountain."

Mr. Meyer smiled. "I remember telling him that story."

"Theo wanted me to ask you a question, and not for your sake. He wanted to know your answer. He asked if it was any easier for a mother eagle to watch her babies fly away than it is for an adopted mother goose."

Mr. Meyer lowered his head and when he looked up, tears were in his eyes. "You tell Theo that it's even harder for the mother eagle than it was for the goose. The mother eagle knows how cruel the world is to eagles. The goose misses her babies but only feels bad because she can't go with them. The mother eagle could go but she needs all her strength to let her babies fly into the world alone when all she really wants is to keep them home and protect them. But if she does that, her babies will never be free, never know how high they can fly. Her love for her children has got to be stronger than her fear. Even if it means . . . " Mr. Meyer's voice cracked. "Even if it means her children flying into harm's way."

"I'll be sure to tell him that. Can I tell him you passed the letter along?" Mr. Meyer nodded.

Willard got up, leaving Mr. Meyer to stare at the letter.

When Liza and Dave got back to their country home, the house seemed brighter. Liza began to move their collectibles into a storage shed behind the barn. Three weeks later, her period was late. Two weeks after that she woke up laughing at her own nausea because, after all of the previous drama, it seemed too stereotypical to have a simple case of morning sickness.

Full of questions, Karen read the last word and gently placed the manuscript in the center of her precious coffee table. She had been carried along by the story, but she would have to read it at least once again to more fully understand it. The one thing she did know for sure was that, in spite of herself, she loved it. She floated out of her office and quietly asked her shocked secretary to call Liza and invite her to a lunch meeting.

Liza stepped out of the elevator, her bladder calling to her even more urgently than her previous visit, another one of the curious but welcome changes in her body. From an open door, an excited voice called her into the office. Karen sat on the sofa, patting the upholstery for Liza to sit next to her. Liza noted the delicate china tea set on the coffee table as she sat down. Karen had found a cup that was a pretty good replica of the broken one.

Karen smiled warmly. "Not exactly a story for the romance section of the bookstore."

Liza nodded, waiting for the sword to be drawn. "Agreed. Not enough French lace and roses, and no ripped bodice."

"Yes, but it does have that certain something that makes a girl sit up and pay attention." The women sat staring at each other in silence. The spark of sisterhood that had always been between them, but that had been dominated by their growing adversarial relationship, suddenly resurfaced. Karen poured tea into the porcelain cups. "It certainly is a special story. I think if you work on it, it could be worthwhile."

Liza shook her head. "You don't understand. I didn't write it."

Karen smirked. "Tell the truth. It's about you and David, so who else could have written it?"

Liza shrugged. "When I found out I was pregnant, I started dreaming, fantasizing about the baby. One day, I was playing with names to choose. I remembered that old book we had bought at the flea market and went to look for it. Several days after the accident, David went back to the wreck and filled a box with everything he could salvage. The car was a total loss. The tow truck couldn't get near enough to tow it out. Our cell phones were smashed, but the GPS that had gone berserk made it through without a scratch. And the map that started it all was strangely missing. I found the book at the bottom of the box. I started going through the list. Some of the names were totally crazy. Agamemnon, Archibald, Algernon. I only got halfway through the 'A's. The pages were stuck together on purpose. Someone deliberately cut out the middle. You know, like prisoners do with Bibles to sneak things into jail."

"To hide weapons or pocket helicopters."

Liza chuckled. "Yes. But inside this book was a manuscript and a letter." Liza took an envelope from her pocket and slid it across the polished surface of the desk. Karen put on her glasses and began to read.

"Congratulations. If you are reading this letter it means that you are pregnant. That means that it is time for the book to be published. Good luck. P.S. Sorry about cutting out the pages. You only needed the section on 'J' names, anyway. Name him James, for your father-in-law."

Karen stared at Liza. "You didn't write this?"

Liza shook her head. "I just told you. I found it inside the book we bought at that flea market. The book that came with the map that nearly cost us our lives."

Karen put her teacup down. "You mean someone who knew what had happened to you broke into your house and slipped this into the book?" Liza shook her head. Karen felt her face grow hot. "Well, what you are saying is that someone, that man who sold you the map and book, knew beforehand, that you would . . . and then you . . . and now you're . . ." Liza's smile grew as she nodded, agreeing with Karen's frustrated attempts at putting the puzzle together. "This is the craziest story I have ever heard, and if it were anyone else telling it, I would toss them out my window and run down to kick them after they hit the sidewalk." She paused, sipping the tea to wet her throat that went suddenly dry. "Is it all true?"

An impish grin spread across Liza's face. "If you mean does the manuscript give an accurate accounting of the facts as they occurred and a fair representation of the characters involved? In my opinion, the answer is 'yes'. There are those who might disagree with me, my obstetrician included, whose tunnel vision doesn't allow for possibilities that aren't listed in his medical textbook. If you are asking me for an explanation of how such a thing appeared in my hands before said events occurred, I will have to disappoint you. I don't know how it was written, when it was written, or who wrote it. I wonder what would have happened had I opened up the book right away and read it before the crash. However, not only is that a moot point, but I don't really care. A miracle happened, actually two miracles happened. I am pregnant, and I am ecstatic about it. Somehow, someone who was involved in those miracles asked me for a favor. I don't know if the favor includes making sure the book gets published or if I am off the hook once the book is in your hands. Do what you want. I am on maternity leave, starting today."

Karen stroked the cover of the manuscript on her lap, as if for good luck. The front cover said The Hope Merchant: Free Wish With Every Purchase.

She looked up. "You think it has a chance??"

Liza nodded. "It's good, definitely good enough. But after all my years in the business, the one thing I am sure of is that you can never be too sure. What I do know is that this book already has some serious mojo working."

Karen thought for a minute. "I won't make any promises and I certainly won't give you a snap decision right now. But I am considering it. What about the author? How do I get in touch with him?"

Liza had a strange smile on her face. "Well, I told you. He put the manuscript inside the book. I went back to the flea market but he wasn't there and nobody knows who he is."

Karen hesitated. "I need to speak to him because we can't publish without his consent."

Liza nodded, reluctant but eager at the same time. "It shouldn't be too much of a problem. Call the building superintendent and tell him the smoke detector in your office is broken."

Karen's mouth dropped open. "What? That crazy old coot?"

Liza nodded. "I think so. I've only met him once before and I wasn't really paying attention."

Karen shook her head in disbelief. Her voice became strangely hesitant and her eyes kept darting back to the manuscript. "Not that I believe any of this, but if I do decide to publish it, do I get a free wish?"

Liza smiled. "Put it in the contract and we'll haggle over it. But what could a liberated, accomplished woman like you possibly lack?"

Karen took off her glasses. "You would be surprised by the dreams that lie beneath this cold veneer, hidden in this frosty heart of mine. Why don't we go out to lunch and I'll tell you about them?"

THE
BOOK
OF
DREAMS

LILLY

L illy left her office, irresponsibly early by her standards. It was a holiday weekend and her boss would certainly not have objected. But today, she grudgingly packed up her desk, worried that she would not have anything to eat if she didn't shop before the stores closed. Leaving work was nothing less than negligent when the crushing load of work that came at the end of the year was looming just ahead, a few short weeks away. Thanksgiving was only an inconvenience.

Ending the day early meant more time alone and less time that she desperately needed at the office. All morning, she watched with growing annoyance as her co-workers, exchanging good wishes, took advantage of the holiday to leave early. Lilly was double-checking her afternoon's figures when she suddenly noticed the office was silent. Looking out her door, she realized that she was alone in the building. She hesitated, looking at the pile of work on her desk. She would have stayed even longer, but she reminded herself that her refrigerator was almost empty. Reluctantly, she grabbed her coat and hurried outside.

It was still early but the streets were empty. Most of the city's inhabitants had already hurried home for the long Thanksgiving weekend. She glanced at the houses, imagining them full of families, snug and comfortable, enjoying being together again. With pictures of colorful fall foliage, the calendar promised "autumn", but winter was definitely arriving a few weeks early. The sky was uniformly gray and bleak, unrelieved by the few leaves still hanging on. Even though the temperature was well above freezing, a bitter wind made it feel much colder. Alone on the empty streets, Lilly felt she was the only one experiencing this first taste of winter. Head down and hunched over against the wind, she struggled to close the top buttons on her light spring coat.

She wanted to shout at the sky, demanding that she had a few more weeks of warmth coming to her. She felt cheated, shivering in her thin coat, angry as she argued with no one in particular that autumn is spring reversed, so the clothes should be the same. Despite the heat, she was partial to summer when it was still light long into the evening. Autumn always gave rise to a somber mood.

During the bus ride home, her thoughts drifted back to last year when her mother had done the shopping and cooking. She bought enough food for a large family and spent the entire day in the kitchen. The meal was still hot but noticeably dried out in the oven when Lilly finally came home. Lilly tried to remember what they ate. Had she known it was to be their last holiday supper together, Lilly would have been more attentive and pleasant. She couldn't remember anything of the meal except being aggravated at her mother for cooking too much food, as usual. Lilly had arrived home feeling worn and brittle from the office. She was looking forward to losing herself in the pages of a new romance novel. When her mother's attempts at pleasant conversation pulled her attention from the book, Lilly made a half-hearted effort to be polite, but the conversation quickly became a monologue with Lilly speaking at length about her efforts to get promoted and the many obstacles in her way. Her mother tried to follow and feigned interest but since she had no work background, the nuances of corporate structure and infighting that dominated her daughter's life left her feeling confused. Her questions and suggestions, intended to convey her heartfelt concern and empathy, seemed irrelevant and silly. Lilly quickly became annoyed at her mother and couldn't hold back from calling her ignorant of the ways of the world. They finished the holiday meal in frustrated silence. Her mother turned down her hearing aid while Lilly absorbed herself in her novel. Rushing home to her empty apartment, Lilly dismissed these uncomfortable thoughts and hurried off the bus into the store. Quickly selecting a few items, she ignored the clerk's holiday greeting as she hurried through the aisles.

The bouncing bag of groceries kept a steady beat against her thigh as she walked from the small store to her apartment. Cans of corn, peas and some cold cuts would hold her over until Monday morning. It wouldn't be festive or even tasty, but at least she wouldn't be hungry. She would survive the holiday, eating alone, watching some TV, and reading before she fell asleep.

As senior accountant at the firm, she was known for burning the midnight oil and politely declining invitations to most office parties. She had been working towards a promotion that always seemed imminent, but never materialized. Lilly could not remember exactly when, but at some point over the last year, her dreams of a brighter future in the company had been disappointed, and she reconciled herself to endless monotonous days punching out numbers on her adding machine. From sheer habit, Lilly continued to work the long hours, though she no longer had any expectations of climbing another rung up the corporate ladder. She was stuck in the confusing career doldrums of the middle aged, somewhere between the fierce determination of youth and the palsied fear of losing job and pension that precedes retirement. She distinctly remembered being optimistic last year about her prospects, when she was telling her mother about her job over the holiday supper.

Lilly struggled to remember the exact point in time when she gave up hope of a promotion and developed a malaise about her current position. Over the course of the year, even though she worked the same long hours, her enthusiasm disappeared. Though her credentials were impeccable and her resume impressive, the prospect of looking for a new job terrified her. She had lost a measure of confidence, feeling her skills were a sham, and was sure an interviewer looking closely would laugh in her face for pretending to be something she wasn't. Every time she sat down at her computer, she had trouble working up the energy to update her résumé, and when she looked through her closet for a power suit to wear to an interview, her clothes looked hopelessly out of fashion. She spent her days avoiding her supervisor, afraid he would decide to fire her because she didn't fit the image of the company.

Lilly pulled her collar tight. She pushed against the gusts of wind that were blowing through her coat and billowing around her. The coat was thin and poorly made, and like so much else lately, it was too much effort to replace it with something more weather-appropriate. Lilly knew that going through the winter with the coat was a sure prescription for catching a cold. Besides being insufficient for winter weather, the coat seemed drab and she felt frumpy whenever she noticed her reflection in a store window. She knew she had more than enough money to buy a decent, even fashionable, wardrobe, but she had cultivated this image of being practical and serious. Now, everything she owned, even her summer clothes, were either black, brown or grey, sensible, non-descript, and cheap. It occurred to Lilly that she was becoming obsessed about saving money and she wondered whether she was becoming eccentric.

The straps of the shopping bag cut into her right hand as the left one pulled her collar tight. Her tearing eyes squeezed shut as an icy blast caught her full in the face. Lilly walked a few steps blinded, but stopped short as she bumped into someone she had not seen a few moments before. She opened her eyes but her vision was still blurry. She could make out the lumpy outline of an old woman in a brown felt overcoat. Her heart skipped as she thought she saw her mother standing in front of her. She blinked the tears away and looked again. The woman was about the same age her mother had been when she died, but she was more solidly built. Lilly tried to step around her but the old lady grabbed her sleeve and held it tightly.

"Where's the Hope Merchant?"

Lilly clenched her teeth. She wanted to jerk her arm away and keep walking, but the old woman's grip was surprisingly strong. "I'm sorry but I don't know what you are talking about. I've lived here for ten years and I've never heard of such a store."

The old lady didn't let go of her sleeve. She stared up into Lilly's face with intense blue eyes. "It's right around here. I went to him twelve years ago when Father passed away. My little Billy was going through such hard times. Mr. Meyer fixed me up good. I need him again. Can you help me? I can't remember where the street is."

Lilly tried taking a step away but the old woman's grip was too strong. "I'm sure he's closed for the holiday."

"No, not him. Holidays are his busy season."

Lilly gently pried the lady's hand from her sleeve one finger at a time. "I'm sorry but I can't help you. I really must be getting home." She hesitated. "My family is holding supper for me."

The old lady looked up into Lilly's face, making her uncomfortable at the lie. The woman seemed to see something that made up her mind, and her wrinkled face folded in on itself. Pursing her lips, and increasing her wrinkles, she nodded grimly as she released Lilly's arm, giving it a gentle pat. "Of course they are. You go ahead and hurry on home. But do an old lady a favor. When you see his store, stop in for me and tell Mr. Meyer that Mildred needs him, but I lost his address."

"I don't know where the store is. Even if I did, do you think he would remember you after all this time?"

"He'll remember. Just make sure you remember." The old lady turned quickly and hustled off, her heavy brown coat barely moving in the bitter wind.

Another icy gust forced Lilly to close her eyes. She felt the shopping bag pull at her hand, spin around, and slap painfully against her leg. Suddenly, a blast of the wind yanked it from her hand, sending a jolt of pain up her arm. The bag fell to the ground, its contents spilling onto the sidewalk. She opened her eyes, expecting to see the back of some young hoodlum running off with her groceries. Her eyes stung but all she could see were leaves and newspapers twirling in the wind. Lilly dropped to her knees, scrambling to grab the cans before they rolled away, and watched her new paperback skip across the street. Lilly groaned, thinking of the long, lonely weekend without something to read. Throwing her groceries back into the bag she chased after the book as it made a sudden right turn into an alley. The wind, even stronger in the narrow alleyway, blew the book down a short flight of steps. She stooped to pick it up, straightened up, and saw before her a storefront she never noticed before. She stared at the plate glass window wondering how a business could possibly exist in a basement hidden in an alley. The window was full of dusty bric-a-brac, and inside the store it was dark, as if it had been closed for a very long time. Undoubtedly it was out of business, and with good reason. Looking inside gave Lilly an eerie feeling. She was just about to climb the stairs and hurry out of the alleyway when the sign on the door caught her eye.

> *Thelonius S. Meyer*
> The Hope Merchant

Both her conscience and the manners she learned from her deceased parents, dictated that she at least convey the old woman's message. It should only take a moment to speak to this Mr. Meyer and then she would be on her way. She reluctantly leaned against the door, hoping that it would be locked. It was, after all, late on Thanksgiving Eve. But the door swung open, a bell tinkling pleasantly. She stepped into the darkness and clutter, blinking the grit out of her eyes. At first glance it looked like any other down-and-out bric-a-brac shop that would not attract customers looking for authentic antiques. The place seemed deserted, but as she turned to leave, her hand on the doorknob, she stopped. Something seemed familiar but she couldn't place it. She stared at the shelves. Surely she had never been here before. Then, slowly, it dawned on her. The strong smell of patchouli filled the back of her throat, and made her smile.

Patchouli was the smell of Lilly's adolescent search for freedom and feminine mystique. She had never been brave enough to wear patchouli, and her mother would have frowned on such a daring, provocative scent. Their neighbor, Mrs. Ross, was an original flower child, a true hippie even in her old age, and she wore patchouli. Mrs. Ross loved wild, brightly printed muslin skirts and gypsy scarves wrapped around her head. Lilly was awed by her audacious femininity. Unpopular with her peers, and repressed by her mother, Lilly became Mrs. Ross's shy admirer. The lady was an artist, and Lilly had made a few attempts under her tutelage. Lilly still loved patchouli. She stood still, taking deep breaths, with thoughts of a difficult adolescence and Mrs. Ross' strong Mother Earth influence that had been such a comfort. Suddenly overwhelmed by sadness, she realized how painful it must have been for her mother when she so obviously preferred Mrs. Ross' company. Now, too late, it hurt to think of how much remained unsaid between mother and daughter. Last year, this night would have been the perfect time to rectify that, but Lilly had come home tired and frustrated from work. This Thanksgiving holiday she would dine alone, in silence.

A voice came out of the darkness. "Can I help you?"

Startled from her thoughts, she looked up to see an old man standing in the entrance to a back room. He had his back to her as he secured a velvet rope across the entrance. When he turned around, a pair of blue eyes stared out of the darkness, transfixing her, glowing in the dim light of the shop. The sides of his head were covered with fine wisps of white hair that stood on end, and waved gently, like seaweed underwater, as he came towards her.

"Well, no, I . . . I don't need any help."

"How very unfortunate for you. I can only hope your condition will improve."

She was momentarily shocked into silence by his strange response. She expected him to laugh and explain that he was joking, but his face maintained its serious expression. "I came here for a friend."

He nodded. "You would like to purchase a friend? It is not a simple thing and will probably be quite expensive, but I think we can arrange that. They do happen to be one of our specialties. I may even have an old one lying around somewhere that I could lend you until we find a suitable match. So many people these days are in need of a friend but don't have the knack."

She waited for him to acknowledge his joke but he stood there silently. Her face grew warm with embarrassment and confusion. "I'm afraid you misunderstood. I came here on an errand for someone else."

He continued nodding. "I understand but you must realize that everyone says that. I never understood why people are embarrassed to ask for something in their own name."

"No, it is true, I am on an errand. I met an old woman on the street today and she asked me to forward a message if I ever came into your shop."

He waited expectantly. "Yes?"

"Her name is Mildred. She asked me to tell you that she lost your address and needs you."

His forehead wrinkled in concern. "What an odd message. Why didn't you tell her my address?"

She stammered before answering. "I didn't know it."

"But here you are."

"I found the shop by accident."

"Finding something you need is never an accident. Even if you didn't know you needed it." He rubbed his chin in thought. "Are you certain her name is Mildred? I don't remember her. A former customer, you say? I must investigate."

He went behind a high oak counter with a glowing white marble top and struggled to pull out an enormous ledger. He flipped pages so quickly that Lilly found it hard to believe he was reading. He mumbled a list of names while he turned the pages. She watched impatiently, wondering how long it would take him to find one name in such a massive book and whether she was expected to wait until he did. She put her bag of groceries on the floor and decided to look around the shop. The variety of merchandise was remarkable, and Lilly was hard-pressed to figure out exactly what type of store she was in. Enormous rainbow-colored lollipops, absurdly large and festooned with ribbons, were on display next to the cash register. On closer inspection, some of what she thought was junk might just be valuable.

It looked like the store was randomly organized. A bucket of seeds and a burlap sack of potting soil sat incongruously in the middle of the shop next to wooden crates of ceramic pots. In the back room she glimpsed a dollhouse in the making, one that would have fulfilled any little girl's dreams. One corner of the store seemed to be dedicated to small decorative boxes and another to beautiful glass bottles. Rough, hand carved boxes, were displayed next to delicate pink crystal boxes. She leafed through a large, leather-bound Bible on a tall wooden lectern. As she gently fingered the pages, recalling the biblical stories of her childhood, she wondered whether the letters on the page were hand written. It looked like something she saw in a museum once, though she couldn't believe something so rare would be on display for sale alongside lollipops and fake flowers. The shelf behind the Bible was sagging with Korans, Bibles in every language, and several books written in what looked like ancient Hebrew. Another box contained an assortment of pens. She sorted through them, finding antique fountain pens with gold nibs mixed in with feathery quills and cheap modern ballpoints.

She glanced up at the shopkeeper and saw that he was now flipping through his ledger in the opposite direction. She saw a shelf of books and went to see if there were any romance novels for sale. The books were different sizes and colors, piled haphazardly and covered by a thick layer of fine dust, as if no one had touched them for years. There were no titles on the spines, and she soon discovered that the pages in all of the books were blank. There were boxes of fragrant candles and a cabinet that made her dizzy with the overwhelming musk of a large selection of incense. She rolled a small vial labeled 'patchouli' between her fingers before putting it back on the shelf, a pang of regret making her fingers slow and clumsy. Delicate blown glass perfume atomizers were arranged on one shelf, while the shelf below displayed an assortment of kaleidoscopes. Hanging from the ceiling in one corner were hand-painted talismans fastened to strings of colored glass beads. The beads had pictures on them that captured her attention, though they didn't seem to make sense; a dog in jockey silks, a boy in a yellow rain slicker, a zebra. One antique bead had a picture of a bright red flower. She reached out to touch it, feeling she had seen it somewhere before. Her reverie was broken by a noise behind her. She glanced over her shoulder and saw the old storekeeper flip the book over and begin reading the book upside down. She was looking through a kaleidoscope when he slammed the book shut and cleared his throat.

"No, I am quite sure. There is no Maggie."

"Her name was Mildred."

"Well, of course there is no Mildred. I told you that already. That is strange but I am not interested in strange things. Strange things have no purpose. I am interested in amazing things and what I find amazing is that there is also no Maggie. I don't understand how such an oversight happened. I must fix it at once." His shaggy white eyebrows came together as he inspected Lilly closely. "Your name wouldn't happen to be Maggie, would it?"

"No. My name is Lilly."

"Like the leaves floating in ponds where frogs rest their cold and slimy derrieres while waiting for tardy princesses to finish putting on their make-up?"

"Umm . . . most people think of the flower."

"How very strange. I never knew a frog to sit on a flower while waiting for a princess. I imagine it would make their bottoms smell better, though any thorns could lead to immediate and painful consequences. For the frog, of course. Princesses tend not to notice such things."

Lilly looked at the old man, waiting for him to smile but he remained quite serious. She carefully returned the kaleidoscope to its place on the shelf. His eccentricity was becoming tedious, and she was about to pick up her bag of groceries when the old man appeared at her side.

"Didn't you find what you were looking for?"

She was startled and couldn't understand how he had crossed over the counter so quickly. "I didn't come looking for anything."

"That doesn't mean that you aren't looking for something now." He looked at her eagerly for a few moments before shaking his head and wrinkling his forehead in deep thought. "You said that you came here for a reason, though I can't seem to remember what it was."

"I came here for someone else."

He nodded. "Of course. And what did she say she needed?"

"Nothing."

He looked confused. "And what do you need?"

"I don't need anything, either."

"I can't stay in business that way. We'll both have to try harder. You mentioned that you don't need anything but that is not the same as saying that you don't want anything. I may not be able to supply you with what you need but I am sure I have something you want."

Lilly thought for a moment, deciding it was best to humor him until she could get out the door. "That's all true. I should have said that I don't want anything."

He looked deeply concerned and worried, tears appearing at the corners of his eyes. "You poor girl. Things couldn't possibly be all that bad."

"You don't understand," Lilly insisted, "I only came to give you the message."

"I'm having a special discount sale today. Everything in the store has been marked down."

"There are no prices marked at all."

He winked at her. "So true. I guess everything is free."

"So how could it be marked down?"

"You aren't much of a bargain hunter, are you?"

"How do you stay in business?"

"As the saying goes, I lose money on every sale but I make it up in volume."

"That's ridiculous."

"Of course. But business often is."

This statement made Lilly angry but she chose not to argue the point. She looked around the store. "Okay. How much does the kaleidoscope cost?"

The old man looked shocked. "I couldn't possibly sell that to you again."

"You haven't sold it to me yet."

"Which is why I couldn't possibly sell it to you again."

"That doesn't make sense."

"I always thought so. I'm so glad we finally agree on something. I can tell already that we are going to be the dearest of friends again. Don't you think so, Maggie?"

"My name isn't Maggie. It's Lilly."

"I know that but I just thought that old friends like us should have pet names for each other. I thought Maggie would be nice because it almost rhymes with Lilly. Now, my dearest childhood friend, isn't there something you would love to buy?"

"What about . . ."

"Of course not. I couldn't bear to part with it."

"You don't know what I wanted to ask you."

"Well, neither did you two minutes ago. You told me so yourself. It seems to me that we have quite a bit in common."

Now totally exasperated, Lilly grabbed her bag and started for the door. Her hand rested on the brass doorknob. She thought of the long, lonely night ahead of her and hesitated. She turned and saw the old man looking at her with the gentlest smile she had ever seen. It reminded her of someone, but she couldn't remember whom.

"Yes? Can I help you?"

Lilly looked around the store and a childish urge overcame her. She pointed at the enormous candy-striped lollipops. "How much?"

He clapped his hands together and laughed. "How wonderful. You see, I told you that you wanted something."

The old man seemed so delighted that Lilly was forced to smile. "Okay, so I guess you were right after all. How much do the lollipops cost?"

He looked surprised at her question. "I couldn't possibly sell you a lollipop. Perhaps a lost group of children will wander by and be in need of serious laughter and joy. If I sell you a lollipop, I might not have enough for them. How will that one child feel, if he's the one whose lollipop I sold? A person should always be prepared for such emergencies."

"Enough," Lilly snapped at him. "What can you let me buy?"

Mr. Meyer pointed at the bucket of seeds. Lilly went over and looked down at the mixed selection, amazed at the variety. She was used to seeds coming in sterile packets, pre-sorted with a picture of the plant on the package. This box was a gardener's nightmare. No two seeds looked alike. They came in a variety of colors and sizes, ranging in size from tiny poppy seeds to one enormous pit that was wrinkled and velvety to the touch. She reached out her hand but stopped short of touching them. Although Lilly seemed very much a city person, she had been raised in a small town surrounded by farms. Her mother had been an avid gardener and Lilly always connected the smell of freshly plowed earth with good feelings. She vaguely remembered hugging her mother, burying her face in her earth-scented apron. Lilly had moved away from her hometown and settled in the city to advance her career. After her father died, Lilly's mother reluctantly left her garden behind and moved into Lilly's third floor walk-up apartment. Lilly always kept an eye open for a garden apartment or one with a balcony large enough for her mother to have a small garden, but the opportunity never materialized. She looked down at the seeds and thought of how wonderful it would have been to surprise her mother with a bag of seeds, an assortment of pots, and to help with the planting. It would have been a nice present to bring home for the holiday.

The old man's voice floated across the shop. "Go ahead, Lilly of the flower, not of the pond. Go ahead and touch them."

Lilly reached out as if in a dream and scooped up a handful of seeds, letting them sift through her fingers. She smiled as she watched them falling. The wind howling outside accompanied the old man's singsong voice.

"Lilly of the flower has come to find her dream. She has filled her hands with seeds but she may only choose one. Choose carefully, for a seed hides its heart well. The smallest acorn may grow into the mightiest oak but not all dreams are made of oak. Some dreams lay hidden in the hearts of roses and others laugh in the breeze as they play amongst the wildflowers. The oak makes a fine house, sturdy enough for many generations of children. A rose fades quickly, leaving its luxurious scent as it wounds the lover brave enough to bleed for his lady fair. Choose your dream well and then hide it in the earth. Pray for your dream to live, as it lies sleeping under the ground. Water it with tears lest it dry up and die."

One seed caught her eye. It was hard, oval, and indented on one end. Light red, bordering on pink, it looked almost like a tiny heart. Lilly plucked it out of the bucket and held it close to inspect it. It seemed warm in her hand and smelled pleasantly of something she couldn't quite recall. She held it out to the shopkeeper. He seemed about to say something but stopped himself and smiled instead. He took the seed from her and placed it in a brown paper bag then filled another bag with soil. Lilly looked through the crates of clay pots and was surprised to find one of pale blue porcelain. It seemed that it had been carelessly thrown in with the assortment of rough clay pots. It was shaped like a miniature Grecian urn with the raised silhouette of a woman's face in alabaster. Lilly held it out to the shopkeeper. He looked at the pot and pursed his lips, shaking his head slowly.

"Your seed may not grow. What good would such a fine pot be without a flower? What use is a pot full of soil? It would be a shame to leave it empty and even worse to fill it with pens and paper clips."

Lilly didn't want to put the urn-shaped pot back. It seemed so precious. "Could you perhaps put it aside for me? I really like it. When my seed grows I'd like to come back and buy it for my plant."

"Perhaps your seed is an oak and you will need to move to a cabin in the mountains to watch it grow. Perhaps your seed is a cactus, and it will require that you move to the desert and don Bedouin robes and ride your camel, searching for a hidden oasis where you can collect water for your precious plant. Perhaps your seed is a flower sent to you by an admirer who is too shy to give it to you, so he left this seed here for you to find for yourself. Perhaps it is dead inside, having been left here too long ago and forgotten. Perhaps after thinking about your seed and choosing so carefully, you will find that you don't like what grows from your seed and you will throw it away and then spend the rest of your days looking for another one just like it. Wait until it grows and then come back." He held out the two small brown paper bags and gently took the urn from her. The bell tinkled as she opened the door to leave the shop. Suddenly it occurred to her that she needed to pay for the seed.

"How much?"

The old man's eyes twinkled. "I told you, everything was marked down."

"So how much do I owe?"

"Yesterday it was free."

Lilly was confused. "So what could it possibly be marked down to?"

He shrugged his shoulders and giggled.

"Yes, but I can't just take it."

"It's just a nasty old seed, not even good enough to eat. It may turn out to be a weed. Then you would say that the Hope Merchant is nothing but a huckster selling worthless junk that only looks pretty to the eye. Take the seed. The first wish is always free. If you like it, you may pay me later or bring me two seeds in its place. Plants are like that, you know, so generous with their blessings."

She slipped the small paper bag with the seed into her pocket and turned to leave. "Excuse me." She turned to face the old man. He held a small paper bag out to her. "Don't forget to take your bag of soil." She took the bag from his hand and nervously hurried out of the store.

Night had fallen and the wind was not nearly as fierce. Lilly walked home quickly, trying to avoid looking into the brightly lit houses where families were gathering together for the holiday. The strange encounter with the odd shopkeeper put her into a different and unfamiliar frame of mind. She heated up her simple meal but then, on a whim, carefully arranged the canned food on a fine china plate and ate by candlelight. She poured apple juice into a wineglass, complimenting the waiter on its fine vintage.

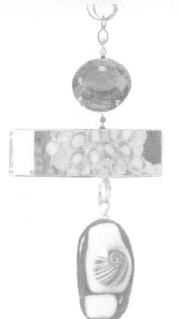

MAGGIE MAE

The weather was unseasonably mild all weekend, and the day was already warm when Lilly left early for work, to get a little exercise walking through the park. She decided to plant her seed in her office so she could watch it grow. The walk was pleasant at first, but she soon felt uncomfortable walking alone. Many people had taken advantage of the weather. The park was overflowing with families, young couples, baby carriages, and clusters of laughing children.

She fled the festive atmosphere of the park and jumped on a crowded bus. Forced to stand, she could not read her novel on the way to work. In the office, hanging up her coat, she felt a lump in the pocket. Reaching in, she pulled out the seed and the bag of soil. She found an old, cracked coffee mug in her bottom desk drawer. It would have to do until the cranky old storekeeper agreed to sell her the beautiful little urn. A return to the shop would be unpleasant but she very much wanted the urn, it was the first thing she truly wanted to buy in a long time.

Lilly was suddenly afraid the seed wouldn't grow. Despite years of watching her mother, any attempts to keep houseplants inevitably ended in either forgetting to water the plant or neglecting to give it enough sun. She told herself that if her seed didn't grow, she would buy a plant somewhere else and tell the Hope Merchant it had grown from the seed. He couldn't possibly tell the difference. She filled the mug with earth and gently pushed the seed in until it disappeared. She poured water on it, biting her lip as she thought of the old man's warnings. It just had to be a flower. What if it turned out to be a tree or a weed or a cactus? But it mustn't. The week dragged by and the seed remained hidden under the dirt. Lilly didn't expect it to grow quickly, but she felt nervous, and silly for being excited about something so inconsequential. On Friday she considered taking it home but was afraid the chill and the shock of being carried around would kill the seed, so she just gave it a little extra water before she left the office.

Monday morning she awoke early, eager to get to work and anxious about the seed. She hung up her coat and had just finished watering the seed when her boss rang, asking to meet with her immediately. Mr. Chin was young, attractive, and successful, and when he first signed on with the company, she had fantasized about dating him. He was over qualified, with a law degree as well as a degree in business and marketing, and the company was lucky to have him. He was younger than she, and that made the chances for her being promoted less likely. She went out with him socially, but he immediately established that there would be no more than a professional relationship between them. She had since become embarrassed in his presence and their working relationship become strained. She hurried to his office, though she dreaded going, thinking of possible reasons he might be angry with her. It disturbed her that she didn't know what he wanted. She would have liked to prepare responses to any possible accusations. He had a serious expression on his face when she entered and sat down.

"Good morning, Mr. Chin."

"Good morning, Lilly." He looked at her for several seconds making Lilly wonder if her makeup was on straight. "We've been working together for two years. You can call me 'Simon.'" She nodded mutely, uncomfortable with the sudden familiarity. "I have a special project and need to know how your workload stands now."

If she said that her workload was light, then it would look bad and seem that her position in the company was redundant. If she said that she was very busy, than he might think she was overwhelmed and incapable, and she might miss an opportunity for a project that would bring her to the attention of the board of directors. She tried to think of the best response but became confused and exasperated. "Umm . . . it's okay." She added as an afterthought, "Simon." How stupid all that must have sounded to him.

He seemed not to notice her discomfort. "Great. I need you to start clearing everything out and delegating the everyday stuff to one of your assistants. The board of directors has decided to start looking into branching out and diversifying operations. They are going to need a complete report on the assets and fiscal health of the company. They want to start moving on this in six weeks. They need your report in order to begin."

Lilly felt herself go numb. The amount of work required would be staggering. "Ummm . . . I don't . . . " Her voice trailed off. On one hand, she wanted the project and the attention it could bring to her. On the other hand, she was worried she wouldn't be able to handle it.

"Lilly, are you okay?"

She nodded. He reached into his top drawer and pulled out a folder, handing it to her. "This is a brief outline of what we want to know. Feel free to come to me any time for clarification. Okay?"

Lilly nodded and stood up to leave.

"One more thing. This project is very important to the board and I know it's too much for one person. I'm reassigning a bookkeeper from another department to assist you. His name is Willard. He was hired as a temp to help straighten out the books in advertising but since this project came up, we can use him a little bit longer. He got very good reviews from his previous boss."

"I don't need an assistant."

"He's a special man. I think you will find him invaluable."

"What do you mean special? Is he one of those . . . charity cases?"

Simon smiled and Lilly resented him for looking so attractive and confident. "No, not at all. I think you will get along with him. I've known him for several years."

"I don't . . ."

"This is an important project. There is no leeway for lagging behind or not getting it done. Willard is very good and I insist."

She pulled out the files she would need, the conversation with her boss replaying in her head. She had the feeling he wasn't being totally straight with her, sensing an ulterior motive. She paused, thinking this would be a perfect pretense for him to replace her with a friend of his. She would spend the next six weeks training her assistant to replace her and showing a stranger everything he would need to know to take over her job. Furious at what she thought was a probable scenario, she slammed the files down onto her desk, sending her pencil rolling over the edge. She bent down to pick it up but somehow it rolled backwards, coming to rest under the desk.

"Excuse me. I'm looking for Miss Lilly Preston, the head accountant."

She rose quickly, banging her head on the desk. He was a middle-aged man whose rugged good looks caught Lilly off guard for several uncomfortable seconds. His thinning, wavy brown hair was longer than office protocol dictated, but standards were relaxed for temps. The sleeves of his white shirt were rolled up to his elbows revealing beefy arms clutching a cheap briefcase to his chest like a football. She pretended to read a random sheet of paper on her desk and realized that it was actually his application. Glancing at the form, Lilly assumed he must not be a very good bookkeeper since he never landed a steady position. Suddenly she remembered that he might be here to take her job, and she looked at him with disapproval.

"I'm sorry. I didn't mean to startle you." His eyes were an unusual shade of gray.

Lilly rubbed the top of her head. "You didn't startle me." He gave her a wry smile that made her feel like a bashful little girl. Lilly bristled, resolving to establish herself as the boss at the outset. "You are Willard?"

"Yes."

A strange thought came to mind, making her realize that the situation was already inconsistent with office protocol. "Is that your first or your last name?"

She was surprised at how such a seemingly average man, a merely competent bookkeeper, could have such a sparkling smile. "Would you believe both?"

She looked puzzled. "Your name is Willard?"

He laughed. "No. My name is Willard Biggins. I just wanted to see if you would believe it." He was looking over her shoulder into the distance as if his office work was hardly his main concern. Lilly found it disconcerting and struggled to maintain her control.

His easy familiarity annoyed her and made her anxious to establish boundaries. "Shall we get to work, Mr. Biggins?"

He nodded his head but his soft gray eyes continued to focus on something behind her. He hesitated a moment before speaking. "What is it?"

"What is what?"

He crossed the room and walked around her desk, standing uncomfortably close to her. He reached over her shoulder and picked up the cracked mug from the shelf behind her. She was about to snap at him when she saw the tender green shoot curling up from the dark potting soil. She was speechless. This morning when she watered it, there hadn't been anything. Now, two hours later, the seed had sprouted two-and-a-half inches and there was a tiny bud on top. He turned the mug around in hands covered with calluses. She wondered where a bookkeeper would get calluses. He held it tenderly, staring for several moments with a smile on his face.

"Please put it back."

He looked startled but complied. "What is it?"

"I . . . I don't really know." She stammered.

"You bought seeds and you don't know what kind?" He gave her a curious look.

Lilly bristled at his impertinence. He was a temporary employee and she was a senior department head. She didn't think she should be the one to feel defensive. "Gardening is neither important nor relevant. Shall we get down to business? We have a great deal of work ahead of us."

He nodded, a half-smile remaining on his face. "Let's get to it, Miss Preston."

Lilly spent the rest of the morning explaining her system and the guidelines for the project. He learned quickly and was able to spend the rest of the day in his office, working independently. He left the office at five, but Lilly, as project head, worked until eight. When she got off the bus, she decided on a whim to pass by the Hope Merchant and see if he was open, wanting the blue porcelain pot. Now that the seed had sprouted, the shopkeeper would have to sell it to her. As she turned into the alley, she was surprised to see a dim light in the Hope Merchant's window. The shop was deserted so she went straight to the crate full of ceramic pots, digging through them until she was quite sure that the pale blue urn was not there. A noise from the back room drew her deeper into the store. Velvet curtains barred its entrance. A voice called out from behind her, making her jump.

"Can I help you, Miss Maggie?"

The old man was sitting behind his register, looking at her with a warm smile. She was sure he had not been there a moment ago.

"My name is Lilly, and I would like that blue porcelain pot, for the seed I purchased here two weeks ago."

"Oh. How wonderful! What did it grow into?"

"I'm not sure. It just sprouted today. It's still very tiny."

"I'm so excited. And now you want to purchase that very special blue porcelain piece for your plant to grow in?"

"Yes."

He clapped his hands in joy. "Excellent."

They stared at each other. Lilly finally broke the silence. "So?"

He looked confused. "Excuse me?"

"Could I have it?"

"Have what?"

219

"The blue porcelain urn."

"I'm so sorry. I just sold it. Two weeks is a very long time to wait and expect the merchandise to still be on the shelf."

Lilly looked around at the dusty store. "It seems to me that most of your merchandise has been here for quite some time. I should think that two weeks is a relatively short turnover for you."

"Oh, I don't know. Some things seem to fly through the store, barely touching the shelf before they are snatched away. Some things seem to have been sitting here since the beginning of time, as if the store had been built around them. That blue jug was a fine antique that was specially ordered and set aside for a Miss Maggie. She never came back for it so I sold it to a nice young man. You shouldn't worry. These things have a tendency to work themselves out."

"I am Miss Maggie. You just said so yourself."

"And you very kindly corrected me. I believe you said your name was Rose."

"Lilly. It's short for Lillian."

"Of course. But certainly not Maggie."

"No, not Maggie."

They stood staring at each other for a minute, the old man grinning while Lilly gritted her teeth.

"I wanted it."

"Then why didn't you buy it?"

"You wouldn't let me."

"That's silly. This is a store. I sell things to people who want to buy things. You must not have wanted it very much or I would certainly have sold it to you. Was it too expensive, perhaps?"

Lilly stared into his light blue eyes, trying to see if he was laughing at her. He was serious, almost too serious, with a child-like simplicity. She realized that arguing would be futile. She buttoned up her coat and turned to leave.

"Isn't there anything else you want?"

She turned around. "Not this time. You caught me last time in your crazy game." Lilly picked up a large colorful lollipop. "How about?" The storekeeper looked startled and shook his head. Lilly jumped across the aisle and picked up the kaleidoscope. "How about this lovely . . . ?" The storekeeper gasped, shaking his head vigorously. "What's the point? What kind of crazy store is this? Oooof!" Annoyed with herself for forgetting how obnoxious he was, she turned again to storm out of the store.

He coughed. "Excuse me, Miss Maggie."

She spun around, furious. "What?"

He seemed embarrassed and confused, reluctant to speak. "I was just wondering . . ."

"Yes?"

"Who took the ribbons from your hair?"

She stomped over to him, poking him in his chest. "You are a crazy old man."

She turned and lunged for the brass doorknob, twisting it sharply. The brass became liquid in her hand. It flowed around her wrist and solidified, locking her arm in an icy grip. Just as she was ready to scream, she was overcome by emotion as an image came to mind of herself as a young girl, sitting in front of a mirror, feeling her mother's soft fingers weaving ribbons into her braided hair. The memory was so strong it was as if she were actually there, by her mother's knees, feeling her warm breath. She felt so special, each touch of her mother's fingers like a loving caress. Suddenly, she felt transformed, seeing herself in the mirror as her mother had seen her, as a beautiful princess. Skipping off to school, she was smiling as she thought of the blond-haired boy she had a crush on. Then, she saw herself running home from school, crying, her hair loose, and the ribbons left behind. Her mother had scooped her up into her arms, hugging her. "Who pulled the ribbons from your hair?" Between sobs she told her mother about a bully who tormented everyone. She blinked her eyes and watched as a tear dropped from her cheek, falling slowly to the grimy floor. Who had pulled the shiny ribbons from her hair? She remembered how the blond boy laughed, his cute mouth twisted into a cruel smile as he and the bully yanked out the ribbons, ignoring her cries of pain.

Lilly looked up to see the shopkeeper reflected in the glass of the door. She turned. He stood behind the counter and seemed to grow until he filled half the store, glowing, while the rest of the store grew dark. His bright blue eyes were fixed on her like laser beams.

"Will you run from me? Do you dare? Would you run from the only thing that stands between you and a life without meaning? I am the Hope Merchant. You believe that you come here to buy trinkets, objects, and pretty little distractions. The hope shop seems quaint to you. Yet when you leave my store you have left richer by far, whether you know it or not. I give you trinkets because you don't want to see the truth."

Lilly wanted to yell out in anger but instead, her voice shook in fear, absorbed by the shop's walls. "I see the truth. The truth is that you are totally insane."

He shook his head sadly, and when he spoke, his voice echoed as if he were standing in an enormous cave. "My poor little Maggie, you aren't ready yet. Your eyes see objects on a shelf, but you are totally blind to a part of your heart that you have hidden from yourself. Every time you leave my store, old dreams and hopes long abandoned reawaken and struggle for your awareness. You have chosen a most minimal existence in the cold winter of life, and your imagination is a bleak and empty field where joy and enthusiasm cannot flourish. Sometimes you have a brief glimpse of something more for yourself, but most of the time it lies buried. Sometimes, on a spring morning, you suddenly have an urge to have a picnic with a dear friend whom you have yet to meet. Sometimes you have a silly urge to walk barefoot, listen to poetry, take a long walk alone in the forest, and maybe even burst forth in song."

Angry tears blurred her vision. "Barefoot walks? Poetry? You have the wrong person. I am an accountant. I crunch numbers. Your lousy little shop isn't worth one page on my balance sheets."

His smile grew. "My merchandise is worth more than all the gold in the world because a man can dream of greater things than his hands can reach. Yet what do I sell? Wishes? Hope? They are less than nothing. They are what you don't have. They are your weaknesses. They are the things that you fear you will never be able to achieve. So you wish. So you dream. And your wishes and dreams take on a life of their own, continuing to grow until they are larger than the dreamer. They are your darkness, your shortcomings, everything you lack. But they are also your strengths and the wrinkle in your soul that redeems the human spirit. I ask 'Can I help you?' knowing that I am the only one who can. You came to me without dreams, without hope. Shall I give you a dream so large that it looms over your head like a mountain too high to climb, leaving you frostbitten and broken in the middle of the trail? Or shall I grant you a small wish, a sweet little dream that will gently awaken the child in you who still remembers how to hope?"

"Nothing has happened to me. My memory is perfect and I am the same as I have always been."

"Oh really? What has happened to you Lilly? Have you forgotten the grandmother who smelled of vanilla and taught you to lick the drop of nectar from the honeysuckle blossom? Have you forgotten the grandfather who called you Maggie in his lilting Irish accent?"

"What? How did you . . . ?" Memories came at her in one big rush. Her grandfather had called her Maggie, in memory of his younger sister. After her grandfather passed away, there was no one to remember the long gone sister and the pet name had faded away.

He continued, ignoring her half-hearted protest. "Have you forgotten your dreams? Have you forgotten the one dream, the most special dream? Remember how you hid it away from the bitter old teacher who took your poetry and scribbled all over it in red ink? The wise little girl, who mourned the grandfather, knew that they would come in the middle of the night to steal her dreams, every last one. They would empty her hope chest and refill it with the dry sand of 'realistic and proper ambitions'. Wishes are like witches, they told her, and should be burned before they cast their ugly spells. She knew they would come and destroy her dreams, so she took the most precious one and hid it where no one would ever look. But she hid it too well. She hid it so well that even she couldn't find it years later when she needed it the most. The little girl tossed and turned in her bed at night, searching her dreams for the key to a memory she could no longer find. One night, the little girl knew that she couldn't hold on any longer. She must become a woman and forget her dreams forever. That night, from within a deep sleep, she sent a letter to me, asking for help, entrusting me with the safety of her last, and dearest dream. I have come to return the dream that was lost to the little girl. After all this time, after she has squandered so much and had even more stolen from her, will she still accept it? Will she still recognize it as her own? Has her heart grown a shell around it so thick that nothing can penetrate it? Or will the shell fall away like the hard covering around the seed that has sprouted?"

He held out an open hand with something small in it. She tried to identify it, but her eyes were full of tears and her vision was blurred. His voice took on a lilting Irish accent. "Take it, my wee lassie. Take it, Maggie Mae."

Freed from the brass claw, she reached out, snatching the object, and ran from the store. She ran down the darkened street, not stopping until she stood panting, safe inside her apartment, leaning against the locked front door. She held up her hand and opened her fingers to find a tiny blue glass box, shaped like a heart. Perched on top, legs grasping the silver metal frame, was a butterfly made of twisted gold wire and clear glass. Held up to the light, the glass glittered with rainbow sparkles that changed design as the box tilted. The wings, held by tiny springs, fluttered gently in her hand. She slid to the floor, careful not to drop the small package. She sat on her knees, crying, trying to call forth memories of a grandfather who passed away when she was still a child. Snatches of memory came to her, rough hands, the smell of pipe tobacco, and the accent she believed was a secret language he used just to speak to her. She stayed on the floor until her tears ran dry and she was empty of memories. She went into her bedroom and lay down, falling asleep in her business suit.

MR.
WILLARD
BIGGINS

The next morning, she was late for work for the first time in almost two years. She put the heart-shaped glass box with the butterfly in the middle of her desk. She tried to remember the exact words of the Hope Merchant. She had all but forgotten her grandfather. No one else ever called her Maggie and she had long since buried the memories associated with that pet name. She remembered her tiny hand disappearing into her grandfather's large rough hand as they walked together. Family lore related how he had been a carpenter in the old country but couldn't find work when he came to America. Eventually he landed a job as an iceman, driving a truck and delivering large blocks of ice.

How strange that would seem to people today who have refrigerators that dispense ice at the press of a button. She had vague memories of his lilting, gravelly voice coming to her through the dark as she lay in bed, telling stories of fairies and 'the wee ones'. She tried remembering something she knew was important, but her attempts were interrupted by a knock at her office door. She put her hands over the tiny glass butterfly box as the door opened and Willard stepped in carrying a box of files.

She was feeling tired and drained but she tried to sound crisp and professional. "Can I help you, Mr. Biggins?"

"Yes, Miss Preston. I collected the copies of the files you needed from the other departments. I need to know which of these files are relevant and which need to be returned to the other departments."

She had not expected him to finish collecting the files until the afternoon. She would need to overcome her fatigue and stop thinking about the crazy incident at the shop.

"Thank you, Mr. Biggins. Please leave the box by the door. I'll return them to you as soon as I've looked through them."

He put the box down. "I was wondering if I could speak to you for a moment." She considered telling him that she was tired and would rather not deal with people this morning but realized that her position as department head didn't afford her that luxury. She nodded and he blurted out, "Do you have to call me Mr. Biggins? I'd much prefer being called by my first name."

"Of course, if that is what you prefer." She began to feel awkward, holding her hands together in the middle of her empty desk. It must be obvious to him that she was hiding something. "Is that all?" He seemed indecisive, stopping in the doorway and turning to face her. He opened his mouth to say something but stopped.

"Would you prefer that I call you by your first name?"

She frowned. "I prefer being called 'Miss Preston'. I feel that it is more appropriate given the nature of our working relationship."

He frowned. "Sure." He looked past her and said, "It's almost ready to bloom."

Startled, she twisted around to look over her shoulder. Her plant had grown another two inches overnight. It was still only one slender stalk with two leaves, but at its peak was a tiny bud, tightly closed. She hadn't even noticed the plant when she came in this morning. She quickly turned back to face him.

"Yes, I guess it is. Will that be all? I really must be getting to those files."

He hesitated again but finally left.

Sorting through the box to make sure it contained all the necessary files, Lilly realized that one very important file, from the regional sales manager, was missing. She was ready to jump up and reprimand him when, chagrined, she realized she had neglected to include it on the list. She went to see Sally in the sales office. Sally and Lilly had been close friends when Sally's boss was an up-and-coming executive and Lilly was trying to get a date with him. The up-and-coming exec had up and left, and their friendship faded into a nodding acquaintance. The secretary handing Lilly the file said, "Was that your new assistant that was just up here?"

"Yes."

"He's cute. Don't you think?"

Sally, recently married to a bearded, classical guitarist was clearly hinting at Willard as a prospect for her. But Lilly disapproved of Sally's taste in men. Her husband was attractive and pleasant to chat with at the occasional office party, but marriage was a serious arrangement and a woman needed to be responsible about her future. Classical guitar was hardly a promising profession. Sally was popular and Lilly was sure that this would be the beginning of the new topic of office gossip, spicy stories about the spinster boss abusing her power over the mountain man hunk. Lilly couldn't bear the thought that she would be the butt of silly jokes. Certainly the match was absurd, but she could practically write headlines for an imaginary office newsletter, posting the scuttlebutt above the coffee machine. Lilly, the perennial passed-over-for-promotion wannabe, hooking up with a burly Neanderthal never-gonna-be. Lilly almost huffed. "It's not something I think about. Good day."

She was still steaming when she got back to her office. She tore into her work and spent the morning fighting back fatigue and an unusual desire to run away from the office and never return. Rather than spend lunch in the company cafeteria, she put on her coat and slipped out of the building. A light rain was falling interspersed with snowflakes. She avoided the local restaurants where she might encounter her co-workers. Instead, she lifted up her collar and wandered, gazing into store windows.

One store's name was written in rainbow colored letters, "Deeply Dreaming of Blue." She always felt uncomfortable passing by this store. The name seemed to be a code understood by some alternative-lifestyle subculture, making fun of conventional people like her. The store sold crystals, statuettes of unicorns, wizards and guardian angels, guidebooks to self-acceptance and forgiveness, tarot cards, and a surprising array of eye-catching exotica. She had never gone in but always stopped outside to listen to the snatches of Celtic fusion music and smell the incense that wafted out whenever customers opened the door. She dismissed the store as being a cheap Mecca for adherents of the latest trend in New Age consciousness parading as spirituality. Seahorses and dragonflies never seemed to go out of style. Even so, a nagging feeling that she lacked the freedom of spirit to go in and shop plagued her. She became aware of her hand gently clutching the glass box in her coat pocket. A shudder ran up her spine. A gust of wind reminded her that winter would curtail her wanderlust, limiting her window-shopping to short spurts. She found herself inside the store before she realized that she had even moved.

She browsed absent-mindedly, just enjoying an unfamiliar, light-headed feeling of abandon, and stopped at a glass shelf with kaleidoscopes and Dragon Eye pendants. She touched a brass kaleidoscope, almost identical to the one in the wish shop. As her fingertips came in contact with the cold, oily metal, a small voice in the back of her mind reprimanded her, "I couldn't possibly . . ." She quickly withdrew her hand, immediately angry with herself for doing so. The queer old man in that horrid little shop had caused her enough aggravation. She refused to be intimidated by him in his absence. She took the kaleidoscope and went to the cashier, a young woman with purple hair and wearing more earrings than Lilly had ever seen.

"Can you sell me this kaleidoscope?"

"Excuse me?"

Lilly placed the kaleidoscope on the counter. "Can you sell me this kaleidoscope?"

"Of course, I mean, that's why it's here. To be sold."

Lilly realized how strange her question must have sounded. "How much is it?"

"It isn't marked? How peculiar! Just a moment, I'll have to check." The girl pulled out a large notebook covered with iridescent rainbows and began to leaf through the pages. Lilly had a strange sense of déjà vu but she dismissed it.

"I'm sorry. A gentleman came in yesterday and put a deposit on it. I usually take things off the shelf when that happens. I don't know why I didn't. I can order another one for you, if you'd like."

Lilly felt slightly dizzy. She wanted to ask the saleswoman if he had been a strange old man with light blue eyes, but she decided she that didn't really want to know the answer.

"Can I interest you in anything else?"

Lilly looked at the saleswoman and then glanced outside. A light rain was falling. She had another twenty minutes until she was expected back at her desk, but she didn't want to wander around the city in the cold rain.

"I think I'll just look around."

She meandered through the shop until she found herself in front of an open display case with buckets containing hundreds of crystals and semi-precious stones. She picked up a handful of the stones and let them fall through her fingers, enjoying their cool, smooth surface and the solid clicks they made. For a moment she was reminded of the seeds in the Hope Merchant's dusty shop. She cupped her hands together and picked up another handful. As they ran through her fingers, one stone caught her eye, a heart-shaped piece of rose quartz. The color seemed to float just below the shiny surface with a streak of white that ran down the middle like a scar. She reached into her pocket, pulled out the glass box, and dropped the heart into it. It fit perfectly, leaving no space for the stone to rattle against the glass sides, as if the stone had been cut to fit the box, or as if the box had been formed to fit the stone. But how unlikely could that be, and even more unlikely for her to find it here. The voice in her head told her to put the stone back, throw away the glass box, and never return to the Hope Merchant or this ridiculous store with its silly voodoo trinkets. Disregarding her better judgment, she walked to the clerk and paid for the rose quartz heart. She stepped out, holding the small glass box in her hand, stuffed deep in her coat pocket. As she stepped over a puddle, she realized the rain had stopped.

Lilly arrived at her office late for the second time in the same day, but she was strangely apathetic about this lapse in her work ethic and gave no thought to the secretary checking her watch when Lilly walked past. She placed the little glass box in her top desk drawer and found herself smiling whenever she thought of it, sitting between her paper clips and spare pencils. The afternoon passed by like a dream, yet she was surprised to see that she had finished the entire pile of folders. Passing by Willard's tiny office on her way out, she noticed his door was open and he was still working at his desk. She tried to hurry past, but he looked up as she walked by and called out her name.

"Miss Preston, do you have a moment?"

She stopped and took a deep breath. "Yes?"

"I was just finishing up here. I was wondering what you wanted me to do tomorrow."

"I finished up the rest of the folders. It should be enough to keep you busy until tomorrow afternoon. We should meet before lunch to discuss the next phase of the project."

Willard shuffled the papers on his desk, avoiding her gaze. "Ummm . . . Why don't we meet over lunch tomorrow? I know a great place."

She hesitated. Could it be that this . . . Willard, was asking her out on a date? Her first impulse was to turn him down flat, but perhaps it was an innocent invitation to discuss business over lunch. Turning him down would make her look foolish. She was unsure of herself. It had been so long since a man asked her out that she might not even recognize an invitation when it happened. Social situations were always uncomfortable but had become even more so, as she became more reclusive. Even socializing at work had become confusing, as she agonized over the correct protocol with her subordinates. It seemed easier to just keep to herself. Before long the other women in the office got the message and even the friendliest among them no longer made any effort to include Lilly in social activities and events. "Yes. That would be acceptable." She turned and left before he could offer to walk her home or something equally embarrassing.

On the way home, she stopped to buy a romance novel by one of her favorite authors. She hurried past the alley, promising herself that she would not look, but she couldn't resist a quick glance. She had vowed never to set foot in the Hope Merchant's store again but she was angry, and felt like giving that strange old man a piece of her mind. She strode into the alley, and stopped at the dark storefront. She considered turning around but a single light bulb glowed over the door as a challenge to her resolve. She grasped the brass doorknob. The locked door frustrated her, but she was a bit relieved that the doorknob didn't grab her back as she let go. She peered in but saw nothing, except perhaps a faint glow where the entrance to the back room should have been. Feeling disgruntled at not being allowed to vent her anger, she turned and strode away, swearing that she would never set foot in the absurd store again.

She arrived at work her usual forty minutes early and hurried past Willard's open office door, catching a glimpse of the semi-shiny top of his balding head. He started to look up as she walked past, but she doubted that he saw her. She put the glass butterfly and the quartz heart inside her top drawer and got to work. She was hoping that Willard had forgotten their lunch engagement or simply dropped the whole idea. He didn't enter her office all morning. She hoped that she could slip out for lunch before he spoke to her. Sally stepped into Lilly's office half an hour before lunch to drop off a request from her boss. As she turned to leave, she looked over Lilly's head.

"What a pretty flower!"

Lilly panicked. She had neglected the seed for several days, forgetting all about it because of her preoccupation with the glass butterfly box and the rose quartz heart. She turned and saw that the bud had indeed blossomed into a tiny but beautifully formed flower.

Sally came around the desk and stood next to Lilly to get a better look. "What kind of flower is it?"

Lilly's first impulse was to remind Sally that she was a very busy department head and not a florist when it struck her that she knew the answer to Sally's question. She recognized the tiny flower from her mother's garden, planted especially for her. Her reply came as a whisper. "It's a trumpet lily."

"I've never seen one so small and so perfect before. It's a miniature just like one of those bonsai trees. And where did you get this beautiful vase?"

Lilly found herself staring, open mouthed, at the blue porcelain pot. "I . . . I found it at a store near my house."

When Sally finally left, Lilly carefully picked up the pot and inspected it. There was no doubt that it was the same one she had seen in the Hope Merchant's store. Had he been to her office? She should have been angry, but she smiled despite herself. The pot was even more beautiful now with the tiny lily growing out of it. Willard stepped into her office carrying a small daypack.

"Are you ready to go?"

"I think maybe it would be better if we stayed near the office. This project is too important to be taking time off."

Willard looked at her for a moment. "Aren't we ahead of schedule?"

"Yes, but . . ."

"Don't we deserve an hour away from our desks?"

"Yes, but . . ."

"Do you like the pot I got for your flower?"

"Yes, but . . ." Lilly was stunned and stopped to absorb what he had just said. "You got me the pot?" He smiled shyly and nodded. "Where did you get it?"

His gray eyes dropped for a moment. "An antique shop not far from where my mother works sells the nicest little knick-knacks. Do you like it?"

Lilly imagined Willard wandering around her neighborhood and poking around in that strange shop. She shuddered to think that she might have bumped into him after working hours.

"Well? Do you like it?"

"Yes," she admitted grudgingly. "It's lovely. I was looking to buy one just like it."

He laughed and she was surprised that his laugh was deep and pleasant. "Fine. Then let's go celebrate."

"Celebrate what?"

He smiled, his eyes twinkling, "We can celebrate the good work we have done on the project up until now."

"I don't think . . ."

"You're right. We are going to celebrate the emergence of a brand new lily into the world." He walked around the desk and took the flowerpot from the shelf. Lilly, surprised once again by his thick and muscular arms, was suddenly uncomfortable to be standing so close to him. He walked to the doorway of her office and turned.

"Shall we go, Lilly?"

"What about my plant? Aren't you going to put it back?"

"Not at all. It obviously needs fresh air and sunshine almost as much as we do."

She followed him down the corridor, forgetting her overcoat and also forgetting to object to his using her first name. She wanted to go back for her coat; the morning had been dark and cloudy, threatening rain. But once outside, she was surprised to see the blue sky breaking through the clouds. The air was warm with only the slightest hint of yesterday's chill. He led her to the park. She was strangely pleased with such a glorious day outdoors that would normally have passed her by. People strolled around the park and Lilly thought how days like this used to aggravate her. The office seemed to grind to a standstill with the arrival of nice weather. She was a bit put out when Willard led her to the top of a grassy knoll overlooking the duck pond. He carried the flowerpot from the office. She was anxious watching his large, callused hands grip the delicate blue porcelain pot. His grip was strangely gentle, surprising her, and the flower arrived safely, seeming to perk up in the sun.

"Is this the restaurant you had in mind?"

Willard smiled. "I come here all the time. The service is definitely lacking but you can't beat it for atmosphere."

"How's the food?"

Still smiling, he pulled a blanket out of his pack. "You tell me after dessert." She helped him spread it out, but he insisted that she sit down while he served. She felt strange trying to find a dignified way to sit on the blanket. She gave up after a few minutes, taking off the jacket of her business suit and lying down on her side. Willard gently placed the pot in the middle of the blanket. He pulled out small containers of food and a bottle of white wine. He even packed plates, wine glasses, and silverware. She sipped her wine, amazed. She didn't usually indulge but she found it to be refreshing and light. She picked up the bottle and read the label as he served food onto her plate. The label read 'Chateau Willard' and there was a picture of a man standing in front of a rustic cabin waving. The label had been printed out on a low-end printer but the picture was hand-drawn in crayon. She looked up to find him smiling as he topped off her glass.

"Chateau Willard?"

"I have a little cabin in the mountains that I built myself. Nothing too fancy but when I moved in, I found wild grape vines. I cultivated them and make wine. I usually get a couple of dozen bottles every year. It doesn't take too much effort and it is usually quite nice. This year was especially good."

"Where did you learn to make wine?"

"My grandfather used to make wine, but he passed on when I was still young. I read a little and jumped right in. The first couple of years were awful, but I think I finally got it right. Do you like it?"

She took another sip. "Yes. You're right. It's really quite nice." That would explain his muscular arms and calloused hands. She found herself wanting to say more but stopped herself. "Could we get down to business?"

"Shouldn't we eat first?"

She looked down at her plate and was surprised to see it beautifully arranged, as if a chef had just been at work. The food looked wonderful and reminded her of a meal at a fancy gourmet restaurant. She looked up to see Willard's amused smile.

"Cooking is a hobby of mine. I am a bachelor who likes to eat well but I have a limited budget. I don't like restaurants very much anyway. They are usually stuffy and pretentious. I enjoy cooking but I don't usually get a chance to cook for anyone beside myself. That doesn't work well for me. I think I enjoy cooking more than I enjoy eating. I guess I'm a loner pining for guests."

Lilly, realizing she was starving, forgot all about business and enjoyed every bite. Indian summer was making a belated appearance, and it was pleasant to just sit back in the sun and watch the people in the park. How long had it been since she felt like a participant rather than an outsider? She was surprised when Willard poured out the last drop of wine into her glass. She was barely aware that she had been drinking at all. She felt a little tipsy and a bit drowsy so she lay back and watched the clouds drift overhead.

"Willard." Her tongue felt heavy and she had to struggle not to slur her words. "You seem like a pretty sociable guy and you don't seem to be too much of a loser, I mean loner."

"Thank you. It's actually my life's ambition, to not be too much of a loser. Or a loner. When I graduated college, I got an award for the guy most likely to not be much of a loser. I think maybe you've had a little too much Chateau Willard."

"No, really. I mean it. Okay. Maybe I wouldn't be saying this if I didn't drink three glasses of wine."

"Four."

"Okay, four. But it's true. You finished those files very fast and you seem to be pretty good at your job. Thanks to you, we are going to finish a week early. Next Friday you can say goodbye and never be bothered with this corporate stuff ever again and return to making wine."

"Is there a problem with that?"

She flipped over onto her side and looked him in the face. "Yeah. Why are you just a loser of a bookkeeper? At your age you should be head of a department somewhere. I could understand it if you were incompetent or lazy, but you're not. What's the deal? Are you afraid of success? Can't deal with the stress?" She surprised herself that she was so outspoken.

He packed up the dishes, avoiding her gaze. "None of the above. It just isn't important enough to me to dedicate all my energy and time just to make more money. What I do in the office doesn't do much for me in ways that I find lasting or significant. Being a temp suits me just fine. I take a job when I need one and do my best until it's over."

"Come on, Willard. Be serious."

He glanced over at her but continued with the dishes. "I am."

"What else is there? A career is just about the most important thing a person can put his mind to. It's what you do with most of your time and energy."

He looked at her sharply for a moment. "Not me. A few weeks here and there are quite enough for me. Enough to pay the bills. More than that and it gets in the way of things that are really important to me." He zipped the backpack and sat down on the grass. His gray eyes made her giddy and uncomfortable. "Are you serious? Is work that important to you?"

She picked up her wineglass, hoping to have a few sips to delay her answer, but the glass was empty. She hesitated before answering. "Yes."

"Do you have a hobby?"

She winced. "I read a lot. It doesn't compare to making wine, gourmet cooking, and building cabins."

"I also spend a lot of time meditating."

"You mean like yoga?"

"No, not always. I spend a lot of time walking in the woods, working in my garden, teaching myself how to do things like carpentry and sewing."

"And making wine."

"Yes, that too. I also spend a lot of time with my family."

"It sounds like a full schedule."

"It is. What about you?"

She flipped over onto her back again, staring up at the clouds. "What about me? I am the head of a department."

"Is that it?"

"It's enough."

"Is it really?"

She rolled over onto her stomach so she could look at him. "It's a full schedule. It certainly pays more than making wine, and staring at clouds. Or temping as a pocket calculator."

"I am sure it does. But is it enough?"

"No, of course not. I want to move up the ladder."

"Is that it? What if you get to the top of the ladder and the only thing you find is more ladder? Or a bigger fall with no one to catch you?"

"I'm quite happy with my career." She was beginning to feel defensive.

"You know, you're surprised that a man like me is satisfied with no great career advances. I'm kind of surprised that a woman like you would be satisfied with just that."

"Why?"

"You are a beautiful and caring woman whose heart is suffering, trying so hard to stay warm in the cold world you've built for yourself. You've bought into a system that doesn't sustain you in the ways that matter deeply."

Lilly felt the wine drain out of her system. His words sounded so much like something someone else had once said to her. She sat up and searched for her coat. She fumbled around, searching under the blanket, before remembering she had left it at the office. "I think this conversation is over. I thank you for lunch. It was delicious, but if we aren't going to keep this on a professional level, I must insist that we leave. There is a load of work waiting for us at the office."

Willard put his hand on her arm. "I apologize. I didn't mean any offense. Why don't you ask me what you were going to ask me?"

"What was I going to ask you?" she snapped at him.

"You were going to ask me about the porcelain flowerpot."

She sat back down, all the energy drained out of her, feeling as if she would have fallen were it not for the light touch of his hand on her arm.

"He sold it to me."

She heard a roaring in her ears. "Who sold it to you?"

"The Hope Merchant. He didn't say that it was for you but when I saw that your lily had bloomed, I knew."

"You've been to the Hope Merchant?"

"Yes. We have an arrangement. Sometimes I build things for him, and sometimes he gives me things. A lot of times we just sit and talk."

"That explains a lot. He's crazy and he nearly succeeded in making me crazy. I can see he was more successful with you."

Willard laughed. "Just the opposite! He's the sanest man I've ever met since my father died."

"Does anything . . . strange happen to you when you're there?"

"Yeah, sure. I feel really happy every time I walk through the door and I don't know why. Maybe it's the incense he burns."

"Incense?"

"Sure. Didn't you notice the smell when you walked in? It smells almost like burning pine logs in the fireplace. It reminds me of when my pop and I used to go up to the cabin to fish when I was a kid. I usually hate incense but this stuff smells nice."

She thought of the Hope Merchant and his cluttered shop. She thought of patchouli and wondered why she had never bought some for herself. Finally she stood up, nearly forgetting her shoes. The grass felt so good that only after taking a few steps did she realize she was barefoot. "I'm sorry if I was rude. Thank you for the picnic. It was lovely. Even so, we should be getting back to work."

They worked together for an hour, organizing the next stage of the project. Lilly was pleased at how easy it was to work with him and didn't notice that she forgot to put her business jacket on when she returned to the office. There were actually many things that Lilly didn't notice. She didn't notice that the blue porcelain pot had changed places and now sat in front of her, on a corner of her desk. Even stranger, the little heart shaped glass box with the butterfly had taken its place next to the blue vase, though she couldn't remember taking it from its hiding place. She also didn't notice that she no longer thought of Willard as a competitor out to steal her job. It was the last day of the workweek so she checked their progress against her project timeline. They were even further ahead of schedule than she thought. She wouldn't have to come in on the weekend after all. She didn't know why, but she found herself dreading the weekend. It was still early but she had an errand to run. She packed up her desk and left the office, the receptionist watching her leave with a look of surprise on her face.

She walked straight to the shop, somehow knowing that it would be open. The store window was decorated with twinkling, colored lights. She pushed the door open and stepped inside, her nose twitching from the cloud of patchouli. The shopkeeper was hopping around, stringing more lights around the store. When he heard the bell over the door announce her entrance, he turned around and shouted, "Happy New Year!"

She tried to restrain herself, knowing that she would regret any comment she made. But she couldn't hold back and blurted out, "New Year's is still a month away."

"I know that. Of course I know that. I was just practicing. Such an important day needs a lot of preparation. This was just a rehearsal." He started walking around the shop, taking down the decorations.

She watched him for a few minutes. "You gave my porcelain flowerpot to Willard."

He stopped taking down the lights and looked at her, and with an injured expression said, "You had a porcelain vase?" Lilly was determined to keep their exchange on a rational level.

"No, I wanted to buy one from you but you wouldn't sell it to me."

"So it wasn't yours?"

"No, it was here in the store."

"Why are you upset? If it was in the store, then anyone has the right to come in and buy it."

"Then why wouldn't you sell it to me?" Lilly was exasperated with his infernal word games.

"I wouldn't sell it you? How very strange."

"I thought so too."

"What did Mr. Willard do with it?"

"He gave it to me."

"How delightful! So what exactly is your complaint?" She opened her mouth but was unable to reply. "What can I help you with today?"

"I am looking for a brass kaleidoscope."

"How unfortunate. I just sold my last one."

"Who did you sell it to?"

"That's privileged information."

"So you won't tell me."

"Of course I will. But I wanted you to realize how privileged you are."

He went behind the counter and pulled out his enormous ledger. He closed his eyes and opened it, running his finger down the page blindly. "Aha! Here it is. I sold it to a friend of mine, a former apprentice who has a store in mid-town."

"What's the name of the store?"

"Hmm. 'Deeply Dreaming of Blue.'"

"I should have known. They don't have any. I checked."

"Of course they don't. That's why he needed to buy one from me."

"They had one but someone went in and put a deposit on it. You wouldn't happen to know anything about that, would you?"

"Actually, I do. I bought it."

"You sold it to them in order to buy it back."

"Correct. That is why I couldn't sell it to you."

"And since you needed to buy it back they couldn't sell it to me."

"Of course."

"Where is it now?"

The old man pulled an enormous feather duster from behind the counter and began dusting the shelves. "I sold it."

Lilly followed him. "Who did you sell it to?"

"That's privileged information."

"I'm privileged."

"Who said so?"

"You did."

He slammed the enormous book shut. "You aren't that privileged."

She glared at him overwhelmed by anger and fear as she realized how adept he was at playing with her mind. She turned to leave and was almost at the door when he called out to her in a sweet voice.

"Would you like a lollipop?"

She turned to face him. "Excuse me?"

He held out an enormous lollipop with swirling colors and a bright red bow. "Would you like this one?"

"You wouldn't let me have it last time I was here."

"That may be true or it may not, but now I am giving it to you."

"Why? What's different now?"

"I need a favor."

"Of course you do. What is it?"

"I need something delivered."

"I don't have time."

"Please?"

She let out a sigh. He was treating her like a child and whether by hypnosis or some other trickery, she felt powerless. It was as if he knew that his request would summon up the vision of her parents, who were very strict about respecting elders. The old man's eyes twinkled. She let out a deep breath. "Okay."

He clapped his hands. "Good." He reached under the counter and pulled out a box, wrapped like a present. "Be very careful. It is fragile and very expensive."

"What's in the box?"

"A kaleidoscope."

The box hung suspended between them, her hands just about to take it from him. She drew back. "You want me to deliver the kaleidoscope that I wanted but you wouldn't sell to me?"

"Of course not. That would be cruel and malicious. The kaleidoscope that I wouldn't sell to you, I sold to my friend at 'Deeply Dreaming of Blue.' This is the kaleidoscope I bought from him. You wanted to buy it from him, but he had already sold it to me. In the meantime, I sold it to someone else. Now, I need it delivered."

"Forget it."

"What about the lollipop? Don't you want it?"

He held the lollipop up to the light and twirled it around. She saw the blinking holiday lights reflected in the cellophane wrapper. The colors of the lollipop began to move across its surface, converging to make an almost recognizable face and then dispersed, only to merge together again. She wanted to leave but felt rooted to where she was standing. A voice came to her. It sounded like the Hope Merchant but she couldn't see his face to see his lips move. Everything outside of the lollipop seemed strangely blurred. Lilly was caught in a tide of emotions as strong as any undertow.

"My little Maggie, what have they done? They have turned your world upside down and made you afraid of your own heart and the truth you feel inside. They have told you that giving is bad and that only things you have earned are worthwhile. Don't you remember how much you loved big boxes tied up in ribbons? Don't you remember the little girl who spent all day making an 'I love you' card for her mother? You need to learn how to give and I can teach you. After you give, then you can begin to receive. The only thing the world ever taught you was how to take. They said that everything was buying and selling. They lied. Buying and selling isn't nearly enough. The clouds and sun give gifts to the earth, and the Earth pays them back with beautiful flowers. Learn to give and the world will become a warm and welcoming place."

The lollipop slowly twirled, the red lights twinkling along its surface. Lilly heard a voice gently calling her name, shifting from one ear to the other. She focused on the center of the lollipop where white petals encircled a bright yellow center. She could avoid dizziness if she counted the petals, ignoring the blizzard of fuzzy lights that spun in the background. Lilly shook her head attempting to think clearly when she realized that she was standing on the street. The lollipop was in her hand, held out at arm's length, the cellophane wrapper reflecting the colors of the setting sun. The package was tucked under her arm and the buttons on her half open overcoat were askew as if a child had buttoned it. She was halfway down the alley, in the middle of taking another shaky step when she turned and walked back to the Hope Merchant. The door was locked and the store was dark. Standing at the door, unsure of what to do next, she decided that she would deliver the package and then take a solemn vow never to return to the shop again. Her life had become topsy-turvy from the first moment she entered the shop. The old man drove her crazy; what was most frightening was the way he could affect her so strongly. Now she was carrying a package under her arm without any memory of having taken it. The Hope Merchant had neglected to tell her where to deliver it. "Ha!" she thought, "Even better." Placing the package on the ground in front of the door, she noticed a card taped to the top of the box and the name 'Bill' written in gold ink. A voice in her head told her to leave the package and go, but the same sense of polite obligation that had first brought her to the shop forced her to open the card and read the address written inside. She recognized the name of the street as being in a quiet neighborhood on the outskirts of town. The bus would take her there but it was a long ride. Even worse, she would be coming home late. She stood at the bus stop thinking that it would really be too late for her to deliver it tonight and maybe she should wait until tomorrow morning. She was still debating with herself when she stepped onto the bus. A romance novel from a hot new author sat untouched in her coat pocket as the bus rumbled across town.

The sun set and the night air was chilly. She checked the numbers on the houses and realized the bus had dropped her off half a block from her destination. A young girl was standing under the streetlight in front of what she thought was the correct address. Lilly approached the child and saw that despite being about ten years old, she was sucking her thumb. Lilly was an only child and always felt uncomfortable speaking to children. The girl looked like she had been crying and would begin again at any moment. Lilly wanted to cross the street to avoid the little girl, but the street was dark and she could not read the numbers on the houses.

"Excuse me. I'm looking for number eight Elm Street."

The little girl raised up a finger to point at the house in front of them, keeping her thumb firmly plugged into her mouth.

"Do you live here?"

The girl nodded mutely.

"Is there a man there named Bill?"

The girl nodded again and tears welled up in her eyes. Lilly became flustered, confronted with a strange child in tears.

"Could you give him this package?"

The little girl shook her head, tears now running down her cheeks. Lilly held out the package.

"Please."

The little girl shook her head and took her thumb out of her mouth. "Can't. I'm never going back. They don't want me."

"What's your name?"

The little girl shook her head. "My mommy said not to talk to strangers."

Without the thumb in place to hold back the rising tide, the little girl launched into a full-blown bout of crying. Lilly knelt in front of her and fumbled in her deep coat pocket for a tissue. The lollipop handle got tangled up in the tissue and came tumbling out onto the grass. Lilly held out the tissue but the girl stopped crying, her eyes glued to the enormous lollipop.

"Where did you get it?"

Lilly picked up the lollipop quickly, suddenly feeling silly to be in possession of such a thing. On impulse, she held it out to the little girl. "Would you like it?"

The little girl drew in her breath and took a step back. "I can't. It's the most beautiful lollipop I've ever seen. It must be for a fairy princess."

Lilly held it out to her. "Well it's magical, and it's only for a special little girl who truly is a fairy princess."

The girl shook her head. "They all said I was a baby and stupid and only stupid babies sucked their thumb." Her thumb disappeared back into her mouth.

Lilly was speechless. She had already struggled through a very strange day and now she had to deal with an emotionally challenged child, who might even be abused. She was tempted to run to the front door, ring the bell, drop the package in, and then dash for the bus without looking back. The little girl was looking straight at her, tears welling up again. Lilly's legs ached from kneeling. Suddenly Lilly felt a warm rush come over her as she remembered another girl, not quite so little, who had also run away.

"I don't think so. I think you're very special. Tell me, have you ever seen such a special lollipop?"

The little girl shook her head.

"Such a special lollipop is only for very special little girls."

The little girl's eyes opened wide as she slowly nodded.

"Someone sent me especially to give it to you. You must be very special otherwise you wouldn't be the one getting this lollipop. Isn't that right?"

The thumb came out of her mouth as she gave a gasp. "Is it really for me?"

"Of course."

"For now and for always?"

Lilly nodded. The girl reached for it and a smile broke across her face.

"I'm not a stupid baby?"

"Of course not. Stupid babies don't get lollipops like this. Everyone knows that."

The girl reached out but as her fingers touched the cellophane, she pulled back. "Mommy said not to take candy from strangers."

Lilly was ready to cry. For some reason, it was of infinite importance to her that the little girl take the lollipop. "We aren't really strangers."

The girl shook her head. "Mommy said."

"I know something about you that nobody else knows."

The girl looked reluctant. "What?"

"I know that you've always wanted a lollipop like this one but you never asked your mommy for it. I know that one time your mommy wanted to buy you one but you said 'no'. You were too afraid. It was too special."

The girl's hazel eyes opened wide. "How did you know?"

Lilly smiled. "Because we aren't strangers. I always wanted one also. That makes us friends. Friends always wish for the same thing." She held out the lollipop and the little girl took it, turning it around in her hand, watching the light reflect off the cellophane wrapping. "Can we show them now?"

Lilly nodded as the girl slipped her hand into hers. They walked up the path to the house. When they got to the front door, the girl pushed it open, pulling Lilly into the strange house. They stepped into a living room full of toys and small faces that looked up at Lilly, suddenly quiet in the presence of a stranger. The girl held up the lollipop for all to see.

"It's special," she proclaimed.

The children crowded around but were afraid to touch a lollipop that was certainly the biggest, most impressive piece of candy architecture any of them had ever seen. A young woman stepped into the living room.

"Can I help you?"

Lilly was embarrassed, realizing that she was standing, uninvited, in a stranger's living room. The little girl turned and faced the woman. "Mommy, this is my friend. She gave me this."

The lollipop was held up as a sign of Lilly's acceptability. "It's special."

The two women shared a look of embarrassed amusement. This seemed to put the girl's mother at ease. "Yes, it certainly is special."

Lilly felt the package under her arm and remembered her original reason for coming.

"I came to deliver a package. It's for Bill."

The woman gave her a strange look. "Bill? I'll go get him."

She turned and left before Lilly had a chance to tell her that she just wanted to leave the package and return home. She heard heavy steps coming down the stairway. She and Willard stared at each other for several moments, both too confused to speak.

THE
KALEIDOSCOPE

The little girl broke the silence. "Look, Uncle Willy. She brought me this. It's special."

"Yes it is." Willard smiled at Lilly. "Hello Miss Preston. What brings you to my neck of the woods?"

Lilly held up the package. "I was told to deliver this."

A puzzled look crossed his face. "What is it?"

"A kaleidoscope."

He laughed. "Now I understand. Mr. Meyer sent it over. It's the last piece I need."

"The last piece you need for what?"

A sly look came over his face. "It's something I'm building for him. It's for his back room. Would you like to see?"

Lilly's hesitation was overcome by her curiosity since she would probably never be allowed into the inner sanctum of the Hope Merchant's back room. "Yes. I would."

He led her outside to a large garage. They climbed a rickety set of stairs to his workshop. It was spacious and well ordered, smelling pleasantly of wood chips and lacquer. A welding machine stood in one corner and there was a small area for working with stained glass. An ornate highboy occupied another corner, nearly complete. In the middle of the room stood a large object covered by a sheet. Willard walked to the center of the room and pulled the sheet away, revealing what looked like an enormous antique radio with a translucent glass screen. He opened the back of the machine and made a few adjustments. He tore open the package Lilly had brought and produced the gleaming brass kaleidoscope, which promptly disappeared inside the contraption. He made a few more adjustments and closed the back panel, stepped to the front of the machine, and ran his hand lovingly over the deeply polished wood inlay. He seemed to have forgotten Lilly's presence until he turned to her and smiled.

"It's a beauty, isn't it?"

"Yes, but what does it do?"

"Would you like a demonstration?"

"Okay. If it isn't too much trouble."

"It's no trouble at all. I need a couple of photographs to make it work."

"What kind of photographs?"

"They have to be photographs of a loved one that has passed away."

Lilly felt her throat tighten up. "I don't happen to have one."

"A photograph or a loved one?"

He seemed adept at making Lilly feel defensive. "I don't make it a habit to walk around carrying old photo albums."

The gray in his eyes glowed, but the softness was gone. "Obviously. But I've noticed that you also don't make it a habit to walk around with loved ones. Do you have any? Is there a special agency where department heads hire actors to pose for their family albums? Maybe you can go there."

Her mouth fell open. "Mr. Biggins! That was entirely uncalled for." But she knew that his words were truer than he could have known. She wanted to leave before the tears came but it was already too late. Willard put his arms around her and she was overcome by an unfamiliar but wonderful feeling, the embrace of strong arms.

He whispered, directly into her ear, calming her sobs. "I'm sorry, but I think that was something you needed to hear. Besides, we aren't at work. And even if we were, I am no longer employed there. You aren't my boss here, so stop acting like it. This is my house and if I wanted you to leave, you would already be on the way out. I like you and I want to get to know you better. I don't know how to lie or play games, so there it is. I guess that's why the corporate world and I don't get along so well. I hate the business world, but I hate it a little less since I met you there. I think we have something we should talk about but that neither of us is able to say. I think Mr. Meyer asked me to build this machine for you just so that we could understand each other. You have no idea how much I need someone I can talk to. Or maybe you do already know how much." His voice trailed off, the words ending as embarrassment took over and the closeness built of the moment ended. She leaned away from him, feeling both relief and disappointment that his strong arms released her so readily.

He turned his back to her, his voice softer and tentative. "I have a few more adjustments to make before it's ready for a test run. My sister lives in town and is driving back home. Why don't you get a ride with her and come back tomorrow. I can let you try it then."

Lilly smoothed out her dress, searching her pockets for a tissue. "I appreciate the offer, but I don't think I can come back."

"I'll cook you a special meal."

"That's very sweet but . . ."

"I have a new batch of Chateau Willard that should be ready for tasting."

"I appreciate . . ."

He spun around, his eyes flashing. "No. Please don't appreciate something that you won't let yourself do or a kindness that you won't allow yourself to receive. I offered because I wanted to give. You won't owe me anything. The payback is in your company and any friendship that comes out of it. I don't keep any other kind of tabs. Please don't compliment me as a way of keeping me at a distance. It's not real, just falsely polite and I hate insincerity. There is only yes or no."

Lilly's immediate reaction was anger but then she realized that she had nothing to be angry about except her own painfully familiar insecurity. "Can I call you and let you know?"

"You can try but I don't usually answer the phone on the weekends."

"Do you ever take no for an answer?"

He smiled, and in spite of herself, Lilly smiled in return. "Of course, but not when it's dressed up in a suit and tie and pretty ribbons and made to look like a yes."

"I will try to make it. I mean it."

"Don't forget the photos."

Willard took her back to the house just as his sister was coaxing the children into their coats for the ride home. As she put on her coat, Lilly felt a small hand slip into hers. She looked down and saw the little girl holding her hand, clutching the enormous lollipop in her other hand. Lilly smiled at her, not knowing what to say.

The little girl smiled back. "My name is Maggie."

Lilly could almost hear the gleeful laugh of the strange old shopkeeper. "So is mine."

The girl's eyes widened. "Really?"

Lilly laughed. "Yes." They walked out to the minivan full of children, half of them already dozing. The front passenger seat was empty with enough room for Maggie and Lilly to squeeze in together with the seat belt over them. Maggie was already leaning her head against Lilly as they pulled out of the driveway.

"Mommy, her name is Maggie too. She came to bring me the lollipop. It's special. She said I'm not a stupid baby and that I'm special." Five minutes into the ride, all of the children were asleep.

The woman glanced at Lilly. "You are Billy's boss?"

"Do you mean Willard?"

She chuckled. "No one has dared to call him that since he was twelve. If you are given a name like that, you either wind up being tough or a loner."

"My guess is that Willard . . . Bill ended up being both."

"Bill? He is strong as a bull, but a loner? Not really. I can't figure out how he meets so many people. You never know who's up in that workshop with him. He seems to know a lot of artist types. He also keeps in touch with most of his former schoolteachers and some of his college professors. Not to mention the time he spends with my kids and their friends." They drove for a few minutes in silence. "Bill told me that your name was Lilly."

"Yes, but when I was a child, my grandfather gave me the nickname 'Maggie'. I haven't been called that in years. Your daughter reminded me that we have something in common. She reminds me of myself when I was that age. I just hope . . ." A truck swerved out from the opposing lane, cutting Lilly off. Her thoughts remained unspoken as they drove on in silence.

Lilly made herself a cup of tea, and settled into bed with her new romance novel. She forced herself to finish the first chapter before she would try to sleep. The book was a big disappointment. The basic plot was predictable, every nuance hinted at in the first thirty pages. Like so many others she had read, it was a story of impossible love that would culminate in an improbable but predictable moment of ecstasy. Lilly already knew that every obstacle that stood between the hero and heroine would be overcome, for nothing stands in the way of true love. She promised herself halfheartedly that she would finish the book the next day.

The next morning, she started reading the book with her coffee, but was bored and found herself eyeing the photo albums on the shelf. She turned the pages, surprised at how young her mother looked in most of them. She tried not to think of how young she herself looked in the photos because it only reminded her how time seemed to be racing by. She picked up the album and put on her coat, telling herself she was only going for a walk, to look at the pictures in the park and to get some fresh air. She tried not to berate herself for sitting down and taking a rest at the bus stop. It was another beautiful Indian summer day.

As she walked up the driveway, she heard banging coming from the workshop. She walked up the steps and knocked on the door. Willard opened the door, looking like he'd been out in the snow, his hair white with sawdust. Lilly was slightly disappointed that he didn't act at all surprised to see her. She thought to protest as he took the album from her but she was too slow. He sat down on a beautiful sofa that seemed to be halfway through refinishing and began to leaf through the album, resting it on an overturned milk crate. She considered sitting down next to him to explain the pictures but the section of the sofa that was cushioned seemed too small to hold them both without having to squeeze together.

"Is this you?" He pointed to a picture.

Lilly humphed and sat down, sitting uncomfortably erect, hoping her body language would tell him that he should keep his distance. She explained the pictures, her body relaxing as he turned the pages. When they got to the end of the album, Lilly wanted to turn back to the beginning and start again. So much of her life was glued onto those pages and it seemed like there were too few photos. She was sure there were some missing but she couldn't remember which ones. Willard picked up the album and carried it to the contraption, opening a panel on its side. He took pictures out of the album and slid them into clips mounted on black velvet. He lowered the ornate wood panel back into place and began to adjust the knobs. Finally, when he seemed satisfied with the settings, he placed a chair in front of the machine and waved Lilly into it. He gave her an antique microphone attached to the machine by a long cord. The microphone seemed heavier than she thought it should have been but she reasoned it preceded the invention of microchips. He put an oversized pair of headphones over her ears and handed her a heavy pair of vintage Red Baron goggles that she slipped over her head. The lenses seemed to be prismatic and initially made her a bit dizzy. With the goggles and the heavy earphones, she felt like an astronaut crammed into a tiny nose cone.

Willard walked across the room and closed the shades, the darkness intensified by some optical trick of the goggles. She heard him turning a crank, and then a whirring sound came from the machine. She jumped when his hands gently grasped the sides of her head and directed her gaze towards the screen mounted in the front of the machine. Stars leaped out at her and suddenly her whole field of vision was filled with a soft pearly glow.

An image appeared. Her mother sitting in her rocking chair, napping. Lilly smiled. She was familiar with the photograph. It was one of her first attempts at photography from when she was ten years old. She had caught her mother napping in her favorite chair on the front porch. This became her mother's favorite photo of herself. The optics somehow made it seem three-dimensional. The image flickered slightly and the field of vision was quite small but the effect was impressive nonetheless.

"Say something."

Lilly held the microphone up to her mouth and cleared her throat. The sound of her voice came over the headphones. "Testing one, two, three."

"No, not like that. Say her name."

"Abigail Rose Preston."

The image shifted. The goggles made Lilly dizzy as the image flickered.

"Say it again."

"Abigail Rose Preston."

The eyes of the image opened and her mother sat up in her chair. She turned her head, looking at Lilly, and blinked. Lilly jumped, her hand flying up to tear the goggles from her face. Willard gently caught her hand.

"Just talk to her. Say anything. Try and keep it light."

"You want me to talk to a . . . picture? Is this microphone even hooked up to anything?"

"Yes. Talk to her like you would to your mother. Just try it."

Lilly cleared her throat. Her mouth was dry and her throat had tightened up. "Hi, Mom." She felt silly.

The image blinked again and the lips began to move. Her lips stopped moving and a buzzing began in the earphones. Willard's blurry shape came into her field of vision, blocking off the image of her mother.

"There are still a few bugs in the system. This should fix it." The view cleared and she could see the image of her mother, waiting patiently, staring right at her. "Try again."

Lilly gripped the microphone, feeling her palms become sweaty. "Hi, Mom."

"Hello, Lillian. How are you?"

Lilly felt lightheaded. The voice that come over the earphones was her mother's. Willard put a steadying hand on her shoulder. "Answer her," he whispered.

She heard her own voice but wasn't sure she had actually spoken. "I'm fine, Mom."

The image of her mother began to rock gently, picking up the knitting that had fallen into her lap as she slept. Lilly could see the trees in the background moving in the breeze. "Are you really?"

"Yes, Mom. I'm still at my job and working hard."

Her mother pursed her lips and Lilly could hear the click of the knitting needles. Her mother concentrated on her knitting. "That's nice." The image blurred and returned.

"Mom?"

"Yes?"

"Mom . . . I miss you."

Her mother sat up in her chair, dropping the knitting into her lap. She smiled exactly the smile that Lilly had loved to see when she was a little girl. Though her mother had died less than a year ago, it seemed like forever since she last saw that particular smile. "Thank you, dear. Remember . . . you were always . . . very special. Your father and I . . . knew that . . . from the moment . . . we first saw you. I wish . . ."

"Mom? What do you wish?"

Her mother opened her mouth to speak but the image froze with her mouth open to answer. The whirring of the machine turned into the clicking of gears not meshing and the image began to flicker and blur. Lilly thought she saw a tear in the corner of her mother's eye before the image disappeared and the screen became white. Willard raised the window shades and helped her remove all of the headgear. He handed her a tissue. Her hands were shaking as she wiped the tears from her cheeks.

He bent over the machine and began to tinker with it, his back towards Lilly. "I'm sorry you got interrupted. Like I said, bugs in the system. Look, I might be a while with this and then I have to get lunch together. Why don't you take a walk in the woods behind the house and come back in half an hour or so?"

As soon as she was enveloped in the shade of the forest, she leaned her forehead against the rough trunk of a tree and began to cry. After several minutes, she continued on, following a trail that led to a small creek and then down to a large pond. Gradually her strides became longer and her pace quickened. She had been dazed when she left, but a half an hour in the cool woods cleared her head and turned her cheeks red. Hunger drove her back to the workshop, where the machine stood covered with a sheet, and a rough oak workbench had been set for lunch, a meal even more impressive than his picnic fare. He told stories about his nieces and nephews, two sisters, and a brother. He was the third child and the most sociable and rambunctious of the bunch. Everyone expected him to marry an attractive, accomplished woman and do something exciting with his life, but their expectations went unfulfilled. Instead, he spent most of his time studying, formally and informally. He was constantly enrolled in college but not pursuing a degree. He took a wide variety of courses, anything that intrigued him. His brother and sisters were breeders, taking turns producing closely spaced children who loved to visit with Grandma and Uncle Bill. When he finished relating all this, he lapsed into silence, a half-smile on his face as if it were now her turn. Lilly felt uncomfortable at first, thinking that Willard expected her to respond in kind and open up about her personal life. She was relieved that he was comfortable with silence. She wandered around the shop, picking up the occasional tool. She put her hand on the polished wood of the machine.

"How does it work?"

"I don't really know. I followed the blueprints and instructions that Mr. Meyer gave me. The optics were installed in his shop and I have no idea how they work, even though I helped put them in. The audio is put together from an old phonograph that works off of wax cylinders, an old music box that was missing a few pieces, and an old telephone. I basically just built the cabinet and pieced it all together."

"How do you think it works?"

"I don't have any idea. That old music box was stuffed in a corner of his storeroom and covered in twenty layers of dust. I'm not sure that Mr. Meyer even knows how it works. Some might call it magic, some might call it worse. I don't care and I don't think it really matters anyway. There's no way anyone could build another, even if you could find the parts. And you weren't the first person to use it. You were the second. I was the first."

"After my dad passed away, I was a mess. He was everything to me. I was spending all my time alone and not feeling too good about it. So Mr. Meyer called me up and asked me if I would take a commission as a carpenter. I don't know how he found out about me. I had never worked as a professional carpenter before. I was all set to say 'no', but for some reason I found myself asking about the details and where to get the parts. When the machine was finished, I had to try it out so I used pictures of my dad. I was spending a lot of time with the goggles on, talking to my dad. It messed me up for a while. It became an obsession; at one point, I got angry and smashed the machine. It lay up here in a corner, broken. Little by little, I started going out. After all the talking I had done with my dad up here, I got used to the feeling and missed it when I broke the machine. I guess something was broken inside of me and needed some fixing. I don't know and I don't really care. What matters is that I'm a lot happier now and people are a lot happier to be around me. Eventually, I had to tell Mr. Meyer what I did to his machine but he didn't seem angry at all. He just asked me to rebuild it and told me to take my time. I was almost finished when I found out the kaleidoscope was broken. Mr. Meyer said he would get me another one, and here you are."

"Would it be okay if I stopped by to use the machine again?" Lilly lowered her eyes and blushed. She feared the answer might be important to her in more ways than one.

"Sure. Anytime you want."

His eager answer lit her defenses. He was presumptuous, perhaps even thinking she was attracted to him. Lilly came close to an angry speech about how her busy work schedule left no room for socializing. After a moment's hesitation, she realized that she would sound silly since she had suggested it in the first place. After another moment's hesitation she realized that she wanted him to think she was attracted to him.

"If you want to come and use the machine, feel free. I'll help you, no strings attached. But I've got to tell you the truth. I'll be looking forward to seeing you."

Her words seemed to have a will of their own. "Do you remember your dreams?"

Willard looked surprised but then he smiled. "Yes. Mr. Meyer had me start a dream journal. He said that without it, the machine wouldn't work."

She looked down into her almost empty teacup. "I still remember when they took my dreams away, and it has been a long time since I've remembered them. When I was a little girl, I used to wake up every morning and tell my mother about them. One day at school I told a dream to my friends, a sweet child's dream, and they laughed at me. I began not to believe in dreams, thinking it was better not to have them than to invite ridicule. I think it was then that I even began to resent my mother for not preparing me for such a cruel world. It's a dull ache that I've learned to live with. I still can't get it to go away and I can't ignore it anymore. Every time I've opened my heart and shared a dream, someone was always there to steal it, rip it out by the roots, not even leaving me a memory. How could they do such a thing? How can people touch my heart if they don't care, or when I didn't give them the keys? And I feel . . ." A sob stopped the flow of words and she watched a tear fall into the dregs of cold tea. "Perhaps I was an especially sensitive child. Over the years I have built a barrier around my heart to the point where I feel threatened by anyone who makes an attempt to break through. Now I can't even get in touch with my own feelings."

Willard moved his chair next to hers. She felt small and vulnerable, and though she tried, she couldn't lift her eyes to look at him. His voice seemed to come from far away. "I have something to tell you." He poured more tea, then stood and searched for something on a crowded shelf, returning with a large album. He opened the album on his lap. The pages were covered in colorful hand-drawn pictures and small handwriting in black ink. Willard read. "This is a story about a little boy, actually about a man who still thought of himself as a little boy because he was in search of his lost childhood. His name was Willard Ray Biggins. His name wasn't really Willard Ray Biggins but that is what every one called him. His real name was Will You Fly Up To The Sky, Are You My Friend, Ray Of Light, Big Heart Inside. Every year he would have a birthday party with all of his best friends. They would sing and dance and laugh but they wouldn't play games because, as everyone knows, when you become an adult you are not allowed to play games anymore except for games that aren't very fun. After everyone went home, he would clean up from the party. Then he would look through his house, peek in the closets, check the basement, and even make sure that nobody had climbed into the refrigerator. He drew the curtains so no one could see in and locked the door. Then he would take an ice-cream cake out of the freezer, put on a party hat, put long sparkly candles into the cake, and sit down to have his real birthday party. He would play all of his favorite party games like pin the tail on the porcupine and bobbing for marshmallows. It was not very much fun to play these games by himself but he always gave out prizes to the winners."

"His favorite game was Slay the Dragon. Now I am sure that you know how to play Slay the Dragon, but he played it differently. Most people want to be the brave knight who comes to slay the dragon and save the princess. Some people want to be the beautiful princess who is trapped and about to be eaten by the dragon. Some, who don't really understand how to play the game, want to be the king who sends the knight to slay the dragon and save his daughter, the princess. Willard always played the dragon, in a long green coat and big galoshes that were as big as a real dragon's feet. He even had a mask that covered his whole head and scared him when he looked in the mirror. Every year, he was the dragon. He would look at himself in the mirror scaring himself, and shouting out in surprise. Every year he would laugh at himself for being scared. He would search all over his house for the beautiful princess, jumping and twirling around to make sure the knight was not sneaking up on him with his sharp sword. He looked everywhere, in all of the closets, the basement, and even the refrigerator. He would run around faster and faster, looking for the princess. He called out to the princess but she would never answer. You see, he was not an ordinary sort of dragon. All that he really wanted to do was to hug the little princess and apologize. He wanted to explain to her that the world seemed to be full of nasty dragons that ate princesses, but that he was different. He wanted to explain to her that it was really her father, the king, who had her tied up and was the source of all her troubles. He knew that if there were no knights or sharp swords, no one would ever think to tie up princesses. Especially not a well-fed dragon on his birthday. So he would run around his house faster and faster but every year his party would end up the same. He would fall down exhausted in a corner and cry, wishing for a princess that never came."

"Did you write that?"

Willard shook his head, opening his mouth twice before an answer came. "My pops wrote this for my tenth birthday. I was having a rough time and he thought this would help."

"Did it?"

Willard laughed. "A bit. Pops and I were close but I don't think he knew the first thing about kids. From when I was a baby he thought God had given him a brand new best buddy. When I was six and he took me fishing the first time, my mom had to come up to the lake to bring me some juice. He thought that we'd just share his beers."

"How was that for you?"

"In some ways it was amazing. My sister was born when I was a year old so my mom was busy with the baby when it was time for me to go to sleep. My dad's idea of putting me to sleep was to lie me down on his belly and he would pass out. No bedtime story, no lullabies. I think he saw me as part of him, like an extra leg. He figured that when he went to sleep, I would go to sleep, too. Until I was ten, that's how I went to sleep. I would lie down on my parent's big bed, part of me on top of my dad, usually my head on his belly, listening to his dinner gurgle and slosh with his heart playing rhythm."

The story made no sense but something in it touched her and she was afraid of where it was taking her. It was carrying her forward against her will but she was afraid not to hear the rest of what Willard had to say. She wanted to yell for him to stop but instead she said, "That sounds nice."

Willard shrugged. "It was and it wasn't. Pops was always there for me. He understood me better than most dads understand their sons. If I misbehaved or threw a tantrum, he wouldn't hit me or get angry. Like if your leg gets hurt you don't get angry at it. I'd be throwing a fit and he would just scoop me up into his lap and hug me until my anger turned into tears. I never got punished. He would just hug me and tell me how sweet I was until whatever was making me angry went away."

"What could be bad about that?"

"It wasn't fair to raise me like that. I assumed the whole world was the same way, that we were all one big happy family. I hated sports because I could never understand why someone had to win and someone else had to lose. And when I started dating it was even worse. I wanted that same closeness and all the girls wanted was to have fun. They thought I was way too serious and intense. And they were right. As long as my dad was around, I never needed anyone else. I didn't have friends like the other kids. Money totally confused me. I just couldn't understand 'this is mine and that is yours.' If I had something nice, I naturally just wanted to give it away so that someone else could enjoy it too. That's why I studied accounting. I needed to learn that things weren't all just one big lump. I needed to learn limits. Accounting helped but I was lousy at business. If someone wanted something, I just naturally wanted them to have it. I stayed at home and never had to worry much about having enough money. I was fascinated by so many things I just jumped from one thing to the other. One week it was pottery and the next it was Zen philosophy and meditation. I never had time for a career because I was so busy learning all these amazing things."

"Like how to make wine and how to create gourmet meals."

"Yes. But like I said, I didn't need anyone else except for my dad. When he died, I lost half the world. I was angry. I felt he had lied to me, built up the world into the beautiful place where everyone loves each other. I couldn't find one other person who saw the world as I did. I tried dating but all the women treated marriage like an extension of their office. They were trying to make the best deal they could, trying to trade their good looks and career for some guy worth at least as much as them. It didn't matter who he was. It just mattered how his assets added up." Lilly felt uncomfortable as his words hit too close for comfort, but Willard seemed not to notice and continued talking. "I wasn't looking for the best or even the best I could get with whatever I had to offer. I was looking for the rest of me. I'm not perfect so there's no way she could be either. It's not a business deal. I can't trade up for bigger or better. I won't be disappointed that I didn't get enough for my money."

Willard suddenly remembered he wasn't alone and glanced over at Lilly. Her hands covered her face and for a few awful moments he thought she was laughing at him as her shoulders shook. "Are you laughing at me? I know I'm a little weird but . . ."

She pulled her hands away, tears streaming down her face. "No! All these things you're telling me, all these things that make you so strange and make it so hard for you, I've needed to hear them for so long. I'm so sick of having to prove myself on paper, to show that objectively I'm good enough just so that maybe someone will look at me. I am so sick of being so . . . alone. Your dad was right. I need to be part of someone else and I need him to be a part of me. If you're crazy, then a big part of me needs to be crazy too. But I am warning you, Mr. Willard R. Biggins, let me down even a little bit and I will rip you into pieces and feed you into my paper shredder."

He put his hand on the sofa cushion. She instinctively reached down and held it.

The dishes were washed and drying in the rack, and though Lilly couldn't remember getting up, she found herself on the couch again. Willard was sitting next to her and she placed his hand in hers, stroking the back of his hand to the rhythm of his voice.

"I've always enjoyed the simplest pleasures but I am missing what I need to be truly happy. I think I finally understand my dad's story. I think it was a message he hid away for me to hear today." He lifted his hand and wiped the back of her hand against his cheek. She was surprised to feel it damp from tears. "I don't need you to act like a princess. You already are. I don't want to go out and slay a dragon because I've realized that any dragons are of my own making. I just want to sit with you and listen to all the dreams that come back to you now that the door is open. I want to encourage your dreams with stories that flow from the springs of my heart and that flourish in the sunshine of your beautiful smile. I want . . ." As if it were his turn to be embarrassed, he stopped speaking and she felt him pull his hand away. She held on, wrapping his calloused hand in both of hers. "If you want, I could leave the machine on the settings you need and show you how to insert the photos and operate it yourself. It's not at all complicated. That way, I don't have to be here when you use it. Please, take my extra key to the workshop. I remember how much I wanted to be alone after I first used the machine."

Lilly felt strange, a dull roar in her ears, as if a great wind had suddenly died away, leaving her adrift on a flat sea. She let his hand go. "That sounds very good. I wouldn't want to put you out in any way." She realized that her voice had taken on the same tone she used at work, making her wince at how different she sounded barely one minute ago. She felt like she had exposed another, totally different personality that was struggling with a stranger that had posed as her identity for so many years.

After putting the dishes away, they went out to the backyard for iced tea. She was afraid that it would be awkward, being together after the deep feelings they shared.

She was aware of the key in her pocket as they walked around the garden and she found the presence of it comforting. Their conversation was light and pleasant, and the silences deep and comfortable. She was surprised to see the sun sink below the trees as they sat on the porch swing. The stars came out and the air turned brisk when Lilly stood to leave, saying that the bus ride home was long and she was tired. The next day, while her paperback romance lay untouched on her night table, Lilly went for a long walk in the park. For the first time, she didn't resent all the families and couples strolling around her.

Monday morning, Lilly jumped out of bed, arriving at her usual early hour but with an uncharacteristic eagerness. By ten o'clock Willard still wasn't in the office. Her secretary stuck her head in saying that Lilly's boss had called asking her to come up to his office. Her usual feelings of dread were gone, replaced by an emptiness caused by Willard's absence. It worried her that he hadn't called.

Her boss seemed anxious. "Lilly, I got a call this morning from Mr. Biggins. Can you finish the project without him?"

Lilly was taken aback. "It will be difficult. He is an efficient worker and a pleasant man to work with. I was hoping we might find him a permanent position in the company."

He raised his eyebrows at the suggestion. Lilly felt her cheeks blush. "He seems to feel that it should be simple enough for you to finish without him. He said that you have been ahead of schedule and all that remains is to double check the figures."

"That is more or less correct. Did he give a reason for not wanting to stay with me . . . I mean, with the company?"

"He said that a new work opportunity arose of a more permanent and lucrative nature. I thought it only proper that we honor his request since we can only promise him work until the end of the week. Unless you have a creative idea how to fit him in."

"No, I can't see any way to fit him in permanently. He isn't the corporate type." She hesitated. "Did he say where he was going to work?"

He looked at her for a moment before answering. "I didn't think it necessary to ask since he didn't request a reference. He mentioned something about a training position in marketing, but he didn't say where. I think it had to do with the wine industry."

Lilly thought she caught a whiff of patchouli mixed with pine. "I should be okay working without him."

He made a few notes and looked up. "Thanks very much for the good work. The board is very impressed. Perhaps you could help me prepare a presentation?"

Lilly thought for a moment and shook her head. "Actually, I was hoping to take some vacation time after this project is finished. I have several weeks coming to me."

He looked surprised, as it was so atypical of Lilly. "Of course. I think we could manage without you. Where are you thinking of going?"

"I . . . I don't know yet. I'm checking out the possibilities."

"Good. It sounds like a great idea."

Lilly was too preoccupied with her own thoughts to notice her boss's smile.

The rest of the week was full of long workdays. Lilly attacked the files with a fury and finished the project on Wednesday night. Thursday evening, before she left her office, she called Willard at home and got his answering machine. She hung up without leaving a message, put on her coat, then took it off and dialed his number again, this time leaving a message.

"Hello, Mr. Biggins. I just wanted an opportunity to tell you that I think you are very talented and a hard worker. It was a pleasure working with you and I . . . I look forward to working with . . . seeing you again. If you ever need anything, a reference perhaps, feel free to contact me. It was also a pleasure getting to know you on a . . . personal level."

She hung up, got her coat, opened the door, and then closed it, and returned to the phone.

"Hello, Willard. I would like to stop by Saturday afternoon, if it's okay. I will need your help setting up the machine and . . . would appreciate if you could stay with me after I finish. I could use your advice and . . . friendship. If it isn't a good time, you can call tomorrow and leave a message with my secretary. I . . . I am looking forward to seeing you."

Saturday afternoon she was standing on the doorstep listening to the sounds of the children. She knocked gently, sure that no one would hear. A short form appeared on the other side of the screen and the little hands pushing the door open were Maggie's.

"I knew it was you. Uncle Bill told me you were coming. He didn't tell anyone else, only me. I'll go tell him you're here." She turned and ran, leaving Lilly standing on the outside of the screen door. Lilly knocked again. This time an old woman opened the door. Lilly thought she recognized the woman but, before she could place her, the woman smiled and said, "It's good to see you again, so I can thank you. My Billy told me that you found the Hope Merchant after all."

"Yes, Mildred. And I passed on your message. He didn't seem to remember you."

Mildred smiled. "That's not important. What is important is that he got the message. I'm happy he did. Why don't you come inside? Billy will be down in a minute. He wouldn't say so, but he has been looking forward to your visit. Maggie is out on the back porch. She fixed you some iced tea with fresh-picked mint. Will you sit down and stay a while?"

A voice from Lilly's old persona objected that this had all been a set-up to reject her and make her feel foolish for getting her hopes up about this uppity out-of-work bookkeeper. But the voice was losing steam until it sounded more like an annoying mosquito in her ear. She smiled and stepped inside.

"Thank you, Mildred. I'd like that very much."

SIMON

S imon was lost in thought. His intercom buzzed twice before he answered.

"Your ten o'clock appointment is here, Mr. Chin."

His brow wrinkled. "Remind me who it is."

He could hear his secretary hesitate. "He is from the District Attorney's office."

Simon smiled. "Not a problem. He's an old college buddy. You won't have to post bail. It's social."

"I'm sure it is."

Even after two years, Simon was still surprised at how reserved Sheila was and by her total lack of a sense of humor. Even so, their shared ethnicity made him more comfortable with her than with many of the other people in the office. After Mr. Jonas fired him, Simon spent several months on a soul-searching journey to understand his Chinese roots. He eventually changed careers and was pleased to discover how much a simple nine-to-five management position satisfied him. He liked his co-workers and appreciated not seeing the people around him as rivals. He hired Sheila as a result of his deeper connection to his Chinese identity, pleasantly surprised that no eyebrows were raised by his choice. Sheila was even more Chinese than he was. He was first generation American while Sheila was born in Mainland China, brought here just in time to start first grade. Sheila had always felt like an outsider, accepting her identity as a Chinese living in America. Simon was just beginning to come to terms with his feelings of not belonging.

He stepped out from behind his desk to greet his old friend with a back-pounding hug. They settled into their chairs and Sheila appeared with two cups of coffee.

"I just wanted to thank you for hiring Willard. It was a favor for a friend of mine but it also meant a lot to me."

Simon shrugged. "It wasn't a big deal. You actually did me a favor by connecting me with Willard. A project had just come up that left us short-handed and he was perfect for the job. I've got a department head that is a workhorse but a difficult fit when it comes to interpersonal relations. Willard smoothed that out for me in a totally unanticipated manner."

"That all sounds fascinating, but what I'd really like to hear about is how you ended up here after Mr. Jonas chewed you up and spit you out. I was pleasantly surprised to get a letter asking me to contact you. It actually found it's way into my hands the day after I got married. I wanted to get together and talk about old times but I was way too busy for more than that quick email asking you to hire Willard."

Simon looked perplexed. "Dude, a simple phone call would have been okay."

"Well, I was in the middle of a sudden career change and also trying to juggle a few other minor miracles. One of them is baby

Ben. I'd love for you to come out to the farm this weekend to meet Hanna and the baby. We have a lot to talk about."

"Sounds great, but no reminiscing about our legal careers and all the glory that could have been."

Jack shook his head. "We have much more important things to discuss. The guy who sent me the letter asking me to contact you about Willard called me the other day. He told me that he knows you. I really need to hear about that."

Simon was suddenly confused. "I thought Willard was a friend of yours that asked you to help find him a job."

Jack shook his head. "I've never met Willard, though he's next on my list. I wasn't kidding when I said that miracles have been happening to me. I just want to know a little more about them. Miracles leave me feeling small and powerless. I don't like having to rely so much on something I don't understand. They all have to do with one person, so I am checking out everyone who knows him."

"So tell me Simon, how do you know Theo?"

After hearing Jack mention Theo's name, Simon needed several moments before he could respond. "You know Theo? How do you know Theo? And which version of him are we talking about."

Jack shook his head. "You first."

"Well, it's all because Mr. Jonas did me the favor of kicking me out of the firm. As I recall, you had one of the front row seats. Besides being humiliated in front of my peers, I was totally devastated. But it turned out to be the best thing that ever happened to me. I'd spent my entire life overachieving, trying to fit in by becoming the all-American dream boy. The real problem was as clear as the nose on my face, right under my Asian eyes. The first thing people knew about me was that I was Chinese. Either they thought they knew what that meant or they tried to convince themselves that it didn't matter, that it was only skin deep. The only people who might have understood me better than I understood myself were the immigrants living in Chinatown, and I avoided them like the plague. I'd been trying to convince myself that being Chinese didn't matter, that it was an accident of birth. However, the fact is, being Chinese is a very real thing. The problem was that I never learned what it meant."

"After Mr. Jonas kicked me out, I couldn't get a job. I had enough money to get by for a while without working. The Chinese are frugal. I heard that a solo trek in the woods was a good way to clear the head and discover your inner self, so I decided to give it a try. Over-achiever that I am, I decided that my hike would be a thousand mile trek with no civilization along the way. Two weeks in, I started hating it. But every morning, before I strapped on that dreaded backpack, I convinced myself that enlightenment was waiting at the end of that day's trail. Then, one day, I twisted my ankle bad and sat down in the middle of a field full of the hungriest mosquitoes God put on this planet. I felt like crying. So then, Theo . . ." he stammered to a halt. " A boy named Theo . . ."

Jack laughed. "Let me guess. A young, redhead about fourteen-years-old who doesn't always wear the same body."

Simon shook his head in disbelief. "I guess you do know. Anyway, Theo showed up with an enormous Native American. Besides being totally lame, I was so bitten up and disheartened that I didn't want to move. His Indian friend carried me to the next overnight spot and then disappeared. Theo put up my tent and stayed with me for three days while my ankle healed. It rained for three days straight, so it was just the two of us stuck together in a one-and-a-half man tent eating rehydrated cuisine."

Jack shook his head. "The big guy is an Eskimo. His name is Brad, or Oogrooq, if you prefer Inuit. You can thank him personally this weekend. He works at the farm."

Simon shrugged. "I'll keep it simple, which is going to end up sounding crazy. We did a lot of talking. Actually, I did all the talking and Theo listened. After my ankle got better and the rain stopped, Theo just left. He didn't even say goodbye. When the sun came out, I just couldn't get myself to put that pack back on. I knew that enlightenment, for me anyway, wasn't just around the next bend in the trail. I dumped the pack in a ditch, headed for the nearest road, called a friend collect from a gas station, and went home. I figured that if I were looking for a place to discover myself, it was probably going to be where people drank more tea than soda-pop."

"I bought a ticket for China. At first I didn't connect with anything. I began to think maybe I wasn't really Chinese. Then I met this student on his way home after graduating from Beijing University. He wasn't in a rush so we toured together for two weeks. He was a few years younger than I, and I kept thinking that if my grandparents hadn't come to America to find work, I would be this kid. His English was shaky so my Chinese improved quickly. It turns out I knew more of the language than I thought. After the first week, he let something slip, something he knew about me that he shouldn't have known. After passing the bar exam I traveled to Europe and fell in love with mayonnaise on French fries. When I was stuck in that tent with Theo, I complained about the non-stop dehydrated meals and kept saying how much I wanted just one small bag of 'pomme-frites' like I had in Belgium. Theo asked what that was, and when I explained that it was French fries drizzled in vinegar and served with mayo, he almost died laughing. After that, anytime I complained about the food, he teased me about mayo on my fries calling them pomme-freaks. I had forgotten about that but when I complained to the Chinese student about how there were no burger joints in the Chinese countryside, he just laughed at me and said that even if there were, they wouldn't have mayo for my fries anyway. At that moment I realized it was no loonier for Theo to be American and Chinese than it was for me to be Chinese and American. I almost started beating on him but he gave me a strange look and walked away. I never saw either of him again. I was camped out by a rice paddy and already going a little crazy. I kept asking myself how these people could live without Internet or Starbucks. But there was a little voice inside me that wouldn't leave me alone, that kept telling me that the Internet and Starbucks were killing me. Life in the legal fast lane with Mr. Jonas had driven me over the edge. It was clear that a piss-poor peasant in a straw hat spending his days staring at the back side of a water buffalo while plowing his field had a better hold on sanity and self than I did."

"I finally lost it, total meltdown. Theo's split personality was the last straw. He was two people and it didn't bother him because inside, he knew exactly who he was. I was one person and couldn't hold it together because I was in total denial of all the different things that were clearly me. After my ego suffered a systems crash, the Chinese kid showed up again, and Theo and I had another long talk. He told me who he was and I was in a dizzy enough space to believe him. It almost seemed logical that a fourteen-year-old white kid spouting wisdom in a tent on the Appalachian Trail could morph into a twenty-three-year-old Chinese student. I remember being angry that a stinking Laowai knew more about being Chinese than I did, even if he did happen to look Chinese at the time. Chinese Theo went home, but I stayed."

"After he left, I went to my grandfather's village and hunted up some total strangers I was related to. For them, there was no question. Family is sacred. Three months later I knew what it was like to be Chinese and I knew a lot more about who I was, for better or worse. When I came back, I went job hunting. I thought my career possibilities were bleak but after a little introspection, I realized that was Mr. Jonas' voice talking to me. He had us all convinced that his way was the only road to success and happiness."

Jack nodded. "Even though he is lonely and miserable."

"Exactly. Once I got his voice out of my head and went looking for what I wanted, I got offered a job here in management. I like business more than law."

Jack took a deep breath. "It will take an awful lot to figure this out."

Simon smiled. "A good bottle of wine might help and I have just the thing. A business associate brought it back from vacation." He opened his desk drawer and pulled out a bottle. The label was amateurish, hand drawn: "Chateau Willard" over a childish drawing of a man and a woman, holding hands, in front of a cabin, surrounded by flowers. The door to the cabin was open and Jack thought he saw the faint image of a child's face peeking out.

THE
BOOK
OF
REALITY

SAMUEL

T he room was small but floor-to-ceiling windows made it seem larger than it was. He had spent the last several years in a small room without a window, as if the same bureaucracy responsible for regulating the size of his office, or choosing the color of his drab furniture also meted out sunlight. The same frugality that denied him a personal window was also responsible for the lack of window shades in this room. He stared out the window while the team of doctors settled into their seats. He missed the sun and wide-open spaces of his youth, but his work demanded uncompromising dedication without distractions. On the other side of the room five psychiatrists arranged around a long table sat patiently, waiting in judgment. Samuel experienced a moment of vertigo when he stood, as the room wobbled with the various, diverse personalities looming menacingly around him. Ironically, the psychiatric team seemed unbalanced with one man on the left, three men on the right, and one woman slightly off center. A committee should be uneven to avoid the possibility of a tie in decisions; however this uneven configuration was deeper than mere numbers. A longer look revealed that the man on the left was a block of stone ballast, easily outweighing the three men on the right. The woman was the pivot, a buffer to protect the three on the right from the one on the left. She was young and pretty, and though she could have easily flaunted her beauty, she was trying to look more professional. The doctor on the left, a graying bulldog of a man, would have no compunctions haranguing and bullying his colleagues on the right, but this simple arrangement meant he would have to go through her to do it. Her youth and beauty, obvious yet unapproachable, made that an unattractive if not impossible option.

Samuel arranged the pages on the table in front of him, channeling his nervous energy away from his thoughts and into his shaking hands. He didn't need the notes to present his thesis. It had taken shape laboriously during many long hours of debate with colleagues, every detail endlessly discussed, examined, and scrutinized under the unforgiving glare of intellectual criticism. The board of psychiatrists wielded power over his future and was about to sit in judgment based on his presentation. This was the cause of his anxiety. Even so, he knew that their decision would be irrelevant. His calling was towards a higher truth that existed in another dimension that was unavailable to these so-called experts. They could get a glimpse of this dimension if they were open to it and could move beyond their rigid preconceptions. Ultimately, it didn't matter. The truth resided in this dimension and it would become obvious, with or without his presentation, with glacial inevitability. It was his thesis that defined his identity and transcended his trillions of cells and chemical reactions.

Samuel began slowly, knowing from experience that the objections would be from a misunderstanding or total rejection of the initial statements that formed the basis for his entire body of work. "In quantum physics, there is the theory of multiple realities based on experiments attempting to determine whether light is a particle or wave."

A voice roughened from years of cigarette abuse growled at him from the side of the room. "I didn't come prepared for a lecture on physics. I left my calculator in my office."

Samuel looked up from his notes to see the woman staring at him. Her eyes seemed to absorb all the light from the windows. She spoke calmly, refuting the doctor without taking her eyes from Samuel. "I think we should hear him out before jumping to any conclusions."

Samuel was surprised that this short comment silenced the older psychiatrist. He waited a moment before continuing. "Quantum physicists have declared that light is both a particle and a wave, depending on how you look at it." A few nervous chuckles came from the right side of the table. "More accurately, it depends on who is looking at it. Observation changes the results. The observer becomes part of the system. Another way to explain this is that before the experiment, before the event occurs, there is the possibility that light is either a wave or a particle. After the event, when one possible outcome is determined by observation, the other possibility has ceased to exist. That is an unacceptable explanation. The light's reality of being either a wave or a particle cannot logically be affected or determined by observation. It can only be observed. That is true if the observer is not a part of the equation, if he is outside of the box, so to speak. This simple experiment has drawn the observer, or at least his consciousness, into the equation and into the box. Since there is proof that light is both a wave and a particle, quantum physicists prefer to say that both possibilities continue to exist even after the test has determined one or the other to be true. They call this the multiple reality theory. Light is both a wave and a particle, but the observer continues to exist in one reality or the other, not both. The problem with accepting this from the perspective of psychology is that the observer is not a passive factor in the equation." Samuel paused and his voice assumed an added emphasis, "In brief, what we see is ourselves seeing."

"The observer is a person: a living, breathing, intelligent individual. To theorize multiple realities is all well and good in the underground cafeteria at a particle research laboratory, but it becomes more problematic when you are sitting in your office with a victim of child abuse. However, I feel that the quantum theory is a reality that must be incorporated into our understanding of the psyche. Scientists have accepted multiple realities and despite years of intensive research into the human psyche, I feel that quantum scientists have a better understanding of what goes on in the molecule than I do of what goes on inside the human mind. If physicists can accept multiple realities, than I feel obligated to follow. In psychological terms, let us say the individual is defined by his consciousness. Jung approached a broadened definition of consciousness but in an incomplete fashion. Let us say that if there are multiple realities, then there are multiple aspects of the individual's consciousness, parallel and separate. We have long been aware of multiple personalities in our patients; we must now acknowledge that our so-called objectivity is actually a function of who we are; objectivity becomes relative."

A growl came from across the small room. "As psychiatrists we already accept that. However we define it as an illness. Are you trying to twist it around, to redefine illness as normal, as a sign of health?"

Samuel fought to retain his intellectual objectivity despite the apparent antagonism. "No. Multiple personalities is a tragic illness but I feel our understanding of it is flawed. There are multiple realities. That is a fact. Let us say that in the experiment set up by the physicists, light flows into one specific reality. Actually, it flows into both realities, or many realities. If the observer is part of the system, he also flows into many realities. He also becomes many; many consciousnesses separated into distinct realities. Multiple reality disorder is caused when more than one consciousness flows into one reality. That is a flaw. Another result is that psychological distress occurs because the consciousness is mismatched with reality. What we see as a disorder may be a perfectly healthy reaction to a different reality. That consciousness is unable to cope with the reality it has been thrust into. And it is correct in its inability. Perhaps trauma is an introduction of a reality that is unsuited to that consciousness and the psyche longs for its proper place, its proper reality."

Samuel knew that he was not speaking to open minds but to a group of professionals who were holding fast to the beliefs they already had before entering the room. Imminent failure made him desperately bold. He pushed on. "The story is told of a certain scholar who studied night and day until he was physically weak and ill. His mentor told him that he needed to travel to a certain institution in order to be cured. That institute was a special place where scholars dedicated themselves to works of charity and merit but also to joyous living. The professor did not tell his student the nature of the institute for fear he would not go. The student left the next day as per his teacher's instructions. The journey was through the forest and, it being a deep and bitter winter, the student bundled himself up to protect his frail health. When he arrived, he lingered outside for several minutes, hesitating to enter. Inside, the scholars were celebrating a wedding. The dancing was at its peak and the musicians had retreated into a corner. The scholars were dancing wildly, tumbling and swinging in a frenzy of joy. The frail scholar standing outside decided to peek in the window. He saw the dancing, but his ears, covered against the cold, could not hear the music. He saw the wild gyrations not as joyous dancing but rather a spastic affliction of the insane. He was suddenly struck with the belief that his teacher had sent him to an asylum. In anger and fear, he left, never to be seen again."

The old doctor slammed his hand on the table. "Are you implying that we simply are not enlightened enough to hear the music?"

"Yes. However it is ignorance chosen under the guise of an educated decision. I feel that we should at least understand that the patient could be reacting to an actual reality that we cannot perceive. This would seem dysfunctional to us because our perspective is based in this reality."

Her voice floated across the room, startling him with the stirrings of emotions that he didn't expect. "You are defining the 'self' as consciousness. Yet consciousness seems objective in your understanding, almost separate from the self."

She had understood him. That, by itself, was worth the struggle to maintain professional detachment. "I am not defining the 'self' as pure consciousness. However, I feel they are tightly joined and co-dependent. Therefore, a shift in consciousness necessarily causes a change in the 'self'. 'Self' and consciousness are joined together, but they are separate from reality. Sanity or wellness is when they are in sync with reality, but being separate, there are other possibilities. The self can be in one reality and the consciousness in another." As she considered his words, a warm feeling grew in his heart, and he recognized it as hope, a feeling that had lain buried and forgotten for too long.

A rough voice interrupted. "Multiple personalities is an illness. The self is a single cohesive unit. I am one person, the same person I was yesterday and the same person I will be tomorrow. To deny this is to be truly insane. Do you expect us to be dragged into your tangled hypothesis?"

Samuel's anger distracted him from his carefully planned speech. "That is precisely the problem. Our definition of sanity and self are written in stone and yet this is clearly and absolutely wrong. Yesterday was different than today so to remain the same is an illness, an illness we call sanity. The world changes each day, sometimes drastically, and we must also. Our survival, in fact, depends upon that flexibility. Even in this single limited reality, I am many people. I am a son, a man, a client, a teacher . . ."

"A nut-job."

"Doctor!" The stern rebuke was softened by the femininity of her voice.

Samuel took a deep breath and continued. "The perception of the self and reality as a single, unified, constant is false yet useful. It permits us to operate in this world, to achieve goals, and to have lasting relationships. These are also measurements of sanity, less valued by classical psychology yet perhaps more useful to mankind. I am not suggesting that we ignore those elements. They have their uses. Just as mechanical, Newtonian physics help us to cope with the physical world and quantum theory may safely be ignored for most of the day, so too can we operate in our day-to-day lives with the classical perception of the self as a unified constant. We can ignore the fact that there are alternate 'I's living parallel lives. Eastern mysticism is the art of connecting with the particular reality that a particular 'I' is sliding into, being in the eternal 'now'. Quantum theory only becomes necessary in extreme circumstances. Even though it is always present, it only becomes relevant in the extreme. A deep emotional crisis can separate the self from the stream of perceived reality. It is quite possible that reality could make a jump sideways farther than the self is able. Part of the self can vaguely perceive what should have been its future while reality is continuing down a different path. The self is left straddling two realities. We, the psychiatrists, perceive that individual from a reality no longer relevant to his self. Quantum psychology is therefore necessary as a tool in understanding souls that are experiencing life outside of our reality."

"Are you suggesting that if I could access that alternate reality then I would be able to shake hands with myself?"

Samuel snapped. "Perhaps in an alternate reality you will have realized what a complete ass you are and would refuse to shake your own hand."

"Mr. Morrison!"

The air in the room crackled, lying heavily in his lungs as if it lacked sufficient oxygen. A smile split the doctor's face like a fault-line spreading across a stone wall. "This is all very fascinating and will make for interesting bedtime stories for pathological children. However, we did not come here today to reconsider our approaches to modern psychology. We came here to judge Mr. Morrison's fitness to re-enter society as a safe and functioning individual. It is my professional opinion that he has proven with his own words that this is not a possibility." Nervous mumbling from the other side of the table was an ambiguous affirmation. Samuel looked for help from the center of the table but her eyes were hidden as she wrote notes in the file in front of her. The rough hands of the attendants touched his shoulders. A gentle voice halted all activity.

"I can't dispute that. However, I do feel that Mr. Morrison's case warrants more attention. His comments were well thought out and insightful; the sign of an active and ordered intelligence."

The doctor on her left slapped the table. "His intelligence is not an issue. He could be the next Einstein and it wouldn't influence my opinion. He is unbalanced and delusional, unsafe to rejoin society."

Her pretty face wrinkled in thought. "I agree. I am not ready to discharge him." Her words hung in the air. The doctor's aggression abated. The encounter was a victory. Samuel smiled as he considered how she carefully qualified her statements. He tried to decipher her deeper thoughts, disappointed that they were hidden from him. His empathetic sense had become second nature to him, something he rarely thought about. He felt as if he had suddenly gone deaf in one ear. She went on. "I would like to take charge of his case." Samuel's heart skipped a beat.

A noise came from the left, something caught between a growl and a laugh. "It's your privilege, but I question your objectivity. Just for the sake of rigorous professional standards, I will also spend some time with Mr. Morrison. Perhaps in a private session he can explain his theories in a way that will not make me question his sanity."

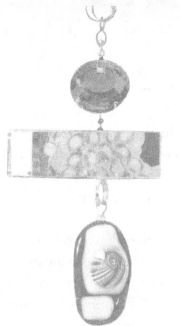

JANET

The attendants led Samuel to his room. The door was open because it was still dayroom hours. He opened a well-worn book and began to read, the words running through his mind like an old song, its melody half-heard but comforting nonetheless. Dr. Richards appeared in the doorway, a thin folder held lightly in her hand. She was about to speak when she realized that he was already aware of her presence, but reluctant to put aside his reading. After a few moments, he stood and returned the book to the shelf, looking at the other books as if to bid them farewell, then turned to face the doctor. His smile discomforted her, putting her off balance. It was relaxed and inviting, an invitation to normal conversation, something that rarely occurred even between patient and staff in this institution. Insanity is a condition so subtle and insidious that the caregivers needed to be ever vigilant against contagion. She knew that all that separated her from the patients were a white coat, a magnetic ID badge, and the knowledge that her ability to differentiate between sanity and insanity, as she had learned it in university, was absolutely correct and unimpeachable. There were days when the picture on her ID badge looked like a stranger, someone who didn't even resemble her, a younger woman whose embarrassed smile was now impossible for her to imitate. She was reluctant to enter. The small room seemed intimate and even dangerous. He sensed her hesitation and stepped out to the hallway.

"Hello, doctor. Have you come to speak with me? I prefer to speak outside on the balcony. Is that okay with you?" He began to walk, not waiting for her response. She followed. He seemed to be moving in slow motion, his strides fluid and loose, but she had to walk quickly to keep up. They stepped onto the balcony garden. It was an oasis of green high above the busy city streets, separated from the sterile white ward by sliding glass doors and wired security glass.

On an average day, the balcony was crowded with patients, many oblivious to the beautiful surroundings. Today they were alone, the garden area strangely empty.

"There is a special television show in the day room. No one wanted to miss it." She looked at him with an incredulous glance. He laughed. "In this program, they interview a group of ecologists who set up an underwater habitat to live alongside dolphins. The experiment ended before the scheduled completion because the scientists were suffering from clinical depression. The scientists that ran the project from the mainland concluded that it was due to the difficult conditions; cramped and pressurized living quarters, physical exhaustion, lack of direct sunlight. But what really happened was the dolphins accepted them and changed their swimming and hunting patterns to be near them. After a few months, all of the participants began to suffer from extreme depression. After many sessions to cope with this, it was revealed that the humans felt that the dolphins were relating to them as inferior. The dolphins would slow down; sometimes even trying to help the ecologists swim faster. Recordings showed that the dolphins communicated at a slower rate when humans were present and used a different, less rich, vocabulary. They realized that they were subconsciously aware of the dolphins' attitude and despite their success in collecting important new data and making groundbreaking discoveries about dolphins, they were depressed. They felt like the dolphins treated them like mentally disabled and physically handicapped cousins. These scientists were all the best in their fields, with multiple academic degrees, most of them doctors or professors. Their egos couldn't handle condescension."

She smiled, not sure to believe him or not. "You've seen it before? Is that how you know so much about it?"

"No. I was involved in the project in an unofficial capacity, after the fact. A couple of the scientists became my clients. I became familiar with the details of the project through my work with them, trying to help them recuperate from the experience."

She resisted the impulse to smile. "Are you a psychiatrist?"

He pointed at the file in her hand. "If I said I was, you would label me as delusional. My file clearly states that I am not a psychiatrist. And I don't consider psychiatry or psychology to be professions."

"Should I take that personally?"

"I hope not. You could probably tell from my lecture that I don't consider insanity to be a disease requiring a cure. Given certain circumstances, I consider it to be the healthiest response to an intolerable reality."

"Is that because you don't consider yourself insane, and feel you have been unfairly institutionalized?"

He smiled in a way that looked normal but his words made her feel as though the rooftop was swaying under her feet. "I am not here because I am insane. I am here on vacation."

He sat in the vinyl chair, its slimy coldness cutting right through his thin pajamas. His bladder felt suddenly heavy and full. He walked slowly, his feet shuffling along the cold tile floor. His eyes never shifted, his path across the room straight and unimpeded. The other patients moved around him like characters in a movie being played at twice normal speed, projected on a screen that surrounded him but remained always beyond his reach. He moved forward through their choreographed motions, wondering how their actions seemed so sure and defined. He reached the bathroom after several minutes of struggling against a current that seemed to push him backwards. He opened the door, a single toilet filling the tiny room. He waited to lower his pants until his eyes made the transition from the blinding sterile whiteness of the corridor to the single bulb semi-darkness of the WC. He stood for several minutes before a tiny stream tinkled out, hardly justifying the pressure that had filled his loins a few minutes before. He turned, hesitating with his hand on the doorknob. He closed his eyes and his lips moved, speaking angrily, spit flying out to land on the shiny white paint of the door. Tears began to flow and his head drooped, his chin resting on his chest. In final resignation he pushed the door open.

The hallway was dark and silent, moonlight filtering through the curtains at the end of the hall. His slippered feet moved silently across the thick carpeting as he walked down the dark hallway. He glanced in as he passed his daughter's room, noting the comforter on the floor. His son's room was next. He was asleep on the floor, his head resting on an oversized teddy bear. He fought desperately but his body was not his to control. He continued walking down the hallway until he stood at the half-open door to the master bedroom. Against his will, his hand reached up to push the door open. The man in the baggy army coat knelt on top of his wife, the knife absurdly large, serrated on one side, shiny black in the moonlight. He had missed that detail when it actually happened but now he knew that it was black because it was coated with his wife's blood. The man with the knife looked up, and suddenly, he was on him, his sour street person smell filling his nostrils, and he could feel the knife sliding into him, stabbing at his stomach, the knife so sharp that it felt like punches with a little pinch added in. A noise from behind him stopped the stabbing in mid-swing. He fell to the floor and felt the carpet sticky and wet with his own blood. He lay there, unable to move, unable to speak, his daughter standing in the hallway, looking right at her father while the stranger stepped over him, moving towards her, the knife held loose and ready against his hip.

He woke to the sound of pounding at the door. An attendant, the fat one with the lisp, was banging on the door, calling his name.

"Hey, yo! Mith-ter Grant! You been too long. What ith wrong witcha? Ith you havin' one of thothe thpells agin?"

A key rattled in the lock, opening it from the outside. A pudgy hand grabbed his arm and pulled him to his feet. He realized that he was sitting on the toilet with his pajama pants down around his ankles. He was pulled into the hallway, stumbling over his pants, aware in a vague way that people were staring at his naked bottom half. He was past being ashamed, that being the least of the emotions hammering at him right now. This had been a bad day. It was a little past lunch and he had already seen his family killed three times today. He felt his pants being yanked up and tied tightly around his waist. A sturdy grip led him gently back to the dayroom and helped him sit back down in vinyl chair that had become even colder in his absence.

❦

They sat under a small mimosa, its light pink flowers just beginning to sprout. "I'd like to discuss the talk you gave to the psychology board today, Mr. Morrison."

Their eye contact grew stronger, and then she looked away, opening the file as an excuse. She looked up when he spoke and felt uncomfortable as his eyes commanded her attention. "My name isn't 'Morrison'. It isn't even 'Samuel', though I kind of like the name Sam. I've grown used to it over the last year."

She returned to the file, avoiding his gaze. "So what is your name?" Her tone carried the slightest hint of disbelief necessary for her professional persona. He chose not to challenge her disbelief.

"My name is Thelonius S. Meyer. My father was a free jazz fanatic, even though it drove my mom and the cows bonkers. He named me after Thelonius S. Monk. He regretted his decision after my first birthday when he tried to fit 'Happy Birthday Thelonius' onto the cake. After that, my mom was the only one who ever called me Thelonius. I think she did it just to spite my dad and gloat over his bad judgment. I'd like for you to call me Theo."

"Okay, Theo." She glanced down at the printed file in her lap, as if to reassure herself that she knew his real name. "Where did you grow up?"

He sighed. "Are you asking me that because you are interested, or are you asking me that to judge whether my version of reality is correct and coincides with what is in that file?" She hesitated for a moment, long enough for him to resume the conversation before she could think of an adequate professional response. "That file is entirely fictitious. It says that my name is Samuel Morrison, forty-three years old, a delivery truck driver employed by a large bakery, divorced for ten years, no children."

"And the file is incorrect?"

"Of course. I am an ambassador from the planet Zoid, ten thousand years old with forty eight hundred offspring, a member of the royal Yark family by marriage." A smile grew on his face, showing strong white teeth in a face that was boyishly free of facial hair. The hair on his head was thick and heavily flecked with gray, but he could pass for twenty-five as easily as forty-five. She was confused and disconcerted by strong unfamiliar emotions. He laughed. "I'm just kidding. Joking is a nervous habit that I'm not very good at." He picked a flower from over her head and inspected it for a minute. "My name really is Thelonius S. Meyer. I was born and raised upstate on my parents' dairy farm. I worked at . . . I had a shop downtown where I sold memorabilia and antiques. My job required changing identities quite frequently. Samuel Morrison just happened to be the person I was when they brought me here. I am actually glad they did that. I needed a vacation and this is a great place to hide from the world. The world won't look for me here because they don't want to know that crazy people exist. Hiding amongst the hopeless is a restful experience for me. There is no background noise."

She wrote a few notes.

Conflicting thoughts pulled her in different directions; clearly, he didn't make sense and yet he didn't sound insane. It was her experience that insane people didn't make jokes, and, in general, lacked the ability to laugh at themselves. She had always been taught that humor was a sign of intelligence and her experience proved it to be true. Humor was in short supply and any jokes the staff exchanged were at the expense of the patients and usually in bad taste. The conversation seemed out of place, unlike any other session she ever had with a patient. She knew they were in the ward, though being alone in the balcony garden made the ward seem incredibly distant. She felt almost like it was a pleasant social engagement and she was getting to know a fascinating new acquaintance. She struggled to maintain the proper headspace. "Mr. Morrison . . ."

He stopped her. "Theo."

She continued. "Mr. Morrison, your story does not make sense. Why would a storekeeper need multiple identities? It sounds to me like you created an entire theory of multiple realities in order to cope with a crisis you were suffering in your life."

She expected an immediate denial, the standard reaction she had come to expect in her work. Mental illness created its own system of self-denial. She was surprised by his silence as he considered her words. "Maybe you are right. In any case, the truth as I know it is a whole lot stranger than anything you would be willing to accept. Even if Theo Meyer is a figment of my imagination, a construct created by an unbalanced psyche, he is a really nice guy that I would like for you to get to know better."

"I'd like to get to know Samuel Morrison. Why don't you tell me more about him? What was it like driving a truck for a bakery?"

He shook his head. "That won't work for me. I need for you to get to know Theo."

She scribbled a note in the file. "Why is that so important to you?"

"Because we are going to spend our years together. And in the sense that I am anyone, I am really Theo."

She put her pen down. "Mr. Morrison, I can allow for some freedom in the healing process; however there are distinct boundaries. I am your doctor. Please do not harbor any romantic fantasies."

He shook his head. "I have a lot of romantic fantasies but this isn't one of them. We are going to get married because the world needs our children, the fruit of our love. If you understood what it is to have children, you would embrace our destiny."

She jumped to her feet, a clenched hand held back ready to strike. "I understand how to have children and I have the power of decision in that matter. Our session is over and if you take one step towards me, I will call the attendants." Her free hand fumbled in the pocket of her white coat, and pulled out a can of Mace.

He sat calmly, a sad look on his face. "Please don't use that."

She held it up, pointing it at his eyes. "Just try me, buster. One shot of this stuff and you'll be at my feet, crying like a baby."

"You have the nozzle facing the wrong way. If you push the button, you might hurt yourself." She sighted down her arm and saw the nozzle staring back at her. Their eyes met again. His voice came to her as if carried from far away on the breeze, but she realized that he was standing very close to her, too close, closer than the rulebook said he should be. Had they met in her office, there would be a desk between them and an attendant just outside the door.

"When I was a boy, my father would take me fishing." His accent changed, his voice taking on a different tone and rhythm. She couldn't pull her eyes away from his and wondered if the peculiar speech was meant to hypnotize her. In any case, she listened so carefully that, years later, she could repeat it word for word. "We would set out early, before dawn, and reach the lake just as it was getting light. We had a little row boat that my dad built himself. It was flat-bottomed and sat low in the water, great for fishing but not much good for anything else. My poppa would row on out to the middle of the lake and I would lie down in the front, my face out over the edge, just a few inches above the water. That time of day, the lake was smooth as glass, not a ripple in sight. I would stare down into the orange cedar water, looking for fish. I could see the first six inches pretty good but deeper than that, the water got cloudy. Once in a while I'd see something, or thought I saw something. And then I knew that the lake could be as deep as God intended and there wasn't anything I could do about it. There I was, in a tiny little nothing of a boat, gliding across the surface like a water strider walks on water, and I just knew that under me was the biggest hole in the world, all filled up with water, and all I could see was the very tiniest little top of it. There could be a whole world of things right beneath me and I would never know it. And those shapes that I would see flitting in and out, they were hints, little glimpses of the tiniest bit of an enormous world right underneath me."

"And as I got older, I kept feeling like that was my whole life. Like I'm walking around doing things, thinking I know what I'm doing, but all I'm really seeing is the thinnest layer right on the surface. Like when I play baseball, the pitcher throws the ball, and I know I'm supposed to swing the bat and hit it. I know how to do it. But as I got older, I got the feeling that it wasn't so simple; that when I swung the bat, a whole lot of other stuff was going on but it was all too deep for me to see. I stopped playing baseball after a while. The other kids were happy about that because I was so busy thinking that I always struck out."

She smiled and realized that she was sitting down again under the mimosa tree, much closer to him than before. "Why are you telling me this?"

"When I became the Hope Merchant, I started operating on an entirely different level. I would be doing things that seemed simple, everyday things. But what I was really doing was changing things deep down in the water, things I couldn't see. And that wasn't all. By changing these things, I was able to fix other things as well, things that I couldn't see. At first I was operating blind, working on a kind of wisdom or insight that just moved me along. Little by little I started understanding more of what I was doing."

"That must have been a relief."

"It was awful. When I was blind, I didn't see how badly things were broken or how much was at stake. When I started to understand what I was doing, that's when I needed a vacation. If a man stays single, it is lonely but he can still live a full life. When a woman doesn't have children, it isn't a great tragedy, unless you can see deeper, see what is happening in the hidden places of her heart and soul. A woman who has never become a mother harbors a silent sadness. A man who doesn't become a husband or a father becomes a stunted tree, deprived of sunlight and rain and unable to thrive. I began to see these things and I guess I went a little crazy. Maybe I do belong here. I see things differently than other people. But the difference is that I don't want to get sane. I have a job to do, a job of fixing the world one heart at a time, and if I need to be a certain way to do that job, a way that the world thinks is crazy, well then, so be it."

Janet felt a need to speak like a doctor, to return to familiar ground. "So, you were seeing things that weren't actually there, disturbing things, things that sometimes left you broken and ill."

"I saw other things as well, beautiful things, more beautiful than you would ever think this world could contain. This world doesn't just include miracles, this world is a miracle. I want to marry you and have children, and if that happens, it will be simple and real, almost too normal to bear. Yet it will be enormous, miraculous, unique, and boundless in what it will bring to the world."

"I don't believe in miracles. I believe in observable facts."

He reached out and took her hand. Her impulse was to pull back and snatch her hand away, but for some reason, it didn't move. He pulled her gently to her feet and pointed toward the setting sun. A small cloud was moving with the wind. She was about to say something, to protest that she had already neglected a full schedule, when she saw that the cloud was moving directly towards them. As it came close she realized that it was shifting shape rapidly and its pink hue was not a reflection from the setting sun. They were suddenly surrounded by thousands of butterflies; their wings light pink, matching the mimosa blossoms. Her hair was covered with gently fluttering butterflies and she turned to see Theo covered as well, a broad smile mirroring the setting sun.

"Being the Hope Merchant is the hardest job in the whole world and it can literally drive you crazy. The hours are brutal, and you have to travel a lot. It is an ongoing identity crisis. But . . ." He held out a hand filled with pink wings gently flapping, "It does have its fringe benefits. Now tell me again, why don't you believe in miracles?"

He sat in the vinyl chair, feeling his bladder full to bursting. The attendants resented the fact that he had recently begun to pee in his pants, but he was willing to accept their anger, which was pleasant compared to what waited beyond closed doors. If he turned too quickly, horrible sights would cruely spring at him. If he didn't watch his food, it turned into the most awful things. He sat staring at the wall, terrified of what lay at the edges of his vision. He became aware of someone sitting down next to him. He hoped it was an attendant but it could have been a new horror: a new vision of the killer or perhaps his wife with her throat slashed and her head hanging at an angle. He felt his hand being gently lifted. A man's voice, not the killer's, spoke to him.

"Let's go, Robert. I'll take you to the bathroom."

He allowed himself to be led to the bathroom but hesitated before going in. A small voice, the tiniest echo of what remained of his sanity, asked how the man knew his bladder was full. The voice was lost in the static, all the white noise that made it impossible for him to think. The man opened the door wide and gave him a gentle push. He hesitated but resigned himself to the inevitable replay of hell. He stood in front of the toilet waiting for his bladder to unclench itself, reluctant because he knew that finishing meant stepping out of the bathroom and revisiting his family's brutal murder. The man's voice spoke in his ear, "It's mighty cramped in here. Why don't you go ahead and finish your business so we can leave?"

A tiny candle flickered in the dark storm that lashed at his soul. The stream tinkled easily, and he knew that with another person in the bathroom, the reality outside the door would not be able to shift. For the moment, he was safe.

ROBERT

Dr. Richards walked to her office but stopped at the door. The door was slightly ajar, though she was quite sure she had locked it. "Do come in, Dr. Richards," Dr. Manheimer's voice called out, inviting her in to her own office. She stepped in, working hard at containing her anger at having her professional domain violated. He sat in her chair reading a file.

"I've been searching for your file on Samuel Morrison. I can't find it."

She was shocked at his audacity. "There is no reason why you should find it. He is my patient and what you are doing violates the patient's rights."

He dropped the file carelessly onto the desk. "The patient is a nut-job, a ward of the state. I am responsible for this institution and all of its patients."

She glared. "What you are doing is in clear violation of procedures. If you want to see his file, you are required to submit a request."

He shrugged and pulled a folded piece of paper from his coat pocket. "This is a copy of the request I already filed. I just thought I would save you the trouble of coming to my office."

His calm made her angrier. "I appreciate your consideration however it is unnecessary. In the meantime, consider yourself notified that I am going to file a formal complaint about this ridiculous breach of doctor-patient confidentiality."

He waved off her threat like a bad odor. "Go ahead. But since I'm already here, why don't you just show me the file. As department head, I have the authority and right to demand it." He pressed the paper into a tight ball and threw it towards her. "And I have already filed the proper form. Let's take a look at that file." Her face grew hot and the blood thundered in her ears. She remained silent, her lips pressed tightly together. His face cracked into an ugly grin. "I'd be willing to bet dollars to donuts that the file doesn't exist. You have been meeting with him every day for an hour. That is a large investment of time, paid for by public taxes. You were supposed to be treating him for delusional psychosis. Doctor-patient confidentiality only covers notes pertaining to treatment, not love letters."

Her shout was heard down the hall in the day room. "How dare you!"

His twisted smile grew wider. "I wouldn't file any formal complaints if I were you. When you open up a case like this, you never know what will come out." He stood up from her chair and walked past her into the hall. "Oh, and I like your perfume. Is it a new scent? And the pretty little pin holding back your hair, is that an heirloom or was it a gift? It looks expensive." He walked away, his shoes squeaking on the polished linoleum. She stepped into her office, leaning back against the door, breathing deeply. She pulled the pin from her hair, pulling a few strands out with it. She was about to fling it across the room but stopped herself.

She slowly opened her hand. The hairpin was a small butterfly, its wings encrusted with pale pink stones, its body a slender opal. She slipped the pin into her lab coat pocket and at some point during the day, without being fully aware of it, she slipped it back into her hair.

Dr. Manheimer went straight to the nurses station adjacent to the dayroom. He had personally chosen the head nurse ten years before. She followed his lead instinctively and ran the ward like clockwork. Their job was tending to the mentally ill but they both knew, by unspoken agreement, that wards like theirs existed to protect society by keeping these people locked away.

She stood up when the doctor walked in. He glanced at the day room, the center of the ward's daily routine, and noted that there had been no changes in staff for several years. He wondered if some of the nurses and attendants felt more comfortable in the ward than in the outside world. "How is Mr. Morrison doing?"

The nurse was a little confused at the question. "I thought he was due to be released. I wish I had more like him. He has been helping us out by taking care of one of the other patients. Do you remember Mr. Grant? He is the man who became semi-catatonic after his family was murdered. Mr. Morrison has been feeding and clothing him. We even moved them into a room together. It is a big relief for the staff. Mr. Grant was sinking deeper into his catatonia, even becoming incontinent. Not only are his needs being met, but his condition is improving, thanks to Mr. Morrison."

The doctor nodded. "I would like them separated. I am going to be making some serious changes in Mr. Morrison's treatment." He pulled out the ultimate trump card. "I believe he is dangerous."

The nurse was confused but she had never questioned Dr. Manheimer. "It will take a few days. We are very tight for space and the arrangement to have them together helped us out a lot."

He gritted his teeth. "Do it as soon as possible. I am going to request that Dr. Richards be taken off his case. I will be taking his case over as soon as the board reviews my request."

The ward was not known for culinary excellence. The food was starchy, cheap and flavorless. Its main goal was to sustain patients for whom chewing could be a traumatic experience. Many had no teeth and few could remember what they had eaten a few hours ago. Robert Grant needed to be encouraged to swallow his food. Theo was doing just that, spooning lumps of mashed potatoes into his mouth. His will to live had been buried along with his wife and two children. Drugs that kept him alive by deadening his thoughts clouded Robert's mind. Their main function was to prevent him from thinking or remembering. It was the closest modern psychiatry could come to showing mercy in a case like his. He had nearly died in the attack, but the medical system, manned by super-skilled professionals equipped with hi-tech hardware saved his life, never asking him if he may have preferred to die. The paramedics kept him alive long enough for the emergency room to take over. The emergency room staff performed all the proper procedures. The killer was dead, shot down by police, what they call 'suicide by cop.' He had run at a group of ten policemen, waving his bloody combat knife, screaming. The entire incident was closed and sealed, the newspapers referring to it whenever a similar act of violence occurred.

But Robert lived on. The body healed but what was left of the man was beyond repair. The best the psychiatric system could do was continue what the paramedics had begun and keep his body alive. In an ideal world, Robert should have died. He was a husband too late to save his wife, too injured to save his children, in an attack that should never have happened in a merciful world. Society expected sanity from Robert yet failed to provide sanity for him when he and his family needed it most. So he was locked away, for his own good. The gates and guards were redundant. He was already locked away, locked in his own mind, forced to step into the reality of that awful night over and over again.

Drugs and his own living hell left him emotionally dead. When Theo had first offered to take him to the bathroom, a glimmer of life entered his consciousness. He felt another presence in his thoughts. He didn't respond, but he did recognize it. What he didn't know was the effect it had on Theo, the dreadful price he paid to connect with this tortured soul.

When dinner was over, Theo helped Mr. Grant stand. They shuffled towards their room, Theo holding Mr. Grant's arm.

"I have a story to tell you, Robert. In the books of Kabbalah, it is said that there are thirty-six righteous people in the world, and it is their merit that tips the scales and allows the world to continue to exist, despite the evil and darkness that abound. Without these unique souls, without even one of them, our sins would consume us and the world would perish in the unquenchable fire of our own hate. Many people know this story, though only a few believe it to be real."

Theo paused, searching Robert's face for a reaction. When there was none, he sighed and continued.

"Robert, what I have told you is true but it is not the entire story. That part of the story was written down and retold. But there is part of the story that has never been told. Once every seven years, the thirty-six righteous men and women gather together and hold a tribunal. They put God on trial. It is the only time they ever come together. The tribunal is terrifying. There are two angels present. One angel dares to accuse God Himself. The other angel comes to defend God, but that angel is too awesome for anyone to behold.

He stands in another room, silent. They put God on trial for His sins, and if God is judged to be innocent, then the world has no recourse. Our sins are ours alone to bear and the world must be destroyed. If God is found to be guilty, then He bears part of our guilt and the world can claim at least partial innocence. God's guilt permits us to live. Every seven years since man was created, the defending angel has struggled in vain to refute the accusing angel's claims against God. Every seven years since the beginning of time, for that one awful night, the world hangs in balance. But for the accusing angel to hold destruction at bay, he needs the tribunal of thirty-six at his side. These holy men and women must be pure in action and courageous in spirit to take on such a terrible task. They prepare themselves for seven years, purifying themselves, in order to live through that one night. But, Robert, in order to perform their duties, in order to give the world hope for survival, they need to call a witness. They need someone who can point a finger at God and bring justice upon his Creator." Robert turned his head and for the first time since the attack, looked at another person's face. "Robert, I have been sent to bring you to the tribunal. You are the witness. Will you come with me?"

Robert smiled as tears streamed down his face. He nodded as his voice, hoarse with neglect, spoke for the first time in two years. "Yes. I will come."

The shop was dusty and dark. Piles of chairs huddled against one wall. A figure stepped in, the bell over the door ringing lightly. The man took off his coat, making himself seem even smaller, so frail that it seemed he was part of the shadows. He tried the light switch, but the electricity had been turned off. He found candles and matches on the windowsill and began lighting them, distributing them around the many nooks and crannies. He was stooped over and his leg dragged when he walked, but his frailty was not due to age. The flare of the match revealed the face of a young man, already lined with trouble and illness. Another figure entered, a large bear of a man, his broad face hidden behind a tangled beard. They nodded grimly to each other and began to distribute the chairs around the room. The room filled up quickly and quietly with silent figures, an odd mixture of races and ages. Although most of them were dressed in the simple clothes of poverty, one woman wore an evening gown, jewels sparkling around her neck in the candlelight. When the chairs were arranged in a semi-circle, they all sat down. They waited, each one lost in his own thoughts, many moving their lips in silent prayer. At one point the candlelight dimmed, as if a wind had entered the room. The candles flared briefly before resuming their gentle flicker, but many eyes now glanced nervously at the heavy wood door in the back of the room. The bell gently announced a new entrance. All eyes turned, silently urging Robert to enter.

Robert had reverted to his previous catatonia. Theo had quickly dressed him and led him to the front gate that sealed the ward from the hospital and the rest of the world. The guard did not look up as Theo opened a gate that should have been locked. A cab was waiting for them, the driver bringing them to the shop without asking their destination. Robert allowed himself to be led, no more aware of the night's journey than he had been of the past two years. A chair was quickly brought to the center of the semi-circle where Theo helped Robert sit down. Theo went to the door, about to exit, when a soft whisper stopped him. An old woman, a scarf covering her hair, called out to him by name.

"We request that you stay." Theo looked around the room. The woman nodded. "We have all agreed that you might be needed. In any case, your presence will certainly not damage our case." She turned to Robert. "Do you know why you are here?" He seemed not to hear her but something in his eyes awakened, like a reflection of the flickering candles. "Is the defending angel present?" A deep chill passed through the hearts of all, wordlessly assuring them that fearsome powers were nearby. The woman stood, looking slowly around the room as she spoke.

"We all know why we are here but the words must be said. We, who love God most, who are in His presence every moment of every day, are here to judge Him. We do this, not in anger, but out of love, since He has commanded it. And here, before us, is the witness we have waited for." She looked towards Robert but he was unresponsive, his chin resting lightly on his chest. She continued speaking to Robert. "We all know what happened to you and to your family. We are filled with sadness and remorse. But you must know that your family had to perish. It was the will of God." Slowly, Robert's head began to sway from side to side. "Your family's death saved the world. Your two children died in order that all of the other children in the world could continue living." The swaying of his head increased, loose and wide, as a moan grew deep in his chest. "Evil is a power in the world and balance is demanded. To pay for the world's evil, to offset it, the good must suffer. It is not fair, but it is this point of God's injustice with which the world was created that permits man to live despite his own sins. It is not how we would have it but so it was decreed from the Creator. Your family's suffering was not in vain. They paid the most awful price but the world was saved." She raised her voice so that she could be heard over Robert's moan. "It is sad beyond words. We feel your pain. But surely you would agree that it is just, sacrificing three souls in order to save an entire world. You were not present when the world was created. You do not know the Creator's plan. Surely . . ."

Her words were cut off as Robert jumped to his feet with a piercing scream that made everyone in the room shudder. His screaming went on for a full minute until his lungs were empty and he had to gasp painfully for breath. "I don't need to know about God's eternal plan! I am a man and I know only what a man knows in his lifetime. But that is enough. My children, my wife, they were worth more than all of the other children and wives in the world. The rest of the world can die and disappear. I don't care. It was wrong that they should suffer. It was wrong that they were taken from me!"

"Surely you can't believe that. The entire world on one side and . . ."

His scream welled up again, like an unstoppable wave pounding the beach. "My wife and my children!"

She straightened her back, her face set in stone. "That is selfish. You only care for your own domestic pleasures. If you believed in God, you would leave it in his hands."

His breathing was like an engine, sucking air hoarsely, his body twitching in anger. "I don't believe in God. I know God, in all His glory and in all His ugliness. I held my children in my hands when they were born, watching them take their first breaths. I crawled to them and touched them as they took their last breath. That puts me on a level with God. I was their father. They were my children. That makes me as powerful as Him when He created the world. He created the world for me in order for that to happen. I knew it in my heart because nothing that beautiful could come from my own hands. And God was in that animal that walked on two legs. He killed them. God did that. And it was evil."

She seemed to grow taller and her eyes spat back fire from the candles. "You dare call God evil? Man is commanded to be good. God is above that."

His hands twitched at his sides. "God is not above anything. He is above and below. He is everywhere. And just as He commands me to be good wherever I am, I demand the same from Him." He took a ragged breath and the fire went out of his anger, replaced by a sadness that burned deeper. "God help me. I think back on my little girl and I think of how much sweetness can be contained in this world. My boy . . . ." His sobs were echoed around the room. "As good as the sweetness was, the evil is even greater. If the only reason for creating me were to bring my children into the world so they could die for someone else's evil, I would have killed myself when I was born. You can say my pain is only one person's suffering, but isn't one person's suffering enough? If God wanted to, he could have held back this evil from the world." Robert looked at the floor for a moment and when he looked up, there was so much fire in his gaze that the woman had to look away. "God could have kept this evil from the world and he chose not to."

A raspy whisper filled the room, taking the breath out of everyone's chest. The whisper came from behind the closed wooden door but it filled the room like a silent roar. "It was a man's hand that wielded the knife."

Robert whirled to face the door. His voice was filled with cold anger. "But it was God's will that made it happen. It was God's hand that brought the knife down. If God made the world, then He can't just walk away. He can't just close his eyes. He has infinite power, infinite knowledge. God is able to save people, to prevent suffering, so He is responsible. Man is a child but God made him the world's caretaker. It was not our choice and we are not in control. Our responsibility was forced upon us." He took several steps towards the door, his hands clenched into fists. He was surrounded by people, gentle hands holding him back. They led him to his chair and sat him down. He was limp and weak, quickly slipping back into his silent world. The figures returned to their places, many of them shaking with silent tears.

The woman's scarf had slipped, revealing thick gray hair. Tears streamed down her lined face. She tried to stand straight but her body shuddered with sobs for a minute before she was able to control herself enough to speak. "The defending angel has spoken. Will he speak again?"

The assembly held its breath and waited. Heads were bowed in prayer, lips moved feverishly, tears dropped to the dusty floor. Finally, she let out a breath. "We have decided. The witness was a true witness." She sat down.

Robert jumped to his feet. "No! This means nothing. Nothing has changed. I demand true justice."

The woman smiled sadly. "There is no true justice in this world. There is no verdict, only life and death."

"Then this was all a lie."

She shook her head. "As I said, there is no true justice in this world, yet as payment for standing witness, this one time there will be true justice." Her eyes glanced at the door for a moment. "What was done until now was because our souls and our Creator required it." Her voice softened. "Now we must act according to the demands of our hearts."

Robert stood, his legs shaking. "I want my family back."

She shook her head, more in sadness than in denial. "You know that can't be. But . . ." She looked at him and something seemed to travel from her eyes to his, flickering across the empty room that separated them. He smiled for a moment before sinking back into his chair. Theo rushed to his side but his eyes slid back into a blank stare. He held Robert's limp hand until all of the people had left.

THE GOOD
DOCTOR

"The concept of the individual is clearly incorrect on many levels. It is an illusion, inaccurate in every aspect. I would dismiss it as a quirk unique to humanity however it is the source of all suffering and death. I believe it would be more accurately classified as a disease, probably communicable, possibly via a sub-atomic virus."

"There is no such thing as a sub-atomic virus."

"We have yet to discover one, however awareness is a product of the individual. It could be that the virus has a survival mechanism that prevents the infected individual from discovering it."

"That's absurd."

"But irrefutable. I base my entire theory on observation, a scientific process that you cannot discount with any level of credibility. To deny observation and deduction, hence the scientific process, is to entomb psychology in the realm of fanaticism. You define truth as a subjective experience unearthed by psychoanalysis, self-validated in murky halls, clearly a by-product of the disease in question. I would like to expand the possibilities of truth to include the improbable and to include phenomena outside of our knowledge. The truth may be unknown but it isn't unknowable."

"When does the individual begin? When his father's sperm enters the mother's egg? Can we not classify that egg, firmly embedded in the mother's womb, as an appendage, a newly formed internal organ, its growth spurred by an infection, or perhaps inspired by an other? It is clearly not a separate organism, an individual. Biologists muse with a chuckle that the single-celled organisms alive today are immortal, multiple incarnations of the original cell that first divided millions of years ago. An individual human can be seen as a symbiotic organization of single cells with an enigmatic spark of the ever elusive, indefinable, 'self' added in. The entire human race can be seen as a multi-celled organism, each person a cell, all brought together in a rather loose collection, in slightly less proximity than usually present in a single organism. Perhaps the human race is an individual organism made up of millions of organs, each considering itself to be separate and independent, when in fact, they are clearly inter-dependent."

"What is your point?"

"A healthy organism displays certain behavior; an unhealthy organism displays different behavior. A zoologist who observes a chimpanzee chewing off its own fingers will naturally conclude that he is observing a pathology. Humans may display extreme cruelty towards other humans and the only thing that allows the possibility that this is not clearly pathological is the illusion that the object of this aggression and hatred is an other. Take away the concept of the other and murder becomes suicide, cruelty becomes masochistic. Permitting others to starve or die through neglect appears as a man applying a tourniquet to his own limb and allowing it to wither and die. Pollution becomes an individual eating his own excrement. The concept of the individual is the arm claiming that it is free and independent of the liver. The heart may be permitted to live because it has a clear and immediate utility. Take away the concept of the individual, replace it with the far more accurate concept of a super-organism, and society will be enhanced. The human race has a chance of survival. The individual will be happier and better cared for. If this perception brings us to a higher, improved level of functionality, then isn't it clearly true? Isn't denial a deadly disease?"

"It is clearly untrue. I can feel pain and you will be unaware of it. I can die and it will not affect any other person."

"Isn't that clearly a symptom of this pathology? We should be so connected that I feel your pain. One of the parameters of sanity is a level of empathy considered normal. And perhaps we are so connected that I can feel your pain. I do not share your pain in the direct sense that I experience my own, however it is seen that those who exist only in their own experiential reality become embittered, ill, and capable of horrendously destructive acts. Over-consumption works fine in capitalistic theory; however it exhibits itself as an illness, a fevered run towards communal death. On a lower level, the human psyche is able to separate itself from its own body, over-indulge until it is ill." He hesitated. "I have been told by parents that they can physically feel a portion of their child's pain." He paused, looking at Janet for support but found none.

"In any case, I deny that we are necessarily separate. It seems to be a choice. Some feel this connection stronger than others. They are called saints or humanitarians. They are not exceptions. Self-denial is not suffering. It is a direct result of expanded consciousness. We are all eating at a buffet. My overeating causes my neighbor to starve."

Dr. Manheimer slammed his hand on the table. "You've turned the individual into an appendage, making him worthless. Murder becomes nothing more than trimming fingernails."

"Yes and no. The individual is an appendage. His worth is determined by his function in the organism as a whole. When a surgeon holds a beating heart in his hand, he is filled with awe. Not for the heart itself, but for the organism as a whole. What are his feelings when he cuts out a cancerous growth? Is it filled with life in the same way the heart is? But I believe the true worth of the individual is even greater than we realize. We are microcosms that contain the macrocosm. The loss of an individual changes the whole. We are all interconnected. If I lift a stone in Vermont, it may save a life in Vietnam. Consciousness is also an action."

"This all sounds very nice and altruistic but as a theory it is unverifiable and undeniable. We are all individuals living separate lives. We all act according to personal interests. To view yourself as part of a super-organism is a false belief." Dr. Manheimer turned to the other board members, pointedly ignoring Janet. "It is clear that the permissive attitude we have taken towards Mr. Morrison has only encouraged him to expand his delusional theories, making them more complex, intricate, and interwoven. It is my opinion that he is so deeply entrenched in a false reality that only drastic means will have any hope of extracting him. As department head, I am taking over his case. It is clear that further reviews will only be a waste of this board's time."

"But Doctor, we haven't heard the board's opinion. We have only heard your opinion."

"And that is enough." He stared at Janet for a moment, making a note that the pretty butterfly pin was still in her hair. "I am taking over his case. There is nothing to discuss."

Janet returned his stare and practically growled. "There certainly is more to discuss, another topic being your pig-headedness and lack of professionalism." Dr. Manheimer's face turned bright red as he snatched up his papers from the table in front of him, spilling half of them on the floor. Theo smiled. This woman had moxie and if he merited marrying her, she would demand his total respect every moment of every day.

He felt the attendants' hands on his shoulders, urging him to leave. Reluctantly, he acquiesced, knowing that Robert needed him in the day room to feed him lunch.

Robert's condition had grown worse since the night of the trial. He barely chewed his food and now wore diapers. Theo had just finished feeding him when Janet walked into the room. She searched for a minute before finding Theo, rewarding him with a smile. She sat down, looking at Robert for a few moments.

"He isn't getting better."

Theo shook his head. "No. He is sinking deeper every day."

She gave him a curious look. "I thought you considered that to be a good thing?"

He shrugged. "On one level, it is. But I am human. My human perspective sees him suffering."

She considered this for a moment. "I am considering your offer but it is a little hard to take seriously."

Theo frowned. "I was never more serious in my life."

She put her hand on his. "I know you were. As crazy as it sounds, I am ready to believe everything you say. But you are ignoring a very real problem." She pulled her hand away and waved it around the room. "Look around. This isn't Disneyland and that big guy in the white suit isn't Donald Duck. You are locked up and considered dangerous to society."

Theo pointed at the butterfly in her hair. "Can I have it back?"

She tried hard not to smile and shook her head. He shrugged and went on. "Society is right. Samuel Morrison is a threat and needs serious help. But I am not Samuel Morrison. I am Theo, the Hope Merchant. Sam needs to be locked up, if for no other reason than to get a rest. But since I am Theo, these bars were not meant for me and therefore could not possibly stop me from going where I need to go. Especially if I were going with you."

She chewed her lip for a few seconds. "I want to believe you but I can't. The facts are . . . ."

A rough hand, nails yellow from nicotine, came down on her shoulder. "The facts are now irrelevant." A thick folder slapped down on the table between them. Dr. Manheimer spun a chair around, straddling it as he glanced back and forth between Theo and Janet. "I hope I am not interrupting."

Janet felt her anger rising but saw that Theo was smiling sadly. Theo sighed and shook his head. "We were having a discussion about the healing process and the doctor-patient relationship. It is certainly not an interruption, considering how deeply you are involved."

Dr. Manheimer grinned like a goblin as he lit a cigarette. "In that case, I really am not involved. And neither are you, Dr. Richards." He took a puff before continuing. "And I think even you have been trumped, Mr. Morrison." He took a folded paper from his coat pocket and opened up the folder that lay between them on the table. "This is your transfer. This afternoon you will be going to a different facility."

Janet watched as he opened the file and placed the new form on top. "You can't do that, Doctor."

He grinned. "It's been done, Doctor."

"I will put in a request . . . ."

"It will be denied."

Theo picked up the form. "Actually, there is a problem."

Dr. Manheimer sneered. "Does something in the transfer contradict another of your absurd theories?"

Theo concentrated as he read. "No. Everything seems okay except for the name." Janet was suddenly aware of what was coming and half stood in panic. "The name of the patient on the form is 'Samuel Morrison.' My name is Thelonius Meyer."

Janet sat down but her voice was barely a whisper, her throat tightening in panic. "Not now, Theo. Don't bring this up now."

Theo's eyes scanned the rest of the page. "In fact, everything about this is wrong. All of the personal details are incorrect; date of birth, place of birth, family history." He shook his head and tore the paper in half. "I'm afraid this is all wrong and you'll have to fill out a new transfer with the correct information." Dr. Manheimer's mouth fell open as Theo tore up the form.

Janet's hands shook as she gathered together the scraps of paper. "Dammit, Theo! You can't tear up official forms. They won't just disappear."

Dr. Manheimer's hand came down roughly on hers. "I think we have several breaches of hospital procedure here, doctor." Janet looked up at him and felt her strength drain from her body. "This piece of paper is insignificant. I have a copy, of course, filed in my office. I am concerned, though not surprised, at Mr. Morrison's delusional claims to be someone else. What deeply worries me is that you, Dr. Richards, called him Theo."

Janet felt dizzy as her blood pressure rose. Her mouth opened but no words came out. Instead, Theo spoke, his voice steady and authoritative, perhaps even a little mocking as he answered for her. "Dr. Richards has studied my case very carefully. She has chosen to address me by a name that I prefer. Since I could legally change my name if I so desired, and since it enhanced and facilitated the doctor-patient relationship, this shouldn't be such a problem. Should it, Dr. Manheimer?"

Janet breathed half a sigh of relief before fear froze the air in her lungs. "But you said all the information was wrong. Not just the name. You can change your name as a legal formality but your past is an objective truth. Psychiatrists must accept that or else be sucked into the patient's delusions. That clearly seems to be what has happened to Dr. Richards. She has lost her professional objectivity." He took the scraps of paper from Janet's hands and deposited them in his ashtray, flicking a long cigarette ash on top. He glanced at his watch. "The ambulance will be here in two hours to pick you up, Mr. Morrison. Since this will certainly be our last meeting, I am willing to humor your fantasies for just a little longer." His sneer widened. "I apologize. I meant to say 'Mr. Meyer'. Please enlighten me. Tell me, Thelonius, what else was incorrect."

"Please don't call me that."

"But you just told me that your name was Meyer."

Theo grimaced. "My name is Meyer. Please don't call me Thelonius. I never liked being called that."

Dr. Manheimer laughed bitterly. "You are a real pistol. This is the first time I have ever heard of someone choosing a fantasy personality that they don't like."

Theo smirked. "I like myself. I don't like my name. I didn't choose it. My father did."

"Well, if you object to the name, you can always change it legally to something you prefer. Might I suggest 'Samuel Morrison'? It has a nice ring to it, wouldn't you say?" Janet watched in horror as the two men laughed like old friends. Dr. Manheimer was having Theo shipped off to some dungeon left over to showcase the evils of medieval healthcare. For all she knew he had ordered electro-shock or medication that would fry every healthy synapse in Theo's brain. From Janet's perspective, Theo was a little boy dancing on the edge of a cliff and Dr. Manheimer was waltzing him over the edge, laughing as he fell down into the depths of a living hell. Dr. Manheimer continued. "Please tell me more about yourself. Samuel Morrison was a delivery truck driver. What did you do for a living? Were you a lecturer in clinical psychology? You certainly graced us with much of your professional insight."

Theo smiled. "No. I had a shop. I was a Hope Merchant."

Dr. Manheimer grinned at Theo like a shark that had just bitten off one leg and was being offered the other as well. "And you sold hope?" Theo nodded, smiling like a child doing well in a spelling bee. "What sort of package did your hope come in?"

Theo settled back in his chair. "Oh, all kinds. It depended on the customer. I remember one guy fancied himself a stud. He broke hearts left and right. He came in and got a pair of sunglasses to wear to the beach. He liked them because they made him look good. But they also made him see what a woman was like on the inside. After seeing a woman look ugly even for just one moment, he could never see her the same way again. Eventually, he found a truly beautiful woman, so beautiful on the inside that he held that vision of her always."

Dr. Manheimer's mocking laughter went on so long that it drew stares from all the residents and staff in the day room. Theo's smile didn't waver. When the doctor quieted down, Theo asked him why he laughed. "That's absurd. You're describing a situation that could not exist in real life. Those would be magical glasses." He poked Theo in the chest with each word, emphasizing his message beyond the point of professional detachment. "And-Magic-Does-

Not-Exist." Theo lifted his hand as if to hit the doctor's face, but reached behind his ear, instead, producing a shiny quarter. Dr. Manheimer looked stunned but Theo's smile had not wavered at any point during the confrontation.

"You see, Doctor, magic has many faces and many names. Sometimes it is called sleight of hand. Sometimes, it is called nature. Sometimes it is called luck, and sometimes it is called love. The important thing is to have the eyes to see magic when it happens in front of you. Not everyone does. I have seen the most amazing magic happen in a crowded room, just like this one, and only one or two other people saw it. To see magic, you need hope. I deal in magic, little wonders that fix the world. And just like magic, I have many faces and many names."

Dr. Manheimer was angry but his voice shook and his face was pale. "Magic is a worthless illusion that doesn't really exist. If you were really a magician, you wouldn't be here. You would have opened up the locks and left."

Theo nodded. "Very soon, I will. But I came here to do something and I must complete it." Theo's smile changed into something Janet couldn't recognize. "Dr. Manheimer, I have a little magic left, a trinket I brought with me from the store. Would you like to see it?" Theo held up his hand and Janet saw a thin silver bracelet glowing on his wrist. She had never noticed it before in all of their sessions. Dr. Manheimer stared at it, transfixed as it reflected the harsh institutional lights, its silver softening them into something else.

"What does it do?" The doctor sounded half asleep, hypnotized by the glittering metal.

"It makes you reveal what is really in your heart."

The doctor coughed out a half-hearted laugh of derision. "That's all?"

Theo shrugged. "I admit it's not my most impressive piece, not a real show stopper, however the effect is more intense for some than for others. For some people, the difference is barely noticeable. For others, well, I have seen some spectacular results." The doctor reached towards the silver bracelet. He shook his head and drew his hand suddenly back. Janet watched as Theo slipped it off his wrist and faster than she could follow, it appeared on the doctor's arm. It seemed to shrink, fitting snugly as if it would be difficult to remove.

The doctor's face seemed to grow older, his skin yellow and dry. He shuddered once before shaking his head, blinking his eyes for a full minute before reaching for his cigarettes. The match shook, dancing around in front of the cigarette gripped in his white lips. He took two deep drags before snorting. "A typical parlor trick, like I expected. Like a Ouija board. Anything I say now will sound so significant and special, even if it is a bunch of lies and nonsense."

Theo nodded. "If that is what you believe."

The doctor's face turned red as his anger grew. His voice got louder as he spoke and heads turned to stare. "That's exactly what I mean. You are trying to twist my words to make them sound significant and deep. But if this bracelet was really magic, I wouldn't be able to tell a lie." He stood up and placed his palm on his chest as if taking an oath. "I am not from this planet. I was born far away on the planet Zoid and sent here as an ambassador of good will. I am ten thousand years old with forty eight hundred offspring, a member of the royal Yark family by marriage. Join with me as I sing the praises of our twin purple suns. Yark, yark!" He was breathing heavily when he finished. He looked around at the room full of people staring at him and gave a crooked grin followed by a half-bow. He spoke as he lit another cigarette from the old one. His hands no longer shook. "You see, Janet, it's all a load of lies. I am supposed to put on a cheap piece of jewelry and get all serious and weepy eyed. Ha!" Janet was staring at him, her mouth wide open. "Stop it, Dr. Richards. This man is making up stories. He has you somehow convinced that his delusions are real. I strongly suggest that after this is over you come in for some serious supervision, perhaps even reconsider your choice of profession."

Janet began shaking her head, small arcs at first, gradually larger as she realized what she had witnessed. Theo's smile grew in direct proportion to her confusion. "How did he know?"

Theo shrugged. "I guess it's like one of those old test patterns from the early days of television. It might have been left over on the bracelet when I gave it to him."

Dr. Manheimer stubbed his cigarette out fiercely on the bare linoleum tabletop. "Stop it, Janet. I was spouting nonsense. It's just some random stupidity that came into my head."

Janet grabbed his wrist, staring at the bracelet. "No it wasn't. There was no way you could have known. Take it off before . . ."

He pulled his hand away from her. He gripped the bracelet but it stayed on his wrist. "Bah! This loony is too slick for you, Janet. If it was really magic, I wouldn't be able to talk silliness. I would be moaning about how my father ignored me and my children hate me. I would be all post-modern, bleeding heart liberal, touchy feely goo-goo glop about my feelings and how I never felt loved. If I did that, it would be amazing. It might even be considered magic. But I didn't. All I did was babble nonsense. And you are so gullible it made your eyes pop out." He was silent for a moment and Janet watched as the right side of his face began to twitch. He shuddered and his eyes rolled back into his forehead, showing horribly white for a few moments. She was sure he was having a massive stroke when, just as suddenly, his features relaxed and he sat forward and began to speak.

"While we're on the subject, let me tell you what really gets my goat. I am sick to death of all these weirdoes. All they do is complain, complain, and complain, about the smallest things that pop into their screwed-up minds. They act like they have it so hard just because a few of their wires got crossed. All they really need is a good swift kick in the pants to get them out of bed in the morning. Instead, they sit around all day, watching television and taking up space. And then I have to listen to them." He scanned the room with a look of bitter hatred. "Take that guy, for example," pointing his cigarette at Robert Grant. "That artichoke hasn't budged for three years. He's too lazy to even go to the bathroom by himself. Okay, so I know I'm supposed to feel sad for him because his family got killed but three years is long enough. He should have shaken it off and moved on by now. Hell, I've got a family and if they got killed I'd even be able to see some good in the situation. That's what I would do. I bet if he got a good scare, a taste of reality, he'd be up out of that chair and making good time." Dr. Manheimer sat for a few moments, glowering at Robert as he sat in his wheelchair, unaware of being watched. "Hey! Hey, Mr. Artichoke!" Dr. Manheimer stood up and strode angrily across the dayroom, pushing aside the patients that strayed into his path. He planted himself in front of Robert and stooped down so they could see each other eye to eye. "Listen, you loser. I am going to tell it to you straight. Your family is dead, D-E-A-D, dead, and you can stop waiting for that to change. So you might as well accept that fact and get up out of that chair." Dr. Manheimer reached down and grabbed Robert around the chest, yanking him out of the wheelchair, holding him up like a life sized rag doll. A nurse screamed and an attendant ran towards the doctor struggling to hold up the catatonic patient. The doctor held up a hand, stopping the attendant in his tracks. "No! I am in charge of this man's treatment and you are about to see modern science triumph over bleeding heart nannyism." He struggled to turn the man around so he was facing the center of the room. "Enough exaggerated weeping and moaning. As your doctor, I command you to walk!" He gave Robert a shove forward and for a moment it looked as if he was indeed going to follow the order. Robert took one step, swaying for a few moments, when he collapsed onto the floor and began to convulse. Nurses and attendants surrounded him but the seizure was violent and uncontrollable. A few doctors appeared, kneeling over him, while the nurses and attendants hurried to clear the room of patients. The head nurse reappeared, leading a strangely docile Dr. Manheimer from the room. A gurney appeared, pushed by a matched pair of burly paramedics. They shoveled Robert onto the stretcher but as they were reaching for the straps, his body gave one giant spasm, arching up off the mattress. The veins stood out on his neck as he gave a long scream of pain, cut off, as pink foam filled his mouth. Robert's body arched twice more but there were no more screams. The paramedics worked quickly but it was clear there was no frantic drive behind their movements. They sweated hard to save the living. Dead is no sweat.

Janet had watched the scene with a strange feeling of detachment. Years of experience in clinical psychology couldn't prepare her for the transformation that she had witnessed in Dr. Manheimer. At some point, Samuel Morrison had become Theo and logic then seemed a less likely explanation for everything than magic. She looked over at Theo, expecting him to be grief stricken at the sight of his friend's horrible death. She was shocked to see him looking in the other direction, watching television. He was smiling, almost laughing out loud, while tears of joy streamed down his cheeks. She was furious and about to confront him when he sensed her anger and turned to look into her eyes.

He smiled at her and said softly, "Look."

Her anger turned to puzzlement at his strange behavior. She turned to look at the television screen in the corner of the day room. The volume was turned low, the screen dusty, smeared with greasy fingerprints. The show was just beginning and the opening credits were beginning to roll down the screen in front of a smiling family sitting in their cushy living room, everyone waving at the camera. She didn't recognize the actors or the program but that seemed normal to Janet since she rarely watched television. Her anger was quickly returning and she was about to grill Theo on why he found sitcoms more engaging than the real life tragedy that had just occurred ten feet from his chair. Suddenly something on the television screen caught her eye and she moved closer to get a better look. Her nose was practically touching the screen before she would allow herself to be sure. The smiling father on the television, surrounded by his happy family, was the man lying dead on the stretcher.

She turned to Theo but her mind couldn't figure out how to ask the essential and obvious question she needed answered in order to hold onto her sanity. Theo smiled at her and shook his head. "This is my favorite television show. It's not so true to life but I learn a lot from it. Do you want to watch it with me?"

"He's dead."

Theo shook his head. "No." He pointed at the body on the stretcher, now alone, abandoned by the paramedics. "He is dead. The Robert you see on the television screen is very much alive, as is his family." Theo pulled over a couple of chairs and they sat down. Theo clapped his hands and smiled. "This is one of my favorite episodes and they very rarely show it. I hope no one comes in to interrupt us."

Janet sat in the chair, watching, too numb to move. The story unfolded quickly. The camera followed an angry man searching for a way to enter the house. The music was ominous, an organ wavering as a kettledrum mimicked a heartbeat. He is clearly planning to do something awful. Crouching in the bushes, he discovers an open window. Robert and his family are soundly asleep and have no idea they are in danger. His little boy, the three-year-old, wakes up to go the bathroom and sees the stranger dressed in black climbing the stairs.

Theo reached over to hold Janet's hand. "This part always makes me want to jump out of my skin."

The man is scared and you just know he is about to do something desperate, but the little boy rubs his eyes and asks the man for a glass of water. He reaches up and takes the man's finger and leads him down to the kitchen. You see the man move his other hand, the one holding the knife, behind his back. In the next scene, you see Robert waking up to a noise. He jumps out of bed and runs down the hall. His wife is not in bed next to him and the kids' room is empty, the blankets thrown onto the floor. He runs down the stairs and sees a light on in the kitchen. He rushes in and sees the family sitting at the kitchen table, a strange man sitting in his place. They are having juice and sandwiches. His wife has a strange look on her face but you see them make eye contact, communicating the important messages through their eyes, as only parents can. Everyone is safe so it is okay to flow with the strange situation. The three-year-old takes charge, explaining that he was thirsty and the stranger had helped him get a cup of juice. He had wanted to show his new friend how he was a big boy and could make his own peanut butter and jelly sandwich. That is when his sister showed up, also hungry and thirsty. The children were shy and proud, a strange balance that only children can pull off. The wife is nervous and confused, but doing better now that the husband is here. The stranger is sitting between the children but he is clearly undecided and he has not removed his black leather gloves. All eyes turn to the father. The background music brings us to the heights of tension. The father and stranger lock eyes and the father nods.

"You could be a lot of things, but here and now, at least for tonight, I'd prefer it if I could call you 'friend'. My little boy has brought me a lot of joy and happiness. I'm hoping you will be just another good thing that he has brought our way."

The stranger seems to chew on his words for a few seconds before a scowl screws up his face. His hand slips behind his back, lifting up the back of his jacket. "Listen, buddy. I . . ."

The father shakes his head. "Please. I . . ." His voice cracks and everything hangs in balance. "I've seen hard times and my guess is you have too. This can go a lot of different ways, some of them good, some of them bad, and some I don't want to think about. There's a lot I can do and a lot more I can't. I think we both understand each other but I think we can come to an agreement. Just for tonight, I want to feed you. I have been blessed with a good family. I want to share that blessing with you and invite you to join us. If you accept my invitation, you'll be doing us both a big favor, probably more for me than for you. And for that, I'd be in your debt."

The little boy reaches up and tugs on the sleeve that is reaching for the knife. "Mister, you're not eating your samich. Didn't I make it good?"

The man looks down at the face of the three-year-old boy and tears appear in his eyes. "Is it okay if I don't eat it? I hate peanut butter."

The boy nodded, using his whole body. "Sure. My mommy says you shouldn't say 'hate'. She says too many people say hate when it's not really what they mean. My mommy makes the bestest grilled cheese samich in the world. Do you want me to ask her to make you one?" The man nods and the mother stands up and walks to the fridge. The ending credits begin to roll as the mother gets busy at the stove. In a strange moment, the father turns and waves at the camera. "He's saying goodbye. I think you should say goodbye back. You won't get another chance. He can't come back to visit, and even if he could, he probably won't. I know I wouldn't."

Janet raises her hand and gently waves back as the screen goes black. Theo turns off the television and stands up, holding out his hands to her. She shakes her head. "How can you do this? I feel like I've stayed the same but the entire world has gone crazy."

Theo gave her a crooked smile, making him look like a twelve-year-old boy in a man's body. "In an insane world, the wise man chooses to be crazy."

"So what now?"

He lifted up her hands, holding them for a moment before pulling her to her feet. "And they lived happily ever after."

"I don't believe in happily ever after."

"So come away with me, be my wife, and teach me what you do believe in. Maybe we'll both be right." Theo looked into her eyes and saw her answer waiting to be said. He smiled and suddenly it was all clear and simple, a choice to be made. And the word came so easily she smiled back at the face she finally recognized. "Yes".

He picked up Dr. Manheimer's discarded lab coat and led her to the ward's exit. As they approached the locked door separating them from the outside world, the burly guard at the desk looked up from his newspaper and frowned at them. Janet hesitated but her hand was trapped in Theo's and he led her forward.

"Who is your guest, Dr. Meyer? I hope you aren't helping one of the patients escape."

Janet was terrified, struggling to cope for a moment before she realized the guard wasn't speaking to her. Theo laughed before answering. "No, not a patient. Janet is a grad student. She thought I might have a few things to teach her about modern mental health techniques." Janet looked up and saw her reflection in the one-way glass in the door behind the guard's desk. She was shocked at how young she looked. The reflection staring back at her was ten years out of date. Theo unclipped the nametag from the white coat's lapel, handing it to the guard.

The guard cracked a smile and handed the plastic coated card back to Theo. "I don't need that. If I don't recognize you after all this time then I'd be worse off than some of those patients." Janet glanced over, noting that Theo didn't look that much younger in the photo. The door buzzed and Theo opened it for her. He was halfway through when the guard's deep voice stopped him.

"I hope I don't see you back here."

Theo hesitated before answering. "You might, but it probably won't be for a while. Janet and I are going to take a long vacation. And then we are going to go into private practice together."

The door began to close but the gravelly voice stopped them again. "Why don't you stop by the farm after your vacation?"

Theo's face tightened and twisted. "I'll think about it." He stepped through, allowing the heavy door to click shut. He took a deep breath and smiled as he took Janet's hand.

THE
BOOK
OF
LIFE

BEN

The key struggled in the lock for a few moments before the door relented. Glimpses of a man burst into the apartment, swinging and dancing as he performed a quick circuit of the room. His well-rehearsed speech was sung in rapid fire while his arms shot out in all directions to point out highlights of the apartment. The target of the spiel was a young man, well dressed, with obvious skepticism on his face. He followed the hyper-energetic realtor for a few minutes before taking a stand in the center of the room. He stood like the calm eye of the storm, silently watching the salesman whirl and spin around him, chattering non-stop with hyperbolic pronouncements about the apartment. The presentation wound down after five tightly choreographed minutes leaving the agent exhausted but smiling and evidently pleased with his performance. His pause was only temporary. He sensed the young man's reservations.

"It's perfect, isn't it? Check it out. It has the very latest entertainment system with the very fastest connection."

The client fidgeted. "Well, it lacks . . . that is to say it doesn't have . . . I was told it would have, well, you know."

The agent slapped him on the shoulder. "Can I call you Stan, friend?"

"Umm, I guess so. But my name is Ben."

The agent slapped him on the shoulder again and laughed. "I knew that. I was just testing to see if you knew that. So Ben, I'll be frank, even though my name is Fred. And that's way too many names for any Tom, Dick, or Harry. What this place lacks you don't need. Not an enlightened guy like you. Downstairs is the indoor pool with full beach simulation all day, every day. What more could you possibly want, friend?" He leaned close, whispering a five-decibel secret in Ben's ear. "This place is so swinging that I've been tempted to spend a couple hours here in an empty apartment just to relive my single days of being footloose and fancy free. Not that I don't love the old ball and chain, but I'm human like every man. Trust me, you won't be lacking anything except time to taste all the fruit on the tree. You'll be running like a rabbit twenty-five hours a day, eight days a week, three-hundred-and-sixty-seven days a year, or until your subscription runs out. " He gave him another resounding slap.

Ben attempted a polite smile, but his face assumed a thoughtful expression. "It lacks room."

The crease in the agent's forehead indicated his confusion, but he quickly reverted to hard sell mode. "This apartment is twenty percent bigger than standard. And if you are feeling claustrophobic, the wall-size 3-D screen is top of the line. You can set it to project any panoramic vista you like."

"Well, it is spacious and very well equipped." Ben nodded nervously. "But it lacks . . . I don't know how to say . . . it lacks a room."

The agent began to sense serious trouble and his smile twisted as if he had smelled something unpleasant. "I don't quite get you, friend."

Ben looked at the floor as he spoke. "It lacks . . . a bedroom."

The smile vanished. "Ours is a reputable firm. We don't deal in those types of apartments." He strode to the door and yanked it open, holding it ajar for Ben as a final gesture of feigned good nature. "I must ask you to leave. We will return your deposit immediately. Have a nice day." Ben walked quietly out of the apartment, looking over his shoulder as the agent slammed the door shut.

The Midnight Bar was packed, though only the bartenders with their special night vision contact lenses could bear witness. Despite being full, the lounge was quiet, hushed conversations barely rising above the textured white noise played instead of music. Tiny pinpricks of light sparkled in the ceiling, imitating stars but giving no light. The bar was a huge aquarium covered in glass, bioluminescent fish swimming calmly under the patrons' elbows. Dark silhouettes huddled around the bar, drinking specially blended glow in the dark liqueurs. Ben went to the corner, bumping through the crowd. As he sat, a cocktail waitress suddenly hovered in front of him, her jewelry blinking red dots. "Do you want to try our ghost juice? It's happy hour and ghost juice is half price." Her glowing green lips curled into a disembodied smile floating in the darkness.

Ben shuddered. "No thank you. It's the radium that makes the liquor glow. Radium causes cancer, especially when ingested." The glowing lips shriveled up into a puckered frown. "Could you bring me a . . ."

"Better dead than bed," she spat out as she literally disappeared. Another ghostly image appeared in her place, taking the seat across from Ben. "What did you say to get her angry?"

Ben shrugged, the gesture lost in the darkness. "I guess she didn't like my drink order."

A chuckle came out of the darkness. "It's a pity. She was cute. I thought I was in love for a minute."

Ben smirked. "You probably were in love for a minute. It would have lasted until the lights went on."

"Who needs light when you have love?" A glowing glass suddenly appeared in front of Ben's companion. "You're late."

"I had to look at an apartment."

"How was it?"

Ben paused. Todd was a good friend, an old friend. Todd was also Ben's boss. They had graduated together but Todd had fast-tracked, working double shifts and more to get the key to an executive office. Despite their friendship, Todd still saw Ben as an eccentric, even a bit of a loser. Ben needed to take this into account when sharing the more disdained aspects of his life. "It didn't have everything I was looking for."

Todd's voice assumed a teasing tone. "You mean it didn't have a bedroom."

Ben jumped at the word. "Ssh! Not so loud!"

Todd laughed. "It's not a dirty word."

Ben grabbed his wrist. "It's the only dirty word left in this twisted and sick world."

Ben could hear Todd's impatience. "So go ahead and quit. Sign up, subscribe already. Either way it doesn't matter. No one minds if you want to miss out on twice the fun in your life. You're only hurting yourself, but that is your choice and this is a free world. Like they say, everything is free except water on the moon. But don't expect to make any friends along the way. And don't expect me to visit you when you are old and ugly and need someone young and vital to change your diapers after you've slept away the best years of your life."

Ben felt his anger rising along with Todd's. "Of course it won't be you. You'll be dead of natural causes brought on very prematurely but precisely according to plan. Isn't that fair?"

Smug in his conviction, Todd tilted back in his chair, spilling green drops onto the unseen tabletop. "Yes, it is precisely fair. And happily so. Twice the vice at half the price, is what I always say."

"So does everyone else. They heard it on the Fair Deal Show."

"You should watch it".

"I can't. It starts after my bedtime."

Todd hissed, "That was too much. You are disgusting. The average Fred subscribes. It's the logical, socially responsible thing to do. In the meantime you are living at the public expense. Old cage . . . I mean, old age homes are an added expense that this world could do without. Why get old?"

"Just a slogan."

"Maybe it is, but it makes sense. I watch the debates. The pro-agers are slow and stupid. They object to everything. They criticize the most profitable and efficient industries, citing irrelevant historical facts that no one remembers or cares about. Everything is a disaster that already happened before. If it were up to the cagers, we would drive twenty miles an hour and everything would be triple tested for safety. And nothing would ever get done and no one would have any fun."

"That sounds like another new slogan for Fair Deal."

Todd's face clouded. "It is. I heard it last night on the show."

"And what's so bad about that. Every two weeks there is a disaster. A factory blows up, or thousands are diagnosed with some disease caused by a product that was never fully tested before being fed to the public. And what would be so bad about driving slower? Do you know how many people die each year in accidents?"

"You would say that. You are a cager through and through." The dark mass that was Todd rose and walked away. Ben sat alone in the dark, waiting for his drink, sunk in self-doubt. How could most of the world be wrong?

Todd was the creative director for a marketing firm that was very hot at the moment. He had a large office and headed two full staffs, one he watched over by day and the other by night. Todd was recognized by his peers as being intelligent with occasional flashes of brilliance. Ben's career in marketing had not only stalled, but totally stagnated. Todd had chosen the Fair Deal path, as did most everyone. Night and day he worked tirelessly, taking occasional two-day whirlwind vacations. Ben worked hard but finished his workday when the sun went down. In theory, given a career that would inevitably span twice the years, Ben would one day achieve the same heights as Todd. That had been his rationale and he planned his career accordingly. Ben always scored well on tests and relied on his keen intelligence to move him to the top in due time. But he had begun to doubt his decision. It was illegal to discriminate against someone for not taking Fair Deal, but everyone understood that was only on paper. The legal age for signing on was nineteen though there was now a push to allow parents to begin their children much younger. One of the social side effects of Fair Deal is that more and more teens were growing up without their parents. Intuitively, Ben wanted to be a rebel but found that his friends, even the brightest of them, lured by a hedonistic way of life bought the propaganda and mocked him for his decision. What began as a theoretical objection on his part, a topic of debate at campus parties when increasingly he was the lone naysayer, became a personal obsession with lifelong implications. Thinking objectively, Ben told himself he could always begin Fair Deal at a later date, but once begun, the course of drug treatment could not be reversed or safely abandoned. He kept putting off the decision to begin until one day, it seemed like the world was full of bright young faces glowing with unnatural health and unusual vigor, and his was the only tired face in the crowd. Fair Deal was a choice, freely made by each individual. Ben thought each side had its pro's and con's. He decided against it for himself, yet every day he found himself more of a pariah accustomed to keeping his reservations to himself.

He thought back about how it all started. He was very young, but he could remember the tense conversations around the dining room table. The words "economy" and "terrible" always seemed to occur in the same sentence.

Ben stirred from his reverie, realizing that his drink had never been delivered. He looked up to see the waitress' glowing lips moving across the room, dancing as she spoke to the other patrons. A low murmur surrounded him and Ben felt suddenly claustrophobic. He could barely make out the other people but he was sure that dark fingers and darker thoughts were being pointed at him. He stood quickly and pushed his way out of the room to avoid a likely confrontation. The street was brightly lit as always and dance music played from speakers mounted on the lampposts. Ben walked aimlessly, ignoring his fatigue in favor of a few more moments of introspection. The low-key carnival atmosphere of the street gave him a false energy that pushed him on but made it difficult to think. A street vendor standing on the corner with a telescope was selling glimpses of the moon. Ben looked up but couldn't see past the klieg lamps strung across cavernous spaces between the buildings. A man in a bulky raincoat and floppy hat stood watching the line of people waiting for their turn to look at the moon.

Ben was walking past the group when he sensed a change in the mood of the people milling about. People had stopped walking, and a crowd was forming, slowly surrounding the man in the bulky coat. The man turned, seeking an opening to flee. Ben caught a quick glimpse of his face and understood what would probably happen, given the crowd mentality. The man was old, his face covered in a scruffy salt and pepper beard, long gray hair straying out from under his hat. Old people were mocked and rebuked, even threatened wherever they went. As a result, they were rarely seen in public. The only ones who did venture out were those who could afford the services of plastic surgeons and make-up artists. Unlike the elderly who hid their condition, this old guy must have suffered from dementia to have wandered out without hair dye and make-up.

All it took was one pointed finger and one voice raised in accusation. "You old parasite. Go visit your friends in the cemetery. You've got no friends here. We don't want you or your kind." Immediately, a chorus of voices rose in agreement. "It's just not fair. It's just not FAIR!"

The old man, realizing the danger, searched for a way out. He tried to push his way through but he was slower than the young, artificially hyped, crowd. Twenty-four hour days left people bored and random violence was becoming a common alternative to the endless channels of senseless programming. The media tried to play it down, but hate graffiti began to appear with slogans like "No fairs are fair game" sprayed all over town. The old man froze in panic when his eyes locked with Ben's. Ben stepped back away from the crowd, ignoring the unspoken cry for help in the old man's gaze. In the sea of angry faces, Ben's ambivalence must have looked like open support but Ben resolved it would go unspoken because the crowd could easily turn on him. The elderly victim began to shout but his voice was lost in the taunts of the crowd. Ben turned to leave. He tried to shut out the sounds of scuffling but winced as he heard the hard slap of a fist hitting flesh. The crowd was quiet, breathless, waiting for the next act, charged with a pre-orgiastic pent up energy waiting to explode. Ben turned and saw the old man on the ground, a young man leaning over him, his arm drawn back to punch again, holding it there for dramatic effect. In that moment, the old man looked up at Ben, one eye swollen shut, and he called out, "Benjy! Help me!"

Ben was stunned but his body began to move with a will of its own. He found himself surging forward, his arms pumping in rage. Caught off guard and off balance, the young tough tumbled off the old man and fell sprawling on the pavement. Ben grabbed the grimy raincoat and felt a lapel rip as he hauled the old man to his feet. He pulled at him desperately, pushing his way through the crowd. They began to stagger away like a strange cumbersome four-legged beast, Ben tangled up in the old man's coat. The crowd let them go, shouting after them with taunts.

"Gray lover."

"Go find some bones to play with"

And the dirtiest word of all followed by childish titters. "Take a walk with your Grandfather!"

Ben blushed, ashamed at the insults despite himself. As they rounded a corner, Ben felt his sudden resolve and fury disappear. His instincts and rage had led him this far and no further. He stood, feeling the old man untangle him from the old raincoat. He tossed his coat in the gutter, tucking Ben's arm under his own.

"You're hard to rouse but a real pisser once you get a head of steam up." He began to lead Ben away with a surprising spring in his step. Ben glanced at him, shocked to see a mischievous grin under what must have been a painful shiner. He tried to yank his arm away but the old man was far stronger than his years should have allowed. Ben stopped short, digging his heels in.

"Where are we going?"

The old man continued to smile. "Does it matter? Unlike all those mindless age-haters we left back there, you don't have to be at work until the morning."

Ben tried to free his arm but the old man didn't seem to notice his efforts. "I need to get home."

The old man patted his arm. "You can say it. I am just like you. Worse, because I look my age. Why do you need to get home?" He waited, making Ben feel like a naughty student who couldn't answer the teacher's question. The old man nodded and filled in the answer. "You need to get home to sleep. I know that. That is why I needed to talk to you. Your dreams brought me to you like the smell of water draws the Tuareg to an oasis." His voice took on an urgent note. "I want to take you to a special place, a place we can talk."

"I don't want to go."

The old man stood looking at Ben. Suddenly he began to grow, as the bright streetlights flickered around him. Ben's neck strained backwards as the old man's glowing eyes transfixed him. His beard grew thick and long like tough vines hanging from an ancient oak. Ben would have screamed but his throat closed up, forcing him to fight for each breath. Ben wasn't sure if the old man actually spoke or if the words just came booming into his mind.

"Of course you will come. Where else can you go? You know the answers but have forgotten all the questions. The sleepless

346

world spins so fast that no one has time for questions anymore. You are the impossible child of dreams, conceived in hopelessness, formed of dust and wonder. Come with me because you have no other choice. Come and discover what lies hidden in your heart." The old man's eyes blazed brightly for a moment, almost blinding Ben. Ben blinked, trying to clear his vision and his head. When he opened his eyes, the old man had returned to his normal state. Ben stood frozen, unable to move. He doubted his own senses and sanity. Had the vision been real? Ben felt a tug on his arm as the old man continued to walk, Ben following meekly, too weak and confused to resist.

The old man led them into an empty office building, walking past a uniformed watchman dozing behind a desk like a mountain of flesh. The watchman's face was deeply lined and though he didn't have a beard, his hair was long and white. He woke up long enough to exchange a nod of recognition with Ben's guide. Ben was shocked. He spent the last few years thinking he was one of the last, if not the final, hold out from Fair Deal. He couldn't remember the last time he had seen an old person, and now in the last ten minutes he had met two. He realized that there must be many, a dwindling population left over from the days when old age was still an honorable alternative and worthy of respect. Like this man standing his solitary watch, they probably gravitated to the unseen edges of society, taking lonely jobs no one else wanted, occupying crumbling neighborhoods hidden from view, living out their lives at a pace too slow to be noticed by the fast-forward youth. The guard took a ring of keys from a drawer and tossed it to the old man. Ben was surprised at how deftly the old man snatched it out of the air, twirling it on his finger as he whistled a tune. He led Ben down the hall towards a freight elevator, the guard following, harmonizing as he walked. He selected a large rusty key and unlocked the gate. He tossed the keys back to the watchman as he pulled the gate shut. The guard yawned, stretching like a rumpled old bear waking up from a long hibernation, his worn-out uniform a shaggy pelt long past its prime.

"They don't pay you to sleep on the job."

"Doesn't matter either way. They pay me if I sleep. They pay me if I don't sleep. I think they pay me to keep out of sight. Fish never come around here anyways. Always running around, they never see anything that stands still. One day they'll blink, or take a nap, and suddenly realize that this old building never got torn down. Then they'll come around and blow it up to make way for an all-night whiz-bang theater."

The old man poked the guard in the chest playfully. "And you in it."

"I wouldn't mind. With the way things are going I wouldn't want to stay around. Fish are all over the place."

He hesitated before pulling the lever. "How's the writing?"

"It's coming. I write three lines and scratch out two. Most of it is garbage. But the stuff I keep . . . ." He smiled and shook his head wistfully.

"What you call garbage is gold. What you keep must be woven of dreams." He reached out to stroke his arm. "Will you finish?"

"That's not up to me. If I finish, it's a blessing, and if I don't, it's a different kind of blessing."

He held his arm a moment longer. "How do you feel?"

"Some days better, some days worse. I'm not gone yet so there must still be a reason for me to be here." The man in uniform stepped back and slid the gate shut.

"I treasure you, my friend."

The guard nodded. "And I treasure you, friend."

The old man slid the brass lever forward and the elevator began to rise. Dark openings slid past, the elevator creaked and groaned, the black shaft rising above the open top, giving Ben vertigo when he looked up and felt he was falling headfirst down an endless mineshaft. He grasped the rough wood handrail to steady himself. The old man reached up and switched on a small electric bulb that swayed with the motions of the elevator. He hummed a different tune, almost familiar, teasing Ben's memory.

Ben was scared and wanted desperately to regain control of the situation. "How did you know my name?"

The old man looked at him with his one good eye "That's not really what you wanted to ask me. Is it?"

Ben's mouth hung open as he searched for an answer. Finally, he sputtered, "Yes, it is."

The old man clucked and shook his head. "No. What you really wanted to ask me was how did I know to call you Benjy?"

"It's the same thing."

The old man shook his head in time with the swinging bulb. "Everyone calls you Ben. Your official signature reads Benjamin. Only one person ever called you Benjy, and he is long dead." He stared at Ben, his one eye glowing in the swaying light. "A name is a powerful thing. It is the key that opens your prayer. Each man has many names but only one true name that he treasures above all else. A name can be a gift or a curse, depending on who speaks it. The one who gave you this name loved you well. He saw much in you. And you loved him back, naming him the keeper of your dreams. You want to know how I called you by a name that was buried years ago."

"I . . ." Ben lost his balance and nearly fell as the elevator continued its slow climb. "Who are you?"

The old man laughed. "Who am I, or what is my name? No matter. I have had many names in my too-long stay in this world. Some have called me Meyer, some Thelonius, and some have even called me Theo. I miss that name. I have been called many things and have had many jobs. The most accurate reading of my name is Thelonius S. Meyer. Most people know me as the Hope Merchant."

"Don't try to sell me. I'm not buying."

The Hope Merchant chuckled. "Oh no. I wouldn't dream of it. In this bleak world where dreams are illegal, you are one of the gifted few with absolutely no need for my services. Never have I been more needed and never have I been more ignored."

The elevator came to a stop at the top floor. Mr. Meyer pulled the gate open and stepped off the elevator into the abandoned ruins of a luxurious office. An enormous desk leaned on two broken legs, its broad top warped. The carpet was ripped and the smell of mold drove them outside. The gaping window frames opened into a rooftop garden, a wall of luxurious, potted plants hiding the view of the taller, more modern, buildings that surrounded them. Mr. Meyer held Ben's arm tightly and led him through what must have once been impressively wide sliding glass doors to a bench set between raised flower beds. The rooftop garden was inexplicably well cared for and in the scented air Ben could hear the rustle of leaves in the gentle night breeze.

Ben looked at the swollen side of Mr. Meyer's face as the old man gazed up at the sky. "You took some a beating."

Mr. Meyer laughed and looked at Ben. "And you most gallantly saved me. For that I am in your debt."

"Forget it."

Mr. Meyer looked perplexed. "Why would a person want to lose a memory of someone saving them? It was an act of compassion. You should never pass by a flower without enjoying it and giving thanks to heaven for the rain that helped it survive. You should never miss greeting a friend or a child, you should never miss a chance to bless or be blessed, and you should certainly never forget how you met and helped your dearest friends."

"We aren't friends."

"For a person who is lost you sound very sure of yourself."

"I'm not lost."

Mr. Meyer smiled slyly. "Of course you aren't. So you've been here before."

Ben shifted uncomfortably, wanting to leave but feeling glued to the seat. "I haven't been in this building before but I know the street. I must have walked past this building hundreds of times."

"But you've never come inside." Mr. Meyer nodded his head. "And now you say you can leave at any time."

It hit Ben like a challenge, but one that was ridiculous. He just had to turn around and take the elevator down to prove the old man wrong. Perhaps that was the real purpose of the watchman, to stop him from leaving. Ben felt young and silly. Instead, he decided to end the pointless adventure and leave the bothersome old man behind. He went into the ruined office and walked quickly to the elevator. He was drawn up short as he almost slammed into a blank plaster wall, old paint peeling where the elevator should have been. His hand hovered in mid-air, waiting for his brain to tell it where to go. He turned back to the open doorway. Mr. Meyer hadn't moved but he was watching him carefully with his one good eye. He smiled at Ben and his teeth, surrounded by beard, shone in the moonlight.

BEN J.

"W"e have a saying in the business: Never turn down an opportunity, or accept one, until you know what the other man actually has to offer. I said I was in your debt. You should not have taken that lightly. I have merchandise that is rare indeed in today's bleak and twisted market place." Mr. Meyer covered his face with his hands and began to rub gently. When he lowered his hands, the swelling was gone and both of his eyes twinkled at Ben. He patted the seat next to him. "Come. We have a lot to talk about and we are both tired. It is way past your bedtime."

"That's not funny."

"No it isn't. I have much to tell you and many things to ask. But first, you have questions."

Ben sagged, feeling suddenly tired. The breeze rustled the leaves around him and Ben realized that the garden smelled differently, as if the air he was breathing was unlike the rest of the air in the city. It was lighter and more refreshing and filled his lungs. He felt tired but the night air, high above the street, was invigorating.

"The guard at the front door . . ."

"My friend. A former teacher and enemy."

"I don't understand."

"Someday I am sure you will."

Ben struggled to understand but decided he didn't have the strength. "He talked about fish."

"That's what we call the masses, the idiots that take Fair Deal. They swim around all day and night, eyes glued wide open, looking for food. One day they float to the top and you flush them down the toilet, go to the store, and buy another fish. They never create anything, anything they do is temporary, and the atmosphere in which they swim begins to stink after a day or two."

"What makes you so different?"

"I am old. I have three children, and I love this world more than my life. I want the world to keep on thriving for my children's sake. I won't build some whiz-bang if it means polluting the environment with poison that hangs around until way after I am dead. Today, the heads of state and corporations, all those in power or who think they are in power, are old men yearning to be perpetually young. They are frightened by any sign, real or imagined, of aging. They have traded wisdom for knowledge. They have increased man's knowledge and ability to do, but have forgotten how to understand what should be done, and what is better left undone. They are afraid of dying. They will produce a million of those whiz-bangs if it means that they can make a profit to buy some new toy that makes them look more important than all the other old-men boys. An old man must reconcile himself to dying, to a world that will go on without him. Children ease that pain. And since I love them so, I will only bring something into the world that is good for them. The fish are like naughty children. They use up everything the world has without any thought for tomorrow. They eat constantly and leave behind piles of their own excrement."

"What does this have to do with me?"

"Why don't you take Fair Deal?"

"Do you always answer a question with a question?"

"Do I?" They both chuckled; their laughter accompanied the rustling of the leaves in the garden. "Questions are what keep the conversation going. It's also the hidden language of nature. A plant asks a question by growing a flower. The bee answers with another question. The answer to both their questions is the fruit. Everything is expansion and contraction, male and female, day and night. Thought is the question, doing is the answer. Balance is natural. Two people meet, there needs to be space for the other. For that to happen, I need to know where I end and where you begin. A question helps that to happen. I can then treasure you for how you fill the empty space where I am not." Ben sat quietly, surprised at how peaceful he felt in the dark. He thought of the glaring streetlights and the perpetual playrooms operating at full tilt in the apartment buildings surrounding them. The artificial darkness, like that at the Midnight Bar, had become a poor substitute for the lost reality of a beautiful night. Open all night like every other club in the city, it was a place where people could forget there was ever something called sleep. It denied the sweeter face of darkness, the power of emptiness that drew the heart forward towards what it lacked, what it yearned for. Night produced dreams, romance, and hope. The old man speaking softly interrupted his thoughts. "Do you know how Fair Deal came into existence?"

"Sure. They developed a drug that kept you awake all the time but shortened your life by half. That's why it's called Fair Deal. It is more logical to live twice as much when you are young and vibrant, more able to enjoy it."

"So you don't know the truth because that is how they sold it to the public, but it is most clearly a lie. Fair Deal was created as a way for workers to stay alert and productive for longer hours. There were jobs that required a superhuman alertness for obscene amounts of time. It was an obvious need in the military industrial complex, and these powers have a history of using their enormous resources to develop what ordinary common sense would argue is destructive. Those in power saw this method as the best way to stay ahead of India and China who were threatening America's cultural and military hegemony. But these countries are fast learning the secrets and before long they will have the same drugs."

"This cocktail of drugs is an absolute failure. Clear thinking indicates that any drug that shortens life doesn't make sense. Only mass hypnosis or hyper-effective advertising could explain how people could believe there is an advantage to living twice as long in half the time. It is cruel and inhumane and, by definition, it is an addictive poison that kills everyone who takes it. The Hippocratic Oath should have prevented medical science from producing such a drug. Once discovered, Fair Deal was used as a tool to enslave men, keep them at the grindstone for more hours than normally possible. But manufacturers want healthy worker ants that will work twenty-four hours a day. Or work at least eighteen hours a day and consume poorly-made giveaway toys for the other six." Ben started to object but Mr. Meyer went on. "A solution was found. A drug was created to lengthen our days, but rejected by its creators because it shortened our years. But the doctors failed to understand that people would choose a glorious failure today over a grim unavoidable truth that awaits us all. The drug became a solution for the frustration science encountered when confronted with death's inevitable victory. More than death, people fear old age. Old age is loathed because it reminds everyone who sees it that their own death is unavoidable."

Ben shook his head. "People want to have more good years. This has been universally true pretty much forever." Ben felt strange defending Fair Deal. He realized that it was the man's confidence that irked him, not his opinion. Ben had never taken the drug, though his decision was riddled with self-doubt. The man smiled before continuing. "There has always been a struggle to live longer but Fair Deal does not belong to that story. Man has always wanted to live forever. The pharaohs of Egypt used mummification, the alchemists sought the philosopher's stone."

"Religion claimed an afterlife."

"No. That was not a desire to live forever. That was a desire to connect God with this world, to release us from the chains of the mundane, or to sanctify the mundane. It sought to give our short lives and ephemeral actions meaning. And it succeeded. Science took up the gauntlet, challenging belief with knowledge, and sought to lengthen the years of our life. Science was not up to the challenge and could never offer the one thing that could truly challenge a belief in life after death. Science could never produce immortality and probably never will. To begin with, humans seem to be programmed to expire. The aged body is more susceptible to infection and less resilient to disease. Also, as they solved the quantitative issues, increasing the number of years most people lived, they ran into qualitative issues. Extended old age is not pleasant, especially if the elderly are not valued. And there was the unspoken social issue. Old people were thought to be an unproductive burden and considered useless even by their own offspring. Of course, it was their own fault. They had accepted a utilitarian survival-of-the-fittest paradigm for society. This was their legacy. The aged could not keep up and for the sake of the tribe were rightfully left behind on the ice floe as the tribe moved ever forward."

"But that is true. Old people are a burden."

"Please don't quote me from the hogwash they try to shove into your brain. Old people are the storehouse of wisdom. But in a society that has ceased teaching wisdom, even the old have become stupid. Wisdom is lost and society has lost its guiding light. New is better and old gets thrown in the garbage, whether it's made of plastic or flesh and blood. Knowledge became king, the ability to manipulate nature, twisting it to serve utilitarian, materialistic purposes. Wisdom is the magic that lies behind the veil of nature. If you have knowledge without wisdom, eventually the machine will grind to a halt or rise up in protest. Man can only deny his natural essence, his God-given mission to be the keeper of the garden for so long. The prospect of death will always remind him that there is something else, something deeper. That brings us to Fair Deal, man's last great tool to cheat death."

"Not true. Everyone who takes Fair Deal knows they will die earlier than if they don't take it."

"Yet they avoid the dying and the dead. At funerals, the dead are painted to look like they are still alive. People eat and drink chemicals dressed up to look like food, but it is actually poison. They play like children, avoiding death, pretending it doesn't exist. The attraction is dying without getting old. They never pass through that final stage of life." The old man took a deep breath. He put his hand on Ben's. "Why don't you take Fair Deal?"

Ben wanted to snatch his hand away but left it, uncomfortably aware of the physical contact. "I just think it's wrong."

Mr. Meyer shook his head. "So you've forgotten that also." He stared into Ben's eyes. "Who called you Benjy and why don't you take Fair Deal?"

"Those are two different questions."

"No. There is one answer but the words are different. They are two stems growing from the same root."

"My grandfather called me Benjy. But that has nothing to do with Fair Deal."

"He called you something else."

"How do you know that?"

"I know it because I have to. What did he call you?"

"He called me his little dreamer. I couldn't concentrate in school. I was always thinking about something else and it drove my teachers crazy. He used to hold me in his lap and for some reason it calmed me down. I would start talking and tell him all the strange things that came into my head. I would go to him whenever I was having trouble in school. But that has nothing to do with why I didn't choose Fair Deal."

"You were his dreamer. Fair Deal would have taken away your sleep. When would you have time to dream if they took away your sleep? Tell me about him."

Ben smiled involuntarily. "Grandpa Jack was an interesting character. He inherited the dairy farm but originally went to law school. He'd been a lawyer for a while so the locals didn't know what to make of him. My grandmother died before I was born, though I got the feeling she was something very special. When my grandmother died, grandpa left the city and moved to the farm. He was a weird mix, part country and part city. I guess my dad was more country than city, which may be why he became a veterinarian. Kind of like a scientist farmer. The locals didn't understand my dad, but they trusted him. I was named after him, Ben Junior. That's why grandpa called me Benjy. Dad was Ben, and I was Ben 'J'. When you're hollering across a field, the subtleties get lost in the wind. I guess I'm a weird fit too. It must be genetic. 'Odd' runs in the family. When my grandfather passed away, my folks moved to the city. Dad went from treating cows and horses to treating pampered cats and dogs. Mom liked it better but I think my dad always missed the farm."

The old man took a ragged breath and Ben was surprised to see tears running freely down his cheeks. "I asked about your grandfather and you've told me about yourself. I would like to get to know you better but we don't have much time. Tell me about your grandfather Jack."

Ben thought for a moment and was surprised when he realized the observation was true. "Grandpa Jack was tough. His father died when he was in college. Grandma was sick and died young, soon after dad was born. All that pain and loss made him love his family even more. If he loved you, you knew it. But if he didn't like you, you knew that too. He used to say people were 'making faces,' acting like they liked you when they really didn't. For a lawyer, he didn't talk much. You would think that since lawyers get paid by the word they would churn up a lot of expensive wind. My grandfather was different; smart in a way I've never seen since. He would think twice and speak once. He didn't talk much, but his words went deep so you really felt them. I was young at the time so I didn't need much talking. I did enough for both of us. I feel like I spent half my childhood walking across a field, blabbering away, with him listening to anything I had to say as long as I kept my little hand tucked inside his big palm. There were nights I would literally talk myself to sleep, sitting on his lap."

The old man smiled, a faraway look in his eyes. "How did your grandfather die?"

Ben shook himself, as if he were trying to wake from a dream. "He died in his sleep."

"Death is sleep's older sister, Ben. So you've told me nothing. Where did he die?"

"He died in the hospital."

"Alone?"

"No. The family was there."

"Were you there?"

"I think so. I guess I probably was."

Mr. Meyer raised a bushy eyebrow. "Probably? You don't remember?"

Ben was surprised as he felt a tear slide down his cheek. "I was a little kid. I was in the waiting room watching cartoons or something."

The old mans brow crinkled. "Or something?" His voice took on a melody and accent that seemed hauntingly familiar to Ben. "When a memory is stolen what does the thief leave in its place? Where were you when he died? It's a simple enough question."

Ben struggled, wrestling to recall a memory. "I was sitting in the waiting room with my folks but they were asleep. I got bored so I went in to see my grandfather. I fell asleep in his room and my parents found me there when they woke up."

"Where were you when he died?'

"I don't know."

"Where did they find you?"

"I was sitting on his lap." Ben jumped at the words. The voice was his but he hadn't spoken. He had never told this story. His memory of his grandfather's passing was different. But once the words were out, Ben knew they were true and that his memory had been altered, influenced by the stories his parents told, molded to fit the version they preferred. He repeated it, to test it, to let the truth sink in and reawaken. "I was with him, sitting on his lap, holding his hand."

"When he died?"

A roaring filled his head as long-locked memories crept out and unfolded, taking shape, filling in gaps he had never questioned before. He remembered gentle hands lifting him from his grandfather's lap, a drowsy child struggling to wake up. The adults had seemed oddly tense and upset. He had always fallen asleep in his grandfather's lap on the nights that his father was away tending to sick livestock. Why would it upset them that night? He nodded, dizzy from the struggle to remember. The old man's voice seemed to come from far away. "How peculiar. I wouldn't think they would allow a child to sleep in a dying man's arms."

"No one stopped me because everyone left the room when he was dying. I was a kid but I felt like I understood what was going on more than the grown-ups. The nurses and doctors were paid to heal people so dying just made them feel irrelevant. They avoided the room as much as possible, but I stayed. He was my grandfather. His dying was no big deal. I felt like a physical part of him was inside of me, so he wasn't really leaving. I knew the way babies were made so I knew that was true. And I knew that one day we would be reunited, two pieces of the same reality coming back together."

"So that is why you don't take Fair Deal?"

"Yes. Death isn't evil. It isn't even a bad thing. It's like sleep. And sleep is good."

"And sleep gives us our dreams." Ben nodded, too afraid to speak. Mr. Meyer smiled shyly. "Lovers sleep together as a sign of their love. It binds their dreams together. Fair Deal has taken that away."

BEN-JAY

Ben remembered sleeping, his face buried in a thick work shirt made soft from sun and sweat. "I loved him." Ben was surprised at the sound of his own voice.

"And he was old."

Memories seeped in, like struggling to recall a dream upon first awakening. "He called me his little dreamer. Fair Deal would have taken that away too."

"Fair Deal took away grandfathers. And you wanted to be a grandfather someday, to pass on what you had received."

"Yes. Everyone seemed so excited about Fair Deal. Never grow old and you get twice as much youth. I didn't understand what was so exciting. I wasn't in any rush to grow old but it didn't scare me either. I saw people running around non-stop, never taking a break, living out a long string of problems. Never changing or growing, always talking but never listening, always laughing but never knowing what they were laughing at, just too afraid to cry."

"Too afraid of growing old."

"Yes. And I couldn't give up sleep. Sleep is like a vacation that takes you away. Life is new and exciting every morning. If you couldn't solve your problems yesterday, it's okay because today is a new day, a new chance. A new . . ."

"Hope?" Ben looked at the old man, suddenly afraid that he had led him somewhere, exposed him. Mr. Meyer reached out and put his hand on Ben's arm. "And dreams?"

"Dreams are . . ." Ben shook himself. "I don't want to talk about dreams."

The old man's blue eyes searched Ben's face for a few moments before he shook his head and looked up. "I had a dream once. I dreamt that a great white bird came to me and carried me away. I dreamt that it flew fast and far, that there was a place in this world yet to be discovered, a secret place where the light came only from the moon and the inhabitants had taken a vow of silence. They didn't speak, they only wrote notes, poems and sonnets to express what they felt in their souls. And they sang songs of grandeur that pierced the heart, songs that had no words, and epic poems that lasted days on end. I dreamt that the great bird took me there." A screech filled the air, making Ben jump. He looked up and saw the moon, large and bright, defying the artificial lights of the buildings around them. A cloud skidded across the face of the moon, impossibly fast, changing shape as it moved, like an enormous bird flying across the sky. Ben looked over at Mr. Meyer, feeling the last shreds of his will fade as the old man held up a large white feather, smiling with tears in his eyes. "Now I have that dream every night. The bird wants to take me away but I can't leave yet. Not until my apprentice is ready." Ben reached out but pulled back as his fingertips touched the feather. The old man put the feather in Ben's hand and curled his fingers around it, making the barbs scratch his palm.

Are you ready?"

Ben wanted to turn and flee, even if it meant flinging himself from the roof. But the old man's eyes had him trapped. His voice, though he barely whispered, rang like a bell, deafening Ben. "I've told you my dream. Now it is your turn." Another screech filled the air. "Tell me about your dreams, Benjy."

BENJY

Ben entered his apartment and fell onto the sofa. Too tired to pull out the thin mattress from the closet, he rolled up his coat into a pillow and fell immediately into a deep sleep. He woke up refreshed, keeping his eyes closed while he enjoyed the feeling. When he finally opened his eyes, he glanced at the clock, horrified to see that he was two hours late. He jumped off the sofa and ran into the bathroom to shower and dress. The commute took longer than usual since it was an off-hour and the shuttles were not running. A note on his office door asked him to come directly to Todd's office. The door opened as he was about to knock, an anxious secretary dashing out, giving Ben a nervous look as she mumbled for him to go right in. Todd was sitting at his desk, typing furiously while talking on the phone. Nodding at Ben, he pointed at a chair with his chin. He stabbed at a button on his desk and the secretary rushed in with a pitcher of supercaff. Todd put his hand over the mouthpiece and shouted after her. "Tell . . ."

She shouted back, over her shoulder. "He's on his way."

The door clicked shut and immediately swung open again as a man rushed in. Ben didn't recognize him but his appearance was shocking. He had piled on white makeup in a vain attempt to hide the yellow tinge that signaled the early stages of Fair Deal failure. Ben guessed his age at forty, old for a Fair Deal subscriber, young to be preparing for death. His eyes were tinged blue with bright red blood vessels sticking out at the edges. This was a more advanced symptom, rarely seen in public. It was impossible to cover up and usually led to blindness. It was probably painful for the man to keep working but there were few alternatives. When the symptoms became unpleasant to others and made it impossible for him to work, the company would send him a form letter thanking him for his service and issuing him a euphemistically named "retirement vacation pass." If he refused, the Fair Deal collections department would show up with a government invitation and take him away. When a young person subscribed, he signed a waiver giving Fair Deal the right to impound him when the termination process began. Most people went quietly before the process turned ugly. The declining stages were painful but Fair Deal was the leader in opiate refining, a service they provided at a reduced price for early subscribers. This man was obviously fighting the process and Ben could see fear and pain in his eyes.

"Ben, this is Jim Stafford, my direct superior." Ben was shocked. He must have seen Jim dozens of times in the office but the makeup and illness had altered him beyond recognition. "He'd like a few words with you and he asked me to be present, if that's okay with you."

Jim nodded. "You see, Ben, I have very little experience with employees that choose half shifts and Todd said he was a personal friend of yours. I thought that might help us achieve our goals in a more amicable fashion."

Ben bristled with indignation. "I don't work half shifts. I work full shifts."

"That may have been the terminology when you were hired but company policy is being reviewed and updated to keep up with the times. You are considered a half-shift employee, and that effects pay scale, promotions, and tenure." He opened a file. "You were late this morning."

Ben spoke before thinking, immediately regretting his outburst. "I overslept."

Mr. Stafford grimaced. "That was uncalled for. I am aware of your condition but there is no reason to flaunt your perversions in public."

Ben looked to Todd for support. Todd was inspecting his watch in a pathetic attempt to avoid Ben's gaze. In that instant, Ben understood the situation, adding to his anger. He realized that Todd was vying to replace Stafford, knowing that the ailing man's days were numbered. Firing Ben would be a shoe in the door, garnering points without actually getting his hands dirty. It was a done deal, decided in the middle of the night while he slept. Todd poured the concentrated coffee, placing the tiny cups on the desk in front of them, Stafford trying to hide a small pill he slipped into his own cup. Ben realized that his condition was probably further advanced than he had thought at first. The pill was probably a semi-legal pain killer, prescribed by a greasy physician for a fictitious ailment, a little something extra to buy the executive more office time than he really had coming. Ben's anger turned to pity.

"I appreciate your taking time out of your tight schedule, Mr. Stafford. I understand your position completely. Firing me outright would open the company up to a law suit for discriminating against sleepers." Stafford began to object but Ben cut him off. "Don't worry. I have every intention of leaving quickly and quietly. It's a pity. I was beginning to look forward to many more years of improving my skills at this job, a long and fruitful career with a pleasant retirement at the end. I just have one question for you, and I feel you owe me an answer for smoothing this out for you."

Mr. Stafford took a large sip of his coffee and Ben watched as the painful wrinkles in his eyes relaxed. "I don't feel that I owe you anything, however as a courtesy to a former employee, I will try to accommodate you."

Ben smirked. "What do you get out of it?"

Stafford fiddled with his tie, trying to ignore the pain so he could appear professional. "There were rumors flying around, and criticisms because our numbers have been sliding lately. There is about to be a biannual review and I wanted to iron things out before the facts got put to paper."

Ben nodded. "I understand. You saw the writing on the wall. You wanted to go out with a bang, make a splash at my expense. You wanted everyone to say how amazing you were. Of course, by the time they see the review, you'll be gone and forgotten. It's a shame. The best you can do at the end of your life is a good quarterly review. It's not much of a legacy for a man to leave behind, a few numbers in the ledger that will be forgotten in the rush to boost next month's profits. That's really sad." Todd began to object but the false sympathy in his voice made Ben shoot him a look of hatred, his finger pointed like a knife inches from his former friend's chest. "Don't say a word. You're a bottom feeder, the worst kind of fish there is. You're just waiting for him to step aside so that you can have your turn at bat. And you're willing to toss me out to get it." He turned to Stafford, his voice turning soft. "Well, if it's important to you I don't mind helping. It's only my career, a pretty worthless thing when you look at the big picture, something I can do but you can't. I am going to live a long, full life. You settled for the condensed version. This job was getting old, and much of the time I was bored. There was no one here to learn from anymore. I've had some ideas lately for what I want to do with my life. I've got some plans for the future, and unlike you fish, I've got one." Ben stood up and left, leaving the two men wide eyed and gaping. He laughed quietly. "Just fish."

He went to his office to collect his belongings, and realized that the only thing he really needed to take with him was his coat, and that had a big rip in it from the scuffle outside of the Midnight Bar. The receptionist appeared in the doorway, afraid to enter. He tossed the coat in the can and laughed. "You can come in. I'm unemployed but it isn't fatal or even contagious."

She wavered, looking uncomfortable and uncertain. "A man came to speak to you."

"What did he want?"

She lowered her voice to a whisper. "He was old!"

Ben laughed. "That's not contagious either, though I wish it was. It would make the world a better place. Did he leave a message?"

Held at arm's length, she gave him the note, pinched between two fingers. "He wouldn't let me beep you. I suggested leaving a message, recorded like any normal person would, but he insisted on writing."

He looked at it. It was the name of a hospital with an address he didn't recognize. The note was written in a careful script. "My dear friend is dying. I need you." At the bottom of the page, separated by a wide space, "Come now" was scrawled in what seemed like a different hand. Ben had never heard of the hospital but that was not unusual. Hospitals were situated out of sight in obscure corners of most cities. After Fair Deal revved up the body's metabolism and fed it an array of feel good chemicals, mind and body became addicted to an energy level that was pure manic. Before long, no one could remember what it felt like to be tired and the experience of sleep was as offensive and disgusting as cannibalism had been to past generations. Years back, no one would have believed that New York's proud claim to being "the city that never sleeps" would become literally true for the entire population.

All considerations of ethics and morality were subordinate to levels of productivity and to the cult of the individual's expression of what passed for creative genius. The drugs, which were dispensed at no charge and passed out like candy, were necessary to perpetuate the belief and actual experience that the virtual universe was far superior to reality. In this constant fast-forward mode, there was no time for meditation and reflection. Anyone viewing this scene in city after city would think that "fish" was an appropriate metaphor for the mindless frenzy of perpetual motion. Food that contained more chemicals than organic matter fueled the fever and there were no blessed hours of sleep to recover and recoup. A minor illness or small infection could send the body spiraling into a tailspin of disease that ended quickly. Under the influence of mind altering drugs, illness and infirmity inspired revulsion rather than compassion. Ambulances had become hearses, sirens usually turned off. Cars were overpowered and flimsy, a reflection of the adolescent desires of the consumers, driven at speeds that were unreasonable and unsafe. Sports resembled playful brushes with suicide, ongoing attempts at increasingly bizarre events. Despite the forward march of science, medicine was no longer devoted to prevention and healing but had become the servile handmaiden of the drug industry, dedicated to developing new and improved versions of concoctions that turned human beings into robots. Pharmacology was pathetically specialized, producing a range of anesthetics to deaden pain and speed the dying process, but little else. There was no need for the true healing arts when the stakes had dwindled from a full lifetime to a few short years.

Fair Deal turned hospitals into mausoleums. Visiting patients in the final stages of Fair Deal was discouraged, even for the surviving children. It would have been bad for sales. Fair Deal Corporation included in its contract a final waiver, permitting physicians to use opiates and other exotic chemicals that were lethal but purported to induce a state of euphoria. This claim was difficult to verify since the drugs induced a deep stupor making communication impossible. In any case, the subscriber was guaranteed what he most wanted; a quick, painless end in his sleep. Funerals, memorial services and other rites of passage from this world to the next had long been dispensed with. Most parents passed away before their children were old enough to get to know them. The children were whisked away to state run children's homes or raised by adoptive parents for a contracted period of time. Extended families were mythical, siblings a random result of concurrent contracts. Grandparent was a scatological insult, its true meaning barely remembered and of no practical use.

Ben didn't know the location of the hospital so he took a taxi, trusting the driver's knowledge of the city. Lulled by the motion and already feeling exhausted, he fell asleep in the back seat. He woke up on the floor as the cab slid to a screeching stop. They were parked on a dark side street. Ben was drowsy and confused. Hospitals were large buildings with brightly lit entrances. Ben's door was pulled open and a strong set of hands pulled Ben out of the cab, throwing him to the hard pavement. A hard kick to the ribs left him gasping for air. Ben struggled to sit up as the driver returned to his cab. The young man paused with his door open, looking at Ben with disgust.

"I don't care what you do in your own time, but I don't go for that disgusting stuff in my backseat. Sleepy is creepy and makes me puke." The driver jumped into his cab and drove away, tires squealing.

Ben limped to the end of the alley, hoping it would intersect a major thoroughfare. The alley opened onto a wide street that should have been bustling with traffic but was strangely silent. To Ben's eyes, long accustomed to a city kept bright around the clock, the neighborhood seemed strangely dark. There were sufficient streetlights but their glow seemed to be on a dimmer setting. Ben touched his side, wincing at the pain, just as set of oncoming headlights blinded him. The car moved slowly, weaving slightly as it approached. Ben was relieved to see the familiar yellow triangle on top indicating a cab for hire. He waved, almost breaking into laughter as it stopped in front of him. He jumped into the back seat, calling out the name of the hospital, half-expecting the driver to object. He heard a deep sigh from the front seat and looked up. The back of the driver's head was covered with patches of hair that had been crudely dyed to an absurd shade of yellow. Blue eyes surrounded by a solid web of blood stared at him from the rear view mirror. One eye was cloudy with cataracts. Ben realized that his driver was half-blind, probably drugged to avoid the pain. He had never witnessed such an advanced case of Fair Deal Failure. Most people this far along in the process were taken away quietly and efficiently, thanks to friends and co-workers who called the company, and then jockeyed to take possession of the dead person's effects. This cab driver was sicker than anyone Ben ever saw before. Ben wondered how many there were like this wandering the city like soulless ghouls, unsure of how to stop moving how to just lay down and die, moving, forward with eyes glued open. 'Like fish,'

Ben thought. He realized, with a shock, that he had received a precious gift from his grandfather. His grandfather had taught him how to die, to surround himself with loved ones and leave the world with grace.

Ben became aware of a pulsing sound that seemed to come from all around him. He was shocked when he finally located the source. The cab driver was groaning, his exhalations desperate acts of pain, the life-breath driven from him in excruciating waves. Ben saw a large building half a block in front of them, the letters "FD" painted three stories tall across its facade. This was a hospital, hopefully the one he wanted. A lone figure stood under the street-light in front of the hospital. As the cab staggered forward, Ben could make out Mr. Meyer's silhouette, slouched under the light. Ben breathed a sigh of relief but was immediately thrown back into his seat. A scream came from the driver as he leaped, his head hitting the roof, his back arched painfully. The scream was word-less and without meaning, a mechanical result of grotesque full body muscle spasms. The cab surged forward as the driver's foot shot ahead with an uncontrolled kick, pushing the accelerator to the floor. The driver was beyond feeling as the cab slammed into the steel lamppost. The cab spun into the air, shuddering like a marlin fighting the line relentlessly reeling it in to die. Ben was tossed around inside the cab, bouncing off the upholstered inside of the cab and then suddenly free in the open air.

He woke up on the asphalt, a dozen meters in front of the cab. The windshield had exploded outwards, littering the street with small shards of broken glass. He stood painfully, shaking tiny slivers of glass out of his hair and clothes. He was in pain but it was a general soreness, no worse than what he felt after the beating he received from the first cabbie. He checked for blood saw none. When he ran his fingers through his hair, more glass fell to the ground. Ben was shocked by the undeniable realization that the windshield had been broken by his own body flying through it. He limped to the wrecked car, twisted around the immovable steel post. The driver was standing upright in the front seat, his head jammed against the roof, his eyes wide open dripping blood like tiny red tears. Ben touched him but was sickened by how stiff the body had become.

He heard a groan from the other side of the car. Ben limped around the front of the car, slipping on oil that pooled on the street, as if the car was a casualty no less mortal than the driver. Ben saw Mr. Meyer lying on the ground beside the hospital's front door. He limped quickly to him, kneeling next to him but afraid to touch the old man.

He knelt over him, looking into his eyes. "Are you okay?"

Mr. Meyer smiled and Ben saw with horror that his teeth were coated with blood, a thin red froth in the corner of his mouth. "I am wonderful. I am dying."

Ben tried to think of a response, some words of comfort, but Mr. Meyer indicated he was actually happy. Words seemed superfluous, as a wrinkled hand wrapped itself around his. Ben wanted to pull away but he didn't want to deprive Mr. Meyer of this human contact in what were clearly his final moments.

The old man smiled sweetly. " Your grandmother believed that children are the answer to every dream. I almost missed that lesson but she made a believer of your grandfather overnight. I knew them when they first met each other. I miss them." Pain rippled across his face. Like the sun suddenly reappearing, his smile returned, his teeth painted red.

"I will tell you a secret. Underneath everything, I am an angry man. I believe that every man is required to argue with God, to scream at Him that He got it wrong. Every man must scream in his own voice. That is what your grandmother taught me about prayer and hope. The prayer for good health speaks of hope, it places the scepter of kingship firmly in the hands of the great Other. Yet at the same time, in the same breath, it accuses the Creator of creating sickness. I guess that as the Hope Merchant, it was my job to focus on the good, but I was a bit of a failure. If God made one in every million hopes go unrealized, one in every hundred thousand prayers go unanswered, I could have rested easy. I could have stopped screaming, closed up shop and gone home. But every person in the world has a heart half full of unanswered prayers." Ben was amazed that he still had the strength to keep speaking.

"I knew a man who grew up without a father. His father died from a painful illness while he was still a young child. His father's last words were "I took care of him until now. From now on, I leave him in God's hands." The boy grew to be a lonely man. He grew up in want and need, his mother suffering from loneliness, poverty, and shame. And now that man is dying, leaving behind more orphans, but he is too sad and confused to repeat his father's final plea. If that man's voice cried alone, I would sing with him and be content. But every day a great chorus rises up from the earth, challenging heaven."

A smile creased his face as blood seeped into the hairs on his cheeks. "I can hear that chorus more clearly now. It is painful in its sadness." His hand squeezed Ben's as a wave of pain passed through him. "Pray for me, Ben. Pray that when I am standing before the Splendor, that I will remember this world and not forget that pain and suffering are ugly when seen from below." Mr. Meyer paused and Ben waited for him to continue. He waited a full minute before he realized that Mr. Meyer would not speak again.

Nurses and doctors stumbled out of the hospital, confused at the sight of blood. Ben was pushed back, standing on the edge of the circle of light cast by the streetlight that had killed Mr. Meyer, its light still flickering despite the crooked lamppost and the beating it had taken. The cab driver was quickly body-bagged and taken away, his death by Fair Deal Failure fitting the hospitals routine. Finally, the hospital personnel approached Mr. Meyer's corpse, confused and intimidated by his age and the violent manner of his death. Relieved that they would not be required to attend a medical problem they were not trained to cope with, they carried the old man away.

Ben stood watching as both bodies disappeared. The only disturbance was a tow truck hauling the taxi away. Ben stood there, asking himself why he could not leave, wondering if he had a concussion. Regardless, Ben knew with an inexplicable certainty that he had been spared from injury by some odd miracle. He had no practical reason to be anywhere, now that he was unemployed. This was clearly true, however, he was suddenly struck with the overpowering compulsion that he had unfinished business in this spot and that he was waiting for someone, as if he had an appointment to keep.

He looked up to see two people exiting from the alley. One was a very large man, growing larger as he approached. The other was a much smaller boy, blond and freckled. The large man waited in the dark as the boy stepped into the light, and held out an envelope. Ben's full name was written across the front. He opened it with steady hands that refused to shake, it disturbed him that he was so calm. He looked up as the odd strangers left, the boy looking back for a moment to wave and smile, leaving without having said a word.

The envelope contained a business card and an oddly shaped key, heavy and roughly made. The card was thick and textured, but pleasing to the touch. Gothic letters in black ink announced "The

Hope Merchant". The address was written underneath in the same calligraphic script. The name under the address made his head spin. "Mr. Benjamin Jackson". Jackson was not his last name but he understood that in a very deep and real way, it was more his name than any other. Grandpa Jack was never far from his memories. Ben slipped the key and card back into the envelope, and put the envelope in his pocket. He looked up and down the street for a cab. The street had remained empty since the tow truck drove away, and no people or vehicles were anywhere in sight, though he could hear music in the distance and see a red glow on the horizon. Ben noticed that the sky above his head was gray, just a few minutes away from morning. He began to walk. He had no idea where the street was, how far or in which direction, but somehow he knew that he would find it in time to have a cup of tea before falling asleep in his new bed.

THE
DREAM

Ben was still breathing deeply, trying to shake the feeling that he was caught in the mist between dreaming and waking. He opened his dream journal and jotted down a few notes.

His dream had been relatively tame, trekking through forests and climbing a bare mountain. The one strange experience occurred just before he awoke. He had reached the peak of the mountaintop and stood at the edge of a cliff admiring the vista. Then, out of the north, a large white bird appeared, landing at his side. It burst into flames and, unlike the phoenix, immediately crumbled into a pile of gray ash. Ben sifted through the ashes until he found one pure white feather, untouched by the flames. He lifted it up to inspect it but the feather crumbled in his hand. Suddenly, tiny white feathers began to sprout from the hand that was holding the feather. The feathers spread until his entire body was covered. He gave one wordless shriek and leaped from the cliff, spreading his wings, but saw they were only hands. He jumped up in bed with a muffled scream in his throat. He shuddered, sliding out of bed and dressing quickly. Rushing to escape his dream, he failed to notice the feather on his pillow, which could have been from the down stuffing escaping through a few loose stitches.

He spent the first week at the shop writing a careful inventory. He worked hard, busily preparing for customers who never came. This could have been more distressing, but Ben had no idea what the job entailed and how many customers he could reasonably expect. Mr. Meyer had left no inventory, list of suppliers, or price list. Even if customers did discover the shop in this dark, out of the way alley, he wouldn't know what to charge or how to replenish the stock. Anyone would have thought his career was doomed to be short-lived and hopelessly unprofitable. The workshop behind the curtains had an antique roll-top desk overflowing with papers. Ben tried establishing some sort of order, searching for invoices, bills, receipts, anything of a business nature. He searched every corner of the old desk for an electric bill, rental agreement, tax form, any invoice or cancelled check that might be a clue to the history of the shop. The papers were stories, fanciful fiction, each written in a different hand. Ben tried organizing them but was always distracted by some irresistible snippet that would draw him in. Despite his efforts, the desk remained a mess, and Ben learned to avoid it if he didn't want to become distracted.

He had expected the inventory to take a few days and a modest section of a notebook. He quickly discovered that the shop looked small but was long and narrow. Three steps led to an alcove that opened up into another large room lined with count-less shelves. What had appeared at first glance to be a quaint, tiny shop was in fact quite large with a small warehouse attached. Undaunted, he began methodically taking an inventory of all the odds and ends that filled up the store's shelves. He could not determine any system or preference that may have governed the acquisition of the countless items. There was a large bucket of mixed seeds, smelling fresh and earthy despite being covered with a thick layer of dust. A small box contained a jumble of keys, some old and rusty, others of modern design with emblems for automobiles. Ben puzzled over this. The shop had been closed for years yet many of the keys were current. It would seem that Mr. Meyer had come periodically, ignoring the dust, yet updating select items of stock. Even more puzzling was the question of what to do with the keys. Was there a parking garage nearby full of vehicles, antique and modern, set aside for his shop? He found a long shelf of journals handwritten in languages he didn't recognize intermingled with empty journals, some leather bound with thick woody pages, others wrapped in lace with paper that was thin and colored like butterfly wings. Each day left him with more questions than facts. But the most puzzling dilemma occurred in the second week. A name scribbled in one of the journals seemed strangely familiar. He copied it in the margin of his inventory list, intending to investigate when he had a few moments. At the end of the third week, a search on the Internet brought up the name of an artist, unknown to the general public in his own time, yet hugely influential after his death. His paintings were still being discovered in forgotten attics and sold for small fortunes. Ben ran down the stairs into the shop. He searched for the journal but the journal had disappeared. In its place was a bin of art supplies, paints and tools for working with clay. An ancient mallet and wood chisels sat in a rough wooden box in precisely the spot the journal had been a week before.

He rarely left the shop. Every morning, he walked down the stairs into the back room, opened the curtains, and was drawn into his work like a diver plunging into murky waters. The only item in the shop that seemed immovable, always in the same place, was the chipped porcelain teapot that Ben used every morning. This morning, he sat sipping his tea, contemplating his new business. In a strange way, it suited him as nothing ever had before. He was perpetuating the family legacy of being 'odd', and this was just fine with him. He strolled around the shop with a feather duster, using it as an excuse to inspect his ever-changing wares. He found a small shelf that had inherited some of the lost journals. He picked a random book and opened to the middle. One page showed a pencil sketch of a leaf floating in a pond, remarkable in its attention to detail. The facing page contained just one sentence written in fanciful Edwardian script. "Fall without clinging. Float without sinking. The river is one." He searched the book for a name but only found the word 'Oogrooq' scribbled on the inside cover.

Ben was holding the journal when the door opened. A young woman slipped in, pushing the door open barely enough to enter. She looked around the shop with eyes that darted from side to side like a small animal helplessly caught in an unfamiliar environment. Her coat was too large for her and too warm for the season. Her hair was windblown though no wind accompanied her as she entered. She froze when she saw Ben watching her, her deep brown eyes opened wide with fright. Ben smiled and carefully replaced the journal to its place on the shelf.

"How can I help you?"

"I need . . ." Ben thought she had finished speaking when another word appeared, completing the sentence but leaving even more unsaid. " . . . something."

No further explanation followed. "Perhaps you'd care to look around. I'm sure you'll find something, maybe even something you like."

He opened the journal and began reading from the beginning. It wasn't a diary. It was more of a primer with short lessons meant to be memorized. The lessons were cleverly worded and the hand-drawn pictures so engaging that after a few minutes he could recall them effortlessly. He was engrossed in his reading and didn't notice the young woman standing in front of him until she cleared her throat to catch his attention.

He looked up into deep brown eyes. "Can I help you?"

She shifted from one foot to the other. "I'm finished. I'd like to leave."

Ben felt disoriented for a moment as a picture of a plant flashed through his mind. He couldn't remember if she had asked to leave, or asked for a leaf. He looked in the corner where the bags of seeds usually appeared. Ben felt mildly disappointed that his first customer was leaving without a purchase. "I'm sorry you didn't find what you were looking for."

She shifted again, her eyes darting around the shop. "I'd like to leave."

The picture of the leaf flashed through his mind again. "Of course. Is that an immediate leaf or can you wait for it to grow?"

A tiny spark of anger appeared in her eyes. "The door is locked. Don't try anything. I have a can of Mace in my pocketbook, and I can scream louder than you would think."

"I can't think very loud so I am sure you are correct. Why would you scream? Is it something you particularly enjoy doing?"

"No! But you locked the door and now I can't get out."

"I assure you that I did not lock the door. It may have done so on its own. That sort of thing has been happening quite a lot,

382

lately." Ben closed his book and came out from behind the counter. He tried turning the knob and was only mildly surprised to find it unyielding, although it had been unlocked when he arrived and he never thought to lock it. Just this morning it had opened for him in a courteous non-key manner when he took out the garbage. He turned to face the young lady. "I'm sorry. It does seem to be locked but I have no idea where the key is." Her hand reached into the pocketbook, searching for the mace. He held up his hands in self-defense. Incongruously, one of his hands held a can of mace that Ben was sure had not been there a moment before. He quickly placed it on the counter between them. "I am being quite honest with you. I know it sounds strange but I didn't lock the door and I don't know how to unlock it. There is a back entrance, so let's try that." He turned and led her through the curtains to the work-room, but the service entrance was also locked. When he turned to explain the situation, he was looking at a spray canister pointed at his face.

"Is there another exit?"

"I am new here. There might be a service entrance in the back-room. It is quite dark and I haven't fully explored it." He led her up the stairs and into the back of the store. He was relieved to find another door, half- hidden behind a shelf, but panicked when he tried turning the doorknob and found that it too was locked. At the foot of the door was the box of keys. Hoping to buy time before getting a face full of mace, he picked up the box and began to sift through the keys. A quick gasp from the young woman made him look up. She was holding a small brown glass bottle in her hand and was reading the label intensely.

Her face was even paler than when she had entered and the hand holding the bottle shook visibly. She set her lips tightly and closed her fingers around the bottle. "I'd like to buy this before leaving."

Ben put the box of keys down and smiled warmly. "Of course." As he spoke, the dusty door swung open, hinges squeaking. He closed it and they walked to the front of the shop together. When they arrived at the shining brass cash register Ben was reminded that he had no idea how much to charge. He reached for the bottle and she reluctantly handed it over. He gasped when he read the glued on label. Two words were written in bold red letters: "Arsenic. Poison."

"I'm sorry. I can't sell this to you."

The girl shrieked and pulled the mace from her purse again. "That's what the pharmacy said. I thought that since it was on your shelf, you would sell it to me. This place seems seedy enough." She prepared to press the button on the spray. "If you don't sell it to me, I'll just take it."

A sudden dizziness hit him. He felt like he was spinning down a river, and even the lights in the shop flickered as if he was seeing them through rippled water. When his head cleared, he was calm. "I apologize for the misunderstanding. Of course I will let you have it. What I meant is that since I am so new, I don't know the price. Why don't I just take down your name and phone number and when I find out the price, I'll give you a call and you can come back and pay for it?"

Her eyes flashed and the sparks became fire. "Are you stupid? Can't you read the label? Don't you know what this stuff does?"

"Of course. However I simply can't see any other way of dealing with the situation. I can't give it away. That's not good business. And I refuse to overcharge."

He pulled out his inventory book and opened to the last page. He wrote carefully. 'One dark brown bottle labeled Arsenic. Price unknown. Sold to . . .' He passed the book and pen to the young lady. She snatched the pen from his hand but paused, to put away the mace before taking the book. She wrote, her hand shaking as the pen scratched angrily from too much pressure, almost tearing the paper.

"Do you realize how ridiculous this is, buying poison on credit in order to commit suicide?"

He took the book back, reading her name before closing it. "I'm sure some would consider it an odd way of doing business, however I am in an odd business. Thank you, Miss Emily Wells. Now, if you don't mind my asking, where were you thinking of taking the arsenic?"

"What business is it of yours?"

"Consider it part of our customer service."

"I was going to go home and die in the shower where no one can hear me scream."

He clucked his tongue and shook his head. "If you don't mind my saying so, that lacks grace and style. It is also cold and uncomfortable. Rigor mortis would make your body stiffen in that position. Do you really want them to bury you bent over?"

"Why should I care how they bury me?"

He considered a moment before nodding. "A point well made and well taken. Why not in bed? It would be more comfortable and your corpse would be posture perfect. You may not care but it would be a consideration to the pallbearers. The ceremony would be statelier, less like taking out the garbage."

"Don't be rude."

"I didn't intend to be. I was merely being practical."

"I'm no perverted sleeper. I don't have a bed."

"Please forgive me. I didn't mean to imply any insult. Since I am providing the means, I am curious as to the reason."

She stood glaring at him, breathing heavily. "It's not my fault."

"I am sure it isn't."

"I've tried everything but it nothing works." He nodded. "Half the time I was allergic and the other times it just didn't work." He nodded again, questioning only with his eyes. "The company even tried experimental versions. I signed waivers, letting them use me for research. They told me that I was one in a million for whom the chemicals, even double doses, were like a placebo. I would get all excited but two days later I would make an absolute fool of myself, falling asleep in public. It was embarrassing beyond words. I've slept on the floor for ten years, always afraid someone would come to my apartment and see that I have a bed. Can't you understand? Last week, Fair Deal wrote me a final letter of apology, explaining they had exhausted all their options for me, and two days after that I was fired. I haven't ever had a boyfriend stay around for more than two months. I would make excuses, schedule dates only when I could be awake. But eventually they would find out. I can't go on like this. In a few years, all my friends will start dying and they'll notice. Then I'll start to get old and everyone will notice."

Ben nodded. "It seems like you have certainly tried everything. In any case, I would like to offer the services of the establishment. We have a very comfortable bed in a quiet and private room."

She was close to tears, wrung out from her confession. "Please, just give me the bottle and let me leave."

He smiled. "The bottle is in your hand. The door is open. But my offer still stands." She wavered for a few moments, her eyes shifting nervously between Ben and the front door. "You might also consider that I know how to administer the drug. You might make a mistake. Too large a dose might prove horribly painful. Too small a dose and you will wake up sicker than you can imagine. The most tragic suicide is the one that survives."

Her chin lowered as tears began to flow. She put the brown glass bottle on the counter and slid it across to Ben's waiting hand. He led the way to the apartment.

The porcelain teapot sat on the table as Ben heated the water. The instructions on the package warned against boiling the leaves. Ideally they should be allowed to steep in a closed pot. He poured the tea while Emily used the bathroom. She came out, carrying her heavy overcoat. Her dress was unfashionably modest, to the floor, to her wrists, and all the way up to her neck. The dress was severe and forbidding but the lace trim softened the effect, drawing attention to her deep eyes. She sat down, watching him pour the tea into her cup, staring with morbid fascination. "Is it . . . ?"

He smiled. "No. This is just tea. I wanted to be hospitable. Would you like a biscuit? Guaranteed poison free." She shook her head.

She watched him over the rim of her cup as she sipped her tea. Ben sat calmly munching biscuits, comfortable in the silence. When the cup was almost empty, she sat staring at it, afraid to finish. "It was awful. You have no idea what it was like. People whispering about me, calling me 'sleeper', and worse. The Fair Deal Show was always coming up with new slogans, new names for people like me. And people were always trying them out on me to see which ones hurt the most. It was cruel. I was even spat at once. I know it is wrong to sleep but I can't help it. It's an unfair use of public resources. I would stop if I could."

"It's no such thing."

She slammed the teacup down. "You have no idea what it was like."

"Actually, I know exactly what it's like. Why do you think I have a bed?"

"What . . . ?" She stared at him for a few moments until it sunk in. "I didn't mean to . . . I didn't . . ."

He waved his hand. "No matter. I thoroughly agree. I also found being a pariah unbearable. I've decided that I too cannot go on." He held up the bottle. She could see the kitchen lamp through the brown glass. The bottle was empty. "Arsenic is known for adding a slight almond taste. I found it to be quite nice with the tea, didn't you?" She stared at the bottle, watching as he slipped it into his pocket. "Please don't feel that I lied. When I made my poison free guarantee, I was referring to the biscuits. They are all natural, no preservatives. The tea, however, is past its expiration date though I don't think that will hamper the poison from achieving its desired effect. I suggest we retire to the bedroom, unless you'd prefer your original choice, the bathtub. Mine is quite large, an antique, and you might not end up totally crooked. Personally, I prefer my bed. There is room for you, all totally platonic, you understand." He stood and held out his hand. She hesitated before taking his hand and allowing herself to be led into the bedroom. She paused in the doorway with Ben standing next to her. "As you can see, the bed is oversized. In these dismal days, when beds aren't even commercially produced, and every week there seems to be another bed burning, it would be impossible to find another one like it. It would be considered a gross display of a personal perversion. Considering our present situation, you can be assured I mean no impropriety. You can lie on one side and I will lie on the other. There will be plenty of space between us." He paused. "Or, if you prefer, I will retire to the bathtub. My sense of hospitality over-rides my personal preference for deathly posturing. I don't mind being a hunchback corpse. I'll just leave a note asking them to bury me on my side."

She shook her head. "That's not necessary. I think I would prefer it if you remained with me. I'm scared and I would like it if you held my hand."

"I already am."

She looked down at their joined hands, as if seeing them for the first time. "Please don't let go."

"Till death do us part."

She looked into his eyes and the joke died on his lips, tears streaming down his cheeks to match hers. They parted for a few moments, sitting on opposite sides of the bed, backs to each other, as they slipped off their shoes. Lying on their backs, tears wetting their pillows, they reached out and clasped their hands together. They remained silent, feeling an aching weariness settle into their limbs, making it impossible to move.

She sobbed once. "I almost wish . . . ."

He squeezed her hand. "Never almost wish. Wish all the way and the wings of your dreams will take you there."

Her words were slurred, her lips numb. "I almost wish I won't die."

"I guess in this sleepless world of no dreams and little hope, a half-wish will have to do." He gathered his strength to roll over and hold her. He held the bottle close to her eyes so she could see it through drooping lids.

"Do you hate me?"

Her face relaxed and she smiled sweetly, using the last of her strength to shake her head. The white label had peeled off, revealing another label, smaller and older. "Meyer's Original Formula Sleeping Potion. Guaranteed many hours of dreamful sleep."

His head drooped and his mouth rested on the pillow next to her ear. He whispered, "Dream of everything your heart can hold. Dream enough to last a lifetime and more. And when we awaken, I will tell you my dreams too. We will grow old together, making those dreams real, discovering new dreams along the way. And we will find that dreams are only the seeds for what happens when we are together. Our dreams are seeds, brought by angels, sent by God, seeds that will grow into trees, bearing sweet fruit to heal a hungry world."

His breathing grew heavy and his arm rested across her. They slept for many hours indeed, and dreamed dreams for thousands of years.

THE END

Publisher's Note: *We asked Adam to write an 'About the Author.' He couldn't. Instead, what we received appears on the next three and a half pages. You can skip it if you like.*

HUMORING THE AUTHOR

Arctic wolves abandoned me as a baby in a maternity ward in Philadelphia where I was adopted by a kind hearted Jewish couple who still claim to be my parents. I have, through judicious doses of cosmetic surgery, lost most of my lupine physical traits but am left with an unfulfilled desire to chase rabbits through the snow. Recognizing their adopted son's need for open space and plentiful game, my parents moved to the wilds of suburban New Jersey where I was free to roam the well tended lawns and golf greens. The conservative Jewish private schools were strangely suited to my animalistic needs. The academics were dog-eat-dog, the school lunches freshly killed game, and the Chassidic rabbis were open to howling at the moon as a valid outlet for expressing my Jewishness. The centerpieces at my Bar Mitzvah, made from road-kill peeled from the asphalt of the Garden State Parkway, were a big hit.

My success in Jewish day school led me to the mistaken belief that, despite my odd beginnings, I could somehow fit in. I was forced to drop out of Rutgers in my senior year when it was discovered that my non-human anatomy would never be able to adapt to drinking liquids through a funnel and my clawed feet ruled out business shoes. Finally, in my senior year, I left in protest, furious that my double major in Cafeteria and Game Room had been discontinued due to academic cutbacks. Pac-Man had been invented and pinball, my raison d'être, had become an anachronism. I toyed with the idea of returning to my roots but years of living amongst humans and stalking my prey in shopping malls had domesticated the animal I should have been. The local bagel shop refused to allow me to strip down and stalk my meals in their aisles. It was a classic case of adapt or die. I toyed with nihilism before settling on a cooking career. I moved to New York to apprentice in the most exclusive French restaurants. In between sips of vintage wine, I developed a taste for the specific brand of ultra-violence and debasement found in the East Village after midnight. There was bare bones truth that exposed the lies of the American dream. Hell's Angels were prophets and I became a part-time disciple. Ozzy and Harriet lay dead by the side of the highway, bloated from cholesterol filled junk food, killed execution style by roving hordes of rogue debt collectors. At some point in my drunken stupor, I became sick to the very core of my existence. I had switched over from mosh-pit existentialism to the brink of hard-core hedonism. I was disgusted with myself and angry at my Creator, or the other way around. I couldn't continue and I couldn't go back to the 'burbs. The Wizard of Oz was a closet queer and Dorothy had an unnatural crush on Toto. At the age of thirty, I had burned my moral roadmap and gone spiritual off-roading at light speed. I was due for a very ugly crash.

Lost and alone, I followed the Grateful Dead on summer tour, living on reds, vitamin C, and cocaine. I whispered my questions into a small vial of LSD and finally got some clear answers to life's trickier issues. The vial whispered back "Why have you always lived someone else's dream? Listen to your own heart". I found a tiny guardian angel hiding behind a mushroom. He was fragile as glass and wore a yarmulke, but I could tell he could kick any biker's butt. He told me to go to Israel. They threw me out of the official Israel office for not wearing a tie or taking a shower. I reasoned that Moses would not have been accepted under those conditions. They were okay with that. Desperate, I found the kibbutz office in a soon-to-be renovated factory building and the mustachioed representative said my biker boots were perfect for farm work. He was happy to sell me a ticket to socialist heaven. Through a divinely orchestrated misunderstanding, I ended up on a religious kibbutz, Sde Eliyahu, pork grease still glistening on my chin. There, I was informed that my background in haute cuisine and overpowered motorcycles made me a prime candidate for the dairy sheds. I traded in my chef's hat for gum boots and spent five years acting as a surrogate mother for sabra Holsteins. Tractors were the agro-placebo for my motorcycle itch and riding half-wild Arabian mares around the Jordan Valley was an acceptable substitute for being chased by New Jersey state troopers down interstate highways. My aggressions and occasional need to drink beer and brawl, were met by futile attempts at cow tipping. The cows never seemed to notice.

The same wisdom prevailing in the IDF (Israeli Defense Forces), I was trained as a combat medic, soldiers treated as a herd animal. The oxymoron created by carrying a gun and bandages had a calming effect, cancelling out any doubts in my own personal existentialist validity. The long hours of lonely guard duty in the Negev Desert finally convinced my internal dialog that it had nothing relevant to say and that it was time to shut up and listen to the desert where my forefathers dwelled.

At the end of five years, I left kibbutz, firmly committed to leaving religion and dairy farming behind. I was going to drop my sorry excuse for a soul at the lost and found in the Egged bus station and be done with spiritual journeys. That decision led me straight to yeshiva in Bat Ayin where conflicting bus schedules have made it impossible for me to leave. Ten years of studying ancient legal texts in Aramaic has pretty much straightened out all the misconceptions western education instilled in me.

I woke up this morning to discover that I have been married to a wonderful woman and have four religious Israeli children. All of those facts seem unnatural, or at least unlikely on a cosmic scale.

My wife tells me that I have returned to cooking, the children and home in the hills are all ours, and that I am happy. Believing her keeps me sane, for the most part. So I believe her and write my doubts in journals that I keep to myself. My threats to retire to the Arctic to hunt small furry animals are met with a sweet smile and shake of her head. Moments of quiet introspection lead to bouts of insomnia and dizziness so I save them for Saturday nights. I look back on my life in disbelief that curls my peyos. Not only can't it be mine, but most of it doesn't make sense. My biography is difficult to believe, absolutely contradicting many laws of nature and most rules of logic, but for lack of evidence or explanations to the contrary, and with so many people who are dear to me confirming it, I have no choice but to believe. Perhaps I was not as genetically inclined to wolfishness as I think, but I am so ill-suited to be a productive, SUV driving, suburbanite, that I might as well have been born with grey fur and fangs. My body may be from Jersey but my soul fell from Mars. I've been trying to dance to the music of my soul but it's a difficult half-step boogie with a bit of techno-polka thrown in. My dream is to keep being me, but with more time to write and much less time spent in commercial kitchens cooking bad food for people who like it that way. I want to build a shack in the woods with an espresso machine and beer on tap, where anyone can come and sit long enough to tell me a story, preferably their own. Every person is a once-in-eternity expression of God's wonder. It sounds kitsch, but I asked God and he said it was true. I would disagree but arguing with God gives me a headache. Every person I have ever met really does have a story to tell, and the only reason to get out of bed in the morning is the stories I have yet to hear.

Publisher's Note Part II: Then, as we were preparing the book to go to press, we asked again. "Come on Adam," we cajoled. "How about a real About the Author." This is what we got.

ABOUT THE AUTHOR

Adam Eliyahu Berkowitz was born in Philadelphia and is a dropout from Rutgers University, through no fault of his professors. He prepared delicacies in Manhattan's finest classical French restaurants for ten years, before moving to Israel in 1991. He lived on a religious kibbutz for five years raising calves and milking their mothers. Adam also served in the IDF as a combat medic. He moved to the community of Bat Ayin, in the rolling hills outside of Jerusalem, where he pursued Talmudic studies, and was the chef in the yeshiva there, for eight years. He is married to Devora Gila, they have four blessed children, and reside in Bat Ayin where he built his own house on a stunning tract of rocky earth. He has recently and reluctantly returned to the professional kitchen as the head chef at one of Jerusalem's landmark restaurants. He would like to be employed as an author, and that is entirely up to you, the reader. He thanks you for helping his dream come true.

ABOUT THE COVER

The cover for *The Hope Merchant* began with a walk by the water, when our senior editor and her husband wandered into a lovely shop in Fell's Point, Maryland. Captivated by the shop, they looked at one another and said, 'Hope Merchant.'

Luana Kaufmann's collages begin life as compilations of found images, created with scissors, paper and glue. They are discoveries of believable fantasy and impossibly-grounded dreams. Next, they become the "printing plates" for a new generation of "old papers", as they are scanned and meticulously remade to be giclees, or archival pigment prints. The incorporation of this exquisite print medium creates the ultimate cohesion of once-disparate parts, as well as renders them to be archival, gallery-quality works.

In addition to creating these initial collage worlds, Luana has discovered derivative offspring. For example, her talismans are wooden blocks covered with fragments of her collage images and embellished with hanging beads and miscellany. They offer aesthetic pleasure and healing energies.

The concept of the cover design for *The Hope Merchant* celebrates the apparently endless process of layering and births of new collage generations. With the publisher's suggestions and guidance, Luana has chosen and customized particular collage image fragments and created a two-dimensional illustration of the three-dimensional collage talismans.

Will it ever end? Hopefully not!

ABOUT THE ARTIST

Luana Kaufmann grew up in the Greater Washington area and graduated from Sarah Lawrence College in 1979 with a Bachelor of Arts degree, having focused on modern dance, cultural histories, and literature. For over a decade, she enjoyed compiling multi-media dance-theatre elements. Her kinetic-theatrical beginnings have been one of the informing forces in her found-imagery collage work.

In describing the experience of creating collages, Luana says, "A couple of images gravitate to each other and suddenly state the impending theme. What was unknown and spontaneous, metamorphoses into the known and deliberate. Allowing the components to have that initial free rein offers a mystery, a conceptual palette of infinite range, and access to the grand land of the psyche. And then, as pseudo-architect, jeweler, social director, interior designer, florist, landscape-designer, milliner and chef, I do enjoy a little tyranny with my commands of placement. I guess it's a waltz of chaos and order. Or preferably, a samba."

Luana has exhibited and sold collage giclees and talismans in numerous festivals and shows in the Baltimore-Washington area and beyond. Some of the more notable venues were Artscape, Surtex, Nordstrom, and the American Visionary Art Museum Store & Holiday Market. She now has her own gallery-shop, Emporium Collagia in Historic Fell's Point in Baltimore, Maryland. The shop is a collage in its own right, offering an eclectic array of fine goods and accessories, as well as her collage giclees, custom-designed-meditation card decks, and necklaces. Luana can be reached at luanakaufmann.com.